The Best Thing I Never Had

ERIN LAWLESS

Harper
impulse
we've got the love

Harper*Impulse* an imprint of
HarperCollins*Publishers Ltd*
77–85 Fulham Palace Road
Hammersmith, London W6 8JB

www.harpercollins.co.uk

A Paperback Original 2013

First published in Great Britain in ebook format by HarperImpulse 2013

Erin Lawless asserts the moral right to
be identified as the author of this work

A catalogue record for this book
is available from the British Library

ISBN: 978-0-00-757550-3

This novel is entirely a work of fiction.
The names, characters and incidents portrayed in it are
the work of the author's imagination. Any resemblance to
actual persons, living or dead, events or localities is
entirely coincidental.

Automatically produced by Atomik ePublisher from Easypress

To my friends;
old, new,
ex, and those yet to come.

but mostly:
for Oli,
who once upon a time kissed me in the snow,
when he wasn't supposed to.

Prologue

February 2012

Nicky took the proposal in the same undemanding way in which it was offered. You know I love you, he had said, followed by: please – twice. It was like receiving a promotion when you were the only applicant in the running; she was grateful and excited, sure, but she couldn't really say that it had been 'unexpected'.

She stretched restlessly in bed the morning after – one day into being twenty-six years old, one day into being engaged – watching the dust dance in the slant of dawn from the skylight window. She watched as the fixtures and furnishings of the little studio flat grew pale and distinct and – rather disappointingly – looked just the same as ever. Beside her Miles lay sprawled on his front.

Nicky pulled her arm behind her head and thought back to the first bed they had shared; a single, he had not been able to sprawl then. So that first morning they'd woken spooned together, a curiously intimate position for a one night stand. He'd kept his hair longer then and it curled around his cheek and tickled at hers. She'd lain there, cramped and uncomfortable, and wondered how to get him to leave without seeming rude.

She had been laden down with Tesco bags that evening, her housemate opening the front door for them, when they both caught sight of the post-it note at the same time. Nicky had dropped one of the carrier bags to the ground and reached to peel it off the glass of her window; a little blue ink heart on the yellow square, stuck facing inwards to her bedroom. And, just in case she had hoards of men leaving hearts stuck to her window, Miles had thoughtfully added an M and an x for a kiss in the corner.

She still had it, somewhere, in a box with old text books, perhaps.

* * *

Leigha had, as her mother always put it, done very well for herself. She had her nails done every two weeks and her hair every four – whether they strictly needed it or not. Home was a minimally furnished leasehold apartment in a Georgian mansion block off the Gloucester Road, which she spent very little time in.

So, true to form, she wasn't at home when she got Nicky's text: she was in the office and already on her second latte and paracetamol combination of the morning. She read it three times before fully absorbing the content and breaking into a lazy smile.

Dear Nicky. She couldn't remember the last text she'd had had from her, couldn't put a finger on the last time they would have seen each other. Leigha rarely ventured out of London these days. Nicky belonged to a different place, a different time; one where she used to sleep until noon, ironed her hair poker straight every day without fail and, as a rule, only drank fruity cocktails – as wine used to give her a headache.

But still, here it was in black and white on her Blackberry screen: Nicky was calling in a years-old promise and Leigha was called to be a bridesmaid.

Dear Nicky, she thought again, absently, as her attention flicked back to her computer screen. I must give her a call after work.

* * *

Sukie was vaguely aware of her phone going off from downstairs but persuading her two particularly unwilling teenage sisters into their uniforms and onto the bus was taking up the majority of her attention.

Twenty minutes later, the table had been wiped clean, the dishwasher stacked, the laundry put on and Sukie went back to bed, tugging her mobile free from the charger cable as she climbed in. She felt a flicker of anticipation as she read the text. Always a little quicker off the mark than Leigha, she could immediately follow Nicky's thinking.

She tilted back on her pillow to better see the cork board that hung at the head of her bed. A digital photo printed out on paper, so many years ago now that the ends were curled completely over on themselves: herself and her three university housemates, all in pastels, pale, thin arms looped around and around one another like the rings of a magic trick. Sukie knew that if she had received a text asking her to be a bridesmaid, then Leigha had as well and so – it could be assumed – had Harriet.

Sukie fired off an appropriately excited and congratulatory response to Nicky and dropped her phone to her bedside table. She pulled herself up to her knees and reached to smooth down the curling edges of the photo. Harriet smiled out from the middle of the group, one arm around Sukie, one arm around Nicky. Sukie brought her hand away and the white edges sprang back.

* * *

Johnny cast a desperate look at the closed en-suite door. Was it worth a dash to the communal bathroom up on the second floor? Risk running into one of the abundant flatmates? No, surely she'd be out soon. He shuffled from foot to foot on the spot. What had possessed him to stay the night? He knew this would happen. He was going to be so late for work and look like shit to boot.

There wasn't even a clock in here. He grabbed his mobile from the bedside table and turned it on. 08.38. Fuck.

He was so distracted that he read the text that had popped up twice before he really registered its content. When it did hit home, he sat down heavily on the end of Iona's bed, scratching at the stubble on his chin absently.

At that moment Iona came out of the bathroom in a cloud of warmth and steam, her body and hair wrapped in matching hot pink towels.

'I'm so glad you're here to get me up early,' she spoke through her yawn, as he dashed past her into the bathroom and shut the door. 'I've really got to get to the library by eleven. '

Eleven! Bloody lazy students. Johnny made a face at his reflection as he wiped the condensation off the mirror with the flat of his hand.

* * *

Harriet read the text whilst waiting for the lift, her mobile in one hand, a cardboard tray of Starbucks' coffees balanced in the other.

During their last dinner together, back before Christmas, Nicky had drunk too much rosé and confided in Harriet that she expected a proposal within the next six months. Miles had, at long last, finished his PhD and would finally be making money. What better way to express his gratitude to the girlfriend who had upped-sticks and moved across the country with him – then financed five years of him researching one of the more obscure battles of the Wars of the Roses – other than purchasing an appropriately sized diamond with his first few doctorate pay cheques? Harriet had thought Nicky was damn right to expect it.

She automatically pressed Reply, backed out of the Reply screen to read the message through once more, pressed Reply again, and paused.

She had herself almost convinced; surely, after almost five years, she was the only one stupid enough to still be thinking about it? Things could never be like they were before, but maybe, at the very least, they could stand there for one day in identical dresses. They could share old smiles, clasp arms and sing along to old songs. Maybe Adam would seek her out, look at her up and down in that old way he had of looking at her that she would never forget.

Harriet began to tap out her reply with the side of her thumb: Of course, of course I will be your Maid of Honour!!

* * *

Adam had his text from Miles the night before. He had felt his iPhone buzz in his suit trouser pocket – apologised to his companion for bad date etiquette – and read the text with appreciation.

'She said yes!' he grinned at his date, on an automatic impulse to share the moment. She stared at him blankly, thrown by the sudden change in conversation. 'My mate's proposed to his girl,' Adam clarified. 'I'm going to be best man!;' and suddenly she was off, talking a mile-a-minute about all the weddings she had attended over the last year, and wasn't it funny how everyone seemed to be getting married lately?

It suddenly struck Adam that there was finally going to be a wedding. He'd spent months knowing Miles was going to propose on Nicky's birthday. He'd even gone ring shopping with him, helped him book the chapel on their old University campus. Now the ring was on the finger, quite literally speaking, and they were all on countdown for an Easter wedding.

After the purchase was complete they'd gone for a pint, the ring with its respectable diamond quiet in its plush black box on the table in front of them. Miles had scratched under his chin in that nervous way he had. 'I assume… she'd want… the other girls. You know, as bridesmaids?'

Adam had taken a long sip from his pint while he arranged his answer. 'I guess.' There was no point pretending he didn't know which other girls Miles was referring to.

'So it will be, like, a reunion,' Miles had said carefully, taking a long draught of his lager himself.

'To be honest mate, it's about time,' Adam had answered, and had meant it.

He drew his attention back to his date, describing the halter-neck bow that had been on her dress for her sister's wedding. Her arms were held up above her shoulders, bent backwards at a strange angle as she laughed at herself for not being able to articulate what she meant. She looked very soft, very sweet, and suddenly Adam felt an impractical urge.

Let's leave the rest of the bottle – he wanted to say to her – let's go for a walk along the river. Let me tell you a story, from when I was young and stupid.

'That sounds really nice though,' was what he said instead, re-filling her glass with wine.

PART ONE

September 2006 – June 2007

Chapter One

September 2006

The Nokia rumbled against the table; Nicky was up like a shot, grabbing the phone and pulling the charger cable taut against the screen of the TV. Leigha immediately made inarticulate sounds of protest through a mouthful of dinner.

'Miles?' Harriet asked.

Nicky didn't bother to take the phone off charge, instead reading the text message standing slouched against the wall. Her mouth twisted; she tapped her thumbnail against the side of the phone nervously before looking up at her three housemates, who were looking back at her expectantly, eating momentarily forgotten.

'He's found somewhere,' she said finally, though she still chewed absently at her bottom lip.

'Hurrah,' Sukie replied, with probably a little more feeling than was tactful. Leigha shot her a quick look.

'Cool, nearby?' she asked Nicky, who had placed her mobile back on the table without sending a reply. Nicky's lip-chewing intensified.

'The high street, actually.'

'Wow, that's lucky!'

'It's above the estate agents,' Nicky interrupted, before the impression that this was a good thing could cement.

'Well, that doesn't mean it's not still really convenient,' tried Harriet.

'It's with two blokes he's never even met, and they're undergrads.'

'Oh no, however will he cope? It's not like he's dating one. It's not like he's just been squatting in the house of four all summer.' Sukie rolled her eyes, helping herself to some more rice from the foil takeaway container on the floor.

'It's only three hundred, and that includes some bills,' Nicky continued – although nobody had asked – 'so maybe we'll still be able to have something put away by graduation.'

'Not if you keep getting Chinese takeaway,' Sukie said through a mouthful of rice. Nicky ignored her and returned to her place on the sofa, looking about herself for her fork.

'When does he move in?' Harriet asked, tilting her head back to better see Nicky's face from where she sat on the floor in front of the sofa.

'He can from tomorrow.'

'Means I can start walking around in my underwear again!' Sukie laughed.

'Yippee,' mumbled Nicky, pulling her fork from the gap between the sofa cushions.

* * *

So, here he was, back for his final year at university. It seemed like no time at all since he'd been an embarrassment of a Fresher and now it was the beginning of the end.

Shaking off the rather uncharacteristically maudlin chain of thought, Adam immediately made himself at home, giving the most cursory of goodbyes to his damp-eyed mother (always emotional during the return-to-term farewell) and lugging his suitcase up the stairs, leaving it unopened just inside the doorway to his bedroom, where he was pretty sure it would remain until at least Reading Week.

The room smelt warm and musty from being shut up the whole summer but otherwise looked and felt much the same. At the foot of his unmade bed was a neat pile of envelopes, post that had arrived for him over the summer. Adam suddenly felt a little flare of annoyance at the presumption, the embarrassing politeness, at what he assumed to be the work of his new housemate.

He and Johnny had harboured serious hopes that their landlord wouldn't be able to let the box-room after their mate Mike sodded off on his placement year in industry, and their third year would just be the two of them. Of course, it was too much to hope for, that the guy'd be able to overlook the rent being short by a couple of hundred quid each month, and unsurprisingly, he'd rustled someone up. All Adam knew was that it was a guy, a postgrad, and his name was Miles.

It transpired that Miles was indeed embarrassingly polite, just the sort of guy that would sort a stranger's post for him and leave it in a neatly right-angled pile in his room. Nice enough, but he seemed so terribly old and serious; when he was at home he was closeted in the tiny box-room studying. Not that he was often at home. Because what Adam and Johnny found most irritating about Miles Healy was that he wanted to be there even less than they wanted him there.

Miles, it came as surprise, had a girlfriend, Nicola, who lived down the road. He'd spent the summer living there with her, being fussed and cosseted over without having to pay a penny towards rent or board; by all accounts, quite a jammy git. Miles' abrupt deterioration in circumstance to a rather damp, lacking in furniture, second floor flat above the estate agents' on the high street was purely down to the girls' landlord belatedly working out that he had an unofficial tenant. It contravened the tenancy agreement, he blustered, and Miles was out on his ear. It was two weeks before the start of term and every last measly room in the main town and the neighbouring student village had gone; apart from, of course, their box-room. Probably something to do with the fact that it hadn't had a carpet. Or a window that opened.

And eventually, after a tactful few days for the boys to acclimatise to one another, the girlfriend arrived, with a housewifely smile and a casserole in a Perspex dish. Johnny and Adam were – surprised. She was dirty blonde, tall and coltish, with a shy, unexpectedly pretty face.

'Talk about Legs Eleven!' Johnny whispered to Adam the second Nicky's attention was on serving out the food. Adam subtly held up his two middle fingers in agreement: their private sign for 'that bird has cracking pins'.

Nicky had let the boys dominate the conversation, interjecting here and there to encourage Miles to tell specific anecdotes, keeping the beer flowing, nurturing what had initially felt reasonably formal into easy chat. And then, at the end of the night, as Nicky pulled on her shoes, Miles hesitated.

'I think I'll stay here tonight, pet,' he said, haltingly, looking over at Johnny. 'You need to show me this so-called "dream team" on your Pro Evo!'

'Ah, mate, it's a work of art!' Johnny had been banging on about the particular merits of his carefully crafted digital football team the entire evening. 'I'll bring my Playstation downstairs.'

Nicky smiled to herself as she finished tying her laces. 'Okay, love. See you tomorrow?' Miles gave her a distracted smile and kiss on the forehead before bounding up the stairs with Johnny to help him disconnect his console from his bedroom television.

'It was nice to meet you, Nicky,' Adam said politely, upon being left alone in the lounge with the girl. 'That dinner was great. Feel free to come back, any time!' he teased.

Nicky laughed. 'Oh, I'm sure you'll be seeing me around!' She paused at the head of the stairs that led down to street level and the flat's front door. 'We're having a party, me and the girls I live with, across on Dell Road? A sort of "back to school" sort of thing.' She used her fingers to mime satirical quotation marks. 'On Saturday. You guys up for it?'

'Er, yeah.' Adam stepped back to let Johnny through, trailing a quagmire of black cables. 'We'll definitely try to make it.'

Deciding that it was infinitely cooler to turn up a couple of hours late, making it seem like they'd had 'another thing' on, Adam and Johnny had sat in their lounge drinking Carlsberg and playing Pro Evo for the first half of Saturday evening, before pulling on their shoes and making the five minute walk into the heart of the student village.

The door was open, with people spilling out into the front garden. A slight, Oriental girl looked up at them quizzically from where she was sitting on the crumbling garden wall – mid-way through bringing a cigarette she had bummed from her companion to her lips – but didn't seem bothered enough to object to their entering the house. They pushed past the bodies congregating in the hallway and at the foot of the stairs, coming through to a large, open-plan kitchen–diner. Adam nervously adjusted the bottle of cheap wine he was holding by its neck.

A brunette girl in a dark pink skater-style dress had turned away from her conversation, throwing her hair over her shoulder as she did. She smiled at them.

'Beads!' she said, very matter-of-factly.

'Sorry?' Adam thought he must have misheard.

'Beads,' the girl repeated, her smile growing wider. 'And a

punishment shot. You don't come late to our parties.' She had turned to a shoe box on the kitchen worktop which was filled half-way to the top with necklaces of plastic beads, delved her hand deep into the clicking mass of them. She untangled two necklaces, draped them around his and Johnny's necks and was turned back to the worktop in a flash, the short skirt of her dress flirting around her upper thighs as she twisted.

'So, who do you belong to?' she asked conversationally, pouring generous measures of Sambuca into two comedy shot glasses.

'Er, Miles,' Johnny answered, quickly. 'Er, I mean, not that we, I mean-'

'He's moved into our flat,' Adam supplied, with a touch more poise. He shot the rosy-faced Johnny a look.

'Aha!' the girl said, looking back at them with renewed interest, spinning the lid of the Sambuca bottle tight against the flat of her hand. 'Well, welcome guys. I'm Nicky's housemate. I'm Leigha.' Then she held out a shot glass to each of them like a handshake.

'Hey. Adam,' Adam said, taking the shot without complaint.

'Johnny,' Johnny introduced himself in the most nonchalant tone imaginable, whilst his fingers fumbled as Leigha passed over his shot glass; he had to suck the spillage from between his thumb and forefinger.

'And this is Harriet,' Leigha gestured behind her to the girl she had been talking to when they arrived, who had been leaning against the fridge and smiling a small smile throughout the whole exchange. She was petite – downright boyish in frame, especially standing next to her curvy friend – with dark, dark hair cut short at the nape of her neck.

'Hiya,' Adam nodded to the girl politely, which Johnny echoed before downing his shot as manfully as he could manage and handing the empty glass back to their hostess, whose attention had already drifted across the room.

13

'I recognise you,' Harriet said. Adam looked at her quizzically. Their campus was a small one; after two full years, it wasn't too unlikely that she might know his face. 'You do English with me,' she finished. It wasn't a question.

'Er, yeah.' Adam searched her face again; she had eyes as dark as her hair. He didn't recognise her.

'You guys!' Nicky was suddenly there, her fair hair in a fat plait over one shoulder, and clearly slightly drunk as she launched into a series of clumsy hugs. 'You made it!'

'Yeah, we thought we'd drop by,' smiled Johnny, although he turned his head away to watch as Leigha moved away from them across the kitchen and started to converse with somebody else, the girl who'd been smoking in the front garden, who turned a liquid gaze upon them.

'So, you're the fresh meat,' she said, baldly, as she stepped closer to them. Adam blanched and laughed nervously.

Nicky, swaying on needlessly high heels, spoke before he had a chance to retort. 'Johnny, Adam, this is Leigha, and Harriet, and Sukie.' She gestured with a lazy flick of her hand to each of the girls who were gathered around them as she spoke. 'My housemates,' she finished, with an indulgent smile.

'Okay, so everybody knows everybody,' Sukie said, impatiently. She reached behind Johnny for the half-empty bottle of Sambuca. 'I thought we were here to have a party, not a debutante ball.' She began to form a line of sticky, empty shot glasses ready for the stream of Sambuca that was yet to come. 'Now, is anybody up for a game of Twenty Ones?'

Chapter Two

October 2006

The front door blew open, slammed shut, the clatter punctuated by the dull thud of a handbag hitting the floor: Leigha, obviously. 'Guess who I saw at the bank,' she began, without preamble, leaning against the worktop with one hand, reaching down to pull her shoe off with the other. Harriet didn't look up from her magazine.

'Elvis?' she asked, purposefully making her tone as weary as possible as clearly Leigha was dying to tell her something.

'No!' Leigha flapped her ballet pump at her like a teacher wagging a finger at a naughty child. 'Seth.' Harriet forced herself not to eyeroll.

'Wow, I am so supremely uninterested.' She turned the page with an exaggerated flip to underline said total indifference.

'You'd care if I'd seen him with a girl.' Leigha pulled off her other shoe and tossed them both under the table. That did it; Harriet's eyes flicked upwards and narrowed.

'I would be naturally curious. As to how he's gone from suicidal to lothario in since I last spoke to him.' Leigha turned her back to flick on the kettle. Harriet lasted about thirty seconds. 'So?' she pressed, admitting defeat and leaning back in the chair.

'So what?'

'So, was he with a girl?' Harriet clarified with great impatience.

'Of course not!' Leigha laughed, reaching two mugs down from the cupboard. 'Not that you care either way, right?' She shot Harriet a challenging look.

'Curiosity,' Harriet repeated, her mouth twitching. And it was the truth; she was glorying in her new singledom, the space in her life, her bed! 'And pride,' she admitted. Leigha stirred the sugar around in the tea with a little more force than was necessary, the metal of the spoon chiming off the ceramic.

'Pride! You bitch. Poor guy. You really shafted him,' she said, her tone lighter than her words.

Harriet flicked a page over again. 'I don't want to hear this again, especially from you.'

'What?' Leigha placed the two mugs on the table and slid into the chair opposite.

'Yes, you. You know jack shit about it. Your longest relationship so far—'

'Don't say 'is breakfast',' Leigha held up a hand in warning.

Harriet smiled. 'You don't eat breakfast.'

Leigha ignored her, wrapping her hands around the mug to take away the last vestiges of the chill of the October day. 'He loves you.' She spoke quietly, her tone strange enough to make Harriet look up again.

'I didn't love him,' she answered, deliberately pitching her voice louder.

'Shame.' Leigha took a sip of her tea. 'Such a waste.'

'Stop going on.' Harriet's eyes were back on the glossy pages.

'I'm not going on. It is a shame,' Leigha whined. 'I just want you to be happy, Harry.' Harriet looked up again, confused.

'I am happy – *now* – you numpty. That's the point.'

'In love happy!'

'Christ.' Harriet closed the magazine and reached for her tea.

'Who says there's any such thing?'

'Miserable bitch,' Leigha said, with great affection, reaching for the magazine herself.

After Harriet ran out of the door almost late for her 4pm lecture, the house fell silent and chilly. Listlessly, Leigha stood up to re-boil the water in the kettle for another cup of tea, something to keep her hands focused, if not her mind. She had a paper due, should really focus on it in these quiet hours before the house filled up again, but knew it was pretty much impossible that she'd get anything done today. Seeing Seth always put her out of sorts.

Seth had always been a middling, background sort of character at school, until Year 11, when he returned from the summer break a good four inches taller and probably just as broad again besides. To Leigha, who had privately nursed a crush since midway through Year 9, it was a not unwelcome shock. She herself had just moved to contact lenses, cut her hair into a bob that made it sway and shine; she knew all about the power of personal reinvention.

So she spent the last year of her GCSEs dragging Sukie, Harry and the rest of their pack around, a little trail like ducklings: them following her, following him. She turned up at every sporting event, each party, forced the inevitable until they were all one big group, her girls and Seth's guys.

And then during the summer before Sixth Form, there was a text from Harriet, and her careless amusement just dripped from every word. Seth had had her round the back of the sports' centre; no joke; you couldn't even make it up.

And so Leigha watched them for years, watched him teach her how to drive, watched him chuck her under the chin when she was low, watched their eyes flash with glares as they argued with one another over stupid, little things. She was privy to each excruciating detail when they first went to bed with one another, had to hear how afterwards Seth had gathered her up in his arms and told her he loved her, loved her, loved her, would never love anyone as much as he loved his Harriet. And even after three whole years, she never quite shook the feeling that this wasn't meant to be, that something had gone terribly wrong and her heart ached, ached for the waste – that she had privately given up her love for this boy for what turned out to be no reason at all.

Because - during their second year at uni - something happened, although Harriet was never very articulate on what that something was. Either way, by the end of it, lovely, sweet Seth was crushed into something very small, something that couldn't look Leigha in the face because she reminded him too much of how things had been before. It was the way he'd been in the bank, his eyes sliding across her like she was so much air – as usual, frustratingly heedless of the fact he made her heart sit up and scream inside her chest.

Adam came back into the room, throwing his mobile phone on the sofa with no small degree of irritation. Johnny didn't look up from his laptop screen.

'Y'alright?'

Adam didn't answer, instead throwing himself down full-length on the sofa. The mobile made a muffled buzz and Adam swore under his breath as he fished underneath his legs for it.

'Tell her to piss off and leave you alone!' Johnny advised. 'Tell her you've got shit to do.'

'If you speak like that to women it's no wonder you don't have a girlfriend,' Adam retorted as he located the phone, turned it right-side up and opened his message inbox.

In the girls' house on Dell Road, Sukie had her disapproving face on.

'Miles says Adam has a girlfriend back home.' She stood with her arms folded in the middle of Leigha's bedroom floor, as if she thought sitting on the bed with the rest of them would be collusion.

'And?' Harriet scored. 'She's sent him a casual text, not a picture of her -!' She was cut off by a scandalised squeal from Nicky.

'Yeah, so casual it's just taken you three ten minutes to draft it!' Sukie shot back. 'I don't even get the appeal of this guy, are you this bored?'

Leigha did her lips-pressed-together smile, the sort of smile that looks like it would rather be a laugh. 'I just want to see!'

Adam was holding his phone like it might try to bite him. The uncharacteristic silence finally drew Johnny's attention away from his coursework.

'Lauren?' he asked, giving Adam about five seconds to decide whether or not he was going to lie to spare his friend's feelings.

'No, Leigha,' he admitted, wincing mentally as Johnny's brows snapped together.

'Oh yeah?' He abruptly turned back to his laptop in an attempt to look as unbothered as possible. 'She hasn't replied to my message from last night. What's she saying?'

'Not much. Asking me if I'm going to the Union on Friday.'

'That's exactly what I asked her yesterday!' Johnny immediately looked surprised at the aggression in his tone. Adam didn't respond, just drummed his thumbs against the buttons of the keypad distractedly. 'What are you gonna say, are we going?' Johnny asked, in a slightly more reasonable voice.

'I can't be arsed really, can you?' Adam sighed, tossing his phone across to the coffee table with Leigha's message, still unanswered, on the screen. Johnny's face was faintly mutinous. Adam hurriedly snatched up the controller from next to his phone. 'Pro Evo, mate?'

'But I think he's interested. I mean, I wouldn't think he's interested if I didn't have reason to think he was interested, therefore, he's probably interested, yeah?'

Harriet brushed muffin crumbs from her hands as she tried to follow Leigha's logic. 'I guess,' she said reluctantly. 'But it doesn't matter anyway, he's got a girl at home, remember?'

Leigha shrugged indifferently. 'Shows he's not a commitment-phobe, I take it as a good sign.'

'Ley, if he came in here right now and told us he's engaged, you'd somehow take it as a good sign. You're set on this, why are you even asking my opinion?'

Leigha hushed her hurriedly, eyes darting around the café. All walls have ears on campus. 'Because I want you to make me feel better about having a wildly unsuitable crush on an involved man,' Leigha whispered. 'Tell me that he'll probably break up with her for me!' Harriet leant back in her chair and considered Leigha objectively for a moment. She was beautiful and obviously sexy with it: face, hair and body all soft and inviting touch. Men always wanted her, because she automatically acted like they would, and it captivated them.

'He's very like you, I think,' she said, choosing her words carefully. 'Confident, I mean.' Leigha tilted her head slightly as she considered this.

'I think I know what you mean,' she replied. 'He's got a real alpha male thing going on. I like it.'

'Does that make you an alpha female, then?' Harriet asked sarcastically as she balled up the baking paper case her muffin had come in.

'I would definitely feel like one on his arm,' Leigha laughed.

'Then you deserve one another,' Harriet decided, mock-serious. 'And I wish you a long and happy relationship together. Better get rid of the existing girlfriend though love, she might cramp your 'alpha' style.'

'Harry, the way he talks about the poor girl – when he talks about her at all! – I don't think I need to worry. To hear him tell it she seems to have the personality and allure of a teaspoon.' Harriet couldn't help but laugh at her friend's audaciousness. 'She's a placeholder girlfriend,' was Leigha's brutal final analysis.

'Poor cow,' Harriet agreed, dropping the balled up muffin case into the remnants of her takeaway latte like a full-stop.

Nicky was in a photo-taking mood, the camera case swinging from her wrist by its cord, getting in the way. Sukie and Harriet snapped to attention each time she aimed the camera anywhere near them, arms flying around one another, lips pouting, over and over again. Johnny gave Leigha bunny ears in one shot, did the 'wanker' fist in the background of one of Miles and Adam, lifted Sukie – the birthday girl – up level with his shoulders, her legs pointed straight out like a burlesque dancer in the finale of her act. When she wasn't taking photos, Nicky was kissing Miles, long, drunken kisses that were more tongue than lip.

Leigha was drunk on too many buy-two-get-one-free VKs. 'I love this song!' she'd shout over the music with each and every track change. 'I fucking *love* this song!' Nicky laughed, taking another photo of Leigha swaying with her arms in the air, a bottle in each hand.

'She only really swears like this when she's drunk,' she explained to Adam. He laughed, taking a swig from his room temperature beer.

'It's cool, she's funny.' He twirled Leigha around with his free hand and released her pointed towards Harriet, who immediately pinched one of the bottles of alcopop, taking a mouthful. Leigha threw her now free arm round her friend and the two swayed together, shouting out the lyrics over the throb of the speakers. Sukie turned from Johnny to Harriet, reaching deftly over to take

21

the bottle and a drink from it in turn, three dark heads together as they danced and sang.

Adam looked across at Johnny, the three girls between them still singing, drinking from the same bottle. Johnny cocked his plastic glass towards Adam in mock salute before his eyes slipped back to Leigha, striking in a forest green dress.

'Adam!' she suddenly shouted over the music, catching his eye-contact and bouncing her way closer, 'Adam! Have a picture with me!' Relinquished now of both bottles, she slipped both hands tight around his bicep, the side of her thigh pressing above his knee as she went up on tip-toes to speak into his ear. 'Have a picture with me,' she repeated, squeezing, pressing.

The censorious silence on the other end of the line was quite possibly the loudest thing Adam had ever heard.

He had planned on continuing to avoid ringing Lauren for as long as possible, but her fourth text of the evening had acquired strings of exclamation marks along with capital letters on its significant nouns and he felt she could no longer be safely ignored.

'So how late were you going to leave it? Until I was on the train? At your front door? In bed with you?' she asked. He couldn't tell if the tremble in her voice was from anger or anguish.

'Obviously not,' he assured her. 'I'm sorry I didn't call you earlier, I really am, but – you know, it was a hard decision for me…'

'Oh, poor baby!' Lauren immediately spat. 'You're right, of course, and nasty old me, I haven't even asked how *you're* feeling!'

'Lauren…' Adam patiently tried to talk over the tirade of sarcasm. 'Look Lauren, it's just a break. I just need to be alone for a while, focus on myself and the course and life down here, you know?'

'Don't you think I know the difference between a break and a break-up?' Lauren's voice had lost the obvious anger and was back to the tremulous softness of before. 'And do you think I'd want you back after you've fucked whatever slut you have in mind?' Adam made a noise of protest but Lauren cut him off before he could object. 'I know you. It's like last year. Someone's caught your eye again. Someone's made you wish you were free and single. Well. Lucky for you then that you are.' And then, with a dignity that surprised him, she simply hung up.

'Lauren?' Adam spoke stupidly into the dial tone. 'Fuck,' he half-laughed, returning the landline handset to its base with perhaps a little more force than he meant to. 'Fuck!' he repeated, louder.

After only a few seconds of silence there was a hesitant knock on his bedroom door. Adam's stomach spasmed guiltily; whoever it was wasn't even pretending that they hadn't overheard.

'Yeah?' he called.

The door opened and Miles stood there, nervously twisting one of his hands in the other. 'You okay?'

'Ah, mate,' Adam replied, rubbing at his hair with the flat of his hand. 'I think I was just dumped.'

Miles' eyebrows disappeared under his fringe. 'Seriously? You alright?'

'Yeah, I'm alright. To be honest it was because I was saying we should take a break and – to be fair – it's not the first time I've put her through it. I'm not a very good boyfriend.' Adam smiled sheepishly. 'Especially not a long-distance one.'

'What, like, you cheat?' asked Miles, perching on the desk chair opposite to where Adam sat on his bed. Adam scratched under his chin hesitantly.

'I wouldn't call it cheating,' he answered finally.

Comprehension dawned on Miles' face. 'Oh I see. So that's the reason for the breaks.'

'Kind of.'

Miles shook his head incredulously, disapproval and admiration mixing on his face. 'Surprised you got away with it that long, to be honest.'

'Yeah, me too!' Adam laughed. Miles laughed too.

'You've got some nerve man – you like, schedule in affairs!'

'What can I say?' Adam winced self-consciously. 'I like my cake and to eat it too?'

'Unbelievable!' Miles burst out laughing. 'Unbelievable!'

'Only to you, mate!'

'What do you mean?'

'Well, you're a rare breed. You're a totally one woman guy. Or at least you do a convincing impression of one,' Adam replied.

'Of course I am!' Miles protested. 'I *love* Nicky. I mean, I'm sure, you know? That she's the one.'

It was Adam's turn to shake his head incredulously. 'Mate, we're too young to have 'Ones'.'

'I'm older than you,' Miles reminded him.

'Yeah, but still too young for all that,' Adam retorted.

Miles just smiled placidly before returning to his own room, leaving Adam alone to reflect.

He and Lauren had been a thing – albeit on and off – since he was fifteen years old. She'd always been there in the background – usually unobtrusive, often unconsidered, sometimes unwelcome. An anchor of sorts, keeping him grounded, but also tied down. Her final shot at him rankled. She was wrong, this time anyway; there was nobody specific in mind.

Unwittingly, his brain gave him the image of Leigha in the Union Friday night, the white length of her legs glowing like bone in the UV lights, disappearing under the darkness of her dress; the smell of her hair as she pressed close to speak into his ear; the territorial squeeze on his arm and the answering pulse in his groin as he realised that he could have this girl that very moment, if he cared to.

Adam switched on his laptop, its hum as it booted filling the silence that had been left in the room following Miles' departure. Whereas his relationship status on Facebook had been neutral thus far out of deference to Lauren, Adam suddenly felt the urge to publicly announce his new Singledom. After all, the game was on.

Chapter Three

November 2006

Harriet paused on the stairs as she spoke, damming the flow of people trying to make their way down to the front of the lecture theatre.

'No wonder I've never really clocked you before now,' she said.

Adam smiled up at her lazily. 'All the cool kids sit at the back,' he assured her.

'It's not a bus,' she answered, titling her dark head to the side. 'But alright. Can you guys move down?'

Adam chivvied his course-mate along, sliding his A4 pad and single pen across the desk that ran in front of the line of fixed seating. Harriet and a pale blonde he recognised dimly from the start of term house party slipped into the vacated seats.

'You don't have a copy of the book,' Harriet pointed out.

'I never have a copy of the book,' Adam replied.

'Have you even read the book?' she tried.

'I have read the SparkNotes online,' Adam answered gravely. The corner of Harriet's mouth twitched as she tried to suppress a smile. Adam's friend snorted.

'Well, you two can have mine and we'll share,' she said, pushing the heavy book towards the boys. 'For appearances at least, yeah?'

'Oh, he can't see whether or not we have the book from all the way down there,' Adam's friend scoffed, referring to the lecturer, who had just arrived on the dais below and was tinkering with a projector.

'Then you *don't* just sit all the way back here to look cool,' Harriet grinned.

'Astounding!' her blonde companion laughed.

Adam felt warmth rush to his face. He wasn't used to being laughed at. 'Can you stop your nattering now then, ladies?' he mock-sighed, opening the loaned book. 'Some of us are here to learn a little something about the works of Alpha Behn.'

'Aphra Behn,' Harriet corrected, with that funny little twist of a smile.

Johnny was so surprised by Adam's appearance in the lounge that his spoon dropped back into his bowl with a splash.

'Bugger me, mate.' He swiped at the droplets of milk on the table with his sleeve. 'Has someone died?'

'No, why?' Adam sat on the arm of the sofa and cracked the ring-pull to his breakfast of a can of Pepsi.

'I don't think I've ever seen you down here before ten o'clock before,' Johnny said.

'There's a viewing in the library at nine.' Adam took a swig from his can. 'A German film adaptation of *Hamlet*. From the sixties.' Johnny sniggered into his cereal.

'You lame-ass English students sure know how to have fun. So sorry to give it a miss, but – damn it! – I've got a seminar.' Adam shrugged and downed the rest of his drink.

'Your loss,' he grinned as he crushed the empty can to a concave shape. 'Hoping I can base one of my courseworks on it and look intelligent.'

'That *would* be a nice change for you,' Johnny agreed, solemnly.

Adam pitched the can at his head.

Harriet dotted little blobs of concealer under her eyes. Leigha sat on the edge of her bed, bundled into a lilac dressing gown and blinking blearily over the rim of her cup of tea.

'And you're sure you want to come?' Harriet repeated doubtfully, clicking the lid back onto the makeup pen. 'Gotta leave in about ten...'

Leigha wordlessly waved a hand at her and took another deep drink from the mug. 'Yeah, yeah, I'll only take five minutes, don't worry.'

'You know it's only going to be a shitty little TV set up in one of the reading rooms,' Harriet said, blending the makeup with the tip of her index finger. 'And it's in German.'

'Yeah you said. I told you, sounds interesting. You know I like to do —' Leigha was cut off by a resounding yawn — 'different things.'

'Well, if you're sure.' Harriet checked the time on her mobile phone display. 'But please get dressed.' Leigha laughed.

'We've spent our fair share of time wearing pyjamas in that library.'

'Yeah, we lived on campus then. You wanna walk through town in your dressing gown, be my guest.' Harriet combed her fingers roughly through her short hair.

'Guess I'd better start getting my face on,' Leigha agreed, leaving her mostly-empty mug on Harriet's beside table and strolling unhurriedly out of the room and into her own.

Feeling exhausted already, Harriet flopped down on the recently vacated bed. Sukie's face appeared around the side of the bedroom door, which Leigha had left ajar.

'She going with you?' she asked.

'Apparently.'

'Isn't this film in German?'

'Well, yes, but it's not like it won't have subtitles!' Harriet answered, impatiently.

Sukie was silent for a moment, uncharacteristically thoughtful about what she was about to say. When she did speak again she pitched her voice lower. 'Is Adam going to this?'

Harriet looked up at her sharply. 'Yes, we're picking him up on the way. Do you think that's why she has suddenly decided to come?'

'Well, I don't think she developed an interest in the German film industry in the time it took her to make that cup of tea.'

'I agree. Eurgh, I'm going to be a right spare part.'

'Practice for when they're a couple,' Sukie agreed. 'I can see Ley being a super clingy girlfriend.'

'Fun, fun, and more fun.' Harriet rolled her eyes. 'So you think he likes her then?'

'*Das ist die...* question,' Sukie answered, raising her eyebrows.

Leigha looked longingly at the reflection of her bed in the mirror as she rubbed tinted moisturiser into her cheeks in vigorous circles. She heard a sudden burst of giggles from Sukie and Harriet across the landing.

'What's up?' she called.

'Hustle it, Webster!' Harriet bellowed.

Adam's phone chimed its message tone and he lazily fished it out of his pocket.

'Oooh,' he smirked, waving his mobile phone tauntingly in Johnny's face. 'Leigha's coming along with Harriet. Bet you wish you were coming to see this 'lame-ass' film now!'

'Oh fuck off,' Johnny growled, lobbing the Pepsi can back across the room for good measure.

The well-known intro carolled through the house. Sukie's eyes widened in disbelief.

'NICKY!' she screeched, slamming her glass of water down onto the coffee table for emphasis. 'Not bloody yet!' Nicky ignored her, instead pitching her voice high as she started to sing along with the track.

'Don't be a Scrooge,' Johnny admonished from the kitchen, where he was helping himself unconcernedly to a glass of someone else's orange juice.

'It's November!' Sukie glared

'And tomorrow,' Leigha laughed, 'it will be December.' And she and Johnny joined in enthusiastically for the end of the chorus.

'Baby, all I want for Christmas, is you!'

The entire group had waited around undecidedly for almost twenty minutes, before someone had the smart idea to run across to the department office and ask where their seminar leader was; sick, apparently. Harriet and Adam wandered aimlessly outside into the sharp winter sunshine. Harriet hefted her bookbag up onto her free shoulder with a grunt.

'What a waste of time.'

Adam, who could never have imagined anyone being disappointed by the cancellation of a class, couldn't help but laugh at her. Harriet shot him a withering look.

'Here, let me carry that,' Adam reached for the bulky bookbag. Harriet handed it over with a smile.

'Purple is totally your colour,' she told him, straight-faced. Adam posed effeminately with the bag thrown over his shoulder and Harriet laughed. 'What now then? Want to head to the library?'

'I so do not,' he answered, rolling his eyes. 'Let's just head home. Johnny should be back at yours already, its board game night tonight.' Harriet didn't answer straight away. She rubbed her palm over her hair, sending it momentarily into little spiked peaks. Adam found himself mirroring the gesture, uncomfortable in the unusual silence.

'It's like suddenly having ten brothers and sisters,' Harriet said, finally. Adam immediately grasped what she meant.

'And sometimes, you just want to be alone?' he supplied, with a sidelong smile. Harriet nodded in silent agreement. 'Well,' he rearranged the bookbag again, 'I am not going to the library. Or back to yours, yet. I'm going off on my own for a cheeky one at the Armstrong.' He tilted his head at her quizzically. 'Want to come be alone with me?'

Harriet responded by turning smartly on her heel and striding towards the east side of campus, where the pub was. She turned and walked backwards a few steps as she answered him.

'As long as you're carrying the bag.'

Harriet groaned as Adam turned around and revealed what he had just bought at the bar. 'I said one more drink, not one more *pitcher*,' she called across to him. 'We're expected home already!'

'Listen to yourself, woman!' Adam said incredulously, reaching the table and putting the jug of Snakebite down. 'They're not our parents!'

'Yeah, but – its board game night, 'The Game of Life'…' Harriet said, stupid with her share of the two jugs of Snakebite they'd imbibed already.

'Fuck 'The Game of Life',' Adam replied, with great delight, refilling their pint glasses with a clumsy slosh from the pitcher. 'I always get the shit jobs anyway.'

'Leigha will be cross,' Harriet predicted, taking a deep drink regardless. Adam's eyebrows rose.

'With you or with me?' he asked. Harriet shot a look at him through her eyelashes.

'Both,' she replied, neutrally, reaching forward and drawing shapes in the condensation on the swell of the pitcher with her forefinger.

'Let her,' Adam stretched out his legs casually under the table. 'She's not my keeper.'

'Shows what you know,' Harriet said; her tone was light and playful but Adam glowered at her in response. Harriet rolled her eyes and reached forward for her glass again, the drink making her indiscreet. 'Christ, any other bloke would be falling at Leigha's feet for one iota of the attention she's bestowing upon you.' Adam redirected his glower towards his drink, which he then saw off with slow, careful swallows. Harriet was not to be deterred; 'what's wrong with you?' she persisted.

'Nothing's wrong with me! I just don't like this whole sense of ownership, it's so obvious that you guys totally assume me and her will be getting together.'

'And what's so odd about that?' Harriet challenged. 'You're single, she's single, you clearly fancy one another. Get on with it. Stop messing her around.'

Adam inhaled sharply, incredulous. 'Messing!'

'Yes, messing!' Harriet's eyes narrowed. 'Unless you're the sort of guy who's just after one thing.'

Adam reddened. 'Of course not.'

The swift and emphatic denial seemed to take the wind out of Harriet's sails; she fell silent but looked him square in the face, exasperation still showing on hers.

'Never mind,' she said, finally, standing up. 'Look, I'm going to go to the toilet and then we really should head back home.' She was away from their table before Adam could even reply. He sat back against the dark leather backing of the booth, feeling entirely unsettled, eyes on the swing door to the Ladies' which Harriet had just disappeared through. For the fourth time that evening, he ignored the persistent vibration of his mobile ringing in his jeans pocket.

After first being informed that Harriet and Adam had gone to the pub for a quick one, Leigha had thoughtfully nipped across to the shop and bought a six pack of the lager that Johnny advised was Adam's favourite.

Johnny was on his third can, feet up on the coffee table, uncaring of the abandoned game board beneath them.

'Maybe they're caught up with people from their course?' Sukie yawned, legs curled under her on the couch. 'Shall we just watch a film?'

'Shall I try Adam again?' Johnny asked, reaching for his mobile.

Leigha didn't answer, just crossed the open-plan room to the kitchen cupboards, adding a generous glug of Malibu to her glass of juice.

'Let's just watch a film,' Sukie repeated, frowning.

Chapter Four

December 2006

Nicky shrieked in concern as Harriet balanced precariously on the arm of the sofa in her attempt to restick a rogue piece of tinsel. 'Come down from there, you idiot!'

'Yes, let someone taller do it, short stuff,' Miles agreed, lending Harriet his shoulder to stabilise herself and allow her to hop down to the cushions and then to the floor.

Sukie craned her neck to see what strange concoction Leigha was mixing in their house's one good saucepan.

'You're not ready yet,' Leigha observed mildly.

'You're ready way too early,' Sukie countered, leaning forward to sniff at the pungent cocktail. 'We really should have bought a jug.'

'We've been saying that for years,' Leigha laughed. 'And this works just as well really.'

'And what's one of our house parties without your famous Pan Punch?' Sukie agreed.

'Infamous more like!' Nicky corrected from across the room.

'The first time I drank that stuff I ended up spontaneously inventing and performing a dance routine to 'My Humps',' Miles frowned.

'Oh God!' cried Harriet.

'I'd forgotten…' Nicky laughed, burying her face in her hands.

'Don't worry Miles, there's not as much tequila in it this time,' Leigha called, winking heavily at Sukie. Sukie grinned.

'Shall we crack some out now?' she asked, reaching for the ladle.

'Uh uh uh!' Leigha snatched it up out of her reach. 'No cocktail for ladies not in their cocktail dress.'

'Ley, it's not even five thirty yet,' Harriet moaned.

'It's New Year's Eve, what does that matter?' Leigha countered, dropping the ladle into the saucepan with a splash.

'Wow.' Adam coughed in surprise. 'This drink doesn't taste as girly as it looks.'

'That will be the bottle and a half of tequila Leigha put in it,' Harriet answered sagely.

'On top of the vodka and Archers, of course,' Sukie added.

'Oh, of course!' Adam coughed again.

'Trust me, three of these, and you'll be totally bladdered,' Harriet assured him.

'All the same, I think I'll switch to beer when I've finished this one,' Adam said.

'Oh that won't do at all!' Sukie dropped her voice mischievously, leaning past him to refill her own glass of cocktail. 'She wants you druuuuunk tonight.'

Harriet smacked her friend on the upper arm, causing her to jolt and splash the ladleful of drink over the counter. Sukie groaned and reached over to the kitchen sink for the dishcloth. Adam and Harriet's eyes met as Sukie leant down between them to swab up the sticky mess dripping down the face of the cupboards and pooling on the floor tiles. Adam's face was embarrassed; Harriet's apologetic. Leigha had been a no-go area of conversation between them all month, since their evening together in the Armstrong.

Harriet suddenly grabbed Adam's glass and with one quick

movement poured the remainder of his potent cocktail back into the saucepan. 'I'll get you that beer,' she smiled

Leigha's cocktail was doing its work and she was well on her way to being seasonably tipsy. She periodically nodded enthusiastically in agreement with whatever it was her companion was talking about; as she was wearing a Santa hat complete with working bell, this proved quite irritating and said companion shortly made her excuses and went to join the queue for the bathroom.

Immediately Johnny slid into the vacated space next to Leigha. 'Hey you,' he said, looking at her with his usual soft appreciation.

'Hey yourself!' she smiled, twisting at the waist in order to face him.

'You're drunk,' he teased, drunk enough himself to reach out and push back the fall of her hair to behind her ear.

'It's New Year's Eve,' Leigha rolled her eyes.

Johnny smiled. 'So it is.'

Johnny hesitated, leaving his fingertips brushing the skin of her neck a little longer than was polite, mesmerised by the fluttering sensation of her pulse there. She didn't pull away, rather, she pushed her head against his hand like a cat wanting to be stroked and smiled up at him, all red lips and white teeth.

Just as suddenly, she had pulled away, and was reaching forward to grab at Nicky's dangling hand, leaving Johnny sitting back, breathless with that curious feeling she always gave him, like he was heavy as stone and lighter than air, all at once.

I probably love her, he thought, miserably, feeling tequila twist and burn in his stomach.

Johnny wandered over to join Harriet as she clumsily scooped slivers of a broken glass into a damp dishcloth over her hand.

'Mind yourself,' she said, automatically. Johnny ignored her, bending down to pick up the larger shards that had fallen to the floor.

'Is Leigha serious about Adam?' he asked, without preamble. Harriet faltered, dropping most of the little splinters that she had managed to collect. She glanced around to see who was in earshot before replying.

'What are you talking about?' Johnny straightened up, throwing the glass he had collected carelessly into the kitchen sink.

'I just want to know. Is she just flirting or,' he coloured, 'does she want something serious with him? Does she want *him*?' Harriet frowned as she deliberated how best to answer.

'What business is it of yours anyway?' she said finally, meeting Johnny's eyes. Johnny didn't drop the eye contact, but leant heavily against the kitchen side, uncaring of the wetness or the fragments of glass.

'Because *I* want her,' he answered simply, the rawness of the honesty causing Harriet to pause.

'I don't know how she feels about it all, really,' she lied. 'And besides, Adam's not exactly into her, so even if she did have a thing for him –'

'Not into her?' Johnny interrupted with a harsh laugh. Then wordlessly, he took her shoulders and spun her around so she faced down the corridor to the front of the house. In the gloom by the main door she could just make out the smudge of redness that was Leigha's dress, a dark tallness that was Adam, a burst of white caught in Leigha's hand: the bunch of mistletoe, commandeered from its place affixed in the upstairs stairwell.

And the longer Harriet looked the more was brought into focus, Adam's hands, one pale against the darkness of Leigha's hair as he held her face to his, the other roving and plucking at the hem of her dress, Leigha's free hand invisible, slid up under Adam's shirt. Discomfort shivered queerly against Harriet's skin.

'Happy fucking New Year,' Johnny said – more to himself than to her – before picking up his bottle of beer off the side and saluting her with it.

Leigha awoke on New Year's Day, 2007, still wearing her tights, lips bruised from kissing, a wicked hangover fogging her sense and memory. Cautiously, without raising her face from the pillow, she stretched her fingers out across the bed, whipping her arm back underneath her when they touched the warm body of the other occupant.

Her companion groaned and stirred, rolling over and away and taking most of the duvet with them. Through her eyelashes, Leigha recognised the person and found herself exhaling in relief; the short hair had thrown her for a moment, but it was only Harriet. She scooched closer, pressing her forehead in-between Harriet's shoulder blades.

'Who's in your bed?' she whispered. Harriet groaned again.

'I have no idea,' she answered groggily. Leigha laughed softly.

'I love New Year's Eve,' she murmured, settling her head down on Harriet's pillow. Harriet only grunted in response.

Chapter Five

Nicky placed her elbows on the table and buried her face in her hands. 'Poor Johnny,' was all she could muster.

'Poor Johnny indeed,' Sukie agreed, dismantling her toasted panini to remove unwanted tomato.

'I mean, it was obvious he quite fancied her,' Harriet said, dolefully. 'But he's got it bad.' She dropped her voice. 'He thinks its love.'

'They always think its love,' Sukie rubbished, pausing to lick mayonnaise from her fingertips. 'He just wanted to bone her, like they all do, and he's pissed off that Adam's getting there first.'

'You're a heartless cow,' Harriet glared. 'He could *very well* be in love with her!'

'Adam too for that matter,' Nicky added, reappearing from between her hands. Harriet frowned down at her lunch. She hadn't yet shared her concerns about Adam's vacillating interest in Leigha with the others.

'And you're a total hypocrite!' Sukie argued, jabbing a chip at Harriet, breaking her out of her introspection. 'When you were breaking up with Seth, what was all that crap about love being invented by Disney?'

'Oh yes, in collusion with Hallmark,' Nicky remembered,

arching her eyebrow. Harriet rolled her eyes.

'You didn't see his face,' she insisted. 'It was heart-breaking.'

'Well, our Leigha *is* a total man-eater,' Sukie said with affection, dipping a chip into Nicky's ketchup.

'And coming up right behind you,' Nicky warned, voice pitched low. Sukie and Harriet turned to see Leigha pushing through the glass doors into the café. The three girls looked up at their friend expectantly as she dumped her handbag under the free chair and began extricating herself from her scarf, gloves and hat. Her cheeks and nose were red with the cold, her hair was touched by the sleety rain and was hanging stuck to her face.

'What?' she snapped peevishly.

'Nothing!' Sukie dabbed another chip into Nicky's ketchup; Harriet couldn't stop herself from asking…

'Weren't you meeting up with Adam at the Armstrong?' she said, tentatively.

'No,' Leigha answered, pulling her handbag onto her lap and busying herself trying to find her purse within it. Nicky and Sukie exchanged a meaningful look.

'He standing you up already, Ley?' Sukie asked, with characteristic directness. Leigha scowled.

'He's not *standing me up*,' she hissed. 'He's going to the library, he said he's really got into the flow of his dissertation this week.' Harriet managed to hide the utter disbelief on her face by dipping her head just in time.

'Well,' Nicky answered after a moment's awkward silence, 'that's good. Looks like you are starting to rub off on him,' she nodded at Harriet. Leigha shot Harriet a livid look, before wordlessly walking over to the food servery. Harriet exhaled nervously.

'Christ!' she said. Sukie made the screeching *Psycho* noise in eloquent agreement.

Adam could have sworn that Harriet had hesitated in the aisle, that her intent had been to keep moving through the lecture theatre, however her companion Lucy – perhaps already too accustomed to their seats at the back of the hall – slid in beside him as usual. A heartbeat too long later, Harriet followed suit. Adam leant forward awkwardly to speak across Lucy's chest.

'Morning, trouble.'

Harriet shot him her routinely condescending look, but perhaps it was a little more loaded than usual.

'I hear your New Year's resolution is going well,' she said in a careful tone, pulling her book and notepad from her bookbag and laying them on the desk. When she was met with a quizzical silence from Adam she continued, 'cracking on with your dissertation, I mean.'

The very tips of Adam's ears went pink, a fact that surely did not escape Harriet's notice. She continued, airily. 'Which idea are you going with then?' Adam just glared at her mutinously, well aware that she knew he hadn't given his thesis a second's more thought since New Year's Eve.

'I'm still playing around with some options,' he answered drily. Harriet nodded sarcastically.

'Good idea.' She lay her biro perpendicular to the notepad and sat back against the back of her chair, staring out at the lectern ahead of them. Adam strained across Lucy a little more.

'Bloody hell, stop it, let's just swap seats!' Lucy demanded, before duly obliging by standing on the chair momentarily whilst Adam squeezed past her and into place.

'Look, I was busy,' he said, without preamble, knowing full well by this point that yesterday's cancellation on her best friend was most likely at the root of this strange hostility. Up close, she still smelt like being outside, sharp and cold and wintery.

'Do you remember how you *promised* me that you weren't just

41

after one thing with Leigha?' Harriet asked him, lowering her voice as the lecturer walked into the room.

'Yes, and I'm not!' he groaned.

'You're not?' Harriet scoffed, 'you snog her face off, then it takes her – what? – five texts before you agree to meet up with her? Then you cancel on her at the last minute?'

Adam had no immediate answer; the tips of his ears were pink again. 'I got busy,' he repeated, finally, dropping his voice to a whisper as the lecturer began to speak. Harriet stiffly turned to face front, uncapping her pen and reaching for her notepad. Adam let out a loud sigh of frustration, rubbing the heels of his palms against his brow.

Harriet glared at him and pushed her notepad towards him, where she had scribbled the words: *You've made your bed, now you bloody well lie in it!!*

The year rushed on and the slushy, sleety January drew towards its end. Leigha finally stopped texting Adam, her limit of humiliation reached by the umpteenth weak excuse received in response.

Taking their cue from Adam and Johnny – who seemed to have decided never to talk about 'what happened' – the others fell delicately back into place and routine was restored between the seven of them; game nights, movie nights, quiz nights.

Harriet watched Johnny watching Leigha watching Adam; Leigha started to pour spirits into all of her evening drinks and laughing always slightly too loudly. One or other of the girls was always on hand to pull Leigha's fingers from her mouth when she bit at her nails a little too long, Harriet looking sidelong at Adam as she did, her annoyance with him clear to read in every line on her face.

She had warned him – no, worse – *asked* him – not to play this game with Leigha. For all her bluster and posturing Leigha was no easy flirt; for whatever reason she did not trust without effort and most of all was terrified, absolutely terrified, of rejection.

Harriet had been wary but happy when Leigha had first set her sights on Adam; a friend, already a friend, someone she couldn't just kick out of her bed and pretend didn't exist. Someone she already had a relationship with; that, Harriet had known, was likely the best shot of Leigha ever having one at all and she so, *so* wanted her best friend to be happy, to relax, and lose that strange kernel of hardness and fear that she carried around inside of her.

Adam met her hard look with a maddeningly assured smile. It was like trying to be angry with a puppy that didn't understand what it had done wrong. Harriet cupped Leigha's hand in her own and resolutely looked away from Adam, keeping up the conversation in a falsely bright voice.

Like he had done countless times before, Adam gave Harriet's slightly ajar door a perfunctory knock and pushed it open.

She looked up at him from where she sat, cross-legged on her bed with her laptop balanced on her thighs, hard-read books lying open to their broken spines around her. She was listening to the new Fall Out Boy album that he had lent her. He smiled broadly. She looked back down at her screen, expressionless.

'Come to ask me to do your *bildungsroman* coursework for you?' she asked. Apparently uninterested in his response, she began typing again. Adam faltered.

'Er. No. Just wondering where you were, what you're doing holed up here when we're all downstairs.' He flashed what he considered his most charming of smiles. 'But the coursework, well, if you're offering…'

Harriet's typing got harder. 'Something to do with *Catcher in the Rye*?' For the first time since she'd started typing again she looked up at him. 'Actually, you remind me of Holden Caulfield.'

Adam, not knowing whether this was an insult or a compliment, decided to change the subject. 'Are you coming downstairs?' he asked.

'Nope.' Harriet paused in her typing, reaching round to swipe at a paragraph in one of the books with a yellow highlighter. 'Unsurprisingly, I've got to do my *bildungsroman* coursework.'

Adam stared at her, bemused. 'Harry,' he began, feeling a sudden swell of panic, 'are you really *this* annoyed with me?'

Harriet's answer was to pick up a slim paperback from the mounds around her and toss it at him. Adam caught it flat to his chest: *The Catcher in the Rye.* He looked up at her, nonplussed.

'You can take my copy,' she said, turning back once again to her screen. 'I'm not referring to it in my essay. I hate that book.'

Adam stood there stupidly, speechless, holding the book weakly in his hand.

So say, what are you waiting for? Kiss her, kiss her, Fall Out Boy sang out into the tight silence. Harriet stabbed at a key on her keyboard and the CD skipped to the next track.

'Well, Harriet's shitting bricks and Johnny looks like he wants to cry, deck me, or both whenever we're in the same room.'

With this abrupt and uninvited entry into Miles' room, Adam threw himself dramatically down on the bed.

Miles pushed himself back on his desk chair and surveyed his prone friend. 'Honestly? I don't blame either of them.'

'Oh, cheers mate! I knew I could count on you to cheer me up!' Adam moaned, flinging the back of his arm over his face.

'You can't keep avoiding Leigha,' Miles advised, seriously. 'It's really obvious and it's embarrassing her to hell. Harriet's probably angry because all she hears at home is Leigha whining about you playing her – and Johnny's annoyed because you pulled the girl he fancied for no apparent reason, because you sure as hell don't seem to care about her or want to go out with her. Can't you see why people are pissed off at you?'

'Well… yes, obviously.' Adam sat up and rubbed his face tiredly. 'This is *exactly* what I didn't want to happen.'

'Well you shouldn't have bloody kissed her then!' Miles exclaimed. 'No sympathy from this corner. Bad show.'

'Oh yeah, like you would have said no, to her, like that, in that dress, holding freaking mistletoe, and after a skinful of beer! If you were single…' Adam added hurriedly at the sight of Miles' supercilious expression.

'I certainly would have,' he answered grandly, 'especially knowing what a nightmare it would cause. Seriously, you're going to HAVE to take her out on a date. That'll calm down the girls. Johnny – well, put it this way, it won't upset him any *more…*'

Adam groaned into his palms. 'I don't even like her that much. She can be so annoying. I don't know what got into me,' he admitted.

'A skinful of beer, wasn't it?' Miles clapped a compassionate hand to Adam's shoulder.

Chapter Six

February 2007

The weather was typically February foul and Harriet seemed to have brought along a mood to match. She didn't remove her scarf the whole journey into Waterloo, her entire lower face concealed behind a wall of plaited, coloured wool.

Adam had never been to Senate House – the University of London's central library – before, preferring instead, like Johnny, to use the online catalogues. The girls had instantly been appalled, berating the piss poor effort he was putting into his studies, predicting – in typically dramatic fashion – the complete and total failure of his degree each and every time they saw him until finally, worn-down, he agreed to tag along with Harriet the next time she went into the city.

The girls had waxed so lyrical about this great national epicentre of learning that Adam was a bit underwhelmed at first sight of the grey Art-Deco building looming pale on the London skyline. The inside wasn't much better, emphatically hushed, like a graveyard, and decorated like a gentlemen's smoking club.

Harriet disappeared into the stacks as soon as they came to the right section, mutely waving her hand to indicate the catalogue computers that lined one wall. Before the log in screen had even loaded for Adam she had reappeared to pile musty books on the reading table where she had discarded her handbag, scarf and coat.

'Harry,' he tried.

Shush, she wordlessly flapped her free hand at him. Dispirited, he typed a few vague searches into the engine: Blake. Shelley. Romanticism. Didn't bother to scroll down the list of several thousand entries that generated. Giving that up as a bad lot he returned to the reading table, shifting Harriet's one precarious pile of books into two more stable ones. He glanced down the aisle. Way at the end Harriet was sitting on one of the portable steps, consulting the bibliography at the back of a thick, yellow-paged book.

Adam hesitated at the entrance to the aisle, feeling rather the unwelcome visitor left loitering in the doorway. He knew she knew he was there and sure enough, within thirty seconds she turned her head to him, eyebrows knitted together.

'What?' Only the fifth or sixth word she had spoken to him all day.

'Help me.' Pathetic, but genuine; he couldn't help but smile ruefully, and – as he had hoped – neither could she. Harriet shut the book with a dull thud, hugging it between her chest and her crossed arms as she stood and came to him.

A move of the mouse as she sat down called up the results list and she started weeding through it with the efficiency he hadn't been able to muster.

'Romanticism,' she muttered to herself, as if it were the most ridiculous focus for a dissertation in the whole world.

Adam moved to stand behind her, hands flat in support on the arms of the computer chair, his stomach pressed to its back. He noticed he could feel a rumbling vibration through Harriet that was her murmuring under her breath as she read through the catalogue list. He noticed how the very tip of her tongue appeared between her lips as she concentrated. He noticed how her hair smelt like the rain that had fallen on them during their walk from the tube.

And then he noticed those unfathomable kicks again, the ones he had felt churning up the Snakebite in his insides that night in the Armstrong; one low down that he recognised well – that was lust – and one higher, that was something more. He pulled back from the support of the chair, frowned, fidgeted.

'How far in to this do you want to research?' Harriet asked, seemingly oblivious to Adam's growing discomfort. 'How many books shall we get you?'

'As many as it takes to for me to get started,' Adam replied, frowning harder as he felt the tell-tale burn of a blush rising on his neck.

Despite being the native Londoner, Harriet was passive and let him pick their spot on the platform at Holborn. She was still quiet, but it was a silence of a different quality now. Her eyes were soft again, her oversized scarf looped around and around the handles of her handbag.

Adam didn't want to take her home, not yet, back to that house and the other girls, who'd sharpen her back up against him in no time. For the moment they seemed to be friends again, and whilst Adam wasn't too sure what about his company today had caused it, he certainly wasn't going to look a gift horse in the mouth.

He suggested going for Chinese food; he knew it was her favourite – she knew he knew, and smiled at him gratefully.

'Look,' Adam said suddenly, interrupting himself, 'look.' Harriet followed the line of his pointing arm to where a tiny brown roundness scuttled parallel to the rails and away out of sight. She clutched at his elbow.

'Oh,' she breathed, her voice small against the rushing sound of the oncoming train. 'You know, I've never actually seen one before.' She looked so decidedly pleased at something so ridiculously commonplace as a mouse that Adam couldn't help but laugh. She smiled up at him, uncaring of his soft ridicule.

They alighted at Piccadilly Circus, out of breath and flushed in their winter layers by the time they made it to street level, where a squall of rain buffeted them immediately. Harriet yelped, unconsciously drawing closer to the shelter and warmth of Adam's body, wrapping their arms together tightly as if he were another one of the girls. They navigated the flow of tourists, heads together and down, on towards Soho and Chinatown.

'Did you know,' Adam turned his face to murmur into her ear, 'that it's not Cupid?' Harriet gave a preoccupied half glance back at the familiar statue in the centre of the circus.

'It's Eros,' she agreed.

'No, it's actually Anteros,' Adam corrected her, pleased with himself. 'Unrequited love.'

'Fraternal love,' Harriet retorted immediately; there was an edge back to her voice and Adam pulled himself up immediately.

'Yeah, something like that,' he agreed convivially as they moved forward towards Leicester Square, her fingers still pulling distractedly at the sleeve of his coat.

Now he had noticed Harriet, and the strange solar-plexus wrenches she seemed to incur, Adam found he could notice nothing else. She slipped in front of him, to better see the screen of the quiz machine in the pub, standing so close he could feel the warmth of her body heat all the way down his front; everything on his body involuntarily tightened.

The stake was £2 and rising, and it was a football question. Sukie delicately declared herself without a 'fucking clue' and Harriet tilted her head backwards, looking up at him expectantly for the answer.

His mind went blank.

'Adam!' Sukie cried, grabbing at his arm in a panic. 'What's the answer?'

'Man United.' Johnny appeared out of nowhere to save the day, reaching clumsily over Harriet's head to punch the correct answer on the touch screen with just milliseconds to spare. Sukie exhaled in relief; she took her quiz machine investments very seriously; after all, £2 could be a small fortune to a student the wrong side of Reading Week. The display changed to the next question, the now £3 pot flashing tantalisingly in the corner of the screen.

Q. Who was the first poet to be buried in Poet's Corner in London's Westminster Abbey?

A. Keats   B. Wordsworth

C. Chaucer   D. Shakespeare

Sukie looked eagerly at her two tame Literature students.

They were still looking at one another, Adam flushed all the way to the tip of his ears, Harriet's lips slightly apart, so that her bottom teeth reflected a sheen in the light from the flashing quiz machine.

'Guys,' Sukie tried, weakly, 'hey, guys?'

'Chaucer,' Johnny said, decisively, reaching forward to once again select the right answer, startling Adam and Harriet out of their impromptu staring contest.

'At least someone is taking this seriously!' Sukie grumbled, hooking arms with Johnny to prevent him from returning to the table where Leigha and Nicky were sharing a particularly limp looking plate of curly fries.

'Just going to the loo,' Harriet mumbled, to nobody in particular.

Adam watched her slip away and through the swing doors into the Ladies'. He could feel Leigha's eyes on him from the nearby table. He took a long drink from his pint of coke, feeling it bubble low in his throat as it went down too quickly.

You have royally fucked this up, he thought to himself

Chapter Seven

It took Harriet and Sukie three trips between the bar and the booth to bring the whole round over; pints for the boys, a pitcher of an orangey coloured cocktail – almost overflowing with ice – and a bottle of cheap white wine. The cherry on the cake was a tray of Jägerbombs, courtesy of Sukie's ignorant father; she had cunningly hidden the money trail by asking for cashback when doing her weekly food shop on his credit card.

It was the second week of February, a rainy Wednesday, a generous few degrees above zero, and some absolute twat on the Entertainment committee had decided that what the student body really needed was a Beach Party theme night. As inappropriate as the timing may be, they were all loath to miss out on an opportunity for fancy dress and, most importantly, it happened to be Nicky's 21st birthday. The real celebrations would be that Saturday, of course, at a house party where the Pan Punch would be flowing, but Nicky had wanted to mark the actual day by going for 'a quiet one' – meant of course, as ever, ironically.

Sukie gingerly put the tray of glasses down on the table. Nicky literally clapped her hands with glee. 'Right guys, let's play a game,' she ordered. Leigha groaned, tugging up her blue and white bandeau summer dress, oversized sunglasses perched stylistically on her head.

'Never Ever…?' Sukie suggested, with a grin, knowing Nicky was far too prim.

'Bunny?' was Johnny's proposal, complete with hands-above-head imitation of the ears.

'Twenty Ones?' Miles said. Leigha groaned louder.

'No, no! I plan on getting very drunk tonight; I don't plan on calculating… prime numbers or… trying to work out Roman Numerals.' Leigha karate-sliced the air to emphasise her point.

'Let's play Categories then,' Harriet suggested.

'Yeah, Categories!' Adam agreed immediately. Leigha rounded on them.

'Oh yes, that's always great fun,' she snapped, sarcasm dripping from every word. 'Especially playing with you two. What will the category be? Nineteenth Century poets? Shakespearean plays?'

'That could be a good one,' Adam said mildly, as uncomplicated and happy-go-lucky as usual, checking Leigha's rising annoyance. She sloshed cocktail and ice cubes into her glass, spattering the table.

'Whatever,' she said, 'I don't really care.' She sipped at her drink, printing her red lipstick like a signature on the rim of the glass. Harriet, still standing, began to line the shot glasses of Jägermeister up next to their respective tumbler of energy drink. Adam stood to help, resting his hand on Harriet's hipbone briefly as he brushed past to her other side. Harriet jerked at the touch.

'Shit.' Harriet sucked the split Jägermeister from between her thumb and index finger.

'That'll have been yours then,' Johnny crowed. Harriet ignored him, wiping her hand on her sarong-style skirt, leaving a streak of darker material. She dropped the now more than half-empty shot glass into her tumbler and downed the lot before the Red

Bull had even subsided from its froth and fizz.

Johnny followed suit, slamming the tumbler down on the table for good measure; the empty shot glass inside it tinkled.

'Well, whilst you ladies are faffing,' he jeered, standing and wiping his hands on his demined thighs. 'Come on mate, pool table.' Adam quickly saw to his shot and obliged, digging in his pockets for pound coins as he went. Harriet, still rubbing at her sticky hand, slid into the newly vacated space next to Leigha.

'Bottoms up Ley,' Sukie pushed a tumbler and shot glass towards Leigha. 'Happy Birthday Nic.' She saluted Nicky with her shot glass before dropping it into the tumbler. She waited for the effervescing to stop before delicately pinching her nose closed and drinking the concoction in three careful gulps, the shot glass banging against her knuckles.

Leigha watched Adam stretch his long body out across the length of the pool table as he lined up his shot. Johnny groaned good naturedly as Adam's break potted two balls. Adam straightened and tossed his pool cue across from one hand to the other, grinning widely. Even in a ludicrously coloured shirt, left hanging open over a preposterously pink tee-shirt, he was irritatingly handsome. That combined with his obvious confidence and his quick and free smiles ensured that Leigha's weren't the only eyes in the bar on him at that moment.

A crow of triumph drew her attention to Johnny; Adam had sunk the white and Johnny was rejoicing as if he had somehow cleverly been responsible for the gaff.

Johnny's acquiescence to the theme was adding a lei garland of plastic flowers to his white tee-shirt over cargo shorts combination, a straggly survivor from some other fancy dress event. He was taller and broader than Adam, well-built, had alternated between the first and second string university football teams since he was a Fresher.

Johnny caught her looking across at him and beamed at her, before self-consciously fumbling with his pint as if to negate the enthusiasm he'd just shown. Leigha smiled back, took a drink herself; she found herself wishing, stupidly, pointlessly, that she could transfer her attraction to Adam onto Johnny, sweet Johnny – then they'd both be happy.

'Harry.' Leigha jumped. Adam had come back to the table whilst she wasn't paying attention. Harriet was slow to turn to him from her conversation with Miles; Adam plucked at the fabric of her top for her attention. 'Got you another,' he said, placing the components for another Jägerbomb in front of her. 'Cos you spilt yours…' he finished, weakly, visibly wilting under Harriet's inquiring stare.

And, not for the first time, Leigha reflected on how nauseating it was that some men, sometimes, acted so pathetically around Harriet. She flushed with guilt immediately and reached for her previously ignored Jägerbomb to distract herself.

'Cheers,' Harriet said finally, dropping the smaller glass into the larger with a wet clunk.

'What about Sambucas next, yeah?' Sukie asked.

'Yuck, yuck, yuck!' Nicky – hopelessly hyperactive – cried out in delight.

Johnny appeared from nowhere, still brandishing his pool cue. He dropped a pound coin into Adam's pint, causing the beer to hiss. Adam groaned.

'Down it,' Johnny commanded, pointing precariously with the pool cue, 'and come and finish this bloody game.'

Months before, the guys had shared a joke about Harriet sleeping in a bed surrounded by books, like teddy bears. Adam was relieved to see that they seemed to be piled up appropriately on the desk and smiled – he had to remember to tell Johnny and Miles.

It was the first time Adam had been in Harriet's room at night. There was a streetlight directly outside, he noted, and the curtains were cheap and thin; the room was flooded with a stark orange light that the clicking on of the bedside lamp did little to diffuse.

Harriet grabbed a glass from her desk, scowling at the little puddle of musty water still in the bottom. Tipsy and more than a little off-balance, she crossed the room and knelt on the bed, throwing the window wide to empty the glass out of it. The sharp February air rushed in to fill the little room, seemingly in agreement with the weather forecasters who predicted snow before the week was out.

'Leigha,' Adam began, the L sound rolling drunkenly from his mouth, 'will be mad.'

'Leigha,' Harriet replied, closing the window as quietly as she could, 'is always mad lately.' She giggled drunkenly at her audacity, tugging the curtains to and turning to face him. 'Oh I'll replace it tomorrow!' she assured him, taking the three-quarters full litre bottle of Malibu they'd pilfered from Leigha's cupboard and pouring a poorly measured shot of the rum into the glass.

'Never ever, have I ever,' Adam began, ignoring Harriet's snort of laughter, 'gone *skinny dipping.*'

Harriet let out a squeal of protest. 'I told you, that was a secret!'

'It's only us here,' Adam pointed out. Harriet sighed in agreement, and did her punishment shot with a wince and a cough.

'Never ever have I ever,' she said, her voice sly, 'had sex in my parents' bed!'

'Nope,' Adam grinned. 'I've *never* had sex in *your* parents' bed.' Harriet rolled her eyes.

'Oh, stop being fucking pedantic,' she moaned. Like Leigha, she tended to swear more when she was drunk. Adam nobly acquiesced and took the shot she poured for him like a man. The rum burned all the way down. They knew too many of one another's secrets, the result of far too much time spent together – both en masse with the rest of the group and alone, distracting each another from research, in libraries and study pods; this game wasn't going to last long.

If he kissed Harriet, right then and there – he found himself thinking, drunkenly, crazily – that both he and she would taste like rum; maybe they would burn one another.

'Never ever have I ever,' said Adam, the words running together in one vague sound, 'given out a fake name or number in a bar?'

'Oh Christ!' Harriet laughed. 'Loads of times!' She poured out the accompanying shot.

'Would you have given me a fake number?' Adam asked her suddenly, before he could stop himself, his face surely glowing in the dark with the sudden rush of drunken mortification.

Harriet finally seemed to sense that her silence had lasted a little too long. 'Oh I don't know,' she said lightly, with a wave of her hand and a slosh from the Malibu held by it. 'Impossible to tell now, you know?' Something about this answer rankled. Adam fixed her with a hard look.

'I guess,' he answered, coolly. 'Your turn.'

'Never ever,' Harriet drew the words out as she tried to think. Adam could almost see the two shots of Malibu at work, slowing her down. 'Have I ever... oh, fuck it, played football,' she gave up. Adam raised his eyebrows.

'Not even at school, like in PE?' he pressed. Harriet's eyes fluttered closed at the realisation that she'd now have to do a double shot.

'Fuck,' she repeated.

'It's alright,' Adam said, reaching for the bottle and pouring himself a small amount. 'I'll let you off.'

'Wait, no, I've got another one,' Harriet interrupted him. 'Never ever have I ever snogged Leigha Webster.'

Adam placed the already considerably emptier bottle of Malibu down on the bedside table, trying desperately to think faster than the night's drinking really facilitated.

'Ha!' he blustered, finally, 'whatever! I've seen you plant plenty of smackers on her! You girls are right lezzers sometimes.'

'I've never had my hand up her skirt,' Harriet shot back in an instant, suddenly impossibly, impossibly angry with him. Adam met her glare with a look of complete bewilderment; he thought they'd put all this him and Leigha stuff behind them. He was getting really sick and tired of these mood swings.

'Harry,' he said finally, 'chill out, mate. You're drunk.'

'And whose fault is that?' Harriet grumbled, but her rage was already deflating, quick to anger, quicker to calm as ever. Slowly she stretched out, snaking her feet past him to rest them on the pillows and curling herself to fit around where he sat on the single bed.

'Poor Leigha,' she mumbled, half to herself.

Adam frowned. 'I don't think she's as poor as she likes you to think she is.'

'Oh, but she is,' Harriet insisted. 'Poor Leigha. She's my best friend.'

'Hey,' Adam said, poking her on the sliver of skin of her back that showed where her top had ridden up. 'I thought I was your best friend,' he teased. Harriet closed her eyes and smiled.

'You're one of them,' she answered, simply. 'You going down to the couch, or trek home?'

'I'll stay here, if you don't mind,' Adam answered, leaning back against the pillows next to Harriet's feet. 'Top and tail, yeah?'

'Just don't kick me in the face,' was Harriet's reply and just minutes later her breathing was the deep and regular one of sleep. Adam lay awake listening to it most of the night, alone with the burning in his chest.

Harriet woke that Thursday cramped and disorientated, feeling like she had a tumbleweed stuck in her throat. She stretched out her legs, disturbing Adam, who had been using her calf as a pillow. He protested faintly and threw his arm over his face to block the light. They were curled around one another's legs like yin and yang.

Harriet sat up completely, slipping her legs from underneath Adam's chest, scrabbling around on the floor for her mobile phone. It was out of battery. She swore, hauling herself up – unsteady due to pins-and-needles – and went out onto the landing, leaning over the banister of the stairs. She could hear someone in the kitchen.

'Hey, what's the time?' she called down, voice hoarse.

'Morning,' Sukie called back. 'About twenty to ten. Do you have Adam up there? His shoes are still here by the door.'

Harriet ignored Sukie, having started to rush back into her room before she'd even finished the sentence. She rat-a-tat-tatted her palm on Adam's hipbone.

'Up, up,' she demanded, 'we've got twenty minutes to make the *bildungsroman* lecture.'

Supremely unbothered, Adam just rolled over to his front and put his head full under the pillow. 'Water,' he croaked.

'When you're up,' Harriet snapped, wriggling frantically into a pair of tights under the sarong-style skirt she'd slept in. 'Get up!' she repeated.

'I'm not going to a lecture dressed like a Hawaiian pimp.' Adam's voice was muffled through the pillow. 'Definitely giving this one a miss.'

'Well I'm not!' Harriet snapped, spraying herself liberally with deodorant. 'And you shouldn't, you've missed so much this term.' She could hear the snort of Adam's laughter.

'What are they going to do, write home to my parents?'

'Adam!' Harriet cried, exasperated. 'For crying out loud. This really is your third year at University, not a practice go at it. You're

going to fail your degree unless you start *trying*. You've got to try.'
She was met with obstinate muteness from beneath the pillow; she
sighed. 'I'll treat you to a plate of curly fries afterwards?' The pillow
slid to one side as Adam begrudgingly heaved himself to his feet.

Dressed as he was in a practically fluorescent pink tee-shirt and
denim shorts cut at the knee, Adam drew his fair share of odd looks
as he and Harriet hurried through the sleet from the lecture theatre
to the campus refectory. He made a solemn vow to never again
take the piss out of guys unseasonably dressed – they too might
just be poor sods doing the walk of shame after a theme night.

True to her word, Harriet ordered him a double portion of
his favourite curly fries, and he immediately coated them in salt
and drowned them in ketchup as she picked up her cutlery and
gingerly cut into a shrivelled jacket potato.

'Last night was fun,' he said, with his mouth full.

'Tell that to my poor head,' Harriet answered, scraping some
cheese and baked beans onto her fork.

'Gotta be on it again for Saturday,' Adam said. Harriet made
a non-committal noise through her mouthful of potato. 'I've got
drinks tomorrow night too. My poor liver!'

'You're going to have to stay in all next week, detox,' Harriet
agreed. 'Maybe even work on your dissertation.' She smiled to
show she that was only teasing.

'Yeah right,' Adam teased back. 'We both know you're going to
end up writing my dissertation for me.' He popped the twist of
a chip into his mouth and gave one of what he thought was his
most winning smiles, the kind that always made Harriet smile
back; she did.

'Adam, Adam!' she sighed theatrically, 'what am I going to do
with you..?'

'Oh, just love me,' Adam answered, just as theatrically; a joke, just automatic banter, but immediately he felt his heart wallop grotesquely against the inside of his ribs. Harriet laughed.

'Everybody loves you.' She dropped her eyes to her plate and carved another chunk of potato. Adam looked hopelessly at the top of her bowed head.

'Oh, I don't know,' he answered, softly, pushing his cooling chips around on his plate with his fingertips.

It was getting busier, noisier, at The Dive, and Adam was having to wait a frustratingly long time to get served. This wasn't one of his usual haunts: a small, dingy campus bar built into the rafters of an extension on the main Student Union building, mostly frequented by Drama students; he could probably count the number of times he'd been in here on one hand.

He finally made eye contact with the frazzled bartender, receiving the briefest nod of acknowledgement in response; he'd be next. The bartender stuffed notes into the till, counted out change at lightning speed. Adam cleared his throat in preparation to shout his order over the din.

Quick as a flash, somebody took advantage of his hesitation.

'Three bottles of orange VK, please,' the girl bellowed, leaning the whole of her upper body across the top of the bar. Adam wheeled around, set to prodigiously tut his annoyance at this poor bar etiquette, but stopped in his tracks as he realised it was Sukie; she grinned at him. 'And a pint of Fosters and two cherry Sourz, please,' she appendixed to her order. 'I presume you're on the Fosters?' she asked Adam.

'Cheers, mate!' Adam nodded his assent. 'You girls out and about tonight too then?' He peered behind her through the mass of people trying to get near the bar.

'No,' Sukie answered, 'just me and some guys from my course.' She started to count out change, almost three full years buying

61

similar rounds ingraining in her the exact cost of various drinks. The bartender shouted out the total as he poured red Sourz into two slender plastic shot glasses and Sukie tipped the precise amount into his open hand, glittering shrapnel full of five and ten pence pieces. 'We're out for a birthday.' She nodded Adam towards the second shot glass, and he picked it up appreciatively.

'Oh yeah? Me too.' In unspoken agreement they shot their Sourz right there at the bar, rather than risk spillage during the push through the crowd. Adam took a hurried swallow from his pint to drop the level of it down below the rim before following Sukie through the horde of Friday night revellers to the space of stools and high tables beyond.

'Daniel Masterson?' Sukie turned back to him, as soon as they were clear.

'Yeah! How do you know Dan?' Adam asked.

'Does Drama like me, doesn't he?' Sukie answered, apparently possessive of this newly discovered-to-be-mutual friend. 'How about you?'

'Same halls in First Year,' Adam replied. 'Yeah, he's a good guy.'

'Yeah,' Sukie agreed, slowing as they reached a particular table. 'Everyone! This is Adam,' she announced, parking two of her three bottles of alcopop on the table. Adam smiled through the round of introductions – managing a particularly brazen 'nice to meet you' at a girl he was pretty sure he'd pulled the previous year – confidently claiming a spot at the table with his placed pint glass.

Three hours and seven rounds later, people started to slip away – home, or into the Union proper, where an R&B night was just starting to get busy. Adam and Sukie – without tickets or the inclination to attend – drank up and shrugged into their coats, Adam gallantly insisting that he walk Sukie all the way back to Dell Road, and Sukie not bothering to politely decline.

The streets on campus and into the student village were deserted. Everyone who was going out had already made their journey, and everyone else was entrenched indoors with the heating on full-blast. The sleety rain and correlating cloud cover of the day had blown away and the winter sky was at its deepest, inkiest black, the air glacier sharp. The heels of Sukie's boots rang out against the pavement as they walked through the silence, hands stuffed in coat pockets, shoulders hunched against the cold.

Sukie dumped her bag onto the low wall of the graveyard as they approached it, the easier to rummage around in it.

'Ciggie?' She offered one to Adam with a deft flick of her fingers. He declined by holding up his hand. Sukie regarded him in silence for a minute. 'Something stronger?' She pulled a suspiciously fat roll-up from the depths of her bag. Adam laughed, both at Sukie and at his immediate reaction to say yes. He was always reckless, but he was a little more reckless than usual lately.

'Go on then.'

Sukie put the spliff between her lips as she held her lighter underneath it before inhaling. She sat down on the damp wall, wrapping her arms around herself to keep warm, blowing out a thick, pale rope of smoke towards the sky. Adam sat down next to her and plucked the roll-up from Sukie's fingers, inhaling from it with an embarrassing hiccup, his throat closing up against the unexpected sear of the smoke. They sat in silence for a few minutes, passing it back and forth. On his third drag, the back of Adam's neck started to feel agreeably fizzy. On her fourth, Sukie exhaled with a long, satisfied sound, as if a weight had been lifted from her shoulders.

'So, what's the plan, Mr Chadwick?' she asked him leisurely, passing the spliff.

'The plan?' Adam asked, confused. 'Finish this and go home?'

'No, not the plan for tonight,' Sukie explained, slowly, as if he were simple. 'Your plan for *life*.'

'Bugger me, bit deep?' Adam laughed. 'Hopefully scrape a degree? Then move back in with the folks? Take the first decently paid job that comes my way and try and get whatever fun I can out of life.'

'Nobody gets out of it alive,' Sukie agreed sagely, waving her arm to encompass the field of mouldering bones behind them. 'I'd like to fall in love,' she informed him, matter-of-factly. 'That's all. You ever been in love?' Adam screwed up his face. 'Apparently it's wonderful. Apparently it makes you feel high.' She laughed, taking another deep drag. 'All the time. That would be nice.' She passed the roll-up again. 'So, do you think Johnny really is in love with Leigha?'

'Who knows?' Adam replied, with a shrug, his words starting to slur and blend a bit. 'I know he's totally mad for her, can't go a day without seeing her.' The fizzing on the back of his neck turned into a prickle. Who was he even talking about? 'Does that sound like love to you?' Suddenly shaky, he took his deepest drag so far, pulling the heat deep down into his lungs.

'Fucked if we know, right?' Sukie answered, a little sullenly.

And suddenly – whether it was the booze, the weed, or the strange pressing quality of the night – Adam suddenly felt like he was going to burst open, unless he said the words that were massing on his tongue, shared this sudden epiphany with Sukie right then and there, a Pandora opening all the boxes in the world. He opened his mouth and the sentence dropped into the space between them like a stone.

'But the way Johnny feels about Leigha… is the way I feel about Harry.'

Sukie didn't say anything, not right away. She took several shallow draws on the spliff without offering it back to him.

'You sick bastard,' she said finally, although her tone was not unkind. 'Do me – and yourself – a favour, okay? Never repeat that. Not to Harry and certainly not to Leigha.' She pinched off the burning end of the roll-up with practiced fingers and put the half or so that remained back into a pocket in the lining of her handbag. 'I'll just assume it's the wacky talking, okay? Now come on, walk me home already.' She stood up decisively, hoisting her bag to her shoulder – 'it's fucking freezing out here,' – and a rather shell-shocked Adam complied.

Chapter Eight

February 2007

Sukie sat at Harriet's desk in front of the mirror, trying in vain to get her heavy hair to curl using Nicky's heated tongs. Harriet – already dressed in a black beaded dress – had her knees up against her chest and her foot planted on her bedside table, and was leaning forward to paint her toenails a bright coral colour. With a mournful noise, Sukie gave up, switching the tongs off and smoothing the heat kinks out of her hair with her palms.

'That's why I keep my hair short,' Harriet observed, without looking up. 'None of this hassle.' Sukie made a face and reached for her glass of water. Usually she, like all the girls, started on spirits and mixers whilst getting ready – Harriet already had a glass of something-and-lemonade set on the bedside table beside her – but Sukie was still hung-over and dry-mouthed from the excesses of the night before and had never really been a great believer in the Hair of the Dog approach.

Adam's face – earnest and bone-white in the moonlight – flittered across Sukie's memory. She pushed aside the compulsion to spill the beans to Harriet that came along with it, reaching for her false eyelash glue. Once she'd applied both of the lashes, she looked back at Harriet, head still bowed to her foot as she dabbed on the nail-varnish. Behind her the bedroom curtains were still open to the dark evening beyond, the window-panes rectangles of black reflecting the points of light in the room. Outside, tufts of snow collided soundlessly with the glass.

'It's snowing,' Sukie said. 'Shit, I hope people can get taxis okay.'

Finished with her first foot, Harriet bent forwards even further to blow ineffectually on the wet nails, before craning her head back to see out the window.

'Don't worry, it'll still be a good night. Especially now that things aren't so tense in the Johnny-Leigha-Adam triangle,' Harriet laughed, shifting her other foot onto the edge of the bedside table.

At the mention of Adam's name, the desire to tell all pressed all the harder. Sukie drained her glass of water and then reached for Harriet's something-and-lemonade, taking a deep gulp: vodka, it transpired. Then she stood and quietly closed Harriet's bedroom door.

'Okay, I've got to tell you something and you totally can't let Leigha find out. And I mean totally, for your own good.' Harriet looked up at Sukie, her interest piqued, replacing the lid on the nail-varnish bottle.

'Go on then,' she said finally, weighing up her loyalty to Leigha with her curiosity. 'What's up?'

Leigha was impatient and straightening her hair even though it wasn't quite bone dry yet, her bedroom smelt warm and damp. Harriet silently perched on the novelty inflatable chair in the corner of the room. Leigha reached to turn down the volume on her computer speakers with her free hand.

'You alright?' she asked Harriet, watching her in the mirror. 'God, I love that dress. You look hot. I have no idea what I'm going to wear and you've just totally upped the ante.' Harriet looked down at her dress as if she'd never seen it before.

'Oh, I don't think I'm going to wear this actually,' she said, touching the beaded panel across her chest with her fingertips. 'Do you want to?' Leigha put her straighteners down on the desk rotated her chair on its casters to look at Harriet properly.

'What?'

'I'm not in a very… sequiny mood,' Harriet said. 'You wear it. It looks better on you anyway, you've got the boobs for it.'

'Well, if you think…' Leigha replied, a little nonplussed.

In one swift movement Harriet pulled the dress up and over her head, throwing it across the room to land in Leigha's lap. It smelt like Harriet's perfume and was pleasantly warm from her body heat. Harriet crossed the room and pulled Leigha's lilac dressing gown down from the hook on the back of the bedroom door, folding her bareness away into its thickness. Leigha fingered the beaded material on her lap.

'I do love this dress,' she repeated, finally.

Harriet had sat on her bed with her vodka and lemonade, wrapped in Leigha's dressing gown, until the constant opening and closing of the front door and the swell of chatter from downstairs grew too loud to ignore.

She slipped into the pair of jeans she had earlier discarded; a purple and white silk camisole top was the first thing out of her drawer that resembled party-wear. Her coral orange toes peeped up at her from the hem of the denim and she glared back. How had eight o' clock come so quickly? She needed more time to think, to deconstruct and compartmentalise, to work out how she felt about this massive and outrageous thing.

But all she could think about – in those precious few minutes before someone would come up and force her downstairs – was last week's Shakespeare: Stage and Screen seminar. David Tennant was suitably becrowned, fretting and strutting his stuff upon the stage, projected on the wallscreen in front of the class and drawing everyone's attention but hers. Instead, Harriet was noticing Adam's hand resting on the desk between them. Each fingertip was perfectly squared off – so unlike her own – odd and manly and perfect. And she didn't really know what that was supposed to mean.

Adam was – quite literally – cornered by a girl he'd known in his first year, apparently also friends with Nicky; incestuously small campus strikes again. He sipped from his drink and made feedback noises in all the right places as she prattled on, all the while glaring at the back of Sukie's dark head across the room.

She'd opened the door to him and Johnny half an hour ago and had studiously avoided meeting his eyes, guilt emblazoned across her face with all the subtlety of a neon sign. And Harriet – where the fucking fuck was Harriet? – his bloody heart was in his feet.

Leigha practically danced across the room – barefoot and lovely in a black shift dress that shimmered with sequins and beads – proffering an open bag of Doritos to guests, Johnny a smiling shadow wherever she stepped. It was maddening; he could hear Harriet's voice now, from somewhere out of sight, in the mass of people through to the hallway, perhaps? Someone shifted and he caught sight of the back of her, one elbow resting on her hip with her hand up by her ear, a stance that told him nothing. If he could just see her face, he would know if Sukie had told her, he would know how to play this. And he had to play this. He couldn't let one moment of stoned confusion ruin one of his most important friendships.

He couldn't bear it any longer, giving a rigid but polite excuse to the girl from his first year and pushing away from her through the crowded room, holding up a palm to decline the bag of Doritos that Leigha whirled into his face as he came near. He gripped Sukie's upper arm, a little more tightly than he'd planned to, and she turned from her conversation to glare at him.

'Sorry guys, just need to borrow her for one sec,' Adam grinned out at the group assembled on the couch, affable as ever, before steering Sukie through the kitchen and unceremoniously out of the back door.

Sukie shivered dramatically, wrapping her arms around herself and pressing backwards towards the shelter of the wall, white chips of snow disappearing as they melted into her hair. 'I haven't told her,' she said immediately, 'stop freaking out.'

'Who haven't you told? Leigha? Or Harriet?' Adam demanded.

'Neither!' Sukie shot back, but there had been the slightest flicker of hesitation there that Adam couldn't ignore. He raked both hands through his damp hair.

'Jesus Christ, Su, you're the one that said not to make it into a big thing!'

'I haven't! Harry won't tell anyone—'

'For crying out loud, it's Harriet who I didn't want to know!'

'Oh come on,' Sukie said, trying to make her voice sound as even and reasonable as possible. 'We're all grown-ups here. And besides,' she smirked, 'it's always nice to know that somebody likes you!'

'But I don't! Like her!' Adam moaned. 'Not like that. It's just I was totally mullered. I didn't mean to say it.' *Not to you, not out loud, not even to myself*, he finished the miserable thought. Sukie looked at him levelly.

'Well, if that's the case, you're a bigger dick than I thought you were.' She moved to open the back door, stepping inside the relative warmth of the back porch. 'And I already thought you were quite a dick,' she finished, balefully, moving away and into the bright kitchen.

Harriet strained to catch Sukie's eyes as she walked back inside, rubbing her palms against her bare, goose-pimpled arms and scowling, a cowed Adam following behind and meekly closing the back door against the cold. Sukie gave her an almost imperceptible shake of the head: *we'll talk later*.

To the uninformed observer, Johnny looked like he was having the worst night of his life. He sat rigid on the chair, staring out ahead of him into the middle distance with a faintly sweaty pallor to his face.

Perched daintily on his knee, Leigha rocked backwards as she laughed at someone's joke, her whole body soft and yielding as it pressed against his.

'Soft' being the apposite word there. It wouldn't do to have anything 'pressing back'. And so – whilst Leigha wiggled herself to get more comfortable – Johnny continued to down his beer and mentally recite Manchester United goalies from the sixties to the present.

Nicky and Miles moved as a unit through the party, mingling and chatting like the jovial hosts they were. Every so often a guest would insist that Nicky – as the feted birthday girl – do a shot of their choosing, so it wasn't too surprising that one leg of Nicky's tights was heavily laddered and she'd managed to lose her left earring.

Spying a free space opening up on the couch, Miles opportunistically steered his inert girlfriend towards it and wedged her into place.

'No shots for a while, okay pet?' he recommended, perching himself on the couch arm.

'Are you inferring that I can't hold my drink?' Nicky slurred, smiling up at him. Miles laughed.

'I'm not 'infurrrring' anything,' he mimicked, putting his arm around her. She leaned back into him, a peaceful expression crossing her face.

'When we live in France,' she said, eyes closed, 'we'll drink red wine with every meal. You can get a really great bottle of Merlot for just a couple of Euro. *La bonne vie!*' Miles squeezed Nicky's shoulders, placating.

'Well, then you'd definitely better learn to hold your alcohol by then. Coupla years practice binge drinking should do it, I think,' he joked.

Nicky opened her eyes and sat forwards, pulling away from his hold. 'Couple of years? But we're going next year? I've applied to do TEFL, remember?'

Miles looked confused. 'What the hell is teffle?'

'Teaching English as a Foreign Language.' Nicky sat up, suddenly feeling all too sober. 'Miles, we talked about this a couple of weeks ago.'

'Oh, your teaching thing? I didn't know you had to be abroad for that!' Miles sounded alarmed. 'I figured you could do that anywhere.'

'But, but Miles! How often have I talked about a year abroad? Living in France? Using my Language qualifications?'

'You haven't mentioned living in France for ages!' Miles tried to reason.

'I haven't?' Nicky couldn't quite believe him. 'It used to be all I talked about. I need the TEFL experience to get on a teaching conversion course. You know I can't afford a full PGCE.' Miles was looking at her like she was speaking in French already.

'Nic, pet, you know I'm going to Bath next year to do my PhD. I thought you meant to do this teffle thing up there.'

Nicky couldn't say anything for a minute. 'Can't you take a gap year?' she asked, finally. 'It will only take me nine months or so out there to qualify...?' She trailed off when she saw that Miles was frowning.

'You know I'll lose my grant money if I piss off to France.

You're not making sense. Let's talk about this when you're sober. No point getting wound up at your own birthday party!' He put his arm around her shoulders again, pulling her back into position against him.

Being uncertain as to whether or not she wanted to be drunk, Harriet found herself mixing elaborate cocktails that she then stood swilling around in her glass. Realising this, she sipped at her drink, scrunched up her face: as she had suspected, she'd made it too strong. Across the room, Adam was sitting cross-legged on the laminate floor, safely trapped playing one of Sukie's more indiscernible drinking games. Their eyes met – every so often – seemingly an accident on his part, as every time they did he couldn't look away fast enough; suddenly finding his drink, his companion, or – in one instance, the couch cushion – utterly fascinating.

She felt a light touch to the small of her back; Sukie had extricated herself from the game under the necessity of refilling her glass.

'You can relax,' she murmured, after her back was to the rest of the room. 'It was just his weird, twisted idea of a joke, apparently.' Harriet couldn't help but glance over at Adam again. This time he didn't look away. This time he looked downright panicky, staring her down, eyes pleading.

'Are you sure?' she asked quietly.

Sukie looked at her. 'It's what he just said, in the garden, why? You all broken-hearted over it?' Sukie smirked.

'Just doesn't seem like... his sort of humour.' It just felt plain wrong, in fact. Harriet frowned, slightly, but not slightly enough that Adam didn't clock it from across the room. Suddenly galvanised into action, he put his drink down on the floor against the wall, started to make excuses and pulled himself to a standing position. The hurried movement caught Sukie's attention.

'Oh fuck, speak of the devil…' she rolled her eyes at Harriet, just as he reached them.

'Harry, can I talk to you?' he rushed, glaring at Sukie, who returned one with interest.

'Come play,' Sukie tugged at Harriet's arm.

'In a minute,' Harriet replied, looking at Adam expectantly. Sukie made a tut of disgust and – refreshed drink in hand – moved back towards the crowd on the floor.

'I am so, so sorry,' Adam said immediately, taking Harriet by the elbow, as if the physical contact between them would add weight to his sincerity.

'For what?' Harriet asked.

Adam was stumped into silence. 'Upsetting you, I guess.'

'Did you tell Sukie you fancied me to have a great big joke at my expense?'

Adam shook his head emphatically.

'Well, good,' Harriet said, studying the reflection of the light bulb overhead in her drink. 'That'll teach you to do drugs. Let's forget it.' Adam gripped her elbow more firmly.

'No,' was all he got out before—

'Let's do the Happy Birthday,' Miles called, 'it's not gonna let up out there.' It was a short-running but important tradition at Dell Road that any renditions of Happy Birthday take place in the garden, apparently snow, or no snow. Nicky – from what Harriet could see from across the room – looked a little pallid and tired but agreeable enough.

Several of the guests made a dash for the coat hooks in the hall, although most of the boys seemed willing to put their trust in their beer jackets. Leigha handed Harriet her coat as she passed back through the kitchen towards the back door, grabbing her by the hand and pulling her along as she went.

Harriet glanced back at Adam as she allowed herself to be piloted by Leigha and the rest of the gathering away from him and out into the garden, pulling her arms hurriedly through her coat as she went. She was barefoot though, Adam noticed, bright orange nails appearing and disappearing under the hem of her jeans as she walked. He moved against the flow of people, into the hall, inspecting the vast collection of shoes discarded between the front door and the foot of the stairs. The noise of the house dulled away as the stragglers made the journey into the garden.

Hastily Adam grabbed at a pair of tan Ugg boots, which he thought he recognised as Nicky's, but – whatever – they looked warm and of an okay size for Harriet.

It took him a minute to locate Harriet in the garden; she wasn't where he expected her to be – with her laughing housemates in the centre of the snow-frosted lawn – but stood instead, acceding to her exposed toes, on the strip of patio near the garden fence, absent-mindedly rubbing one bare foot over the other. Adam manoeuvred his way over to her and wordlessly held up the boots. Harriet received them with a grateful murmur, steadying herself with a hand on his shoulder as she pulled them on. From the grass, the first hesitant strains of Happy Birthday carried across to where they stood. As Harriet opened her mouth to join in, Adam bent his head, so close to her that he felt the brush of his bottom lip against the softness of her earlobe.

'You know you said let's forget it?' he murmured. Harriet nodded, gaze focused doggedly ahead on Nicky, who was laughing and putting her hands over her face with the universal embarrassment of being sung to. 'That's fine. That's good, in fact. But I don't want you thinking I'm some total dick. Even though I was wasted, I want you to know that I meant what I said. I think you're...'

He couldn't even bring himself to finish the sentence. Harriet dropped her eyes from the spectacle on the lawn, studying her fingers intently. 'But most importantly,' Adam rushed to continue, 'you're a mate. A really good mate. So can we… you know, forget the former and… focus on the latter?'

Almost as if on cue, a cheer and a smattering of applause broke out from the people in the garden; the song was finished. The colder members of the company started to drift back inside. Harriet didn't immediately say anything. Adam stood awkwardly, head still bent to hers, watching her face as she in turn watched her housemates twirling on the grass, Leigha laughing, with one arm around Nicky, the other arm flung out to the sky.

'Adam,' she said, finally, and the sound of his own name had never been so alarming. 'Let's get out of here. Let's go for a walk.'

'A walk?' he repeated, dumbly. Harriet nodded and – for the first time during the whole conversation – looked up and met his eyes.

'Why not?' she said, 'I don't think we'll be missed.'

Harriet's nerve lasted her the journey around the side of the house, clumsily rolling the wheelie bins out of their way, emerging into the front garden. Wordlessly she hopped the low and crumbling wall and led the trailing Adam around the corner and on to Hatcher Road, coming to an abrupt halt the other side of her house's garden fence.

Adam took her sudden pause as an invitation to speak. 'Look, I don't want for this to be a big deal,' he implored, catching up to her and running his hand down the snow-damp arm of her coat. 'The last thing I want to do is make you uncomfortable, but when you were angry with me about the whole Leigha thing I couldn't bear it, I can't have you angry at me again. I don't deserve it. This time.'

Harriet's mouth twitched into a smile. 'Oh Adam it's just… a bit awkward, you know? I can't… '

'Don't, don't,' Adam cut her off, panic rising in his voice. 'Don't say whatever you're about to say.' Harriet looked at him inquiringly.

'What is it you think I'm about to say?' she asked; she barely knew herself.

'I don't know,' Adam replied, 'but I'm sure it's not good. How could it be good? I only want good things for you, Harry, and for you to think good things of me, but I keep fucking you off. Please, I'm begging you. Let's draw a line, like we did about the me and Leigha thing. Let's pretend it never happened. Let's have a blank slate; please?'

And in that moment, Harriet realised what it was that she wanted.

She wanted Adam to kiss her, grind his mouth into hers hard enough to bruise, dig his fingernails into the skin of her back, hold her so tightly she couldn't breathe. The surprise of it avalanched into her stomach, colder than her cheeks on that snowy February night, colder than the tip of her nose.

And it must have all shown so clearly on her face because only half a breath passed before Adam kissed her, balling his hands into tight fists inside the fall of her hair, tugging at her scalp. It was like rum burning down her throat, a rush to her extremities. She could hear Leigha's voice carry from their back garden – hear her laughing as she twirled with her arms outstretched, catching snowflakes on her tongue – and a panic rose and fluttered in her chest like a trapped bird. As if he could feel it, Adam drew back, still holding the sides of her head.

'Tell me if you want me to stop,' he said gruffly, his face anxious, but the whole thing was so wonderful and insane.

And – for probably the first time in her life – Harriet stopped worrying about Leigha, and kissed Adam back.

Chapter Nine

Harriet awoke lying on her stomach, disorientated, with her face pressed into her pillow; it smelt fusty from where she'd laid her damp hair upon it the night before. She heard the soft rush of her door against the carpet and the soft click as it was closed. The rattle of the handle as it had been opened was what had roused her.

As she raised her head she saw a pyjama-clad Sukie, repositioning the desk chair closer to the bed before sitting on it.

'So he didn't stay over then?' Sukie asked as soon as she saw Harriet was awake, her voice as stiff as her posture.

'What?' Harriet said, still half-asleep and genuinely confused, rolling into a sitting position and pulling the duvet up higher against the chill of the room.

'I saw you.' Sukie looked at Harriet sharply, as if challenging her to continue playing dumb. 'I came upstairs to put my coat and shoes in my room.' The one room in the house with a view of Hatcher Road.

Harriet felt sick. She was awake now. 'Don't tell Leigha,' she blurted, immediately. It was the only thing she could think of to say.

'Fucking hell, Harry,' Sukie hissed, showing how dearly she wanted to be shouting instead, 'what do you think you're playing at?'

'I was drunk,' Harriet answered immediately, the easiest, most understandable lie. 'And, you know, I was feeling…' – she cast around for an innocent enough word – 'mischievous.'

'Mischievous?' Sukie echoed, incredulous. 'You're not a fucking elf.'

'I know, I'm sorry,' Harriet cringed. 'But, look, I know Leigha would be pissed if she'd seen, but do *you* have to be on my case? Consenting adults, lapse in concentration, no big deal.' Harriet mentally crossed her fingers that Sukie had just glanced from her window, as she couldn't imagine her standing there staring down as she and Adam had talked and kissed in the snowfall for two hours. Two hours! Harriet hadn't quite believed it herself when she'd slipped back into the house and seen how much time had passed.

'The guy is a total prat,' was Sukie's blunt assessment. 'I don't want him messing with you like he did with Leigha.' Harriet felt that prickle and flutter again, doubt and shame. She wondered what words Adam had whispered to Leigha as they'd pressed together against the front door. *Tell me if you want me to stop*, the Adam in her head murmured against Leigha's pulse, as his teeth nipped at her throat.

They both froze at the sound of a door opening on the landing; Nicky's bedroom being downstairs, it had to be Leigha. A second later, they heard the slide of the deadbolt on the bathroom door and the sound of running water.

'You won't tell Leigha?' Harriet repeated, voice pitched quieter; she'd meant for it to be a statement but it still came out sounding like a question.

'Of course I won't, but seriously,' Sukie frowned, 'the next time you get a weird… horny little elf urge… warn me, or something, and I'll point you in a better direction!' she smirked.

Harriet swallowed down the nasty feeling that her deception

79

was giving her, and smiled at her friend.

'Deal.'

'Okay,' Sukie said, rising from the chair and hitching up her baggy pyjama bottoms. 'Tea?'

'Oh, yes please!' Sukie nodded, apparently pleased with the outcome of this early morning intervention, and left the room. After a moment or two Harriet could hear her conversing cheerfully with whoever was downstairs, the pressured rush of water from the tap into the kettle.

Harriet quickly threw the covers back and jumped from the bed, snatching up a hoodie from the back of the desk chair to pull on over her vest top. Urgently she inspected her face in the mirror hanging above her desk. Was that faint redness stubble-rash from kissing, or just where the pillow had been pressing? She rubbed away the black flecks of mascara from under her eyes and exhaled tensely through pursed lips.

Her mobile phone sat quietly on the desk next to her, set to silent, but the little green LED flashing showed that at some point during the night she'd received a text message.

'Tea's up!' Sukie yelled from downstairs. With her customary great timing Leigha emerged from the bathroom, the smell of sweet steam accompanying her and wafting in through Harriet's slightly open door.

'Hope there's one for me?' she called down. 'And some paracetemol! Please?'

Harriet grabbed frantically for the phone as if Leigha were about to randomly charge into the room and snatch it up.

Adam Chadwick, 04.51
I can't sleep. I am smiling so much my cheeks hurt !! xx

Harriet deleted the message before setting the phone back down on her desk, then grabbed it up again – double checked it was set to silent, then slipped it into the pocket of her hoodie. Downstairs, Nicky's voice grew louder as she moved down the hallway.

'So, we don't need anything but bread?' she called back to Sukie in the kitchen. There was a moment of silence after Sukie had replied, before – 'Has anyone seen my boots?' Harriet shot an alarmed look at Nicky's ankle-height Ugg boots, discarded at the foot of her bed. The last thing she needed was someone else's' attention brought to the fact she'd been outside last night. She was already anticipating Leigha's interrogation on where she'd been for the later hours of the party.

There was a thud as Leigha dropped something over the banisters. 'Wear mine,' she called down to Nicky, 'and hurry up! I need some carbohydrates in me.'

Harriet felt a phantom vibration against her stomach. Even though she knew it was her imagination – the phone was set to silent, not vibrate – she couldn't help but pull it out of her hoodie pocket to check it.

'Muooorning,' came Leigha's languorous voice, her head appearing round the door, towel-turban balanced insecurely on her head. Harriet gave the most obvious of guilty starts, hand tightening around her mobile phone. Leigha put a hand to the back of her hair towel, steadying it; she didn't seem to have noticed anything amiss. 'I am *hanging*,' Leigha continued, 'what about you?'

'Not really,' Harriet answered, before immediately realising that she, of course, would be dreadfully hung-over if she had been as drunk as she'd persuaded Sukie she'd been. 'I mean, I probably would be, but I went to bed earlier than you guys. I felt a bit sick.'

'Oh, I wondered where you'd gone to. At least you feel better today. I'm good for nothing but perhaps a DVD and a mid-afternoon nap.' As if on cue, Leigha yawned widely.

'Let's get some caffeine,' Harriet said, moving towards Leigha in the doorway, slipping her phone back into her pocket.

'Nicky's boots,' Leigha said suddenly, her eyeline having come to rest on them as she finished her yawn. Harriet felt a strike of that ridiculous panic again. Leigha shook her head affectionately. 'Dappy cow, better bring them downstairs so she'll see them.' Adjusting her towel again, she turned and went down the stairs. Snatching up the incriminating footwear, Harriet followed.

Johnny's bare feet made a satisfying scuffing noise against the cold linoleum of the kitchen floor. He'd already groggily reached up and opened a cupboard before noticing that he wasn't alone in the room. Adam sat at the small circular table, a box of Cornflakes and a pint of milk in front of him, turning his mobile phone over and over in his hand.

'Morning,' Adam grinned, when he saw that Johnny was aware of his presence. Johnny shut the cupboard door.

'And what are you doing up so early?' Johnny demanded, more than a little piqued at having his typical morning solitude invaded.

'It's more like, what am I doing up so late? I haven't slept, so afraid this doesn't count as getting up early, mate.' Adam used his hand to scoop Cornflakes into his mouth, washing them down with milk drunk straight from the carton. Johnny frowned.

'Good, for a minute there I thought you were giving up the habit of a lifetime.' Adam turned his mobile over in his palm again, bouncing the bottom of it off the table.

'That better not be the only milk.' A bleary Miles scowled from the doorway. Johnny turned to him in surprise. Miles had stayed behind to sleep in Nicky's bed, which he did more often than not anyway. He must have come home after them.

'Everything alright?' Adam asked, alarmed, obviously coming to the same realisation. Miles brushed past Johnny into the room, opening the fridge.

'Yeah. Nic and I had a little spat. I think she had too much to drink. I'll go round and see her later, maybe.' Johnny and Adam exchanged a look; this was unheard of.

'Okay,' Johnny said, tentatively. 'Cool. Lads' day, then. Who wants to go outside and build a snowman with a huge cock?' His ribaldry had the intended effect; Miles straightened from the fridge with a laugh and a groan, holding more milk. He pretended to consider the option

'I don't think there's enough snow settled for a *huge* cock.'

Adam's phone thumped irritatingly against the table top again. 'The girls have got a garden,' he announced, as if this was new information. 'We could go round there?'

'Not much of a lads' day,' Johnny commented in a neutral tone.

'I'd prefer to give Nicky more time to cool down,' Miles admitted. 'She was pretty pissed off with me last night.'

Adam fell quiet. Johnny watched with interest as he sucked on the inside of his cheek, checking his mobile display before allowing it to bounce off the table again, as if in punishment for not heralding a message. A nasty feeling chewed inside his empty stomach. Adam had disappeared for a couple of hours last night. Johnny had eventually found him sitting on the front garden wall, face and ears pink with the bite of cold, looking indolently up at the flurries of white flake in the dark sky. If Johnny hadn't been with Leigha for the entirety of the evening he'd think that –

Johnny physically shook his head, trying to rid himself of the ugly thoughts about his best friend, and the girl he thought himself in love with. Miles noticed the slight movement and gave Johnny a rueful smile, as if he could guess the line of his thoughts. Not that it would be difficult; Leigha was pretty much all he thought about, nowadays.

'Bloody girls, ey?' Miles said. Johnny smiled back, a little sadly.

'Bloody girls,' Adam suddenly echoed, with feeling, before

crunching down on his next mouthful of cereal.

Exhaustion had stolen up on him in the late hours of the morning and Adam had welcomed it, retiring to his bedroom.

The sounds of children playing outside roused him several hours later, the room cast into shadow by the early sunset of a February day. Before his brain had even fully processed the action, his hand was scrabbling on his bedcovers for his mobile phone; there were no new messages displayed. Adam lay back on the bed-sheets warmed by his body and for one irrational moment wondered if the whole thing with Harriet had been a dream.

Resolve hardened in his stomach. This was ridiculous. He opened a blank text message, addressed it to Harriet. There was no point being coy now. Embarrassment lurched as he recalled the things he had murmured to her the night before – into her hair, into her mouth – things he'd never said before, things he hadn't even realised he felt until he was telling her that he did.

Adam Chadwick, 17.03
Can u escape tonight? I think that we shd talk xx

Harriet stood in the kitchen in front of the sluggishly boiling kettle and read the short message over and over, trying to discern a subtext. Was he angry that she hadn't replied to him earlier? Was he now sobered up, embarrassed and regretful? Nerves pitched in her stomach. Would she then have to pretend to be regretful, too?

Her silent phone began to flash insistently in her hand; startled, Harriet almost dropped it. Adam was calling her.

Abandoning the tea preparations, Harriet bolted for her bedroom, taking the steps two at a time. Her thumb pressed the call accept button as she was pushing her bedroom door closed with her other hand.

'Hello?' she said into the phone, immediately wincing at how breathless she sounded.

'If you like piña coladas… and getting caught in the rain,' Adam sung softly down the line. Harriet gave a surprised laugh. 'Didn't want to give you the opportunity to keep ignoring me,' Adam told her, voice quiet and deliberately light.

'I'm sorry,' she said, pitching her voice low to match his tone, 'it's just been mad here today…' she lied.

Adam laughed. 'So… come be alone with me?' His tone was teasing. The silence that fell afterwards was tense. Harriet thought back to December, Adam laughing at himself, hoisting her purple book bag up high and over his shoulder: I'm going to the Armstrong. Want to come be alone with me?

And then she surprised herself – she only hesitated for a minute.

'Do you need help with your Shakespeare coursework?' she asked.

'That was handed in before Christmas,' Adam replied, confused. Harriet rolled her eyes to herself.

'I know that – and thankfully you seem to know that – but I don't think the others do, do they?' Belatedly Adam grasped her meaning.

'Oh I see. Yeah, no, I totally need for you to come over and sort out my… footnotes,' he said, mock-serious. 'It's due in tomorrow and I'm… stressing out,' he added, dead-pan. Harriet laughed.

'Well, I can't say no to that,' she murmured. 'I'll be there in ten minutes or so.'

'Thank you,' Adam said quietly. Harriet laughed again.

'What for? I'm not actually compiling any footnotes for you tonight, so don't you dare ask…'

'For coming round.' Harriet couldn't help but smile.

'I'll be there in ten minutes, 'she repeated. 'Bye.'

'Harry!' Adam said urgently, calling her attention back to the phonecall. 'Wait.'

'What?'

'Do I…' Adam paused; Harriet imagined that the tips of his ears were flushed pink. 'How is this evening going to go?' Harriet crinkled her nose in confusion.

'Pardon?'

'Well, you know…' Adam paused to collect his thoughts again. 'Will I be happy after you've left or… you know… shall I go on a quick beer run?'

'I don't drink beer,' Harriet answered with a smile. She could hear Adam chuckle under his breath on the other end of the line.

'See you in a bit then, trouble.'

Harriet held her phone limply against her cheek for a full minute or so after the line had gone dead. The sounds of the house pushed back at her attention – the loud bass of the television, the bell-like pitch of the other girls laughing, the clatter and knock of cupboards and drawers opening and closing in the kitchen, where someone had stepped up to finish making the teas in her absence.

Tossing her phone down to her desk, Harriet quickly scrunched her fingers through her hair, testing how clean it was, staring unblinkingly at her closed wardrobe door in a mild panic. It was stupid, suddenly worrying what she looked like in front of someone who'd seen her in pyjamas, in the gym, falling over herself drunk in the Union. Plus it would probably cast doubt on their coursework excuse if she tripped over there in a full face of make-up, mini-dress and four inch heels... Standard jeans and a top it was then. She flicked some obligatory mascara onto her lashes, and prepared to go downstairs and make her excuses to the others. She pulled her *Adaptations of Shakespeare* reference book down from the shelf above her desk and held it prominently against her chest for good measure.

Adam flung his phone in the direction of the soft landing of his bed, already out the bedroom door before it had hit the mattress. The bathroom door was pulled closed but, optimistically, he tried the handle anyway. Locked. Thwarted!

'Occupied,' Johnny sang out. Exasperated, Adam banged the side of his first against the door.

'I need to have a shower!'

'Alright, alright, I'll not be long...'

'You're sitting there playing Snake on your phone, aren't you?' Johnny laughed, affirming Adam's suspicions. Adam groaned and whacked the door again. 'You're the slowest shitter in the world!'

'This isn't speeding anything up!' Johnny growled back.

'I need to have a shower!' Adam repeated.

'Yeah, I heard you, wait a bloody bit!'

'Harriet's coming over to help me with an essay that's due in tomorrow,' Adam lied smoothly. 'And I smell like armpit.'

'Just Harriet coming round?' Johnny asked after a pause. Adam felt a pang of pity for his friend.

'Yeah, I suppose so,' he said. 'Sorry mate, I know you're mad for her but Leigha's not the go-to-girl for literary brilliance, is she? Come on, hurry up, Harriet'll be here in like, five minutes!'

'Yeah, alright!' Johnny yelled in exasperation. 'I'm coming out. Shall I start the shower running for you?'

'Yes please,' Adam said, reaching for his towel that was hanging over the landing banister to dry. 'And you can spray some air-freshener around too while you're at it.'

Harriet strung out the seven minute walk between the girls' house and the boys' flat for as long as she could, clamping down hard on the embarrassing urge she had to hurry. The student village was muted and peaceful, a Tesco delivery van driving slowly along the main road as Harriet turned the corner into it, the streetlights flickering into life for the evening as she walked underneath one. The slushy high street had been seen to by the council, grey whorls of melting snow shovelled away into gutters and handfuls of grit scattered across the pavement, sharp and crunching under Harriet's shoes.

She could see the boys' flat by then, on the first and second floors above the lettings agent at the end of the high street. Adam's bedroom was one of the windows at the front; the curtains were closed. Harriet slowed down even more.

Harriet was practical to a fault. She knew very well that she should tell Adam straight away that things needed to go back to how they'd always been. She shouldn't even be going over, she should have said as much to him on the phone. Leigha would be so hurt if she ever found out and, anyway, Harriet was more or less certain she'd probably end up just hurting Adam too, like she had Seth. If she didn't handle this, she'd just end up losing two of her best friends, she knew that, she knew it, but still her heart felt huge in her chest and still her breath was catching in anticipation as she reached the end of the road.

She pressed the doorbell on reflex, hearing it chime somewhere inside the building and, a few moments later, the answering heavy footsteps on the stairs down to the front door. She plastered a panicked smile onto her face, but when the door swung inwards it wasn't Adam standing there, but Miles.

'Hey,' he said, 'what's up?'

'Come to do Adam's coursework for him, what else?' Harriet answered, in an overly jokey tone. Miles stepped aside to let her past him and onto the stairs.

'You're an enabler!' Miles laughed, closing and dead-bolting the front door. 'You can't sit his exams for him, you know.'

'He'll be fine,' Harriet threw over her shoulder as she climbed the narrow staircase. 'He passed first and second year without my help, didn't he? And I'm only guiding him, I'm not really doing anything *for* him…'

'Hmmm, yeah well… let's just say if he gets a First I'll be highly suspicious.'

'Hey, Harry,' Johnny raised a hand in greeting from where he sat on the couch with his feet on the coffee table. 'Is it still snowing out there?'

'Nope, and what did settle is melting. Bit of an anti-climax,' Harriet answered, shrugging off her coat and draping it over the back of a chair.

'Adam's in his room; he's just got out of the shower so I'd give him a minute unless you want to catch him in the altogether,' Johnny advised. Harriet felt her entire face burst into flame. Flustered, she opened and closed her textbook for no apparent reason. Johnny looked at her curiously. 'You alright?'

'Poor girl feels ill at the thought of Adam in the nud,' Miles joked, sitting down on the other sofa.

'Oi!' came Adam's disembodied voice from the upstairs landing. 'Fuck off!' Miles and Johnny burst into laughter. Harriet looked up to where she could see Adam's legs through the banisters of the stairs. 'Harry, do you want a cup of tea or something before we… start?' he asked.

'No, I'm fine, thanks.' Harriet flexed the text book nervously between her hands.

'Okay then…'

Harriet winced. They sounded petrified of one other, ridiculously formal. How could Johnny and Miles not realise something was up? A glance back into the lounge showed that the other two boys were oblivious, transfixed by the television. Adam's shins waited impassively at the top of the stairs.

Harriet faffed for a moment more with her handbag, decided it was best to leave it downstairs with her coat and moved to the foot of the stairs. Adam had retreated up into the shadows of the landing. As she rounded the banisters she saw he was waiting for her in the doorway to his bedroom, backlit by the glow from his desk lamp. The words she'd geared up to say gummed in her throat but Adam just ran his eyes down her from head to toe as if those words were written down the length of her body. His hair was still wet from the shower and hung in dark clumps on his forehead. Then he smiled at her as if she was the most wonderful thing in the world and stepped forward.

And then – just like the previous night – he was suddenly in front of her with her face between his hands and was bringing her lips up to his, pulling her gently backwards into his bedroom. As he pushed the door closed behind them he sighed softly against her mouth.

'Adam,' Harriet tried weakly. He pulled away and rested his forehead to hers.

'Don't overthink it, just kiss me,' he instructed. 'This was always going to happen.' Harriet closed her eyes. Her head was spinning.

'This is…'

'Right?' Adam supplied, bumping his nose against hers. 'Come on. For once, don't think so much. Seriously, just shut up and kiss me.'

And whilst she knew it definitely wasn't practical, Harriet couldn't argue that it didn't feel right. She let the textbook fall from her hands and it slid between their legs – coming to land at their feet, pages bunched into curls – and let all her thoughts sink away under the urgent pressure of Adam's mouth and body against hers.

Chapter Ten

February 2007

Harriet had a tiny mole behind her left ear that he'd never noticed before. Adam lazily stretched forward to kiss it. Harriet giggled; he had discovered she was very ticklish around her neck area.

'I cannot believe,' Adam murmured against her skin, causing her to squirm under his arm, 'I have spent, like, five whole months knowing you and *not* kissing you. What *have* I been doing with my time?'

'A lot of Playstation and sleeping?' Harriet laughed, turning her face back round to his so that the tips of their noses touched. Adam's single bed didn't give them much room to manoeuvre, not that they wanted it. Harriet's bedroom was a little more spacious, but they'd felt much more nervous the two times they'd been in there together. The other girls had a habit of walking into one another's' rooms without warning, and a constant state of vigilance for the sound of footsteps on the stairs was not conducive to passion.

'Ah, fair enough, so it wasn't a total waste then,' Adam grinned, kissing her mouth now that it was within his reach. He was getting addicted to kissing her. He was going to slip up sooner rather than later. Secret-laden smiles as they greeted one another when in company could never be enough; he wanted to fling his arms around her and kiss her whenever she walked into a room. Resting their hands on one another's knees under the lecture theatre desk was one thing, but he wanted to stroll around campus with his arm thrown across her shoulders, make his lap a pillow for her as she lay and studied in the grassy quad, introduce her to everyone he came across as his girlfriend.

Finding that chain of thought too tender to pursue, Adam kissed her again, found himself wishing into her as if she were a candle he was blowing out. *Please, decide that I'm worth it.*

Harriet reached for his hand and curled his fingers around hers as he pulled back and resettled against his pillow. Her eyes were a little sad as she looked at him, as if she'd somehow heard his mute plea.

'Happy two week anniversary,' she said, pressing her forehead against his.

He waited for her to tell him that she was going to speak to Leigha, but she didn't.

Miles had made himself perfectly clear. Nicky knew that she was just being irritating now, but with a First Class stamp her application paperwork could still make the deadline and perhaps she wasn't going to accept the inevitable until there was truly no other option.

Miles was dicing up vegetables in the kitchen. Leigha – the only other girl in the house that evening – had made herself scarce, retiring upstairs to her bedroom pleading that she didn't want her hair to smell like onion. More likely she sensed that things were still tense between the couple, maybe she'd even worked out how close the TEFL application deadline must be; Leigha was always intuitive like that. The wet slice and thunk of the knife through the veg and against the chopping board was hypnotic. Nicky stood stupidly in the middle of the kitchen – the bundle of forms in hand – Miles' back to her, resolute as a wall.

'Honey…' she started nervously, moving to Miles' elbow; the chopping noises paused. 'Can we just—'

'Oh no,' Miles frowned, interrupting her as he caught sight of the papers and guessed at her intent. 'Not this again. Nicky, I'm trying to cook dinner.'

'But the deadline is at the end of the week, I really need to be sure—'

'Sure about what? What aren't you sure about?' Miles interrupted again, his usually calm and composed nature worn extremely thin after two weeks of the same argument. 'Because I'm sure as hell I'm *not going to France.*' Nicky fell into a wretched silence. After an awkward pause, Miles began dicing the vegetables again. 'I told you,' Miles said to the chopping board, 'you can go, if it means this much to you. We can try and make long distance work, especially if it's only a year.'

'I don't want to be apart from you for a year,' Nicky said miserably.

'And I don't want to be apart from you either, that's why I asked you to move in with me in Bath,' Miles said impatiently.

'I can't afford to do a conversion course,' she said, 'but I want to be a teacher. What am I going to do in Bath?' Miles put the knife down; the vegetables were as diced as it was possible for them to be by now.

'I don't know, pet,' he said, finally making eye-contact with her. 'You'll probably have to just get a regular job and then volunteer when you can as a classroom assistant.'

The emphasis wasn't lost on Nicky. 'How much money will you be bringing in?' she asked. 'What are you getting in the way of an academic grant?' There was a telling pause before Miles answered her.

'Not much. A little, to help with the rent. Not enough to live on, really.'

Nicky studied him. 'You've been inferring that you *will* have enough to live on.'

Miles shrugged awkwardly, squaring up the pile of diced vegetables with the knife blade. 'I didn't want you thinking I only want you moving in with me because I can't afford to live alone.'

'I wouldn't think that of you,' Nicky answered immediately, hurt.

'Look,' Miles said, 'a couple of years – five, tops – and then I'll get a professorship and we'll have enough money for you to do a conversion course. But I have to go to Bath this year, I'll lose my grant.' He cupped the vegetables between his hands and dropped them into the waiting wok where they sizzled sullenly on the low heat.

'I love you,' Nicky said miserably, uselessly.

'And I love you. I'm just thinking long-term and about what's best for the both of us. I hope you understand that.'

And then there really wasn't anything else for Nicky to say. She put the TEFL papers down on the kitchen side and mechanically opened the packet of stir-fry noodles.

'Do you think there's any chilli powder in the house?' Miles asked casually.

It was snowing again, for what would turn out to be the last time that year. Sukie paused, elbow-deep in the sudsy washing-up water, to watch the snowflakes outside the kitchen window twist direction in the wind.

Her phone vibrated in her back pocket. She reached for the tea-towel before deciding it was too damp, instead drying her palms on her jeans before extracting the phone. In response to Sukie's query, Harriet had replied to say she'd been in the library and was on her way home – and yes, she knew it was her turn to do the washing up, she'd do it when she got in.

Sukie frowned, putting her phone back and immersing her hands in the water again, returning her attention and the dishcloth to a particularly stubborn coffee ring. Their degrees being the two more primarily research-based – having fewer hours of class-time – she and Harriet most often lazed around the house together of an afternoon watching crap television: *100 Greatest Surgery Shockers*, *Best Celebrity Spats* etc etc. Lately Harriet was spending more and more time in the library, or barricaded away in her room with piles of books and an equally preoccupied Adam. There was something like four months until the final year dissertations were due; if Harriet were being this flustered already, Sukie couldn't imagine how bad she'd be come June.

Sukie was putting the last glass back in the cupboard, the damp tea-towel now sodden through, when she heard Harriet's key in the lock.

'Brrr!' Harriet shivered theatrically. 'White Easter, do you think?' She dropped her handbag and bookbag to the floor at the foot of the stairs, shedding her coat as she moved further info the house; little globes of melting snowflake glittered against the darkness of her coat and hair under the kitchen ceiling spotlights, which were pre-emptively switched on against the gloom of the winter afternoon. 'Tea?' Harriet asked, moving across to the cupboard and fetching out two mugs. 'Thanks for doing the washing up.' Harriet checked the water level in the kettle before clicking it on. 'Add it to my housework tab.'

'How's the work going?' Sukie asked.

'Oh, good.' Harriet busied herself adding teabags and sugar to the mugs. 'Long way to go though.'

'Listen, I want you to do something for me,' Sukie said, spreading the tea-towel over the handle of the oven to dry out. 'You've been single for six months now.'

Harriet paused. 'And?'

'And I want to set you up with someone. He's a really nice guy. Been single a little less time than you. Saw pictures of me and you together when he added me on Facebook the other week, thinks you're hot stuff. Which of course, you are.' Sukie prodded for a smile, for any reaction. Harriet had blanched. 'Listen, you're working too hard. You need someone to wine you and dine you, take you somewhere that isn't the library,' Sukie pressed. 'Or your bedroom. Although…!' She wiggled her eyebrows suggestively.

Harriet tapped at the side of the kettle as if it would somehow make the water within boil sooner. 'Now's not a good time, I really need to focus on my coursework and dissertation. I really want that First…' she said.

'Come on!' Sukie squeezed Harriet's arm. 'One date. Dan just wants to meet you on campus one evening, no big deal. It will be good for you. You'll like him, I promise. He's friends with Adam actually, though I don't hold that against him!' Sukie laughed. The water in the kettle came to the boil; Harriet stared at it blankly. 'Look,' Sukie said, reaching for the kettle and pouring the water into the mugs herself. 'I'm not asking you to sleep with the guy, I'm not asking you to marry him. Just go for a drink, see where it goes. What can it hurt?'

Harriet finished making her cup of tea in silence, wrapping her fingers around it thoughtfully. 'I'll think about it,' she said eventually, leaning against the kitchen side and taking a tentative sip.

'Good.' Sukie straightened from putting the milk back in the fridge. Her gaze softened as she looked at her friend, cheeks and nose still raw from the cold, dark circles under her eyes from the long nights she'd been pulling lately. 'We're just concerned for you, Harry,' she said. 'You're turning into a Literature Hermit. Even we hardly get to see you anymore.'

'I know. It's just… you know.'

'Yeah, I know,' Sukie said kindly, although she didn't. She moved towards the sofas and picked up the remote control. 'Shall we see what's on the telly?'

She hadn't expected him to find it funny.

'I never knew Dan had such good taste,' Adam laughed, trailing his fingertips territorially across Harriet's hipbones and down along the curve of her. She twitched away anxiously, even though they were relatively unexposed thanks to the dense forsythia planted in the flowerbed that curved around the walkway.

'Yes, it's so funny,' Harriet frowned. 'I'm going to have to go out on a date with this guy now, it's weird.' Adam shrugged.

'So what? Just go for the drink with him. Better yet, go for the drink with him and while you're there, tell him about us. He'll think it's funny.'

'He'll tell Su,' Harriet scowled. Adam resettled the strap of his bookbag on his shoulder with an uncomfortable expression on his face.

'Yeah, well, don't you think it's time she knew? That everyone knew? It's getting weird, Harry. It's like you're ashamed of me.'

Harriet closed her eyes momentarily as she collected her thoughts. Adam had been building up to this for days now, she'd known it was coming; she just wished he'd chosen a better moment than ten minutes before a seminar.

'It's not like that, you know we've got to be careful with Leigha.'

'She's not a child,' Adam retorted, frowning.

'No, but the situation is delicate because of you!' Harriet shot back, regretting it immediately as a swell of hurt and annoyance flashed across Adam's face.

'Why say that?' he asked her.

'Well, why kiss her?' Harriet couldn't help but reply. Adam's face darkened further.

'You know what?' he said, shifting his bag strap again as he took a step back from her. 'Leigha is just an excuse. You're not sure how you feel about me, no matter what you say in bed, when we're alone. And you don't want to risk pissing off your mates for something that might not be worth it.' Harriet was struck dumb with astonishment – only for a moment – but it was enough. Adam looked at her pityingly. 'I'm so right, aren't I? Whatever.'

'Adam–' Harriet started.

'I wanted you to be a girlfriend, not a fuck buddy.' Harriet winced at his crudeness and at the past tense; Adam started to walk away.

'What about the seminar?' she called weakly after him.

'Like I give two fucks about the seminar,' he responded, without looking back.

Chapter Eleven

March 2007

Leigha got to the café a little early and dithered as to whether or not to queue up and buy a latte; Adam had invited her there for a coffee, surely that meant the drinks would be on him – but then it wouldn't do to be presumptuous.

Leigha remained standing next to the table she had claimed and took her time unwrapping herself from her winter layers, hoping that when Adam made his appearance it would appear as if she had just that second arrived herself. After all, she had learnt the hard way that when it came to Adam Chadwick, it certainly didn't pay to look too keen.

She fully expected Adam to be late, but he arrived a few minutes past the hour, pushing both of the glass swing doors open as he did, smiling his wide and easy smile as he caught sight of Leigha waiting. Her stomach fluttered; the only guy she'd ever known to make her this nervy.

'Hey, Ley,' Adam greeted her with a light touch of his hand to her elbow as he reached the table. 'Do you want something to drink?'

'Thank you – latte, please?'

Leigha finished hanging her coat over the back of the chair and sat gracefully, watching Adam flirt casually with the barista before finally heading back over to the table, exaggeratedly careful as he carried two ceramic mugs brim-full with milky coffee. Mugs, not takeaway cups, Leigha couldn't help but notice. She decided not to pussyfoot around.

'So what's this about?' she asked, before Adam had even pulled his chair out from the table to sit. He blinked.

'Nothing? I just thought – you know – we're both on campus Wednesday afternoons – and we've said for ages that we should grab coffee...' Adam trailed off; Leigha looked at him sceptically.

'But that was, you know, after New Year...' Leigha too let her sentence hang unfinished.

'We're mates though, yeah?' Adam asked, pausing with sugar sachet in hand, and Leigha couldn't be sure if he was stating it as the reason for the impromptu coffee date or in apology for things not working out between them.

'Yeah, of course,' she answered, because there really wasn't any other way to respond.

'Good,' Adam said with satisfaction, shaking the sugar enthusiastically before ripping the paper of the sachet and tipping the granules into his latte. 'So, how's it going? Feel like I haven't been round to hang out for ages.'

'That's because you haven't,' Leigha pointed out. 'That film on Thursday night was really good, really funny, you missed out – holed upstairs with Harry and fifty thousand books.' She rolled her eyes and took a sip of her latte.

'Yeah, well, the department are really getting our cases lately,' Adam said carefully, eyes on his drink as he stirred it slowly. 'Heavy stuff. And Harriet's even worse. She seems to think she can torture a First Class result out of me.'

'Yeah?' Leigha said, arching an eyebrow. 'Don't I know it. She can be a real ball-breaking bitch. She was like this with Seth – with her ex – all during our A Levels. Poor guy was almost in tears when he got Cs, terrified of disappointing her after she spent so much time studying with him. He almost didn't get accepted here. Got through on clearing. He had to—-' Leigha caught herself, suddenly self-conscious; why was she sitting there rabbiting on about her friend's ex-boyfriend? She hated to talk about Seth. She pictured him the last time she saw him, sitting naked on the edge of the bed, his fair head in his hands, his spine an arched ridge. She took another sip of her drink. 'Anyway,' she dismissed the subject, but Adam was leaning forward expectantly.

'No, go on? He had to what?'

'Oh, he had to do a different degree to the one he wanted to do, cos there were no clearing spaces on it. Stupid. But he wanted to be wherever Harriet was. They do say love makes you crazy, don't they?'

'I guess,' Adam echoed, frowning, drawing a zigzag lightly in the foam of his latte with his fingertip. 'Why did they break up anyway?' Leigha paused to consider her response.

'Just grew apart, I guess. He took her on holiday and she came back and told us she'd broken up with him, didn't love him and it wasn't fair on him. To be honest, it wasn't. She should have broken up with him ages before if she felt like that.' Leigha curtailed herself, feeling that old familiar snake of anger rising up. She sipped at her drink; Adam mirrored the action and looked across the rim of his mug at her shrewdly.

'I think,' he said, setting the mug down gently, 'that you guys were all so close she probably didn't want to rock the boat – you know? – maintain the status quo and all that.' Leigha didn't answer straight away. 'You and Sukie haven't really had anything long-term have you?' Adam continued. Leigha frowned in response, unsure what he was getting at. 'Well, I think it must be quite daunting. You girls are like this.' Adam crossed his index and middle fingers together to indicate closeness. 'You date one of you, you date all of you.' He laughed suddenly.

'I don't know what you're on about,' Leigha said coldly. 'You're making me and Su sound like mad old spinsters living vicariously through Harriet's relationship.'

'Am I?' Adam said. 'Well sorry, that's not what I was getting at.' He smiled maddeningly at her, looking like he'd just discovered a secret.

Adam had gone straight from the café to the Armstrong, where had had remained until last orders, comfortably ensconced with a few course-mates and copious amounts of lager bought by the pitcher on the Wednesday night 'Happy Hour' rate. He thought the walk home would sober him up but it still took him three attempts to get his door key into the lock when he arrived.

'Mate?' Johnny was sitting in his pyjamas on the couch, television remote in hand from where he'd just pressed the mute button. Adam went to drop his bookbag before realising that he didn't have it.

'Fuck it,' he groaned.

'You pissed?' Johnny asked with amusement.

'Well clearly, as I seem to have lost my books somewhere between campus and here,' Adam answered with a scowl. 'I just hope I left them in the pub and not in the gutter.'

'I tried to call you earlier,' Johnny said, watching as Adam hopped awkwardly on one foot as he removed one shoe.

'Yeah, my phone ran out of battery,' Adam replied gruffly. Not strictly true. Somewhere around his fifth pint he'd started to lose the fight against the urge to text Harriet. He'd had to rope in a bewildered mate take his mobile and keep it away from him for the rest of the night. Something else that hadn't made it home with him; fuck it!

'Oh, I am having serious pub regret,' Adam moaned, leaning

on the table and shaking his second trainer off of his foot. 'I am going to bed.'

'Adam—' Johnny started as Adam stumbled wearily from the room.

'Bed!' Adam snapped, mounting the stairs.

'Okay then, goodnight!' Johnny said, a hint of a smirk in his voice.

Adam saw the strip of light underneath his door but hadn't really registered it before he pushed onwards into the room. Harriet looked up at him from where she sat against the pillows of his bed, knees drawn up to her chin, open book at her feet. Adam stopped in his tracks.

'Oh yeah!' Johnny called from downstairs with glee. 'Harriet's been waiting for you.'

'Yeah, CHEERS MATE,' Adam yelled back with heavy sarcasm, before pushing his door closed. 'I'm so sorry—' he began.

'I'm sorry, I did try to call you—' Harriet said at the same time. 'Wait, why are you sorry?' Adam sat down heavily at the foot of the bed.

'For getting all in your face and pissing you off the other day. It's none of my business, really,' he answered. Harriet's face softened.

'Of course it's your business. Who else's business would it be?' she said quietly, reaching over to touch Adam's knee. 'It's just my stupid hang ups.'

'You really got whined at when you broke up with your ex, didn't you?' Adam asked suddenly. Harriet pulled her arm back, thrown by the apparently random change in subject. 'I had coffee with Leigha this afternoon,' Adam began by way of explanation. Harriet's face darkened.

'Yes, I know,' she said, coolly. 'She mentioned.'

'Oh, I see!' Adam laughed. 'Jealous, much?'

'No,' Harriet blushed. 'But I don't understand why you had to have a little coffee date with her!'

'I wanted to see how you were and what you were doing without having to ask you,' Adam said, simply. 'You haven't spoken to me in a week.'

'You haven't spoken to me either,' Harriet countered immediately.

'Plus, I sort of wanted to pick your best friend's mind on why you're being like this, what this whole thing is really about. As it happened I didn't need to do much picking. She practically wrote me a book entitled 'Harriet Shaw's Deepest Darkest Secrets.' Adam laughed at Harriet's horrified expression. 'Not really. But she banged on about your ex and how you broke up with him and ruined his life. You must have been made to feel like the biggest bitch in the world at the time.'

Harriet picked at her fingernail. 'Yeah well, we were all really close friends, had been for years,' she said, trying to sound as unbothered as possible.

'And you're worried the same thing will happen with us?' Adam guessed. 'What, that we won't work out and it will mess up everyone's friendships? That the other girls will get too involved? What?' Harriet squirmed uncomfortably.

'How about all of the above? And – of course,' – she shot him a sideways look – 'it's complicated by the fact that you kissed Leigha…' With an irritated groan Adam grabbed for her and pulled her onto his lap, kissing her roughly.

'Shut UP about that already,' he growled, meshing his fingers into her hair. 'Don't you think I don't regret it enough in hindsight without you bringing it up all the time?' He kissed her again, more softly this time.

'I just don't want to mess everything up,' Harriet murmured unhappily against Adam's lips.

'Story of your life,' Adam answered, lowering Harriet's head back to the pillows and leaning over her. 'You can't make everyone happy all of the time, you know that, right?

'I'm sorry,' Harriet repeated.

'Don't be. Now, how long do I get to keep you?'

It was rationally impossible, of course, but Leigha could swear that her birthday somehow *always* fell on a Monday. This caused great logistical problems; having her birthday party before the actual day felt a little heinous, but worse still was celebrating too long after the fact. Then there was the usual dilemma – house party, or the Union? The perennial choices. She tapped her finger against her computer mouse, impatient with herself, the Facebook event page unstarted and empty on the screen in front of her. This was her 21st, after all, she moaned at Sukie; she wanted a night to remember.

Sukie looked up from where she was lying on Leigha's bed, making illegible marks with a pencil against lines in a script.

'Oh, so, have you forgotten all about mine then?' she asked with a tinge of annoyance. 'I went to the Union, Nicky had a house party – they're both perfectly good choices for a 21st birthday.'

'But I want something a little more interesting,' Leigha whined, spinning her desk chair to face Sukie on the bed. 'Let's go out in London.' Sukie made a derisive noise.

'Yeah, like anyone can afford that, Ley. Dinner, clubbing and – what – a hotel too? Unless you want to get the last train and what's the point in that?' Leigha coloured.

'Well, maybe we could make a properly long night of it and then, I don't know, just hang around in Waterloo until the earliest train home? Which will be, what, five in the morning? That's not *so* bad.'

'More like seven,' Sukie answered, twirling her pencil around her knuckles.

'Fine, forget it.' Leigha fell into silence, turning back to her computer monitor and glowering at it.

'I like the idea of dinner, though,' Sukie said. 'Let's go to

Mauritzo's on the high street.'

'Adam doesn't like Italian food,' Leigha replied, absentmindedly. Sukie made an impatient noise.

'Why can't we go all girls? Like we used to? Without Miles even, definitely without Adam and Johnny. They're total… limpets.' She waved her hand dismissively. 'I feel like we haven't done a single thing without one or both of them since we met them.' Leigha laughed.

'We probably haven't!' she said.

'Johnny's like some lapdog,' Sukie continued, rant-mode engaged. 'And Adam's such a cocky git. Pissing about with you and Harry—'

'What's he done to Harriet?' Leigha interrupted immediately. Sukie stalled, her expression awkward.

'Well, you know,' she said finally, 'she's doing all his work with him and probably *for* him. She needs to be concentrating on her own work from now on. You know she'll jump out the window if she doesn't get a First.' Sukie laughed more heartily than her joke strictly deserved.

'Well, I guess we could go for dinner, just us girls, on the actual Monday,' Leigha said slowly. 'That would be nice. We could do the Union on the Friday before then, what's on?' She answered her own question by consulting the A3 student wall planner blu-taced above her desk. 'Eurgh, R&B night.'

'House party it is then,' Sukie smirked. 'If that's going to be special enough for you, Your Highness.' Leigha ignored her friend's sarcasm.

'I need to come up with a cool theme,' she said, more to herself. 'Let's talk themes!' Sukie groaned.

'I need to have read and made notes on this whole thing before 10 o'clock tomorrow morning!'

'Fine,' Leigha said. 'What time is it? When's Harriet home?'

'Harriet should have been home an hour ago,' Sukie said. 'Probably at the library.' She twirled her pencil around her fingers again.

'Boo her,' Leigha frowned, stretching her leg out and reaching with her toes to pull her bedroom door further ajar. 'Nicky! Miles!' she called out. 'I need a good party theme!'

Chapter Twelve

March 2007

'You would not believe how long this hair took,' Leigha was telling one of her course-mates, gesturing at each side of her head, when Johnny and Adam arrived at Dell Road.

'You look amazing,' the girl – dressed as a ladybird – gushed, clasping Leigha's arm. And she did, she really did. Johnny had to pause for a moment to take her in, tantalising in a gloriously figure-hugging white maxi dress, plastic gun belt and holster low-slung on her hips.

'Happy Birthday, Ley.' Adam had moved forward whilst Johnny had lingered in the hall, kissing Leigha on the temple and putting a brightly coloured envelope in her hand. 'It's just a voucher, yeah?'

'Oh, thanks Adam, you really didn't need to,' Leigha answered with a smile, opening the card.

'Shame to see you didn't go with the gold bikini outfit!' Adam joked, an incorrigible flirt as ever. Leigha laughed and opened her mouth to respond, before catching sight of Johnny. Her face hardened momentarily with exasperation.

'Oh, Johnny…' she said finally. Johnny gave a weak grin.

'Great minds…?' he tried. Leigha looked at him helplessly. His insides cringed. He knew she knew he'd done this on purpose.

She'd mentioned going on a shopping trip to a toy store specifically for the belt; she and the other girls had publicly discussed the best way to put her hair up in the buns. Johnny had then spent 45 minutes lost and walking circles in Debenhams until he found a white terrycloth bathrobe that he thought would suit.

Leigha recovered quickly, slipping her arm around Johnny's.

'You look wonderful, young Skywalker,' she said. 'Let's get a photo of the Skywalker twins. Nicky!' A leggy, blonde Lara Croft whirled around, camera in hand as usual.

'And what in the hell are you?' Adam asked, instantly diverted as Sukie walked past him wearing a prom dress and trainers, hair scraped back to the top of her head and hoop earrings so huge they brushed against her shoulders.

'Lily Allen, duh.' Sukie handed him a plastic shot glass with neon green liquid inside. She looked him up and down, taking in his half-arsed costume of jeans and a red checked shirt. 'Lumberjack?'

'Got it in one,' Adam nodded, pulling the small plastic toy axe from his back pocket and making chopping motions in the air. Sukie rolled her eyes.

'Did he do that on purpose?' she asked, nodding towards Johnny, as Adam tossed back his shot.

'What do you think?' he laughed. 'It's not like Leigha has talked about *anything else* other than her Princess Leia costume for the last week.' Sukie looked over to where Leigha and Johnny were posing for an assortment of photos, Nicky snapping away merrily. They were back to back, in James Bond style poses, Leigha holding up the plastic toy gun that had come with her belt, Johnny steepling his index fingers together in an approximation of one.

'He is ridiculous,' she declared; Adam bristled at once.

'There's no need to be such a giant bitch,' he told her archly. 'He's not bloody hurting anyone.' Sukie stared him down.

'No, you're right,' she said, lightly, already moving past him. 'That's your forte.'

Harriet was in the garden with Lucy, who was smoking, both staying close to whatever warmth the open back door was affording them. Lucy twisted her head with each exhale, blowing a pale plume of smoke away from her companion and into the darkness of the garden beyond.

Adam looked at his girlfriend appreciatively; she was wearing what looked suspiciously like an Anne Summers French Maid outfit, but under a knee length polyester cape, candy red. Harriet's dark eyes looked out at him mischievously from underneath the red hood. He felt his arm twitch with the automatic impulse to reach out and stroke her cheek with the pad of his thumb, like he did when they were alone.

'Nice to see you, Little Red Riding Hood,' he smiled, by way of greeting, before turning to Lucy who was twisting her high heeled shoe on her discarded cigarette butt. She was wearing a white blouse and black pencil skirt. 'And you're – what – a Sexy Secretary? That doesn't begin with L.' Lucy swatted at him playfully.

'I'm a librarian, clearly!' she retorted, resetting her fake, thick-framed glasses on the bridge of her nose.

'Clearly,' Adam echoed.

'I'm a freezing librarian,' Lucy revised, rubbing her hands on her bare arms. 'Does anyone want a drink?'

'Yeah, I'll have a beer if there's one cold enough,' Adam said.

'I'm fine, thank you,' Harriet said, indicating her half full glass of cocktail. Lucy disappeared back into the house. Immediately Adam reached out for Harriet and she shot him a look that froze him in his tracks. He let his hand fall and caught up her elbow instead, their contact concealed from any of the windows by his own body.

'Trouble,' he murmured, 'you look amazing.' Harriet smiled, but pulled the cape around herself a little self-consciously all the same.

'Well, that's good, because you *always* look amazing,' she returned the compliment with a smile.

'Harry,' Sukie called, stepping out onto the paving of the garden. 'Fuck, its cold out here!' They were getting better at not starting guiltily whenever anyone came upon them together; Harriet slid away from Adam's hold with a subtle shifting of her body, looking at Sukie expectantly. 'I've got someone for you to meet,' Sukie continued, gesturing back to where a tall blond boy wearing a novelty moustache and a green tee-shirt and cap was standing in the frame of the back door.

'Dan, mate!' Adam said immediately.

'Alright!' Dan said, clasping hands with Adam companionably. 'What are you meant to be then?'

'Lumberjack,' Adam told him impatiently. 'You?'

'Issa me!' Dan answered, in a high-pitched and terrible approximation of an Italian accent. 'Luigi!' Adam's mouth twitched.

'How very... retro,' he said finally. 'Cool.' He looked round to where Harriet was watching the exchange in silence, Sukie in turn watching her.

'Harry, this is Dan,' Sukie said, which Adam felt was quite redundant by that point. 'Remember I was telling you about him?' Harriet smiled, gracious and friendly as ever.

'Of course, hi Dan, good to meet you. Do you mind if we move inside? I'm frozen stiff.'

'Of course!' Dan flustered, trying to move away from the doorway in what he obviously considered a gentlemanly flourish, which succeeded in bumping Miles so violently that he dropped his can of beer, which went spinning and frothing across the kitchen floor. Sukie rushed for a tea towel; Dan and Harriet disappeared inside to the lounge, Dan apologising profusely to a surly Miles.

A second later Lucy appeared at the back door, holding out a bottle of Carlsberg, obviously surprised to see Adam standing alone outside.

'You coming in?' she said, as he took the bottle from her hand with a muttered thanks.

'Yeah,' he said, following her impatiently as she turned back into the house.

Harriet was uncomfortable but was trying her best to hide it. She was being more or less successful, but Sukie had known her for half of their lives and could read her like a book. Her hand fluttered up to touch her neck far too often, a throwback to how she used to nervously curl her hair around her fingers years ago, back when it was long.

Dan was turned completely towards Harriet on the sofa, his knees at ninety degrees to hers, bottle of beer held casually as he listened intently. He laughed loudly at whatever she was saying; Harriet's eyes flicked up and met Sukie's briefly, before turning to someone behind her.

'What makes you think those two are even suited?'

Sukie jumped; Adam had materialised beside her, frowning and picking compulsively at the label on his bottle.

'I thought he was your mate!' she said, accusingly.

'He is,' Adam said immediately.

'Well then, you should agree that he's a good guy.'

'I'm not disputing that,' Adam said tiredly. 'It's just so forced. Leave Harry alone, she can run her own love life.'

'She's been a nun for the last six months,' Sukie declared. Adam's eyes flashed as if he was going to argue the point, but instead just lifted his bottle to his lips. 'Aside from when she kissed you, of course,' Sukie said mildly. She expected a bit of a reaction, but Adam just looked at her thoughtfully. She wondered if Harriet

112

had ever told him that they'd been seen.

'See now, to me, that suggests that she certainly can decide her own love life,' he said finally, pick-pick-picking agitatedly at the shredded edges of the beer label.

'Suggests the opposite to me,' Sukie scoffed. 'Suggests she needs a fling.'

'But you were so against the idea of me and her having a – what – fling?'

'That's because you're mates. She made that mistake at school, with Seth. You don't shit where you eat.' Sukie laughed. 'She needs fresh meat. She needs distraction from work and from how you're always around, mooning over her.'

'I don't moon!' Adam said immediately with a scowl. Sukie shot him a look.

'You're just as bad as Johnny with Leigha, the way you look across the room at her all the time.' Adam remained silent; there was a furious set to his jaw. 'Get over it,' was Sukie's cheerful advice, as she patted Adam sympathetically on the arm. 'If she wanted to be with you, she would be.'

Adam made an incredulous noise, peeling a white curl of label clean from the glass with his thumbnail.

Nothing made Harriet more nervous than seeing Sukie and Adam deep in conversation. The two of them had a strange love–hate relationship and spent a good deal of time moaning about how the other one was impossible. Sukie patted Adam's upper arm in a seemingly consoling manner; Adam *did not* look consoled.

Dan finally seemed to notice that she wasn't making eye-contact with him as she talked. He followed her line of sight past where Sukie and Adam were standing and into the kitchen area beyond them.

'You wanting a drink?' he asked, helpfully. Harriet looked down at her glass and – sure enough – she'd somehow drained the rest of her cocktail during their five minutes of conversation. She smiled weakly.

'That would be great, thanks. Vodka and anything.'

Clearly eager to please, Dan was up and off like a shot, manoeuvring through the other party guests to try and get close to the kitchen side. Almost as quickly, Sukie came forward, perching on the arm of the sofa. Adam had disappeared into the cover of the standing groups of people.

'So,' Sukie pressed, squeezing Harriet's hand. 'What do you think?'

Nicky knew Lucy's housemate from her French classes. She also knew that she was a TEFL applicant and – sure enough – after the obligatory mutual complimenting of each other's costume, Lucy turned the conversation in that direction.

'Katie's applied for Bordeaux,' Lucy said, 'she thinks it will be a 'realer' experience than Paris, you know? Course, no offense if you're going to Paris.'

'I'm not going to Paris,' Nicky admitted with a rueful smile.

'Oh, where are you going?'

'Bath, actually!' Nicky tried to laugh self-depreciatingly, but it came out sounding embarrassingly brittle.

'Bath? Wow!' Lucy said brightly, obviously mentally groping for something to say. 'Why Bath?' she asked finally.

'Miles is doing his PhD there,' Nicky shrugged.

'Oh, I see! So you two are, like, making it official then? Mortgage? Marriage!?'

Nicky laughed. It's what the other girls had said; it's what her own mother was expecting. And – truth be told – that actually made her feel happier about everything. When people told her that she and Miles were sure to get married, her heart started to punch inside her chest, but not out of panic, something more like impatience.

She loved him, she was realising, really loved him – grown up, real life love. She loved someone so much she found herself willing to disrupt her life plan to be with him, and he loved her too, so much so that he wanted her to live with him, that all their friends thought he was going to ask her to marry him. How could anyone be unhappy when they had that?

And so Nicky sipped her drink, and smiled, and told everyone she spoke to that night how excited she was.

About halfway through the evening there was the accustomed rush for shoes and coats as the gathering moved outside to the garden to sing Leigha a Happy Birthday.

A satisfactorily merry Leigha had clung to Johnny as she teetered on the uneven grass in her gold stiletto heels. She'd noticed that his shins were goose-pimpled under his leg hair where his legs were nonsensically bare under the dressing gown he was wearing.

Then suddenly, embarrassingly, there was another Luke Skywalker at the party, one complete with a glow-in-the-dark light-saber and – perhaps more vitally – trousers. Johnny had watched sullenly as Leigha cheered her friend Matthew and proceeded to pose for the repertoire of photos with him, before eventually Johnny had vanished from her side entirely.

So, for the first time since she'd met him, Leigha had to go looking for Johnny.

She found him in the front garden, sitting in a neat row on the more substantial part of the boundary wall with Adam and two girls she knew from seminars. The girl sitting next to Johnny was laughing – loudly and brashly – and as Leigha neared she saw her cuff his shoulder flirtatiously.

Adam saw her first, breaking into his easy smile. 'Hey, Birthday

Girl,' he said in greeting, Johnny looking up at her with the usual mixture of anxiety and yearning on his face.

'Are you guys going to come in, we might play some games...' Leigha said, suddenly feeling incredibly awkward being the only one standing.

'Muggy in there, too many people,' Johnny declined, politely. The other three made noises of agreement. Leigha suddenly got the sensation she hated above all others: that third-wheel feeling. She smiled tightly.

'Okay, well, see you later,' she said, in her most carefree voice, before pirouetting on one golden heel and marching back into the house.

Harriet was aware that she was lolling rather unattractively against the couch cushions, but she couldn't quite bring herself to care. Ditto that she'd probably drunk a bit too much for sense.

She hadn't seen Adam for hours, so when he loped past where she was sat it was a bit of a physical shock. He looked as drunk as she felt, and was as dark and brooding as a storm cloud. She heard a glassy chinking as he presumably tossed something into the recycling crate in the back porch, before walking back through the kitchen to the fridge, where Johnny was excavating its depths for the final few beers.

Leigha immediately disengaged from her conversation and floated over to join the two boys. She touched her fingers to the small of Adam's back for his attention as she spoke. Adam laughed at whatever it was that she'd said, slinging his arm drunkenly around her shoulder. Johnny straightened, handing Adam a beer with a neutral expression on his face.

Harriet Shaw, 03.11
Are you asleep? x

Adam Chadwick, 03.12
No. Thinking.

Harriet Shaw, 03.12
What about? x

Adam Chadwick, 03.14
Dan's stupid cap :)

Harriet Shaw, 03.14
I miss you.

Adam Chadwick, 03.15
xxx

Adam Chadwick, 03.16
I will be round tomorrow lunchtime, I'll pick up some stuff from the little shop on way. If I can't give u a good morning kiss at least I can give u a bacon sandwich xxx

Harriet Shaw, 03.17
You are literally the best. I am a lucky girl :)

Leigha's breathing as she slept was deep and even. It was almost hypnotic.

Johnny's side was going numb, he was going to have to shift positions. Taking excruciating care not to shift the covers more than necessary, he inched onto his back. Leigha slept on.

Chapter Thirteen

April 2007

Adam thought that it was time to tell everyone.

'Nobody gives a fuck that Johnny spent the night in Leigha's bed the other week,' he pointed out, doodling absent-mindedly in black pen on the skin of Harriet's calf.

Harriet rolled her eyes. 'Trust me, a massive fuck is given,' she assured him. 'Nicky's actually really cross with her, I don't think she's actually spoken to her since she found out. And Sukie gave her usual lecture. She told Leigha,' her eyes flashed mischievously, 'that she was messing Johnny around WORSE than you did her…'

'Coming from Sukie, that's one hell of a reprimand,' Adam laughed, re-angling Harriet's leg on his lap to continue his drawing.

'She said that it was only a drunken kiss and that they didn't do anything in bed but pass out,' Harriet continued.

'Which Johnny corroborates,' Adam nodded.

'Yeah, but, I've never known a man to enter Leigha's bed and come out unscathed!' Harriet laughed. 'You had a lucky escape.'

'I really did.' Adam leant forward to give Harriet a kiss. Her face was hesitant when he pulled away.

'What?' he asked, concerned.

'It was… just a kiss, wasn't it?' she asked. 'Just that one kiss on

New Year's Eve? There weren't… any other kisses that I should know about, were there? Or anything… more?'

Adam dropped the pen into his lap and reached out to her face. 'God, Harry, of course not, I would have told you. You know that.'

'I know.' Harriet was flushed and fidgety with embarrassment. 'It's just… like I said. You'd be the exception, not the rule.' She shrugged. Adam kissed her again.

'Exactly. I'm the exception,' he swore.

Harriet tensed as she heard the front door open.

'I'm home!' came the cry.

Sukie was back a couple of hours earlier than she'd said she'd be; luckily, Adam had left twenty minutes before. Leaving her duffel bag parked at the foot of the stairs, Sukie came straight through to investigate who was home.

'Hey,' she said, perching on the free sofa to kick off her shoes. 'When did you get back?'

Harriet shifted uncomfortably inside her duvet cocoon. She was feeling awful – both figuratively and literally. She'd actually been back at Dell Road for the last five days, cutting her Easter holiday at home with her parents short in order to spend a little uninterruptable, guilt-free time with Adam whilst the house was empty.

'This morning,' she lied. 'My brother drove me back on his way into London. Jumped at the offer… I don't feel so well, couldn't face slogging here on the train.'

Sukie leant forwards with her elbows on her knees, scrutinising Harriet's face. 'Yeah, you don't look so hot,' she agreed. 'Do you want something?' She stood and moved towards the kitchen.

Harriet swallowed laboriously; her throat felt raw and puffy. 'Something hot to drink would be nice, my throat's really sore,' she admitted. Sukie looked at her with renewed concern.

'I think I've got some Lemsip or something in my room,' she

said. 'Hang on.' She took the opportunity to drag her bag upstairs; Harriet winced as her headache pulsed in tandem with the thump, thump, thump of the bag hitting the stair lips. She burrowed further into the warmth and softness of the duvet. She imagined she could still smell Adam on the cotton of the sheets.

'Boots' own brand will have to do!' Sukie announced cheerfully, reappearing in the kitchen with a handful of sachets and busying herself with the kettle. Harriet watched her friend as she moved from cupboard to drawer, collecting mugs and spoons. Hey, she wanted to say, I've got something to tell you. She imagined just blurting it all out. How would she start? You know that thing I said I wouldn't do…

After five days of playing house together things with Adam were growing even more serious. Nothing like cooking your daily meals and waking up every morning with someone to put paid to the pretence that you're not a real couple… The knowledge that she'd be alone in her bed tonight – as opposed to tangled up amongst Adam's arms and legs – made Harriet feel a little adrift.

Matters had definitely escalated. And what had she told herself when this all started? The minute she knew it was for real, she'd talk to Leigha…

'Here you go.' Sukie held out a steaming mug, interrupting her thoughts.

'Oh, thank you!' Harriet strenuously pulled herself up to a sitting position and reached out with both hands for the mug.

Sukie gasped. 'Shit, Harry!' she squealed. 'You're all swollen!'

Drawing her hands back, Harriet placed them under her chin. Her skin felt as puffy and hot as the inside of her throat did. She winced. 'Is it bad?' she asked.

The ever capable Sukie snapped into mother mode, thrusting the mug towards her. 'Drink this. Stay there,' she commanded, a little unnecessarily, as Harriet felt like she had lead weights on all of her limbs. 'I'm calling NHS Direct.'

'You've got the what?' Adam asked, voice rising in alarm.

'*We've* got the mumps,' Harriet croaked down the phone.

'Shit! Thought I felt rough.'

'Exactly. So, fluids, fluids, fluids. And stay in bed,' Harriet advised.

'Hmmm, sounds like what caused the problem in the first place,' Adam laughed quietly, voice low and suggestive. Harriet groaned fondly. 'So, how are we playing this then?' Adam continued. 'We were both opposite sides of the country, at home with our folks, and independently return for term with the mumps?'

'There's probably a national epidemic or something,' Harriet said, straight-faced.

'No doubt,' Adam agreed, sarcastically.

'You sure you don't mind being left here alone, mate?' Johnny asked from the doorway to the lounge, his concern genuine. Adam's flushed and swollen face peered out at him from the duvet that was pulled up to his chin.

'I'm fine,' he rasped, sounding extremely wretched. 'Get out of here. Enjoy your takeaway. What are you getting?'

Johnny rubbed the back of his neck awkwardly. 'Chinese.'

Adam shot him a look. 'You hate Chinese.'

'Yeah, well.' Johnny shrugged. 'It's the girls' favourite and it's not so bad.'

'Is it the 'girls" favourite or is it specifically Leigha's favourite?' Adam asked, irritated.

'Whatever, mate – it's not like it matters,' Johnny snapped. Adam sunk into a frowning silence. 'Are you sure you don't need anything before I go over?' Johnny asked again.

'No, I said, I'm fine! Go. You might as well spend as much time over there as possible, stop you catching this lurgy off me.'

'Well, that would be pointless, being as Harriet's contaminating the girls' house,' Johnny scoffed. 'The two of you – couldn't even have the courtesy to only infect one of the houses!' he laughed. 'We should throw Harriet in here to live with you and board up the doors and windows, like for plague victims.'

And as he said it, he noticed that strange look again, tight between Adam's eyes, the one that made him wonder what it was his best friend wasn't saying. But, before he could examine his misgivings more closely, his mobile buzzed dully against his thigh, distracting him.

Leigha Webster, 18.12
HUNGRY!! xx

Adam leant back rather precariously on his chair and pondered the wall planner tacked up above his desk. He tapped the end of his biro against his teeth thoughtfully.

It was April 15th. Adam's eyes were drawn along the columns to where Harriet had filled in a date box in yellow highlighter pen; June 15th. He now officially had only two months to churn out ten thousand words of a passable quality. Still just about doable, but he really had to knuckle down today and at least pick the genre, if not the specific subject and title of the dissertation. He solemnly avowed that he would go no further than the bathroom until that task was complete.

After checking his emails and Facebook account, Adam opened up the Google search engine and confidently typed in: 'what should I do my English dissertation on?' Within half a second he had more than three million results, a veritable wealth of instruction and advice. Feeling rather pleased with himself, Adam decided he'd earned a fortifying tea break before continuing on.

A mug of builders' tea and half an hour of Pro Evo with Johnny later, Adam returned to the results list and started to sift through.

Focus on a topic that you genuinely like and are interested in.

Adam rolled his eyes. Well, obviously. He just needed help discovering what that was.

Choose novels that are more complex and have a higher word count; this way, if you decided to change your focus partway through the process, the book should have enough scope to allow fresh ideas and approaches.

Adam rubbed the back of his neck. He wasn't quite sure he liked the idea of a lengthy and complicated book, not least because it might be a squeeze to fit in both the reading of it and the actual writing of the thesis on it. Poetry, then, maybe? He typed 'poetry' into Google and was rewarded with 300 million results. He sighed impatiently. This really was not helpful in narrowing his options. He do with another cup of tea...Deciding Poetry.com was as good a place as any to start, well, looking at some poetry, Adam clicked onto the site and started to skim read at random. After a wasted hour glazed over as he read Renaissance verse, he found some more modern stuff he quite liked.

'It's quite good, isn't it mate?' he asked Johnny, as he read one of the poems Adam had kept tabbed open on his screen. 'Sort of like song lyrics, aren't they?'

'Yeah, I guess,' Johnny said, uncertainly. 'But, what are you going to say about them?'

'Ah, you know,' Adam shrugged. 'The usual shit. Theme. Tone. Er, the structure.'

Johnny raised his eyebrows. 'The structure?'

'Yeah, you know. How many lines it has. If it rhymes. You know, structure.'

'You won't get ten thousand words out of that though, mate.'

'Well obviously I'll write about more than just the one poem,' Adam told him, scornfully. Johnny's eyebrows were still arched rather doubtfully.

'Okay, I guess,' he said. 'Good work then, mate. Pro Evo break?'

Feeling very virtuous, Adam took his laptop into bed with him that night, continuing to trawl through the archive on Poetry.com, this time with the filter 'Modern' in play. Harriet had sent through her habitual sweet goodnight text and Adam was looking for a piece of suitable love poetry to impress.

In my sky at twilight you are like a cloud
and your form and colour are the way I love them.
You are mine, mine, woman with sweet lips
and in your life my infinite dreams live.

He revolved his mobile in his hand as he used the other to click in and out of other poems by the same writer, satisfaction growing as he realised he found them quite accessible and that – potentially – he'd found a direction for his dissertation. He'd run it past Harriet when he met up with her in the library tomorrow, see what she thought of its prospects. It was the first time they were going to see one another since they'd recovered from the mumps; shame it had to be the flipping library, but – he guessed she was right, they *had* missed out on ten days of study in the final ever term of their degree.

There was a little bittersweet part of him that almost wished they hadn't had the week or so alone together in her house. It was making all the subterfuge and being apart that much harder, being together 24/7 reduced to texting sappy poetry in the dead of night. Adam laughed to himself. If you'd told him six months ago he'd been mooning over love poetry on the internet – much less texting it on to a girl – he'd have said you were barking.

He'd used to tell Lauren that he loved her, not often, and more as an automatic response to her saying it first. He probably wrote it more often in cards than he'd ever said it out loud. Not for the first time recently, he felt a twinge of guilt at how he'd treated the girl. He hoped she'd find someone who would text her love poetry in the middle of the night.

Harriet had responded, very appreciative of both the content and the intent of his text. Adam thumbed onto the Reply screen and, as he had a lot that week, toyed almost absent-mindedly with the idea of texting: I love you.

Chapter Fourteen

April 2007

They deserved to have been caught; if the other girls hadn't been so drunk they might have been. It had just been so difficult to say goodbye; their conversation had dragged on and she found herself still kissing him goodbye at the front door an hour after he was meant to have left.

They hadn't paid that much attention to the sounds outside at first, the purr of an idling car, its doors slamming. But then – unmistakeable – Sukie's drunken giggle and the grating of the rusty front gate being pushed open.

Within seconds Adam had opened Nicky's nearby bedroom door and disappeared into the shadows beyond. As it clicked shut, the noise was echoed by Leigha's key in the lock and Harriet had to step back to avoid being hit by the front door.

Leigha blinked at her in confusion. Sukie pushed past her into the house.

'The music was GREAT tonight!' she immediately informed Harriet, too drunk to be concerned with why her housemate was standing in the dark hallway at two in the morning. 'You missed out, you're lame.'

'We called you,' Leigha said reproachfully, closing the front door and kicking her high heels off and into the indiscriminate mass of shoes that lived at the bottom of the stairs. Sukie had borrowed Harriet's beautiful but uncomfortable red wedges; they'd obviously pinched her too, as she already had them off and in her hands; she tossed them atop the shoe pile.

'Did you?' Harriet feigned surprise. 'Sorry. My phone's been on silent. I've really been in the dissertation zone tonight.'

'Hmmm.' Sukie had moved through to the mirror by the kitchen door and was slowly and carefully peeling off one false eyelash, her other hand to the wall to steady herself. 'Well, this new and unimproved lifestyle of yours better be worth it. What's your current word count?' She stuck the eyelash to the gilded frame of the mirror, joining all the others that she'd stuck there over the past eighteen months, bristling like insect legs.

'Almost eight and a half thousand,' Harriet answered immediately. She'd stopped keeping count of these little lies. She'd actually finished her dissertation completely two weeks ago.

'God,' Leigha moaned. She was sitting on the bottom step peeling off her tights. 'I'm only just on five. Living with you is bad for the academic ego.' She unsteadily stood up on the stairs and from her elevated height planted a kiss on the top of Harriet's head. 'Su, bring me some water up, please! A lot of water!' With her tights dragging behind her like a tail, she clumped heavily up the stairs.

With one false eyelash still fluttering, Sukie dutifully went through to the kitchen, collecting two clean pint glasses from the drainer and running the cold tap. She wouldn't have been able to hear over the sound of the water pressure, but Harriet – still standing by the foot of the stairs – heard the slow slide of Nicky's sash window being pushed up and, seconds later, back down. Then a singular heavy footfall as Adam hopped the garden wall and was away down the silent street.

Half an hour later, Sukie – always hyperactive when drunk – crashed out on her bed, left eyelash still obstinately in place, Harriet returned to her rumpled bed. On her little TV, the DVD menu for the film she and Adam had watched was still on rotation.

She picked up her mobile. She'd let the girls' call go to voicemail; she assumed they'd just been ringing to hold up the phone whilst a particular song played. She was right; listening to the recording she could just make out the tune to the chorus of 'Grace Kelly', a recent favourite in their house. On top of the bass of the song she could hear Sukie's voice, words indistinguishable – perhaps singing along – and then, suddenly, the background sound dropped away as Leigha presumably cupped her hand around the mouthpiece of the phone. She could hear her as clearly as if she was sitting beside her on the bed, palm cupped to her ear.

'We miss you, Musketeer!' Leigha had trilled down the phone. 'Where are you?'

Johnny was in his customary position on the left hand side of the larger couch, be-socked feet up on the coffee table. On the other couch - the so-called 'studying couch', as it didn't directly face the television – Adam was slogging away on his laptop, pausing in his typing every few paragraphs to expectantly hit the Word Count button. It wasn't increasing by much, but the fact that it was increasing at all felt like a mini miracle. Only four days of work and he was already creeping close to two thousand words. With a great degree of satisfaction, Adam hit 'Insert Footnote' and flipped to the front of the book he was referencing to get the publication details.

In the hush that followed the pause in typing, Adam became aware of a weird scratching sound. He looked up; Johnny was staring past the television, eyes unfocused, a strange black shape in his hand that clicked open and closed and scraped along the loose denim of his jeans as it did so.

'What the hell is that?' Adam asked.

Johnny blinked out of his reverie and looked down at his hand as if he too was confused as to what was in it. 'Oh, it's a hair clip thing. Leigha left it here the other day.'

Miles looked up from where he sat at the dining table, bent over a text book and armed with a highlighter. 'I'm going over there to have dinner with Nicky in a bit, I can take it back if you like?' he offered. Johnny frowned.

'No, no, it's okay,' he said, clicking the hairclip open again. 'I'll give it to her when I see her tomorrow. It's fun to play with. It's kind of like a stress ball. Helps me think.' He resumed staring ostensibly at the television once more. Miles arched his eyebrows at Adam across the room; Adam nodded his head slightly to show his agreement, before returning doggedly to his footnote.

Johnny couldn't work with other people around, had never been able to. As he gleefully and regularly informed everyone, his course was primarily test rather than coursework based. He didn't have a ten thousand word dissertation like everyone else, but he did have fifteen rather nasty exams to revise for. He retired early to his bedroom that evening, rearranged his pillows to prop himself up, pulled one of his coursenote folders from his bookcase at random, opened it balanced against his thighs and started to read.

He held Leigha's clip tightly in his hand, feeling its teeth press hard into the softness of his palm. His hand would smell faintly of Leigha tonight, as if he'd just run his fingers through her hair.

The SU was really scraping the barrel for themes this close to the end of the academic year. It was 'Sex and the City Night' in the Armstrong. Harriet could see no discernible difference from any other Wednesday night aside from the fact that they were serving

Cosmopolitans and girls were slightly more dressed up than usual.

Leigha was wearing a cranberry-red dress with a sweetheart neckline and ropes and ropes of shiny, fake pearls at her throat. Harriet was in the black sequined dress that she'd let Leigha wear on Nicky's birthday, the face of each individual bead and sequin glowing dimly under the bar's downlighters.

Leigha plucked the small wedge of lime off the rim of her glass and squeezed it between her thumb and forefinger, adding its juice to her fourth Cosmo before discarding it with its forbearers in the middle of their table and licking her fingers with satisfaction. Harriet surveyed her friend; Leigha's face and neck was flushed the same soft pink as the Cosmopolitan. Harriet could only assume she looked much the same, as for once, she was matching Leigha drink-for-drink.

Leigha was sparkling, as usual, half way through a story about a hideous dress her nemesis had been wearing in a seminar that day. Harriet leant forward across the small table and listened eagerly. She had missed this. She'd really been burning the candles at any and all conceivable ends, finishing her dissertation, keeping up with all of her modules and fitting in an increasing amount of time with Adam. There was nothing quite like spending your food budget on novelty cocktails and listening to Leigha turn what by rights should be an exceedingly boring story into something dreadfully entertaining. Harriet took a large and happy sip of her Cosmopolitan.

Leigha was already on about a terrible joke that Johnny had text her that afternoon – lightning quick changes of topic were par for the course with her – was it okay for her to have found a sexist joke quite funny or was that a betrayal of feminism, or something?

'I swear we've had this conversation…' Harriet said.

Leigha tilted her head to one side. 'We have? When?'

'At school. In like, Year Eleven. I swear!' Harriet professed.

Leigha laughed. 'God, probably. Nothing new under the sun, ey?'

No, there is, Harriet thought automatically. The one thing that I am dying to tell you and the one thing I can't. Not yet. I can't bear to see you look at me surprised and hurt. Not yet. Surely soon there'll be a way around all this. I just need a little more time.

But you're my best friend. I want to tell you about this guy I like. How he's nothing like Seth – remember how I was worried that every boyfriend would be like that? Being with Adam is easy, almost as easy as being with you.

Leigha drained her glass, Harriet automatically mirroring the action. The vodka burned pleasantly in her stomach.

It was a common complaint amongst the Arts students that their library was in dire need of refurbishment. To call the old building shabby chic was being kind. It didn't have automated stacks or self-service machines like the Management and Sciences library the other side of campus and the carpets and bookcases looked like they were probably the Victorian originals.

But on days like this one, where the springtime sunshine streamed in through the high windows and set the dust motes dancing, Harriet sincerely felt that those BSc lot could stuff their vending machines and state of the art study pods. The Old Library was clearly suited for those who had poetry in their souls, rather than numbers in their heads.

Adam certainly had poetry in his soul lately. He sat across the table from her, absorbed in a critical biography of Pablo Neruda, its pages bristling with strips of Post-its to mark points to revisit. Harriet was trying to focus on studying for her Fin de Siècle literature exam, an impossibly long and inaccessible essay on the androcentric hegemony of the 19th Century medical profession leaving her eyes dry and itchy.

'Do you want to go grab some food?' she asked Adam, her

voice pitched to a stage-whisper. Adam marked his place in the text with his forefinger and glanced up at her.

'In a bit,' he answered. 'I want to finish with this book and make some photocopies. It's Reference so I can't take it out.' Harriet smiled at him 'What?' he asked, defensively.

'Oh, how you've changed Mr Chadwick!' Harriet teased.

Adam shot her a wry look. 'I'm just trying to impress this girl, is all…'

Harriet laughed quietly, reluctantly reaching for her text book once again. 'You let me know how that goes.'

'I love you, Harriet.'

She didn't look up straight away. Had she heard him? Had he even said it at all?

He'd had big plans. He was going to take her out to dinner, somewhere far enough away that she wouldn't be edgy about being seen, maybe out in London. And he was going to order a bottle of white, as Harriet was always saying how she wanted to start drinking it. He planned to say it calmly, casually, manfully; she, of course, would say it straight back.

But it was like how it had been the night they first kissed, he just hadn't been able to stop himself saying it. The words were like a live thing, pushing its way from his heart, up his throat and out of his mouth.

Finally, she looked up at him. She looked distressingly calm and casual.

But then she half stood, leaning her whole upper body across the table and took his face into her hands and kissed him softly.

'I love you, too,' she told him, firmly. '*Now* can we get out of here?'

Adam didn't respond for a moment; he felt a little punch-drunk. 'The book,' he said, a little stupidly. 'My notes.'

Harriet rolled her eyes and plucked the Reference book from his limp grasp. 'We'll hide it and come back for it later.'

'I think that ever since we met—'

Harriet cut him off with a groan. 'PLEASE don't say something bullshit like, it was love at first sight,' she sighed. Adam glared at her.

'That's not what I was going to say – you unromantic bitch! – I was just going to say that it feels like, with the benefit of hindsight – that this was always going to happen.'

Harriet arched her eyebrow sceptically and shifted to a more comfortable position with what space she was afforded on the single bed, wedged tightly between Adam's warm body and the cold wall.

'Oh yeah? Go on..?'

'Well, I mean, being in love…' Harriet noticed with pleasure that Adam's ears blushed pink. 'At the end of the day, it's finding a best friend who you sleep with, right?'

After a few seconds to absorb this, Harriet burst out laughing. 'And you just called me unromantic! Jesus!'

'No, think about it!' Adam pressed. 'When you strip it down, that's basically what it is. A friend you love and the benefits of sex!'

Harriet groaned and threw her hands over her face. 'Oh God…'

'Okay, maybe that is making it sound a little… pasteurised,' Adam conceded. 'But I'm basically just saying that it was meant to happen, once we'd spent enough time together. I mean, I fancied you and all—'

'You fancy everyone,' Harriet interrupted again. Adam scowled at her.

'Take the compliment, will you? And then I just needed time to get to know you properly, and fall in love with your personality. Then add sex and boom. Perfection.'

'So you're saying that if Johnny was a girl, he'd be your perfect girlfriend? You'd be in love with him?'

Adam pulled a disgusted face. 'Man, that'd be one ugly girl. So I wouldn't fancy him. So no! Now come here and stop being gross.'

Their kiss was interrupted by the dull ringing of Harriet's phone in the recesses of her handbag; it was the third time it had rung in the last quarter of an hour. Harriet sighed as she broke the kiss.

'Let me up to just check that, it must be important.'

Begrudgingly, Adam disentangled his legs from hers and shifted so she could stand. After a moments' search Harriet extricated her phone from her bag – one missed call from Leigha and two from Nicky; the voicemail icon was flashing insistently. Harriet paced the small room as she called her voicemail and cycled through the menu options, enjoying the way Adam watched her proprietorially from the bed as she did.

The voicemail was from Nicky; she rambled nonsensically for the first twenty seconds of the recording before coming to the heart of the matter. Harriet listened in increasing horror. She was already groping for her clothes before the voicemail had ended.

Adam had sensed her obvious change in temperament and was sitting up against the pillows, alarmed. As Harriet dropped her phone he caught sight of the tears that had begun stinging her eyes and jumped to his feet.

'What is it?' he asked, catching her in his arms. Harriet only relented against him for a second before blindly pushing her way free and continuing to gather up her strewn clothes.

'I've got to get home,' she said, voice tight. 'Sukie's mum.'

Chapter Fifteen

May 2007

The house was disconcertingly quiet without Sukie, who had understandably upped and bundled herself into a taxi before Harriet had even got home. Sukie had been working in the lounge when she got the call from her father. Nobody quite had the heart to clear her stuff away, so one side of the couch was taken up with a collection of dog-eared notes and tatty playbooks, an uncapped biro lying in the spine of the one that lay open.

It seemed wrong to be social, wrong even to sit in the lounge together. As a result, Leigha retired to her bedroom for most of the rest of the week, cruised to 9,978 words and considered it a dissertation well dissertated. Nicky anxiously browsed the Internet to get a feel for both the employment and rental markets of Bath and did not feel encouraged by what she saw.

But Adam was growing increasingly impatient.

'I can't believe you actually think *this* is a suitable time,' Harriet repeated, agitatedly shaking the vinegar canister over her chips.

'Well, obviously, maybe wait till Sukie comes back,' Adam granted, ripping open salt and pepper sachets with a little more force than necessary. 'But for crying out loud, Harry, it's almost been three months. Three whole months. And I love you.'

Harriet flinched. 'I know,' she said, in a voice that was meant to sound reasonable and placating. 'But that doesn't change the horrible timing. Welcome home Su, so sorry again for your terrible loss, how was the funeral, oh, by the way, there's this HUGE thing that's been going on behind your back...'

Adam rolled his eyes. 'Stop being dramatic. It doesn't need to be like that.'

'It sounds pretty fucking dramatic to me.'

Harriet's head whipped up as her heart spiked down to her toes. Johnny was standing there, his face like thunder to match the snarl in his voice. Adam was already on his feet, palm held out in appeasement to his best friend.

'Mate, listen—'

'Oh, I'm listening alright!' Johnny laughed harshly. 'So, what's been going on, guys? Do I need to sit down for this?' There was no answer forthcoming from Harriet, who was still in a stage of mute horror. Adam hurried to pull out one of the empty chairs like some sort of sycophantic waiter.

'Mate,' Adam tried again, as he sat back down.

'You guys have been in some secret relationship for months?' Johnny shook his head in disbelief. 'I knew it, I fucking knew it. You've been acting really odd. You are the only two who caught the mumps. Shit!' He sat back heavily in his chair. 'What are you guys playing at? What's your problem?'

Adam's face flared with anger. 'What's our *problem?* This is our problem. You guys reacting *like this.* We're in love, for fuck's sake, can't you be happy for us!?'

Johnny scowled back. 'Well did you stop to think that it's insulting us finding out how you guys have been having a laugh and pissing about behind our backs? I can't believe this.'

'Trust me, it has not been having a laugh,' Adam murmured, rubbing his temple with his fingers.

'We were just waiting until the right time.' Harriet had found her voice again, and looked across at Johnny pleadingly. This is what she'd been terrified of; the people she cared for most hating her because of this.

'And when, pray tell, do you think that would have been?' Johnny scoffed. 'When the wedding invitations were in the post?'

'Look mate, just calm down,' Adam pleaded. 'Stuff's just been up in the air. We were just waiting for Sukie to come back and then we were going to let everyone know.'

'Whatever.' Johnny's voice had lost a lot of its anger; he sounded more disgusted with them now. 'I can't believe this,' he said again, shaking his head slowly. 'How could you do this to Leigha?' Harriet wasn't sure if he was directing this at her, Adam or the pair of them; either way, her heart squeezed sharply in her chest.

'We're not doing anything to Leigha!' Adam cried in annoyance.

'She's going to be so mad, isn't she?' Harriet said to Johnny, threading her fingers miserably. Johnny gave a mirthless laugh.

'She's going to be so mad,' he agreed. 'You guys... Shit. I can't believe it,' he said, for the third time.

'But this is why, this is exactly why!' Harriet said, her voice rising a little hysterically. 'I didn't want her – didn't want –' She couldn't finish the sentence but Johnny looked at her with a degree of understanding in his eyes nonetheless. He knew the spirit of what she was trying to say; after all, he knew everything there was to know about Leigha.

'So, are you going to dob us in, mate?' Adam said, taking a gamble on humour as he sensed the softening of Johnny's mood. 'Tell Leigha on us?'

Johnny stared at the table a few moments without responding, before reaching forward and taking a handful of Harriet's over-vinegared chips.

'No,' he said, through his mouthful. 'But you guys really need to. And soon.'

'We will,' Harriet said, in a rush of relief. 'Thank you.'

'We're really sorry mate, we really didn't set out to lie to you and everyone,' Adam said, scratching at his cheek nervously. 'It all just, kind of happened.'

'I can imagine,' Johnny said, ruefully, leaning back in a slightly more relaxed position than before and pinching another handful of chips. 'So come on then, let's hear the big love story.'

It had been persistently spitting with rain all day, but by the time the film was over the weather had turned more serious, with heavy rainfall and high wind marbling shapes onto the window glass. Johnny looked out at the squall in resigned trepidation. On the other side of the sofa, Leigha unfurled her legs and stretched like a cat.

'Looks like you'll have to backstroke it home,' she smirked. 'Man, it's really heaving it down.'

'Yeah, I can see that,' Johnny retorted impatiently, rising to his feet and stopping to pick up his glass and empty crisp packet from the floor. He could feel Leigha's eyes on him as he moved across to put them in the sink and bin respectively. The big, square room was dim, but suddenly lit up in stark greys and blues as the credits finished rolling and the DVD returned to its menu screen.

'Fine, just stay here tonight,' Leigha said, sounding distinctly bored. Johnny looked over his shoulder at her.

'What, on the sofa?'

Leigha casually got to her feet and moved to turn on the corner lamp, flooding the room with colour again. 'You know you're too tall for it; did your back in last time, didn't it?' she said. 'Go in Su's room. She won't be back until tomorrow.' Johnny took another look out of the window, considering the offer for a moment.

'No, I don't want to intrude on her space, even if she's not

here, it would feel weird,' he said, begrudgingly. 'Maybe I'll just…
borrow a brolly.'

'Oh, stop being silly. Look, just come up and crash with me,'
Leigha said, moving past him to the sink as if what she was saying
wasn't a massive deal, and pouring herself a fresh glass of water.
When he didn't answer right away she looked up at him playfully
through her eyelashes. 'Come on, Gentleman Blake. It won't be
the first time.'

She didn't wait for his acceptance, but instead moved off and
up the stairs, completely and totally certain that he was going to
follow her. For one brief, mad moment, Johnny felt the urge to
surprise her, to head off into the wet and the dark rather than
spend another tragic night curled up behind – but never quite
touching – the girl he loves.

He followed her upstairs, of course, pausing outside the closed
door to Sukie's empty room for a momentary reconsider. There
was a ruler of light showing underneath Harriet's closed bedroom
door; Johnny felt another guttering of frustration in his stomach
as it brought to mind Adam's fifty per cent success ratio when it
came to this house.

Inside Leigha's room a soft, repetitive scratching noise began.
Leigha sat on her bed, her back to the door – and to him – brushing
her skin down with a long-handled brush. Lazily, she nudged the
strap of her vest top so that it fell aside, and curved the brush
around that shoulder to the back of her neck. Johnny swallowed.
God, she made him crazy, drove him to utter distraction and she
wasn't even looking at him. As usual, he dared himself to just do
it, just climb onto the bed behind her and trail kisses on the skin
that had been scratched pink and warm. As usual, he didn't.

Leigha pulled the heavy fall of her hair over, concealing the
shoulder Johnny had just been contemplating and turning the
attention of the body-brush onto the other. Glancing behind her

as she did so, she shot him a quizzical look, wondering – quite rightly – why he was standing in the doorway like a tense bouncer. Flushing hot with embarrassment, Johnny hurried inside the room and closed the door behind him. Leigha continued rhythmically brushing her right arm. Johnny awkwardly settled himself on the edge of the bed.

'Don't look for a sec,' Leigha told him, in a smiling voice that suggested she knew just how much he'd want to look. Johnny obediently took out his mobile and stared blankly at its little screen. He heard the shuffle and soft thud of – presumably – Leigha's pyjama bottoms hitting the floor, and the soothing sound of the brushing resuming.

She could almost see cartoonesque sweat beading on his forehead; poor guy. But there was nothing quite like watching a harmless romantic comedy to start up that itching inside her head, and Leigha knew she didn't want to be alone tonight. The house was too quiet – Sukie back home with her family, Nicky over with Miles at the boys' flat, Harriet whey-faced and holed up in her bedroom and Adam pleading his dissertation deadline. It was easy - Leigha was discovering – to feel alone, no matter how many people you surrounded yourself with.

She finished exfoliating her legs and – after a moment's thought – decided she didn't need to replace her pyjama bottoms after all. Instead she just swung her bare legs up onto the bed and arranged herself to her best advantage, lying on her side with her head propped up by her elbow. Johnny must have realised the brushing had stopped and that she'd lain down beside him, but he doggedly continued playing on his phone, presumably until she otherwise instructed. Leigha smiled.

'Let's talk,' Leigha commanded from where she lay, perilously close to him. Johnny briefly panicked over whether or not it was okay to put his mobile phone down on her bedside table before deciding that it probably was.

'What about?' he asked, tilting his body casually towards hers and trying to mirror her nonchalant pose by propping his head up too; it wasn't particularly comfortable on his elbow but it would have been too embarrassing to reposition so soon.

'Anything!' Leigha laughed. 'What's new with you?'

Immediately, every single aspect of his life – aside from the hours spent either with or thinking about her – fled his brain.

'Oh, you know,' he said, blithely. 'Revision. And stuff.'

'Ack, revision!' Leigha daintily screwed up her nose. 'I literally cannot wait until it's all over, can you?' Johnny shifted, awkwardly.

'Well, I wouldn't go that far,' he said. 'I'm not exactly looking forward to moving back in with my parents.'

'Well, it won't be like you're underfoot,' Leigha pointed out, readjusting so that one of her bare legs stroked leisurely against the other. Her vest top rode up against her stomach, almost imperceptible, were it not for the metallic flash as her belly button stud became exposed to the light. 'With your internship. You'll be out and about.'

She was right; he couldn't complain. There was gainful employment and roast dinners aplenty waiting for him back in Bradford; he'd managed to wangle the coveted internship on the city's newspaper. It paid little more than expenses, really, but who knew what it could lead to. He'd been so elated with himself the day he was accepted, he'd felt electric. Now, looking across at his beautiful, disobliging Leigha, he just felt vaguely sick. The thought of being four, five hours on the train away from her; sick, sick, sick. Would she even bother staying in contact with him?

'I'm just going to kick back, relax,' Leigha continued. 'Sign up with some recruitment consultancies, see what there is to see job-wise…' Johnny smiled crookedly at her; it was an old topic of conversation between them.

'I don't know how you can just – not have a plan,' he told her. 'Not even have the slightest clue what sort of job you want.'

'Hey, I do so have a plan,' Leigha retorted immediately. 'The plan is just to get the first decent job going and move out into London, back into together. Nothing wrong with that as a plan.'

'You and the girls?' Maybe he and Adam could get a place? How high was London rent? Maybe he could get the same sort of internship down here…

'Yeah, well, Nicky's going off with Miles,' Leigha frowned, waving her hand dismissively. 'And who knows what's going to go on with Su now. She'll probably want to stay close to home for a while. She's got two kid sisters and her dad's always travelled a lot on business, so they'll need her,' she said sadly. 'So, maybe it'll just be me and Harry – at first, anyway. God,' she smiled. 'There's going to be *mountains* of washing up in *that* flat…'

He could picture it. Leigha and Harriet in a cute little flat, he and Adam living only a couple of tube stops away. Things would be more or less the same as now, better even: him and Adam over at the girls' all the time, slobbing on the couches, eating takeaway and watching films, each with their arms around their respective girlfriend. In that split second, it just seemed so fucking achievable; Johnny's chest cavity suddenly burned with an elation that was almost painful.

'Adam and I were talking about getting a flat together in London,' he lied. Leigha's eyebrows arched.

'Yeah? He was mentioning moving to London when we were talking the other day,' she said, nonchalantly. The burn inside Johnny suddenly rushed cold. When was this? Was it just around the house, a conversation that he'd somehow missed? Or had the two of them had lunch together, or another random coffee date?

The way she spoke about him, so proprietary; she always had, he knew, but *why still?* Why, when she knew Adam didn't want her and she knew that Johnny did – God, so, so much? It wasn't so very long ago that they'd spent the night together in this very bed, drunkenly kissing under the weight of the covers, slick with sweat.

She seemed to have sensed his thoughts had turned dark and inward; maybe his brow was too furrowed, or his face suddenly too shaded with hurt. She looked at him quizzically, her perfect, plump lips pursed into a little o of mute enquiry.

Johnny found himself thinking about how, last night, he had sat up with his laptop until the early hours, unable to sleep, bored and methodically clicking around Facebook. Leigha laughing, Leigha pouting, Leigha half turned away from the camera, and him, there in the background, disconcertingly often, chasing the curve of her face.

And then the sentence was out before he even realised he was speaking.

Leigha thought she could actually feel her heart stutter in her chest, if such a thing was possible. For a split second it was like there was nothing inside of her but silence, and then suddenly a roar as she became aware of the blood rushing through her. She felt dizzy, her body impossibly light on the bed. She sat up straight.

Johnny was babbling now. She could tell from his general anxiety and the redness high on his neck that he was panicking, hadn't meant to tell her. She tried to rally her thoughts out of shock, to ask the sensible, practical questions.

'Are you sure?' she wanted to know. 'How long has this been going on? Am I the last to know?'

But as Johnny cringed and cowered in front of her, pleading ignorance and forgiveness, she could only focus on one thing, like there was a marquee scrolling over and over inside her head. Why

143

does this keep happening to me? Why is it always her? Over and over; sharp as glass.

And so, because she felt like she might cry, or even throw up – that she was about to be driven mad by the itching of the anger and embarrassment inside of her – she rolled over on top of Johnny, startling him into silence. Wordlessly, she drew her bare leg up between his, braced her palms flat on the hard plane of his chest and kissed him; anything, anything, so she wouldn't have to think about it anymore. Johnny groaned, deep and low into her mouth. She kissed him harder.

Chapter Sixteen

May 2007

Nicky and Harriet sat cross-legged on the floor in companionable silence as they arranged the damp white clothes onto the laundry horse. Nicky wondered, as she turned a clammy sleeve the right way, if she should broach the topic of Johnny's shoes – painfully obvious at the bottom of the stairs – and that Nicky knew for a fact that he hadn't come back home to the boys' flat last night. But Harriet was uncharacteristically lost in thought, and Nicky was loathed to break the calm and quiet of the house in the brightness of the morning.

As if conjured by her chain of thought, Johnny's heavy tread on the upstairs landing resounded through the house; Harriet arched her eyebrow at Nicky as the footsteps moved to the stairs. Johnny appeared in the hallway, stooping to pick up his trainers, tee-shirt and jeans heartbreakingly unrumpled; there was no way he'd slept in his clothes last night.

He stood there stupidly for a few seconds, gathering his wits as he blinked in the bright light streaming through the kitchen window, before hurriedly stuffing his feet into his trainers, leaving the laces undone and trailing.

'Catch you later,' he said gruffly, nodding rather formally in the direction of the two girls, before turning and slipping out of the front door before they could even consider replying. Nicky turned back to Harriet, who was looking so incredulous that her eyebrows were lost underneath her fringe.

'Bloody... Leigha,' she said finally, placing her final pair of white knickers on the bottom rung of the laundry horse and stiffly easing herself to her feet.

'He knows what he's doing,' Nicky said quietly. Harriet gave a scoffing laugh.

'You know as well as I do that Leigha's the only one in that pair who knows what she's doing,' she disagreed. 'Poor Johnny's just putty in her hands. Like he can—' Suddenly she stopped speaking, her eyes flickering wider.

'What?' Nicky asked, concerned, rising to her knees. Harriet turned to look at the front door.

'Nothing,' she said, unconvincingly, after a few seconds. 'I'm just going to get my phone.'

Before Harriet could reach the foot of the stairs, there was the distinct scrape and jangle of keys in the lock and a flush-faced and bag-laden Sukie pushed her way through the opening door. Harriet immediately flung her arms around her, knocking her slightly off balance.

'I'm so sorry I wasn't here,' Harriet murmured into Sukie's shoulder. Sukie gently extricated one of her arms enough to be able to let her duffel bag slide from her shoulder to the floor.

'I told you already, it's fine,' she said, her voice weary. 'It's just so good to be home.'

'Really?' Nicky asked sympathetically, moving to the kettle on reflex and picking it up to inspect its water level. 'God, Su, it's so dreadful.'

'It really is,' Sukie agreed, pulling her denim jacket off and dropping it down on top of her bag. 'It's just so.... quiet in that house. It's horrible. Don't we have anything stronger?' she asked, nodding to the kettle in Nicky's hand. Nicky replaced it on its stand with a smile.

'I'm sure Leigha must have something somewhere,' she replied, taking glasses from the cupboard instead of mugs.

And just like how she had conjured up Johnny, Leigha's voice came floating down the stairs.

'Su?'

'Yeah, hi!' Sukie answered, busy kicking off her shoes into the pile. 'I'm home.'

'Can you come up here for a second?' Leigha's voice was off, somehow. Nicky saw Harriet and Sukie exchange a glance. Sukie looked up the stairs, annoyance knitting her features. Harriet flexed her fingers and reached up for hair that was no longer at her shoulders; she was nervous.

'I've literally just walked in, can I have a minute?' Sukie called back. 'We're having a drink, come down.' Without waiting for a response, she moved through into the kitchen space, continuing the search through the cupboards for alcohol that Nicky had paused.

Harriet glanced up the stairs, hesitant as if she was about to climb them.

And Leigha appeared on the landing. Harriet had never seen her mouth so small, her eyes so heated, and the staircase between them suddenly seemed as if it could be a mountain. Harriet's breath caught like a solid thing in her throat, her vague suspicion proved true, but before she could fully process the thought, Leigha was at ground level and pushing past her. Harriet reached out and grabbed her wrist.

'Let go of me,' Leigha hissed between her teeth, eyes flashing. In the kitchen, Sukie and Nicky were pouring Pasoa into glasses, regardless of the cataclysm brewing down the hall.

'Leigha, listen to me,' Harriet said urgently, pushing the taller girl away from the kitchen and closer to the front door with the strength that only desperation can provide.

'You're hurting me,' Leigha growled, whipping her arm violently in an attempt to break Harriet's grip on her wrist.

'Can we just go upstairs, just for a minute?' Harriet begged, loosening her hold only a fraction, but it was enough; Leigha dragged her arm away, but as she did, moved her face closer to Harriet's, so close that Harriet thought for a moment that she was going to kiss her.

'You're such a fucking slut,' she said, voice flat and emotionless. Harriet recoiled instantly, that solid thing inside her throat swelling up so fast she felt like she was going to be sick. 'You stay the hell away from me, you – you nasty, *poisonous* slut.' And then she whirled away, her hair fanning out behind her and rushed into the kitchen, forcing herself into Sukie's arms and bursting into noisy, wet tears.

Sukie blinked in astonishment, before tightening her arms around Leigha. 'Ley, what's wrong?' she asked.

'Honey, what is it?' Nicky asked, putting her glass hurriedly down on the side and rushing to rub Leigha's shuddering back. Sukie made eye contact with Harriet over the top of Leigha's head, silently asking her what was up, but Harriet couldn't speak for the horror that was balled tight in her throat, in her chest.

Leigha mumbled something indistinct into Sukie's collarbones.

'What?' Nicky asked. Leigha lifted her damp-streaked face away from Sukie's chest. Harriet finally had the sense to move towards the others, her hand held out stupidly in front of her like she could somehow reach that extra fifteen feet and clap it over Leigha's mouth before she could speak again.

'Harriet's been *fucking* Adam,' Leigha announced, her phrasing succinct and deadly. Even Nicky blanched. Sukie sucked in a breath.

'You what?' she asked, directed at Harriet.

'No wonder he suddenly went cold on me,' Leigha wailed. 'She got her claws into him.' Harriet grabbed for Leigha's upper arm as she came in range, jostling her.

'It's not like that!' she cried. 'Just calm down for a minute.'

'What's been going on?' Sukie asked, voice hard as she moved her hands to her hips. 'Is this true?'

'Don't be ridiculous, of course it's not.' Nicky moved steadily to stand between Leigha and Harriet. 'There's obviously some sort of… misunderstanding… miscommunication or something going on here.'

'Harry?' Sukie pressed. '*Are* you fucking Adam?'

Harriet hesitated; there was no good way to answer this question. 'Well, yes,' she admitted, miserably, 'but—'

'I fucking knew it!' Sukie exploded, cutting off Harriet's feeble attempts at explanation. 'You promised me nothing was going on!'

'You knew about this!?' Leigha rounded on Sukie, who faltered.

'I – I knew they kissed,' she stumbled. 'At Nicky's birthday party. But she begged me not to tell you!' Harriet made an inarticulate noise of protest.

'My birthday!' Nicky echoed faintly.

'I can't believe you didn't tell me!' Leigha railed at Sukie, who put her palms up soothingly.

'Look, don't get mad at me, it's Harriet you should be mad at!' she reasoned.

'Look, everyone calm down!' Nicky cried, echoing Harriet's earlier plea. 'Harry, is this seriously the case? You and Adam?'

'Yes, we're together,' Harriet said, trying to keep her voice as steady as possible. 'It just happened, it wasn't meant to ever become this massive deal—'

'It just happened?' Sukie echoed, incredulously.

'Couldn't you control yourself?' Leigha sneered. 'It had just been so long since Seth, you just couldn't keep your legs closed?'

'Leigha!' Nicky admonished. Harriet was momentarily struck dumb. She'd never been spoken to like this in her life before; the ease at which the insults were flying from Leigha's mouth was shocking. She tried to rally herself.

'God, you're all about the drama, aren't you?' Leigha was continuing, hatred dripping from every word. 'You just want everything to revolve around you, you always have.'

'You think I *wanted* this to happen?' Harriet cried, finally jarred into defence. 'I wanted nothing more than for him and you to be together and for you to be happy.' Leigha scoffed. 'He just doesn't *like* you in that way, he never did. And that's nothing to do with me.'

'Oh, he liked me plenty!' Leigha countered. 'Trust me.'

'Look, I'm sorry if we've hurt your feelings,' Harriet continued, voice softer. 'But it's actually quite ironic you insist that *I* love drama and think the world revolves around *me,* because you're just describing yourself.'

'How dare you!' Leigha cried, outraged, voice cracking like she was about to burst into tears again. Sukie moved forward and put her arm around her. 'I'm the bloody victim here!'

'You're just proving my point. This is about me and Adam, it's nothing to do with you.'

'Of course it has something to do with her!' Sukie barked, eyes narrowing. 'her best friend and her ex-boyfriend.' Harriet raised her arms in exasperation.

'For crying out loud, *ex-boyfriend?*' she cried. 'How exactly is he your ex-boyfriend, Ley? You had one kiss. By that count, more than half the guys on campus can consider themselves your ex.' Leigha burst into the noisy tears that had been threatening.

'God, when did you turn into such a bitch?' Sukie asked Harriet, squeezing Leigha consolingly.

'I can't believe this…' Nicky murmured, clasping her hands

over her nose and mouth like she was praying.

'Neither can I!' Harriet cried. 'This is exactly what I didn't want to happen, can't you see that? Why it was hard for me to tell you guys?'

'Well, that worked out well for you, didn't it?' Sukie sneered sarcastically. 'Lying to your best friends is usually the wrong thing to do, for future reference.'

'I didn't lie,' Harriet professed miserably.

'Well, you've got a very fucking different definition of the truth than everyone else on the planet,' Sukie shot back.

'Everyone calm down,' Nicky ordered again. 'Ley, Harriet's said she's sorry, can't we—'

'I'm not sorry.' The words had left Harriet's mouth before she even realised she'd thought them. Leigha stopped crying and lifted her face from Sukie's shoulder to stare at her. Nicky's mouth hung open. Sukie's face was dark and furious.

'Like I said, I'm sorry you're upset, I'm sorry your feelings, your pride, or whatever, have been hurt,' Harriet clarified. 'But I'm not sorry that it's happened. I think we're meant to be together. I love him.'

Sukie gave a groan of derision, Leigha a bitter laugh. 'Good for you,' she said, icily. 'I hope he fucks you up like you fucked up Seth. I hope you fuck *each other up*.'

'Why do you have such a bloody chip on your shoulder about Seth?' Harriet shouted. 'All this is nothing to do with you. I'm sorry I wasn't in love with Seth, and I'm sorry that I *am* in love with Adam – but you need to get it into that massive head of yours that none of it is designed to make your life miserable.'

Leigha finally pulled away completely from Sukie's hold, drawing herself up to her full height. 'You stay the fuck away from me,' she spat, voice deadly serious.

'I can't even believe you can't see how in the wrong you

are,' Sukie frowned. Harriet ran her hands through her hair in frustration.

'Su, she kissed him one time, drunk at a party. It doesn't make him her ex. It doesn't give her control over him.'

'He told you it was just that one kiss?' Leigha asked, tilting her head pityingly. Harriet shot her a look full of warning.

'I know it was just that one kiss.'

Leigha shook her head. 'He's playing you. And you fucking deserve it.'

'He's not playing anyone Leigha, for fuck's sake!' Harriet cried. Leigha narrowed her eyes.

'Let's just say that I visited Australia. Many times.'

Harriet's blood ran cold for a second. Adam had a strawberry birthmark on his upper inner thigh that he often joked was in the shape of Australia. Her thoughts faltered. Was there any other way that Leigha would know about the mark, other than the obvious, the way that Leigha was clearly getting at?

'Don't come crying to me when you realise what you've done or when he moves onto the next girl,' Leigha told her, all emotion gone from her voice again.

'I can't believe you,' Sukie said, her voice full of contempt.

'Su, you're making it worse!' Nicky cried, almost hysterical.

'Oh no, this is all on her,' Sukie jabbed a finger at Harriet accusingly. 'I trusted you. I covered for you.'

'Come on, let's get out of here, I can't stand to look at her,' Leigha said, tugging Sukie's arm. And she looked directly at Harriet, for what would prove to be the last time, a look loaded with more disgust and loathing than Harriet could ever have imagined, before heading towards the front door.

'Nic, you coming?' Sukie threw over her shoulder as she followed her.

'No, guys, stop, this is ridiculous!' Nicky cried, wringing her hands, but Leigha and Sukie had their shoes and jackets on and were gone before she could say anything else. The bang of the door was the loudest thing Harriet had ever heard in her life. She sank to her knees on the cold, hard kitchen floor, and silently put her face in her hands.

'They'll calm down,' Nicky assured her, fidgeting nervously. 'Don't worry, Harry, please. Oh, don't cry!' she pleaded, as Harriet's shoulders started to shudder. She sunk down on her haunches and wrapped her arms around her. 'Look, even the best of friends have fights sometimes. We'll all sit down, everyone will say they're sorry…'

Harriet raised her flushed face. 'I told you, I'm not sorry,' she said, like it was that simple.

Johnny felt dreadful, a combination of gnawing guilt and a bad night's sleep. He walked the long way home – past Tesco – loading up with beers and chocolate fingers and share sized bags of crisps for what he optimistically assumed would be a night in front of the TV with Adam – maybe even Miles – and a junk food dinner.

He realised as he ascended the stairs up to the flat – made awkward by the heavy shopping – to find Adam standing in the centre of the living room, his phone to his ear and a rather murderous expression on his face, that he had severely miscalculated. Johnny hesitated, the plastic bag handles cutting off the circulation to his fingertips.

'He's here,' Adam said, into the phone. 'No. No, I want to talk to him. I'll call you back. No, I want to.' He continued to stare at Johnny as he spoke. Johnny gave his best, innocent 'what's up, mate?' expression. 'It's okay. I love you,' Adam continued. At a loss for what to do, Johnny began unpacking the shopping and arranging it on the dining table, like the embarrassing peace offering it was.

Adam slid his phone closed. Johnny filled the ensuing silence with the sound of tearing cardboard as he opened the box of biscuits.

'What's up mate? Finger?' He offered the open box to Adam, whose gaze just narrowed. 'Alright,' he conceded, placing the chocolate fingers back on the table. 'I told Leigha, I'm sorry. What's going on?'

'What's going on?' Adam repeated, disbelievingly. 'A massive amount of shit hitting a massive fan. That's what's going on. Exactly what we wanted to avoid. Harriet is devastated. I had to get half the story from Nicky. Leigha went fucking mental.' Johnny winced.

'Well, I'm sorry to hear it mate, I really am, but Harriet's done this to herself to be honest.' Adam's glare tightened even further, but he was interrupted from immediate response by footfall on the second floor staircase.

Miles appeared behind Johnny, face rosy and hair wet from the shower, mobile phone in hand. 'I just spoke to Nicky, what the hell's going on?' he asked, without preamble.

'This isn't my fault!' Johnny stressed, gesturing wildly for emphasis.

'I'm sure Nicky's told you the gist,' Adam answered, ignoring Johnny. 'Harriet and I have been seeing each other. We were going to tell everyone when Sukie was back,' – he glared at Johnny – 'but then Johnny told Leigha and she and Sukie have gone batshit crazy, and say they never want to see or talk to Harry again.' He mimed an explosion with his hands.

Miles blinked slowly. 'Fuck,' he said.

'It just came out!' Johnny moaned. 'I felt sorry for her.'

'That's the thing, isn't it? Everyone feels sorry for Leigha. Everyone babies her, nobody wants to upset her,' Adam scowled.

'Yeah, but, no offense, but you really look like you've gone out of your way to do just that,' Miles frowned. 'What were you two thinking?' Adam gave a grunt of annoyance.

'You know, I thought Harriet was paranoid, keeping everything a secret, but you're all sort of proving her point with your shitty reactions.'

'Bit of a self-fulfilling prophecy there though,' Miles said thoughtfully. 'Because people are probably more annoyed that you kept it a secret.'

'Oh, I am sorry!' Adam said, falsely sincere. 'We should have sent out a bloody newsletter, kept you all in the loop. How dare we not involve you all?' He glared around at his housemates. Johnny picked at his fingernail, feeling a little stupid when he heard it put like that. Then he thought of Leigha's face when he had told her last night, the pink rims of her eyes as they had opened wide, the intensity of her tongue as it had probed his mouth, her fingers pressing on his body, as if she'd been searching for something.

'You should have had more consideration for Leigha's feelings,' he insisted, stubbornly. 'You shouldn't have led her on in January and you two should have sat her down and told her what was going on right at the beginning.'

Adam's eyes flashed. 'Sorry, mate, I know you *love* her…' Johnny bristled at the implied quotation marks around the word love. 'But she's a brat. She's a controlling *brat*. Look at the way she's reacting! Harriet's been her best friend for what, ten years? And the first and only time she does something that Leigha doesn't like and that's just it? She never wants to speak to her again?'

'It is a pretty extreme reaction…' Miles agreed, quietly.

'She's just a very sensitive person!' Johnny contended. 'And she doesn't deserve this.'

'She doesn't deserve a good friend like Harriet,' Adam shouted.

'Oh yeah, she's *such* a good friend, shacking up with you behind everyone's back, knowing what you are to Leigha. Pretty selfish fucking friend.'

155

There must have been a tell – perhaps a sudden tightening of the muscles in Adam's face or shoulders – because Miles was between them in an instant and Johnny saw Adam shakily lower the fist he hadn't even noticed him raising.

'The two of you,' Miles said in disbelief. 'You're behaving worse than the girls. Can't we just agree there's right and wrong on both sides here?' There was a moment of uneasy silence before Adam sank down into one of the dining chairs, as if all the energy had just rushed from his body.

'Sorry, mate,' he mumbled towards his knees.

'Sorry, mate,' Johnny echoed, even though he wasn't sure if they were apologising to one another or to Miles.

'But she's... she's just in total *pieces* Johnny. To hear her.' Adam looked up at Johnny helplessly. 'She loves those girls. You have to believe me, she did what she did because she didn't want to upset them. You need to talk to Leigha for me, tell her. Harriet *loves* Leigha.'

Johnny sat down heavily on the opposite chair, reaching automatically for a chocolate finger that he didn't really want.

'Well,' he said, snapping the biscuit between his teeth. 'Seems like she loves you more.'

As soon as the flare of testosterone had receded and relations between himself and Johnny seemed on steadier ground, Adam headed off for Dell Road. Nicky opened the door to him, so quickly she must have been waiting for his knock.

'What's going on?' Adam asked, without preamble, shedding his jacket as he moved through into the main part of the house. Nicky flitted behind him.

'Sukie and Leigha are still out. Neither of them answered their phones when I called. Harry's in her bedroom.'

'In her bedroom?' Adam repeated, turning on the spot and

heading back towards the foot of the stairs.

'She said she wanted to be left alone,' Nicky explained, tugging at her fingers anxiously. 'I assumed she was going to call you and you were going to come straight over.'

'She did call,' Adam said, 'but I had to talk to Johnny.'

'Why Johnny?'

'He told Leigha. He promised he'd keep quiet and let us tell everyone, but couldn't go twenty four bloody hours.' Adam had to stamp down on the resentment rising up from his core. Nicky looked at him in horror.

'But, you two, you're—?' she trailed off.

'Yes, it's fine, don't worry,' Adam reassured her, impatiently mounting the stairs.

'It's going to be okay?' Nicky called after him. She probably meant it as an encouragement, but it came out sounding way too much like a question. Adam threw a preoccupied smile over his shoulder as he climbed his way up to the landing, opening Harriet's bedroom door without pausing to knock, unsure what he was about to encounter inside.

Harriet looked up at him from where she sat cross-legged on her bed, a battered paperback copy of *Dubliners* slack in her hand, revising even now. Adam felt a wildly inappropriate laugh bubble up in his throat.

'Hi,' she said, in an impossibly small voice.

Adam crossed the room in two long strides and knelt at the side of the bed, enfolding as much of Harriet as he could in his arms.

'I'm so sorry,' he murmured against the side of her head. 'I'm so sorry.' He pulled back to look her in the face. There was already no sign of the earlier sobbing that Nicky had reported; her eyes were unreasonably dry and bright, her face pale and smooth. Harriet squirmed, uncomfortable under his close scrutiny.

'It's fine,' she said, simply.

'It is not fine!' Adam replied immediately, aghast at her apparent acceptance of the situation. Harriet just shrugged, before placing her bookmark of a torn off piece of paper carefully back into place between the pages of her book and putting it down on her bedside table. She rubbed at her eyes tiredly.

'Let's get out of here, let's go somewhere,' Adam urged her. 'How about I take you out for dinner tonight. I'm thinking… Big Mac?' His light teasing was rewarded with the slight twist of a smile, but her silence was still heavy and queer. Adam leant forward and pressed his forehead to hers. 'Tell me what I can do.'

Harriet pulled away gently. 'I'm really tired,' she said, apologetically. 'Plus I don't want to go running from the house like I've done something wrong. If Nicky is right and Ley does cool off and want to apologise… or at least talk… well, I should be here.'

'Fair enough,' Adam nodded. 'How about I get a film in? We could do the walk to Blockbusters, the weather is okay. Or I could go quickly by myself? Bring something from the chippie back?'

'I'm really tired,' Harriet repeated. She pulled her sleeves as far down over her wrists as possible, pulling at the hems distractedly. Adam pulled her into another hug.

'Do you want to talk about it?' he asked.

'Not really.'

'I really think we should,' Adam pressed. She fidgeted against him again, like the little bird he always pictured her as, fluttering and anxious to get away. He grasped her all the harder. 'Please, Harriet, tell me what I can do to make things better. I love you so much.'

All at once she relaxed and seemed to collapse in on herself into his hold, pliant and soft and reachable once again. 'I feel sick,' she admitted in a whisper. 'Oh, it was so horrible.'

'I can imagine,' Adam soothed. 'Come stay at mine, please. I hate the thought of you rattling around this house whilst Leigha and Sukie are being like this. And it might give them more of a chance to calm down.' He felt her shrug listlessly.

'It doesn't matter if they do. It will be pretty hard for me to forget my best friends calling me a horrible slut, that they've apparently always thought I'm a nasty person, who thinks the world should revolve around them, who purposefully set out to upset and… disappoint them.' He could hear the threat of fresh tears catching in her voice. 'No matter what, today I lost my best friends. I know it for certain. How can I ever feel comfortable around them again?' A single tear spilled over onto the slope of her cheek and she swiped it away angrily.

Adam didn't know what to say. His first instinct was, of course, to tell her that everything was going to be okay, but how could he when she had just quite eloquently illustrated how things were never going to be 'okay' – as she had known it – again? Wordlessly he stroked her hair.

'You still have Nicky. And me,' he said, after a minute.

'I don't want them taking this out on Nicky,' Harriet said, immediately. 'And I don't want her caught in the middle of all this stress. For crying out loud, it's our last term. Exams are starting next month. She doesn't need this. Nobody needs this.'

'This isn't your fault,' Adam said, eyes narrowed. Harriet did that little shrug again.

'You can't really say it's theirs, though.'

Chapter Seventeen

May 2007

Johnny and Harriet were to turn twenty-one in the same week; only days ago, the joint birthday plans had been the hottest topic of conversation. Leigha pulled the card and envelope from their cellophane sleeve and penned Johnny's name with exaggeratedly careful handwriting, studiously avoiding thinking about Harriet's birthday present, still in its shopping bag and hurriedly stuffed into her desk drawer. Out of sight, out of mind.

Harriet seemed to have adopted the very same approach; she was holed up in her bedroom even more than usual. Leigha had been woken by the sound of persistently running water at about 2am and realised it was Harriet having a bath. Her top lip bore back from her teeth in a scowl as she thought about it. Slinking around at night like a rat, too ashamed to face anyone. She wrote 'Happy Birthday!' in large letters inside the card, taking up a lot of the unnecessary white space.

She had been the one to open the door to Adam that evening. She and Sukie had exchanged a glance at the sound of the knocking. Surely could only be Johnny, or Adam? Nicky and Miles would have keys. Sukie had motioned that she would answer, but Leigha had put her hand out and Sukie sunk back down on the couch, frowning.

Maybe Adam had expected to see Nicky – it was she who'd been letting him in for the last few days after all. His face was pleasantly neutral when she opened the door, but as he'd caught sight of her it had snapped into coldness.

'Hi,' she'd breathed, in a stupid, casual voice. Ever the gentleman, Adam had graced her with a stiff nod before easing past her and making his way straight up the stairs, balancing brown paper bags of takeaway in the crook of each arm, the warm, tangy smell of Chinese food wafting after him. Leigha had watched him go, disappearing across the landing, presumably into Harriet's bedroom. When she had turned away, Sukie was leaning against the doorframe into the kitchen, regarding her sceptically.

'Hi,' she'd mimicked, in a little girl voice. 'What the hell was that? Why didn't you tear a strip off of him?' Glaring, Leigha had pushed past her back to the couches and the paused DVD.

He was still in there with her now; well, she hadn't heard anybody leave the house. They'd probably watched a film together on Harriet's little telly, littering the bedroom carpet with rice as they tried to eat out of the takeaway cartons with plastic cutlery. She'd even heard laughter earlier – it might have been the television, but it sounded an awful lot like Harriet. How dare she just be in there, with him, laughing, like she'd done nothing wrong? Leigha exhaled slowly as she focused on drawing a decently round circle inside Johnny's card for a smiley face.

She'd always felt safe with Harriet. Boys came and went, they all knew that; Johnny, Adam, even Miles, all transitory. Other girls tended to get the wrong impression of her, to throw around those ageless slurs: bitch, slut. If she chatted casually to their boyfriends at parties, they'd always come up with a reason to call him away. Sukie was volatile by nature, Nicky hadn't known her for very long. Harriet was her one real constant. The metaphorical stab in the back ached at her like a physical injury.

'Lots of love,' she wrote – without a second thought – 'Leigha xxx'

The world beyond the thin curtains was turning warm and pink as the sun rose; another sleepless night. Beside her, Adam was sprawled out on his back, the duvet ridden down and exposing the whole expanse of his bare chest. His arm was thrown back over his head; his fingers were cupped towards his palm as if he were holding an invisible hand.

She'd so wanted this – him, here, and no more secrets.

It had only been muted, never really banished, that mental movie reel of Leigha's red lips at his pale throat, his now so familiar hand fumbling against her naked thigh. Harriet looked down at him from where she sat, wedged between the pillows and the wall; he was growing distinct in the emerging light. She imagined Leigha's pink-varnished fingernails scraping through the curls of golden hair that spread over his chest. She felt like she was going to choke.

Gently she lifted the duvet up, focusing on the darker patch of skin at the juncture of his thigh that was his birthmark. He'd definitely have to be – as he was now – stark naked for anyone to see it.

'Hey, Trouble, what are you after?' Adam murmured suddenly, his voice husky with sleep. He shifted his body towards her and smiled drowsily. Harriet hurriedly dropped the duvet back into place, embarrassed. 'What time is it?' Adam asked, thickly, through a yawn.

'Early. It's early. Sorry. Go back to sleep.'

He had drifted back into sleep before she'd even finished talking, his breathing evening out and fingers relaxing again, not even curiosity at her obvious attention to his groin enough to keep him awake at half five in the morning. He'll probably think he dreamt it, she thought.

The wall she was leaning against was an external one, and it was cold and unforgiving against her back. Harriet slipped down in the bed, fitting against the curve of Adam's splayed body.

What was upsetting her most? The fact that he might have… with Leigha? Or that if he has, he's lied to her about it?

Harriet had loved Seth, she hated herself when she had to hurt him. But she was always going to, because there is a whole world of difference between loving someone and being in love with them.

She had no doubt that she was in love with Adam. He had the power to devastate her even more than she had Seth. Even just sitting awake wondering if he's lied to her about Leigha caused its own miniature devastation, a mushroom cloud spreading through her insides. She considered how long Adam's eyelashes were in profile, felt the squeeze of an urge to kiss his eyelids. How could she love someone but not quite trust them? But then again, she was having a bad run of luck with people she loved and trusted lately.

She'd known Leigha would fuss, and pout, and make a massive deal out of everything. She was expecting things to be a little strained between them for a while, until the fresh start of graduating was enough of a distraction.

'No control,' Leigha had said loudly to Sukie and Johnny the day before, her voice carrying clearly up the stairs, as she clearly wished for it to. 'Like a bitch in heat.'

'I was telling Kim about it today,' Sukie had added, again in a ludicrously loud voice. 'Couldn't actually believe it, thought I was exaggerating. No, I said, she really is that appalling.'

'You think you know a person,' Leigha had agreed, in a gratified tone of voice. Johnny had mumbled something that had a distinctly sycophantic tone, but at least he had the grace to keep his voice at a normal level so she couldn't hear the specifics.

Did they really, genuinely, seriously think these awful things? Or were they just seeing how much cruelty she could take until she broke, landing on her knees in front of Leigha, wrapping her arms around her legs in supplication and crying out whatever level of apology they would deem acceptable?

'Those bitches,' Adam had snarled heatedly when she'd told him about the conversation she'd been forced to overhear. He'd clasped her hand close to his chest, pulled her near, tried to make them an army of two. But Harriet had had ten years of conditioning and had only given a troubled frown.

'Don't call them that,' she'd berated him.

Adam shifted slightly in his sleep and Harriet's body locked in all the closer to his. If only it *was* just the two of us she thought, and kissed his nearest eyelid.

Johnny awoke feeling disorientated and stupid. Leigha sat at her desk wearing her dressing gown, hair pinned half-up like she was about to straighten it. Sensing he was awake she looked up from where she was trying to untangle the chains of two necklaces from one another.

'I can't believe you actually fell asleep on me,' she said conversationally, looking back down at the task in hand. 'You men are all the same.' Johnny sat up hurriedly, subtly rubbing the back of his hand across his chin to check for drool as he did so.

'You tired me out, woman,' he answered, with what he hoped was a roguish smile. It was lost on Leigha either way, who was concentrating on picking at the tiny chain links with her finger nails.

'Obviously,' she answered, in a tone devoid of all inflection.

Johnny rose from the bed and moved across the room to her, steeling himself to be casual with his nakedness. He reached out and squeezed Leigha's shoulder.

'Come back to bed.'

'I can't,' Leigha answered shortly, dropping the necklaces to the desktop peevishly. 'The taxis are coming at seven. I need to do my hair and stuff.'

'Anything I can do to help?' Johnny offered automatically.

Leigha arched her eyebrow at him. 'I don't think I need you to straighten my hair, thanks.'

'Oh, I meant, like, if you need something ironed or... maybe I could take a look at that jewellery or something,' Johnny hastily clarified. He hoped that he at least didn't look as flustered as he sounded.

Leigha turned back to look into his face; her eyes were softer now. 'I think I'm okay. Thanks,' she said.

'How about a kiss for the birthday boy?' he tried, emboldened by her smile. Leigha laughed, finally, the first time he'd heard the sound all day. She reached forward and turned her straighteners on to heat up.

'You have until they beep,' she told him, grinning, snaking her arms under his and looping them tight around his torso, tilting her head back in invitation to be kissed.

Nicky was always ready in good time. At a loss for anything more to do, she slicked on a needless second coat of lip-gloss.

Miles lay sprawled out on her bed, playing on a Gameboy. Without looking up from the small screen he reached for his can of lager before realising its emptiness and putting it back down. It was the third time he'd done it and he was getting on Nicky's last nerve. She dropped her lip-gloss back into her make-up bag.

'Do you want me to get you another beer, or something?' she asked, a little impolitely.

'Hmm?' said Miles, not lifting his eyes from his game. 'No

thanks, pet, I'm fine. I'll see if Johnny and Adam want to have some Morgan's Spiced with me in a bit. When are the taxis coming?'

'Half an hour,' Nicky answered, fingers rifling restlessly through the contents of her make-up bag. 'Do you really not think I should stay here with Harriet?' she asked. It was the third time she'd asked it that evening; she wondered if the repetition was annoying Miles.

He looked up at her. 'No, love, she's said she's fine. She's not a child who needs looking after.'

'I think Adam should stay home with her,' Nicky frowned.

'It's his best mate's 21st birthday,' Miles disagreed. 'It's unreasonable of him to miss it just because of a problem between two other people.' Nicky's frown deepened. She moved her make-up from her lap back onto her desk.

'How can we all just go out without her?' she muttered.

'I don't think she'd want to come even if Johnny had invited her,' Miles pointed out.

'Well, how can we act like nothing's different then? Like it's just another night out?'

'Because, pet, it *is* just another night out. Birthdays do not stop and wait for girly squabbles and bitchings to abate.' Miles looked at her encouragingly, trying for a smile from her. Nicky returned the look coolly. She wasn't sure if he was belittling the situation in order to make her feel better about it, or if he genuinely believed it was some stupid spat that was going to blow over. She didn't know which attitude irritated her more.

Seemingly unbothered by her nonchalant response, Miles pressed a few more buttons and then shut his Gameboy off. 'Do you think the coke will be cold enough by now?' he asked her, not waiting for a response before standing and stretching out his legs and heading towards the kitchen to investigate the temperature of said coke.

Nicky looked at herself in the mirror again. She looked wan and tired, despite her shiny lips. She reached for some bronzer. As she dabbed the powder onto the apples of her cheeks she heard footfall on the stairs, Adam greeting Miles, glasses chinking as they were fetched from the cupboard and the heavy fizzle of rum and coke being poured.

'Oh, pet, do you want a Morgan's?' Miles called suddenly. Nicky turned her make-up brush onto her other cheek. She hated spiced rum.

'No thank you,' she called out in reply, once again thinking about the nights she now wouldn't be spending in Paris drinking dark red wines from carafes.

Miles had left the door ajar; Leigha pushed through it before Nicky's chain of thought had much time to sour. She turned her back to Nicky, pulling her hair over her left shoulder as she did.

'Zip me up, please!' she demanded. Nicky dutifully complied and Leigha shook the fall of her hair back out.

'You look great,' Nicky told her wistfully. Leigha looked as if it were the middle of summer, her hair shining and skin rosy. She was wearing a coral mini dress with a lace panel across the collarbones and was bare-legged in the temperate late May weather. She laughed.

'It's the sex glow,' she confided, in a stage-whisper. Nicky rolled her eyes.

'So I hear!' she teased, gesturing towards her ceiling and Leigha's bedroom upstairs. Leigha laughed delightedly, not in the least embarrassed. 'I'm so happy for you two,' Nicky continued, 'we must get a double-date in before exams start.'

Leigha looked uncomfortable. 'You're uneven,' she said, evasively, gesturing for the pot of bronzer and the brush in Nicky's hands. Nicky tilted her chin up as Leigha expertly brushed more powder onto her right cheek. Her wrist-full of bangles slid to her elbow as she did so.

'So are you official, is it a boyfriend–girlfriend type thing?' Nicky persisted. She hadn't had the opportunity to be alone with Leigha for over a week, Johnny had been stuck to her like a barnacle since the fight with Harriet. 'I see you haven't changed your Facebook relationship off Single…'

'I don't want to label anything,' Leigha said neatly, snapping the bronzer compact closed. 'It's just Johnny.' Nicky looked at her doubtfully.

'Exactly. It's Johnny.'

'Oh, its exams soon, and then he'll be going back up north, what's the point?' Leigha said, crinkling her nose. 'Let's just go with the flow, can't we? He's certainly enjoying himself either way'. She raised her eyebrows suggestively. 'And he knows I'm not the girlfriend type, I've never pretended any other way.'

Rather than answer, Nicky turned back to survey herself in the mirror again. She looked much better for the bronzer. Leigha put her arms around her from behind and air-kissed an inch away from her cheek, always mindful of the red lipstick prints she tended to leave behind.

'You look beautiful,' Leigha told her. 'Malibu?'

She wanted to feel blunted, but she just felt sharp, and growing sharper every day. All the shots she could drink and all the joints she could smoke, nothing seemed to touch the sides anymore.

That was a positive – however fucking sick it was to say that – about the death of a parent. People were uncomfortable with your grief, never knowing what to say, and so instead grew very generous with buying you drinks and sharing their cigarettes and weed.

Sukie rubbed her middle and index fingers together distract-edly. She'd kill to be able to have a fag whilst waiting to be served; fucking smoking ban. She took her phone out of her clutch bag to keep her hands busy, opened her inbox to double check there were no messages that she'd accidentally forgotten to respond to; she was notoriously bad for that. For once everything seemed up to date and so she started to delete message threads to clear space on her phone's memory.

After she'd cleared the first few contact threads, her one with Harriet started to rise up the list; she deleted the whole thread. Almost instantly she felt a little pang; there were probably some old messages she'd actively been saving – but then again, what did it matter?

Her mother's car crash had been the earthquake of her life, cracking and shaking her through to her core, causing irrevocable damage. But rather than being the emergency services, Harriet had taken a sledgehammer to the suffering foundation stone. She'd like to say it was unexpected, but she and Leigha had since agreed that Harriet had always been inclined towards more egocentric tendencies.

She sought Leigha out in the crowd of dancers; she was queening it over by the rear wall of the club, immediately conspicuous in her bright dress, one arm around Nicky and the other around her course-mate, Sasha. It might be Johnny's birthday but Leigha certainly seemed to have been in charge of the guest list.

Leigha, Nicky, Sasha and a handful of other girls formed a loose circle around a pile of handbags, dancing erratically to that new Rihanna song. Johnny hung back – hard to distinguish against the darkness of the wall with his dark hair and black tee-shirt – bottle at his lips, face turned towards Leigha. Adam stood off to his side, face underlit by the glow of his mobile phone; texting Harriet, no doubt. Miles completed their trio, looking abandoned and lonesome whilst his usual partner danced beside Leigha, happily occupying the space left by Harriet.

She was still three or four people away from being served.

Sukie stuck her arm through the ranks of people ahead and laid one forearm against the sticky bar-top possessively. The track changed to Justin Timberlake. Sukie glanced back at her friends. Leigha was drunk already, unsteady as Bambi in her gold high heels. Nicky stretched out her arm to snap a picture of the two of them, cheeks pressed together. Their faces lit up pale in the flash. Leigha staggered apart from Nicky, both of them laughing, both taking another drink from their plastic cups. Sukie felt a sear of protectiveness, of indignation; poor Leigha, betrayed on both sides.

'Why'd you never say you and Adam had been together like that?' Sukie had asked Leigha – after the two had fled the tension of the house in the aftermath of confronting Harriet – ensconcing themselves in the pub on the high street. Leigha had stirred her drink with its straw, slowly, thoughtfully, sending carbonated bubbles rushing upwards. 'You're not normally so reticent with details when it comes to the bedroom!' Sukie had jokingly pressed. Leigha had regarded her soberly.

'Well, Adam was different,' she'd said, quietly, and Sukie's heart had panged a little for her.

Harriet had said that nothing had happened between her and Adam until Nicky's birthday, but that had to be another lie, because Adam had gone inexplicably cold on Leigha right after the start of term. She was a compulsive liar, shitting all over her best friends when they were at their most vulnerable, pissing things up just before exams, the end of term, the end of university in general.

At least, Sukie reflected wryly, Harriet was proving excellent for being angry at, and that was better than the sharpness she felt when she thought about her mother, about what was waiting for her in July, a house with all the heart and soul gone out of it.

The fatigued bartender made eye-contact as she slipped her phone back into her clutch bag. Six orange VKs please, Sukie mouthed over the thrum of the music, holding up six fingers for good measure. The guy fetched them from a fridge behind the bar, flicking the caps off with practiced swings of the bottle-opener's blade. Sukie poured the money into his cupped hands, waited impatiently for her change, and then grabbed the bottlenecks between her fingers, pushing her way back through the queue.

As she approached her group of friends, Johnny came forward to relieve her strained fingers of some of the bottles.

'What, no shots?' he yelled in her ear. Sukie swatted him playfully.

'What am I, an octopus?' she yelled back. 'I can't carry *everything*.' Johnny grinned at her and passed two of the bottles across to Miles and Nicky. Sukie approached Leigha and Adam with the other two.

Adam was quite drunk for once, she noted, evident by the way he was bobbing his head emphatically to the music. He also seemed to know all the words to this particular Backstreet Boys' song, something that Sukie planned on joyfully teasing him about when he was sober. She passed the bottle of orange alcopop into his left hand – he still had one in his right – and he smiled in thanks. Leigha barrelled into her, grabbing at her bottle impatiently. Adam immediately reached to steady her with the crook of his arm, his hands being occupied. Leigha lay her palm flat against his chest and smiled up at him gratefully. Such a gorgeous couple, Sukie thought, bringing her drink to her lips.

'Smile,' she bellowed over the music, extracting her phone from her bag once again and sliding it open with her free hand.

Chapter Eighteen

May 2007

Harriet spent her last day being twenty years old revising in the library with Lucy and Andrew. Adam had a killer hangover and had begged off when she'd rung him that morning to check he was still planning on joining them. She'd not been surprised; she'd heard the state of everyone else getting in at three-thirty that morning, heard someone falling drunkenly on the stairs and everyone else's' sympathetic laughter.

She leafed inanely through book after book, the heavy quiet of the study floor broken only by Andrew's occasional sniff or cough; he was just getting over a cold. Harriet regarded her course-mates over the top of her textbook, both uncharacteristically diligent in their studying in the face of the looming final exams. Harriet was living in silence too often these days; she wanted to talk and laugh. She glanced out of the window in the hopes that the drizzle had stopped enough for them to be able to study out on the grass, but it was still falling in soft, misty whorls.

Silently signalling her intent to her study companions, Harriet moved across to a computer terminal, signing in with her student details. She had an email from one of her lecturers confirming the name of a particular journal article she thought she might find useful to read in advance of the Literature of the Fin de Siècle exam. As this was a module she shared with Adam, Lucy and Andrew she forwarded it onto them for their reference.

The online journal catalogue was slow and buggy and after almost ten minutes of searching Harriet still hadn't found the right entry. Frustrated, she glanced at the clock in the bottom corner of the screen, wondering if Lucy and Andrew would be up for breaking for a spot of food and caffeine any time soon. She sighed to herself. Just because she wasn't in the right frame of mind to get any revision done shouldn't mean she should distract her friends. Giving into the urge to slack, she logged into her Facebook account.

High and proud on her newsfeed was a new photo album; Sukie had created it only minutes before. Harriet was surprised; Nicky was usually the one with the camera on nights out and therefore the one to upload any photos onto Facebook. There were only seven photos though, all blurry and overexposed, most likely taken with Sukie's phone.

In the first Johnny looked startled as Miles poured a stream of drink straight into his mouth. Leigha and Sasha made exaggerated pouts at the camera, lips dark in the whiteness of their flash-lit faces. Miles and Nicky posed with their arms around one another for a shot, pretty much identical to all the other photos of them taken over the past two years. Adam stood tall, smiling his wide, bright smile, Leigha with her arm and entire upper body pressed against his, face blurring as she spun to face the camera.

Harriet stared at the indistinct, pale pixels of that face, her mind replaying that reel of Leigha kissing Adam with her red, red lips, scratching down his bare back with her red, red nails until the depths of her gut was roaring and churning like the sea.

'Hey,' came a loud whisper from behind her. Harriet jumped a mile and immediately minimised the window, as if she'd been caught looking at something she shouldn't have. Lucy looked at her quizzically. 'Do you wanna get some lunch any time soon?' she asked.

'Oh, that would have been such a nice picture,' Leigha lamented. 'Shame I'm all blurry.'

Johnny turned around from his seat at the computer to stare at her. Was this girl for real? What was she doing, posing for pictures like that – knowing how it would make her boyfriend feel – let alone commenting afterwards how nice a picture it is?

Leigha lay on her front on her bed, leafing through handwritten revision notes. 'Nicky'll put the pictures from her camera up soon, probably,' she continued, eyes back on the paper. After a minute she seemed to realise that Johnny was still staring at her in silence and glanced back up. 'What?' she asked, agitated.

Johnny answered with a question, one he'd steeled himself never to ask.

'Leigha, are you my girlfriend, or what?'

She physically flinched away, but it only served to make him bolder. 'Because I think you are, so if you don't agree, then I think we have a problem.' Sighing, Leigha pulled herself up to a sitting position and regarded him seriously.

'I don't want to put a label on it,' she began, in an extremely reasonable tone of voice. Johnny was unimpressed. He'd heard these exact words already; Leigha had said them to Nicky, who'd told Miles, who'd told him. 'It's not a really good time for me to be thinking about stuff like that, what with the exams and with… with Harriet…' she continued. Johnny had a nagging misgiving that the sad little stutter she'd given before saying Harriet's name was an affectation to get him to feel sorry for her. His resolve hardened further.

'I love you,' he said. It was the first time he had. Leigha just looked disobligingly wretched.

'Listen,' she tried again, 'you're going to be moving back up to Bradford in, like, what? Six, seven weeks? I really don't think I'm a long distance kind of girl.' Johnny's jaw clenched so hard his back molars ached in protest. Leigha just smiled apologetically.

'I don't have to stay up north,' Johnny found himself saying. 'I could come back down here, live in London with Adam. Maybe even with you.'

'Johnny,' Leigha groaned. 'You're just being silly. You've got your internship at that paper, doesn't that start in August?'

'There are other newspapers,' Johnny said, stubbornly. 'Magazines, trade publications, copywriters. Maybe London is actually the best place for me to be to get into journalism. Maybe it's not just about you. But it can be. I love you,' he repeated. 'I really believe that I can be the one to make you happy, Ley.'

Leigha ran her fingertips through her hair in silence. 'Well,' she said, finally. 'If you want to move to London it's not like I'm going to stop you.' She smiled faintly. 'Actually, it could be good.'

'Yeah?' said Johnny, hardly daring to believe his ears.

'Yeah,' Leigha agreed. 'It could be really good.'

'So, can I officially say you're my girl?' Johnny pressed.

Leigha's gaze rested momentarily on the wall behind him and the desk, beyond which was Harriet's room. Was she thinking of Adam over there, in bed with Harriet, Johnny wondered; did it even matter at all, if she answered him with a yes?

'Okay,' she said after a long moment, swinging her legs to the floor and moving across the room to give him a kiss. Her face and lips were cool against his flushed face.

Harriet was so funny lately, so passive aggressive.

'I'm telling you, this is fine,' she said, punctuating her comment with a rather fierce dabbing of her french fry into her ketchup.

Adam stared at her.

'This,' he said, with a sweeping gesture of his hand to indicate the greasy formica table-top, 'is brunch. I want to take you out for *dinner*. For Christ's sake, Harriet, it's your 21st birthday. You have to do *something* to celebrate.' She looked up at him sullenly.

'I don't feel much like celebrating, to be honest,' she muttered.

Spring had sprung upon them, all of a sudden. Campus was awash with bare arms and legs, the grass completely yellowed over with daffodils, drooping and bowing with the weight of their heavy heads. Harriet didn't seem to have noticed; she was still pale-faced, aside from the dark prints under her eyes. Did she really sleep when she lay down next to him at night, Adam wondered. She was wearing opaque black tights with flat boots and a dark grey woollen dress. Adam couldn't help but guilty reminisce about the days that Harriet used to wear reds and purples and blues and smiled all the time. That was a good metaphor actually, he realised sadly. All of Harriet's colour was gone.

He reached across the table and rubbed her knuckles with his fingers. 'Please let me take my girlfriend out on her birthday,' he tried.

'Adam, no,' Harriet replied stubbornly. 'You barely have any student loan left and neither do I. There's no point wasting it.'

'Wasting it!' Adam repeated, incredulous.

'Let's just stay in,' she pleaded, grabbing his hand and holding it in hers, almost as if in a panic, as if she'd just realised she might be upsetting him with her mood, her obstinacy. 'Please?'

'Well, it's what you want, I guess,' Adam begrudgingly relented. 'Although at least let me bring something round later.'

'Like what?'

'Like a bottle of wine? Real wine, not that fizzy Lambrini shit.' Harriet looked doubtful. She wasn't that big on wine; in the house, Nicky was the only one who ever drank it. 'If you won't let me take you out for a grown up dinner,' Adam continued, 'at least let's have a grown up drink. I'll also bring lemonade, in case you need to spritzer it,' he teased. Harriet laughed, as he'd been hoping she would.

Harriet had lain awake in her bed with her eyes closed for a good ten minutes that morning. She couldn't quite believe it was her birthday. It had always seemed so far away.

Her birthday had sort of been her last hope, so she'd lain there with her eyes tightly shut, trying to fool herself into believing that when she opened them Leigha would be sitting in the chair – normal and smiling – glancing into the mirror and fluffing up her hair. April Fools, she'd laugh – even though it was May – I was lying. Happy Birthday! A scenario that would give her back Adam, but – although she'd lain there and thought on it for the longest time – she couldn't quite imagine one that would give her back Leigha, too. But then, she didn't want to be friends with her again, did she? – and so the train of thought went round and round.

'I asked for one that was sweet, not dry,' Adam said, looking extremely pleased with himself as he cradled the swell of one of Nicky's wine glasses in the palm of his hand. 'It's quite nice.' Harriet agreed; the wine was cold in her mouth and warm in her stomach and was relaxing her quite nicely. She toyed with the idea of going downstairs to sit in the lounge. She had just as much right to sit down there as Leigha and Sukie, she still paid a quarter of its rent after all. Instead she just took another large swallow.

'I got you something else too,' Adam said, placing his wine glass carefully down on the desk. Harriet shot him a mock-withering look.

'I told you, I don't want any presents from anyone, and that included you.'

'Just stop moaning for a minute and take a look,' Adam grinned, reaching into the tatty canvas shopper bag from which he'd produced the bottle of wine.

It was a matt, black cube – a small jewellery box, and Harriet immediately had to clamp down on the urge to giggle uncontrollably. Adam looked anxious.

'It's only earrings,' he said instantly. Harriet wasn't sure whether he was saying it to play down the expense of the gift or whether he had sensed where her mind had gone to when she'd seen the little black box.

'Oh, Adam. Thank you,' she said, reaching her hand out to take her present. She loved earrings. Nestled in the black suede lining was a pair of drop earrings, little silver silhouettes of birds, backs arched in stylistic flight. Suddenly her eyes burned. She loved them; they were perfect for her.

'They really made me think of you,' Adam echoed her thoughts, reaching out his hand to softly graze her jaw and run his thumb over her ear. Harriet had at least forty pairs of earrings but hadn't really thought to wear any, not recently. Her lobe felt naked and exposed under his touch.

'I love them,' she told him, dipping her head to smoothly slip the hooks through her piercing holes. The little birds span and dangled against her jaw as she straightened her head. Adam smiled broadly, looking satisfied with himself.

'I have great taste,' he teased. 'In women and earrings at least.'

There's your opening, Harriet thought to herself. Ask him again about Leigha. Ask him about his 'taste in women'. Make him swear it when he flusters that he hasn't. But when it came down to it, Adam was almost all she had left and she still hadn't quite worked out what she'd say if he admitted to it.

And let's face it – she told herself crossly, for what felt like the hundredth time – he probably *did* have sex with Leigha. She certainly would have offered it. She is gorgeous, and he's a man, after all.

'Happy Birthday,' he said again, leaning forward to rub his nose against hers before he kissed her. Her heart felt like it was going to rupture. She'd never imagined being in love would be so painful. She couldn't hear that he'd been with Leigha. Even just imagining it made her breath hitch up inside her.

So instead she just kissed him back, admired her new earrings in the mirror, and put off asking him about it for yet another day.

Johnny couldn't decide how to feel after he read the email, so he just settled for feeling flat. He drummed his fingers absentmindedly against his thigh. So that was that then.

Adam either sensed his friend's dip in mood or was overly eager for a distraction from his work. 'What's up?' he called from where he sat at the table with his laptop. Johnny shot him a stern look.

'Eyes front,' he instructed. 'You shouldn't even be working down here. You've got less than a month to finish.'

'Five thousand words in, like, three weeks is nothing. I've only got to write, like,' – Adam squinted as he presumably consulted the calculator app on his laptop – '208 and a third words every day.'

'Wow, you should have studied Maths, mate,' Johnny told him, deadpan. Adam pulled a face before begrudgingly returning his attention to his keyboard.

The email was formal and polite, but the professional veneer didn't manage to hide its writer's confusion. Not that he was surprised. He'd slogged through four or five online tests, submitted an entire portfolio of work, missioned it back up to Yorkshire for two face-to-face interviews and cringed through three ones via telephone to get a coveted place on this amazing journalism internship programme. And with just a couple of weeks to go he had written to forfeit it. Yeah, I'd be a little surprised too, he thought ruefully at the response email.

He minimised his Hotmail window and immediately felt brighter. His desktop background was a picture of him and Leigha. It was from a pub quiz night, a month or so before they'd gotten together. Leigha was posed prettily, her body curving into his; his arm in actuality had been resting along the arc of the booth, but from the angle of the camera it looked like it was thrown possessively around Leigha's shoulders.

On reflex he scooped up his mobile phone, eager to text Leigha with the news. He glanced over at Adam who was staring at his screen with a glazed expression, his fingers motionless on the keys.

'You're still planning on moving into London, aren't you?' Johnny asked. Adam roused himself, blinking.

'Yeah, of course. ASAP mate, ASA bloody P.'

'We should get a flat together. You know, like, rent one,' Johnny said, making it sound as if the idea had just occurred to him. Adam looked doubtful.

'Of course, mate, I'd love to keep living with you – but I'll probably be set up by the time your thing up north is over – it's a year, isn't it? But of course...' Johnny shook his head, looking doleful.

'It's not happening mate,' he told Adam. 'It's not come off. I'm going to check out internships in London after exams are over.'

'I thought you had it though,' Adam said slowly, suspiciously. Johnny just shook his head again.

'Hasn't come off,' he repeated.

'Well, that's shit for you but great for me,' Adam said, breaking into a grin. 'And both Harry and Leigha's parents live in the suburbs so they're both nearby until they move out themselves. Can't see us getting a house the four of us though, not any time soon!' Adam smiled apologetically at the weakness of his joke. 'Wow, cool. Everything's coming together. The end of childhood is nigh.'

'Yeah, unless you fail your dissertation because it's four thousand words short and have to re-sit this year,' Johnny said, nodding his head at Adam's laptop. 'Stop slacking.'

'Hey, you're the one distracting me!' Adam protested.

'Yeah, well, you should be working in your room,' Johnny grumbled, starting on his text to Leigha.

The Facebook group was the straw that broke Harriet's back.

'You fucking bitch,' she snarled as she stormed down the corridor from the stairs to the living room. Leigha froze, startled, gently steaming mug of tea held halfway to her mouth. Against the far wall the TV was tuned to a music video channel, blaring out an inappropriately upbeat song. Johnny rose immediately from where he sat on the sofa beside Leigha, frowning.

'Harriet,' he started, reaching his hand out in a 'stop' motion to still her. Harriet contemptuously ignored him, swerving round him to Leigha, who drew her feet closer to her in alarm.

'Why can't you just... leave me alone?' The anger that had propelled Harriet off her desk chair and down the stairs was already dissipating, the misery creeping back in. Her limbs felt cold. Only one sentence out and already she was regretting this.

'Ummm,' Leigha said, exaggerating confusion, 'I *am* leaving you alone. I was under the impression that I have absolutely nothing to do with your nasty self.' She sipped her tea delicately. 'So why don't you just calm down and go crawl back into your little den up there.' There it was, the ghost of a smile on those glossed lips. The double-entendre was not lost on Harriet; the anger reignited in her stomach.

'Since when do people create Facebook groups about people they are having nothing to do with?' she spat. Leigha's eyes glittered apprehensively.

'I don't know what you mean,' she answered, taking another

defiant sip of her tea.

'The hell you don't,' Harriet sneered.

'And what Facebook group is this, anyway?' Leigha asked her mug of tea conversationally. She had studiously avoided looking full on at Harriet since she'd walked into the room. Johnny looked mildly panic-stricken, standing there with his arm still pointlessly outstretched.

'The one about me being a dog,' Harriet answered through gritted teeth.

'I created a Facebook group about dogs,' Leigha agreed, her tone excessively innocent. 'Nothing to do with you though. Guilty conscience?'

'It's not exactly subtle,' Harriet frowned. '*The Group Against Referring to Slutty Women as Dogs or Bitches because it's Not Fair on Real Dogs?*' she quoted, disdainfully. 'I get it. Okay? I get that you hate that Adam loves me and not you and that that makes me a "bitch" and a "dog" and a "slut".' She made mocking quotation marks with her fingers in the air as she spoke. 'You know very well that I can hear you guys talking when you *stand outside my bedroom door* calling me a dog in heat. I see your Facebook statuses with stupid little passive aggressive comments about bitches. I hear you humming "Beware of the Dog" when I *dare* come down to the kitchen to grab some food or make a cup of tea. I get it. I get that you hate me now and that you're a totally different person, but why did you have to make a stupid Facebook Group and invite everyone we know to join it? Everyone from school, even? God.' Harriet's voice was wobbling dangerously so she broke off and took a deep breath to steady herself. 'Why are you being such a bitch to me? What on earth did I ever do to you?'

Leigha's eyes flashed; she placed her mug down carefully on the coffee table.

'You slept with my boyfriend.'

Hearing the very sentence that she wanted to yell at Leigha directed at herself took the remaining wind out of Harriet's sails. She turned on her heel and left without another word.

'Harry?' Nicky stood in her bedroom doorframe, voice questioning. Harriet shot her a mute look as she rounded the bottom of the stairs.

As if on cue, the television began to play the music video for Jamelia's *Beware of the Dog*. Leigha's delighted laughter followed Harriet all the way up the stairs. Even the slamming of her bedroom door didn't quite shut it out.

Harriet almost jumped out of her skin as the heavy security doors were beeped open, hissing as they pulled apart. Hurriedly she composed herself and stared back at the computer monitor hoping that, whoever this nocturnal student was, they wouldn't try to engage her in small talk.

'What the hell are you playing at?'

Adam was framed against the closing doors, his face pinched, slipping the student card that he'd just used to access the computer lab back into his jeans pocket.

'What do you mean, what am I playing at? I couldn't sleep so I'm working.'

'Working on what, Harriet, you've *finished* your dissertation and all of your coursework.'

'I'm just editing,' Harriet amended.

'And you couldn't do that at home?'

'I didn't want to disturb you.'

'That's utter bullshit, Harriet. It's three in the morning and you can't sleep so you randomly decide to leave me in bed and walk to campus in the rain and stare at your completed dissertation?'

'I left you a note in case you woke up and wondered where I was,' Harriet pointed out, defensively.

'Yeah, and that's another thing, your note said that you were in the computer lab.'

'Yes. And I am.' Harriet gestured around sardonically at the banks of computers.

'This isn't *the* computer lab, this is the English postgrad students' computer lab,' Adam shouted. 'Were you hoping I wouldn't think to look here, when I couldn't find you in the *actual* computer lab?'

'I thought this one would be more private,' Harriet hissed. 'Nice and quiet,' she added, sarcastically. Adam scowled.

'Come on,' he said, at a more reasonable volume. 'Log off. I'm taking you home.' Harriet stared at him. 'Harriet, come on,' Adam repeated, impatiently. 'I'm bloody exhausted.'

'You go home,' Harriet retorted. 'I'm staying here. I can't... I can't work in that house.'

'It's three in the morning!'

'I am aware,' Harriet snapped, caustically. 'I told you, I'm staying here.'

'What's wrong with you?' Adam asked, incredulously.

'What's wrong with *me*?' Harriet repeated, in a tone just as incredulous, before finally cracking and breaking into tears that felt unbearably hot against her cheeks. Adam reached for her in alarm but she was out of the chair in an instant and backing away from him, blotting at her wet face with her sleeves.'

Did you have sex with Leigha?' she asked.

Adam looked as if she'd just slapped him. 'What? When? Of course not,' he flustered, just like she'd imagined he would. Harriet closed her eyes; the disappointment was like an ache.

'In January. She says you did.'

'She's a dirty, fucking liar.' Adam was angry now and reaching for her again. 'You don't believe her, do you?' When Harriet didn't answer right away his expression darkened. 'Do you?' he repeated, urgently.

'Why would she lie?' Harriet said, finally.

'Because she wants to hurt you. She doesn't want us to be together,' Adam answered immediately.

'She knows about your birthmark,' Harriet said, miserably. Adam's expression knotted.

'She's lying,' he repeated, but his voice was quieter, somehow nervous.

'But then how would she know?' Harriet yelled, balling her hands into fists so tight that she could feel the little crescents of her fingernails puncturing her palm.

'I don't know!' Adam yelled back. 'All I know is that she's *lying*. How long have you been thinking this, huh?' he asked. 'Is that why you've gotten so weird with me lately? Is that why you've been acting so different?'

'I've been acting so different because I *am* so different,' Harriet shot back, resting heavily against a desk. 'I don't know who I am any more. You've got to give me a break. The people I trusted most in the whole world have spent the last few weeks making my life into a total hell. Is it any wonder, really, that I can't trust you, when you say that nothing happened between you and Leigha?'

'Nothing happened between me and Leigha!' Adam shouted again. 'I can't believe you don't believe me. I thought that you loved me?' Harriet put her face in her hands to avoid a response. Yes, she was in love with him, but she didn't want to be any more.

'I loved *them*, and that didn't stop them from hurting me,' was all she said.

Adam stared at her in disbelief. 'I know what this is really about,' he said, slowly. 'You *blame* me.' Harriet shot him a look loaded with warning, but the denial he so obviously wanted was stuck, curled in her throat. 'It's easier to blame me than to blame yourself.'

'Well, you have come out of this all rather well,' she managed, finally. 'You've lost no friendships. You're not being deadbolted out

185

of your own house, with songs and Facebook groups being made up about you. You haven't lost anything.' Adam had been shaking his head in disagreement as she spoke.

'I've lost the girl I fell in love with,' he told her, matter-of-factly. 'Because apparently that girl defined herself as Leigha's lackey, a sidekick with no worth on her own.'

'You're over-simplifying,' Harriet snapped, furious.

'You can't just take it out on me. I wanted to tell everyone from the off.' Adam jabbed his finger at her. 'You've made this bed and you can't un-do the decisions you made and what's happened, but you don't have to just hide in your room, wailing that you're a victim, letting those bitches walk all over you and *sabotaging* your relationship with me.'

'And what exactly do you suggest I do instead?' Harriet asked, tone icy. Adam flung up his hands in exasperation.

'Something! Anything! Walk up to Leigha and tell her she is a gigantic bitch and that she needs to back the hell off.'

'I tried that!' Harriet yelled. 'It didn't work. Nothing's going to change. I just need to see out these last few weeks of term and then get the hell out of here. That's all I want so stop trying to make it more bloody difficult for me. Head down, eyes forward, that's all I'm trying to do. And, yeah, maybe it was a bad call for me to decide not to be honest with everyone from the get go, but that *doesn't* excuse you lying to me. I can't – I can't even bear to look at you. Can you please just go?'

'I'm not lying to you!' Adam bellowed; his neck was flushed a dark, frustrated red.

'She knew about the birthmark,' Harriet reiterated.

'If so, then you must have told her at some point.'

'When the hell would I have told her something like that?'

'I don't know!'

Neither of them had anything more to say. They had been

answering one another so quickly, so loudly, that the quiet of the pause was jarring. Harriet thought that the sound of Adam's angry breathing was louder even than their voices had been.

'This is ridiculous,' Adam said, more to himself, practically under his breath.

'What is?' Harriet asked, sharply.

Adam gestured vaguely. 'This. Everything. You.' Harriet scowled at him; her tears were dry on her face now, the skin there felt tight and thin. 'Why are you being like this?'

'I'm not being like anything,' Harriet answered, wearily. 'I'm just trying to get through this.'

'Then why are you pushing away the *one good thing* to come out of all of this? Are you punishing yourself? Is that it? Emotional self-harm? Huh? Or is it that you don't want to love me, because you need to blame me instead, make me the scapegoat for all this? Or maybe you actually think that if you dump me, Leigha and Sukie will want to be your friends again?'

'No, no, no,' Harriet had repeated emphatically whilst he'd been talking. 'No, it's nothing like that at all. Stop making this all about *you.*'

'I think it is,' Adam said, resignedly. 'I think it's a mix of all of the above. Oh, Harriet.'

'Stop being so fucking patronising,' Harriet snapped, standing straight from where she had been slouched against the rear bank of desks. 'This isn't about you,' she repeated.

'Of course it's about me,' Adam said. 'I may not be getting... bullied the way that you are, but anything that upsets my girl-friend upsets me. And the way that you've been acting, the way you've spoken to me tonight, that upsets me too, Harriet. Don't do this. Please.'

'I don't need you on my case like this, making me feel like shit too. I get enough of that at home.'

Adam reached for her again, and this time he caught her, pinning her arms between his, pulling their torsos together, reaching to hold her face in his hands. From this close she could see that his eyelashes looked damp, his rims reddened by the effort not to cry.

'If you do this,' he said quietly, running his thumbs along her jawline the way he always did. 'You'll be throwing away the best thing that's ever happened to you.' Harriet tried to pull away in protest but he held her firm. 'And the best thing that's ever happened to me. We could make it, you and me. We could be the real deal. I've always felt it. I have. But you know what else? All this, all you've been through lately? It will all have been for nothing.'

'Did you have sex with Leigha?' Harriet asked him again; she felt Adam's grip on her loosen slightly. A coldness slipped into his damp eyes.

'Even if I say no again, you're never going to believe me are you?' he answered. He sounded disgusted with her.

Harriet had extricated her arms from his and slapped him before she even realised that was what she was doing. The sound rang out through the room as the burning on her palm and fingers faded. They were now a foot apart from one another, where only seconds ago they had been pressed fully together, like one person; Adam held his hand up to his reddened cheek with an expression of complete disbelief.

'You're not even bothering to deny it anymore?' Harriet laughed, a bitter, small sound. 'Just get out of here. Leave me alone.'

'Harriet—' Adam began, and the fact that he was still trying to ingratiate himself infuriated Harriet beyond belief.

'I don't ever want to see you again!' she screamed, balling her hands into fists again. 'Why don't you try Leigha's bed? I'm sure she'll still have you.' Adam's top lip curled back from his teeth in a offended sneer.

'You know what? You're just as big a bitch as the other two,' he informed her, his voice the coldest she'd ever heard it.

'Oh, fuck off will you? Just – fuck off.'

'I heard you the first time,' Adam jeered, turning on his heel and slapping the door release button aggressively with the flat of his palm before disappearing out into the night.

Harriet waited where she was, stock-still, just for a few minutes, just to see if he'd come back. After a while she realised she was shaking, like everything under her skin was quivering, so she slipped back into the computer chair she'd been sitting at before Adam had arrived. She stared at the Word window of her dissertation's appendix on the screen with unfocused eyes.

When she let herself into the house at 6.15, the only thing waiting for her was the imprint of Adam's body in the bedsheets. She curled up as far away from it as she could and slept her first solid eight hours for weeks.

'I really can't say I condone this decision,' Callahan said, frowning. Adam sunk lower in the chair; his legs, spread out in front of him, took up most of the floor space in the cramped office.

'Like I said,' he told his tutor, 'it's not been an easy decision, but it's the only way to go.'

'You only have two weeks 'til the deadline,' Callahan protested.

'Seventeen days; eighteen, including the rest of today,' Adam corrected him. 'And I've already made a start, look.' He pulled a plastic wallet full of papers out of his book bag and proffered it. Callahan took it, looking doubtful, and began to leaf through Adam's revised dissertation proposal.

'I really have to advise against it. That's my personal and professional opinion, and my opinion on behalf of the University,' he said as he read.

'I understand that,' Adam said. 'I have just really hit a wall with Neruda. I can't write another five thousand words on love poetry. It will be quicker for me to write the ten thousand on a new subject. Trust me.'

'There's lots of literature on this topic in the library,' Callahan granted. 'I've no doubt that if you knuckle down you can get ten thousand words done, but, Adam, the point of the final year dissertation is that you work towards it for the whole year. I'm afraid you won't be able to recreate the quality of an entire academic year's research in only two weeks.'

'Eighteen days,' Adam repeated doggedly.

'Well, you know my position,' Callahan sighed, handing Adam back his papers. 'But at the end of the day, it is your choice. I'm only here for guidance. Are you really set on this change?'

'I am.'

'Then I'll pull the necessary administrative strings, I suppose.' Callahan sighed loudly to further emphasise his disapproval.

'I'd appreciate that,' Adam said politely.

'By way of me giving guidance, I would suggest revising the thesis title,' Callahan said, thoughtfully.

'Revise in what way?' Adam began removing text books from the bag in order to fit the folder back inside, lying flat at the bottom.

'*Holden Caulfield: A Literary Hero* is a bit… vague, don't you think? At the end of the day, your title *can* be a statement but it still needs to be answering a *question.*'

Adam paused, with his dog-eared copy of *Catcher in the Rye* in his hand; Harriet's copy, he mentally corrected himself. He remembered her tossing it at him once, on a day that felt like it had been years ago.

'I'll keep that in mind.'

'Sweetie, you know I love you,' Nicky said, carefully. 'But this is…

just… fucked up.'

Harriet blanched; Nicky hardly ever swore. 'In what way?'

'I agree with Adam. You have pushed him away on purpose.'

'He slept with Leigha!' Harriet protested immediately.

'So what? If he even did, it was ages before you two meant anything to one another. If he *did* sleep with her and *did* lie to you about it, surely it's just because he was frightened of losing you because of something that meant nothing. He was frightened of you reacting the way that you have.' Nicky chewed on her bottom lip, anxiously.

Harriet rubbed at her eyes. 'It's the lying that bothers me, not the – the sex.'

'Really? Because I think it's the thought of him being with Leigha that's worse for you,' Nicky said kindly. Harriet didn't respond. 'Oh sweetie, you were almost free,' Nicky continued, sadly. 'In just a few weeks you'll be back at your parents' and then who knows? You would have been away from all of this horribleness and would have been able to build a life with Adam, if you'd wanted.'

'Well I don't want,' Harriet said, stubbornly. 'What I *want* is a little support from my one remaining friend.'

'Don't be dramatic, Harry,' Nicky chided, frowning. 'You need to apologise to him. At least speak to him.'

'Apologise?' Harriet choked out. 'Not likely.'

'Oh, you're as stubborn as hell,' Nicky told her, frowning deeper. 'Love should be worth more to you than this.'

'Like how love is worth giving up your own life to follow your lover where *they* want to go?' Harriet snapped. Nicky held herself very still.

'Yes. It is.'

'By that argument, you love Miles but he doesn't love you.' Nicky took a calming breath, visibly trying to hold her temper.

'This isn't about me. Don't take it out on me,' she warned.

191

Harriet shrugged churlishly.

'It's about time you faced some home truths; you've really got the raw end of the deal with all this, Nic.'

'You really want to talk home truths?' Nicky snapped, her patience worn thin. 'Because I've got plenty of those for you, Harriet Shaw.'

The two girls stared at one another in silence for a minute or two, feeling the tension in the room swell and then start to abate.

'Sorry,' Harriet finally said, albeit a little begrudgingly. 'I'm all over the place lately.'

'I know,' Nicky conceded. 'But I wouldn't be your friend—'

'My one remaining friend,' Harriet clarified again, with a sad, dry smile. Nicky rolled her eyes.

'I wouldn't be your friend if I didn't tell you that you're making a mistake,' she finished.

'Well,' Harriet said carefully, 'to be honest I could say the same thing to you.' They fell into weighted silence again.

'I think we're going to have to agree to disagree,' Nicky said finally.

'Probably,' Harriet agreed.

'But you really should talk to Adam.'

'I think that might just tip me over the edge,' Harriet said; her tone was jokey but her eyes were serious. 'I just want this to be over.'

Nicky reached forward and enveloped her friend in a hug. 'But unless you face up to everything it can never be over for you,' she murmured against Harriet's hair.

'Don't move to Bath, Nic,' Harriet mumbled against Nicky's shoulder, voice thick. Nicky sighed.

'I have to.'

Chapter Nineteen

June 2007

'Oi,' Johnny barked, rapping his knuckles on the coffee table. 'Focus.' Adam glared at him.

'I am, alright?'

'You haven't typed anything for a good five minutes. You asked me to keep you on task and that I bloody will mate,' Johnny swore. 'You were a total eejit for changing your dissertation topic last minute so now you have to pay the price. And that price is working like a dog. Get to it.'

'I was thinking,' Adam protested.

'Yeah you probably were, but I don't think it was about the book.' Johnny arched his eyebrow knowingly. 'You had a proper moon face on. Stop thinking about Harriet. This is all her bloody fault anyway.'

'Hardly,' Adam objected. 'It isn't her fault I hit a wall with my original work.'

'Wasn't it?' Johnny's eyebrow arched even higher. 'I certainly wouldn't be up for writing about sappy verse if Leigha had done to me what Harriet has done to you.' Adam scowled. 'Don't allow her to indirectly make this worse, man. Focus.'

'You focus on your own revision,' Adam told him rudely. 'Don't bang on about what you don't understand.'

'Oh, I understand alright,' Johnny insisted. 'It's practically all Ley bloody talks about so I'm actually quite well-versed on the emotional wreckage that's been left in the wake of Harriet Shaw.'

'Mate,' Adam said, warningly. Grudgingly Johnny turned his attention back to his revision notes. Adam rested his hands back onto his keyboard and resumed staring into the middle distance.

That morning Adam had walked into a seminar group revision session in the library. Harriet was there; she'd walked straight out without looking at him.

'What is going on between the two of you?' Andrew had hissed into his ear as he'd sat down. Lucy – across from them, next to Harriet's newly vacated seat – had given him the evil eye, but obviously wasn't offended by his presence enough to compromise her remaining revision time by leaving in protest.

Adam had slogged away at his laptop until gone one thirty in the morning before retiring upstairs to bed. It was finally warm enough to have the window open at night, although the fresh air that circulated his bedroom was suffused with the smell of spices from the Indian takeaway two doors down.

The streetlights outside threw a square of artificial light through the open window and onto the bed. Although it felt uncomfortably like a spotlight Adam didn't quite have the energy to get up and draw the curtains against it. He turned his mobile phone over and over again in his hands and thought about the day after Nicky's birthday, where he'd laid there like this, waiting for Harriet to text him.

It was his birthday next week; he wondered if she had thought about that. It was always going to have been too close to the start of exam week and the coursework deadlines to have done anything big, but Miles and Johnny were insisting that they at least go out for a drink at the Armstrong. Would she come, if he asked her? At least as a friend? That's how they'd started, after all. As angry as he had been the other night, as hurt as he was still, he couldn't quite imagine that the end of the year would come and he would never see Harriet again. So much had happened to bring them to one another, the universe surely wouldn't accept them being separated for the rest of their lives?

It was Harriet, at the end of the day; so he texted her, a simple message, one he'd sent countless times before:

Adam Chadwick, 01.48
Are u awake?

and when she replied that she was, he called her.

There was a pause after the call connected, as if she were still at this late stage considering not speaking with him. 'Hey,' she said finally.

'Hey. What are you doing?' He heard the familiar creak of her computer chair as she shifted.

'Working.' He wondered if she was being intentionally monosyllabic or if it was out of deference to the late hour.

'Do you want to talk?'

'Not really.' The creak again; she always fidgeted when she was anxious. 'I'm working,' she repeated.

'You're always working. You'll be working on that dissertation two months after you've already received your marks back.' She made no response to his admittedly weak attempt at humour.

'What do you want, Adam?' she asked him, bluntly.

'I want to talk,' he admitted.

'We are talking,' she replied.

'In person,' he amended. 'I can be outside your house in ten minutes. It's a beautiful night.' Harriet paused again; Adam held his breath.

'I really don't think so,' she said finally; Adam felt his heart deflate a little inside his chest cavity.

'Come on, Harry, don't be difficult,' he said, sadly.

'I'm not trying to be difficult. I'm just being honest.' She sounded sad too. 'I don't want us to hurt one another anymore than we already have.'

'Will you come out for my birthday on Thursday, at least?' Adam pressed.

'Adam—' Harriet sighed.

'No, no, don't say no. I'll see you there.'

'I really can't—'

'Harriet,' Adam interrupted her again. 'I know things are shit and you're just acting to protect yourself, I know that, I'm sorry I haven't been more patient. If you let me I really will try to be. At the end of the day, you love me, and I love you, and I really want to see you on my birthday.'

Harriet was silent again but for her breathing, heavy on the line.

'This is your last chance,' Adam continued, warningly. 'To fight for us. For you to pick me, not being alone. You need to meet me halfway on this. Please, Harry. Please.'

Adam had to stop; his voice had thickened with emotion and he didn't want her to hear how upset he was. She hadn't said a word. 'I'll see you on Thursday,' he insisted. 'Armstrong, seven o' clock. Goodnight. I love you. I didn't sleep with Leigha. I promise. I love you. Goodnight.'

He lay unmoving in the square of streetlight for a while after terminating the call, waiting to see if she'd text or call back. She didn't. Knowing there was no way he was going to be able to sleep that night he resignedly booted up his laptop again; why waste time moping around in bed when he had another seven thousand words to go?

Johnny was over again. He'd always been round their house a lot, but now he seemed an almost permanent fixture. To be honest, Leigha was glad for it. She was lonely, what with Nicky and Sukie entrenched in their respective revision and Harriet, lurking around upstairs like a bad smell, moving around the house like a ghost in the night when everyone else was in bed.

Johnny seemed to sense her thoughts were on him; he looked up with a bright, expectant smile. 'Do you want a cup of tea, love?' he asked her. Leigha couldn't help but smile back; he was so sweet.

'Sounds good,' she replied, sticking her pen between the pages of her text book to mark her place as she tipped it closed. 'But let me help.'

She didn't end up helping much, more sat perched on the arm of the sofa whilst Johnny busied himself with the kettle and the mugs. She watched appreciatively as the muscles in his back bunched when he reached up into cupboards.

Johnny – she was realising – was that rare thing, a person who would never hurt her. He adored her, like she'd always wanted to be adored. He was funny, sweet, thoughtful – had always been a great friend. He was generous and unstinting in the bedroom department, good looking, athletic – fell over himself to assist with her every want and need.

She was ashamed to admit it, but the thing that excited her most of all was that she knew that, for once, she as the one with the power; she could hurt him, but he could never hurt her. She was like Seth or Adam and Johnny – poor Johnny – he was her.

It wouldn't be so terrible though, to love him; it would be a damn sight healthier for her at the very least. Not for the first time, Leigha wished that it could be him. Already she was regretting the day that she would break his heart.

She waited until he'd finished pouring the boiling water, so as not to startle him, before coming up behind him and looping her arms around his back. She squeezed him tight, enjoying the substantial feeling that his firm back against her softness gave her.

I will try to love you, she told him silently, but I can't make any promises.

Johnny turned round in her embrace to kiss her. His expression, as ever, was honest and open, showing how delighted he was with this unexpected attention.

Harriet waited patiently until she heard the click of the front door, the sound of the chatter moving on down the garden path, the protesting squeal of the rusty gate as it was pulled open. She scrambled to her knees on her bed to peek out the window, catching a glimpse of her housemates as they filed from the garden path out onto the pavement. Leigha – as usual – was the most striking, wearing a royal blue pussybow blouse; Harriet remembered she had been there when she bought it. Sukie wore a beaded grey top and jeans, Nicky was sweet and summery in pale pink. They rounded the curve of the road as a unit.

Seeing the flash of Leigha's teeth as she laughed and smiled as she headed off, carefree, to Adam's birthday drinks steadied Harriet's resolve. Her sentiment was under control, matured now, fossilised hard and cold in the depths of her body. She moved away from the window before the three girls were even fully out of sight. She had a lot to do; her father was due in a little over an hour's time. She hadn't been able to make a start earlier in the week, as Nicky surely would have noticed.

Harriet lugged her large suitcase out from under her bed, coughing at the plume of dust that slid out with it. Moving across to her wardrobe she pulled down the stash of plastic carrier bags she had been hoarding there. Where to start? She told herself impatiently not to think so much, to just do it. Her text books and coursenote folders, they were heavy, they were for the suitcase. She placed them in meticulously, according to their size. Her clothes went into the plastic bags, tossed in unfolded. She stripped away the bedsheets that she hadn't washed since the last time Adam slept in them and stuffed them, too, unceremoniously into a bag.

She'd been surviving on junk food lately, loathed to spend any avoidable time away from the sanctity of her bedroom; the little food she had left in the kitchen cupboards was ignored as she hurriedly stuffed strips of newspaper into and around her motley collection of mugs before wedging them in between the books inside the suitcase. With every item she packed away, every plastic bag she filled, she felt a little lighter, a little emptier.

After half an hour she had no choice but to turn her attention to things like the pictures on her wall, the Post-It notes that littered her wardrobe door, things that she knew that she should just throw away but for some reason collected carefully into a box file. At about the same time her mobile phone started ringing, Adam's name flashing incessantly onto the square of the small screen. She knew she had to hurry up before he came looking for her.

Her clunking old computer had to be dismantled, but before she started pulling wires there was something else she needed to do. She logged onto Facebook. Her newsfeed was littered with various friends wishing Adam a 'Happy Birthday'. Quickly she typed a few letters into her search box, calling up the profile page of Mitsuki 'Sukie' Watanabe. Remove Friend. Are You Sure? Yes, she told Facebook, resolutely clicking on. Next was Leigha Webster. Are You Sure? Facebook asked her again. Oh yes, she assured it.

Finally it was the turn of Adam Chadwick. Are You Sure? Facebook asked her knowingly. No, I'm not sure, she thought, but that's why he's the person it's most important to 'defriend'. As soon as the confirmation screen loaded, Harriet pulled the plug on the PC, busied herself with the technical disassembling.

When she finally realised that that was it, there was nothing else to pack, she simply sat, perched on the end of what had used to be her bed, breathing a little irregularly. The room was once again transformed into the faceless space it had been two years ago, when she'd arrived, excitedly, to claim it as her own. It seemed like both a hundred million years ago and no time at all.

Every piece of coursework, even her dissertation, had been finalised and turned in early. She had four exams in the coming weeks that she'd decided to commute back to take; only one of them was Adam down to take too and, hopefully – considering that most of the alphabet lay between their surnames – she wouldn't cross paths with him, even in the examination hall. She reached up and ran the duster along her shelf for the fourth or fifth time. Adam's name still sporadically flashed silently at her from her mobile phone; she slipped it into her handbag so she wouldn't have to keep seeing it.

She jumped out of her skin when the doorbell sounded through the empty house. Once again she knelt on the bed to peer cautiously out of the window, grateful yet disappointed to recognise that it was her father, only her father, right on time to collect her and the suitcase and tatty plastic bags that now contained her life.

As her placid father dutifully ferried bags down the stairs and out to the boot of the waiting car, Harriet walked pointless circuits around the small room, checking she hadn't left anything behind, trying to make her peace.

'Ready to go?' her father called from where he was loitering, uncertain, at the bottom of the stairs.

'Yeah,' Harriet called back, her voice a world stronger than she felt.

Thoughtfully, she placed the dusting cloth back into the

cupboard under the kitchen sink on her way out of the house.

'Because I'm telling you, Nicky,' Adam said as they crossed the last road, 'I can't do this anymore. She needs to *at least* meet me halfway.'

'She will,' Nicky insisted. 'She just needs time.' Adam gave a wry smile.

'Time. That is *exactly* what we're running out of.'

'But we're not out of it yet.' Nicky held his gaze for a moment, willing him to be patient, be resilient. He smiled at her again, a little more genuinely this time.

She started to pre-emptively fumble in her bag for her keys as Adam pulled the gate open for her. She saw him step back and crane his neck to look up at Harriet's window, knowing she was probably watching them from a chink in the curtains.

The house felt odd as she let herself in.

'Harriet!' Adam called, as he passed the threshold. 'It's only us.'

'Sweetie?' Nicky called, bending down to pull off her shoes. As she did so her gaze fell upon a small pile of metal on the bottom step of the stairs. At first she was confused, but quickly recognised what they were. 'Whose keys are these?' she asked, puzzled; they had no keyrings.

Adam glanced at the keys; Nicky saw a muscle bunching in his neck and suddenly he was gone, taking the stairs two at a time.

'Adam?' Nicky called after him, alarmed, before cold understanding dawned and she hurried to follow him.

Adam was standing stock-still, just a few steps in to Harriet's empty room, his breathing laboured from his dash up the stairs. Nicky made an involuntary little gasp of shock before belatedly clasping her hand to her mouth.

'Oh, she hasn't...' she said, redundantly. 'She hasn't.'

She glanced nervously at Adam as he suddenly moved, rearing

back his right arm; there was a horrible wet crack as he punched the nearest wall with all his strength. Nicky screamed and grabbed at his arm as if to stop him from doing it again. Adam's face was bone white, his features tight with the pain he'd just caused himself.

'You idiot!' she screeched. 'Stop it, you'll break your hand.'

'I can't believe her,' Adam muttered through his teeth. 'I can't believe her. That bitch.'

'Adam, come away downstairs,' Nicky said, worriedly. Adam held his injured fist protectively in his other hand and curled his body away from her. 'Let me look at your hand.' Carefully she led him away from that intolerably unoccupied room and everything that it must symbolise to him, resolutely swallowing the lump sitting in her own throat as she concentrated on steering her shaken friend safely down the stairs.

The room seemed smaller, the walls paler, although surely, now free of all of his mess and belongings, the opposite should hold true?

Adam could hear his mother bustling away downstairs as she re-cleaned the already reasonably clean kitchen, banging cupboard doors and running the water cheerily as she filled the time she had to wait for Adam to finish clearing out his room. They were alone in the flat, Johnny and Miles having vacated over the previous weekend, as had the girls, parts of his life stripping away bit by bit. Adam listlessly cast his eyes over his small bedroom again, almost hopeful that there would be something he had forgotten to pack, to clean – anything to put off the moment of departure just a little while longer. But there was nothing else to stay for; Adam gave a wry smile at that thought, because it was the understatement of the century.

'All finished?' Adam jumped at his mother's voice, hadn't heard her come to stand in his bedroom doorway. She looked at him expectantly. He looked purposelessly around his bedroom for one final time.

'Yup, finished,' he told his mother, following her down the stairs.

PART TWO

February & March 2012

Chapter Twenty

Nicky had fallen half in love with Leigha at first sight.

She had turned up at the Languages social during Freshers' Week, wearing two ropes of plastic beads and a denim mini-dress. She had a mouth made just as much for sulking as for smiling and ended all her sentences with a rising intonation, making everything into a question that everyone rushed to answer. Girls like Leigha had never spoken to Nicky back in school. After an hour – when the complimentary alcohol was finished up – Leigha had suggested to Nicky that they head out to one of the campus bars; Nicky had almost fallen over herself in agreement.

Nicky's degree was in Politics, with a minor in Modern European Languages, and she focused her language course time on French. Taking full and sensible advantage of the subsidiary offered her, she had signed up for extra-curricular Italian lessons, keen to expand her repertoire; maybe she'd do German in the second year, Spanish in the third.

As it happened, she stuck with Italian the whole three years as that was what Leigha had signed up for, on a whim at the Freshers' Fayre; such whims were – Nicky was soon to learn – very typical of Leigha. And through Leigha she had been introduced to Sukie and Harriet – girls who had been at school with Leigha – and that was that – a ready-made friendship group. Sukie was the funniest person Nicky had ever met – caustic, but loyal – and Harriet was straightforward and sweet and always there to listen.

They moved into the little four-bed on Dell Road in June 2005; Nicky was the last to arrive, and on that day, as she had rounded the corner in the taxi full of boxes and bags, she had immediately caught sight of the sheets of paper tacked up in the window of her new bedroom: WELCOME HOME NICKY! And a home it had been; those two years had been the happiest years of her life.

Nicky shifted at her desk, aware that she was staring blankly at her screen, her distraction a little too obvious if a manager happened to look her way. The ring on her left hand glittered as she moved it, reflecting the spotlights above.

No managers around, she opened Internet Explorer with a lazy double-click of the mouse, loading up eBay and the three brides-maids' dresses she'd ordered in from China, paying a premium to ensure their delivery within the month; there was just over two to go until the wedding.

Miles knew that she was still very emotionally attached to their old university and the years she had spent there. Back before Christmas, mid-way through saving for the ring itself, Miles had called up the Chaplaincy Administrator at the university and enquired as to the likelihood of being able to book out the chapel and reception space one Saturday in 2012. Apparently there had been a waiting list upwards of eighteen months.

But the administrator was an old romantic, and – after five minutes of Miles' waffling about how much he loved his (hope-fully) future fiancée and how they had met and fallen in love in one of the campus bars – she'd promised to do what she could for the two alumni. So therefore, Miles had not only proffered a ring at the proposal, but the date and the venue as well – Easter

Saturday, in fact, less than nine weeks away.

It wasn't strictly a date the chapel was meant to be bookable – they'd have to arrange their own priest – but it was better, Miles had thought, than waiting two years. There was no time for an engagement party, or to arrange Stag and Hen dos, and the loss of these traditional celebrations needled Nicky slightly. But it would have been churlish to complain, not when Miles had gone to all the trouble. After all, it was nice to know that he wanted to make her his wife as soon as he could.

At least the other girls had always been at least passably fond of Miles; it would have been awful if they'd taken against him. To be honest, their relationship wouldn't have stood a chance if she'd had the feeling that her housemates didn't like him. As it was, they'd been the ones encouraging her to see him again after their drunken one night stand, make a proper date of it.

Nicky had worn white, a dress she'd borrowed from Leigha, and the irony hadn't been lost on her.

'It's okay, isn't it?' she'd asked, worriedly. 'It's not a little, you know, Here Comes the Bride?' Leigha had burst out laughing.

'As long as you don't accessorise with a veil,' Sukie had smirked.

'Or a large bouquet of flowers,' Harriet had added. Nicky had rolled her eyes at her extremely unhelpful housemates.

'It just seems weird, wearing all white, especially on a date,' she'd insisted, twisting her body to better inspect the back view in the mirror. She'd dropped her voice. 'Slutty even.' Leigha had exploded into laughter again.

'Nicky, you're so funny,' she'd giggled. 'The stuff you come out with. Of course white isn't slutty, it's *pure* and *virginal*.'

'And we're back to Here Comes the Bride,' Nicky had frowned, focusing again on her reflection.

'Nic, you're overthinking,' Sukie had said. 'This guy is mega into you. You could turn up in a bin bag and he'd still be salivating.'

'That would definitely get rid of the weddingy impression,' Harriet had pointed out, mock-thoughtfully. Nicky had laughed, rolling her eyes.

'Okay, well how about, if me and this guy get married one day, I'll wear the bin bag then,' she'd pledged. 'That will even it out.'

'And I suppose we – your beautiful bridesmaids – will wear matching Tesco bags?' Leigha had drawled, amused.

'Naturally,' Nicky had agreed, whilst twisting and contorting herself to survey her reflection some more.

'As long as it doesn't start a trend,' Sukie had said, 'like we each have to wear a different shop's bags for each of our weddings.'

'Bagsie Marks and Spencer for my wedding then. No pun intended,' Harriet had sniggered.

'In which case I'll go with Waitrose,' Leigha had put in, immediately. Sukie had rolled her eyes.

'Of course you will, you posh bitch,' she'd teased, affectionately.

Harriet had come to stand behind Nicky, who was still stood in front of the full-length mirror and had clapped her hand on her friend's shoulder reassuringly.

'I think you should pre-warn this Miles guy that if he hopes to marry you one day, he's going to have to deal with three batty girls wearing carrier bags as dresses.'

'I think that's a little heavy for first date conversation,' Nicky had laughed, using the pad of her index finger to blot her lip-gloss a little more.

Her desk phone rang, jolting Nicky back into the present and she fumbled the receiver as she answered the call. And while she jotted down the inane message for her manager with one hand, she wiggled the fingers on her left, making her engagement ring and wink and wink.

Johnny liked being with Iona; it made him feel like a man. She was petite – a good five inches shorter than him – but it was more than that. She let him pay for her, patronise her, made no demands on his time other than what he was already willing to offer. She made him feel nineteen as well, in her bed with sheets that smelt like cheap laundrette detergent, in bars drinking Snakebite from pint glasses still warm from the dishwasher.

'You're as young as the girl you feel!' Adam had crowed with delight when informed about Iona; that was the general reaction amongst his acquaintances, they were all very wink, wink, nudge, nudge about it.

Sometimes on Sunday mornings he would lie in bed watching her back make shapes as she reaches to move her hair straighteners up and down along her dark hair, and feel like a total arsehole for thinking about someone else.

Leigha always used to bite her nails, a habit that grew worse with stress. He remembers once gently taking her hand away from her mouth and rubbing his thumb across her nail to dissipate the pinpricks of blood, red as the lipstick she wore on weekends, like the colour of the dress she'd worn that on New Year's Eve. He remembers Harriet doing it once too, plucking Leigha's fingers from her teeth as she worried at them, curling their hands together in her lap as she carried on talking to him and Adam without so much as a pause.

He liked it: the nail-biting, that is. It made Leigha seem like she needed someone. Sometimes, Iona bites absently at a hangnail and Johnny is startled into looking for something in the angle of her face, something that won't ever be there, then feels a hot annoyance in his stomach that he's ashamed of.

'The thing with you is…' Demi paused to pull the condom off with a snap, 'you want to be all things to all people.'

Sukie, on her second drag of a post-coital cigarette, gasped and spat smoke incredulously. 'You total hypocrite! You're all *cock* to all people. Aren't you worried Rob will smell vagina in this bed?' Demi gave an indolent smile, lighting up himself, apparently extremely unbothered as to what his boyfriend would think if he found out about his – his words – bit of fanny on the side.

'Which reminds me, don't you need to be getting in the shower?' he replied, mildly. Sukie took a third drag, as obstinate as she dared. He was right. She had to be home soon and needed to wash the sex and nicotine from her hair and the creases of her body. She stubbed her cigarette out with a sigh, moved to the edge of the bed and fished around on the floor with her foot for her discarded underwear.

'Did you have fun at the library then?' Demi asked with a mock serious face; it was where they'd met, where her father and sisters thought she still spent her days. Sukie looked over her shoulder at him.

'I've read better books,' she smiled. Demi laughed in delight and reached across the bed to pull her back, but she slipped out of his grasp. 'Demi, I've got to get in the shower!'

'Ah, go then,' Demi slapped her bottom lightly as she stood. 'You've got to get the dinner on, Cinderelly.' Sukie ignored him; turning the shower on hot and full blast she methodically washed lovely, stupid Demetrios off of her. These days he had given up protesting that she worried too much, that she was a grown woman and could fill her days – and bed – with whomsoever she fancied.

Sukie, however, knew better. Her father wouldn't approve of her eating a kebab; she was pretty sure frequent and fairly filthy sex with a Greek bisexual would be rather past the line.

Leigha saw that Roddy had already ordered her a large glass of rosé as soon as she stepped through the door. It sat in front of him, the glass sweating condensation, dainty and blush-pink. She almost didn't have time to banish the frown from her features before he spotted her, jumping from the barstool and pumping his arm energetically to wave her over.

She found him a little embarrassing, the way he shouted and sprung around like a child, all six foot something of him replete in blue power suit and Windsor-knotted tie. That he presumed to order her a drink – and, perhaps more so, that he had chosen correctly – didn't sit well and her stomach pinched uncomfortably.

When she neared him, Roddy hooked her closer with an arm to the small of her back, went to kiss her, missed her cheek, got her ear instead. Leigha scratched at it as she climbed up onto her bar stool; his five o' clock shadow had irritated her skin.

'You look great!' It was Roddy's standard greeting and Leigha inclined her head in mute recognition of the compliment.

'Thank you for the wine, is it a chardonnay?' she asked, reaching for the glass.

'Yes, I remembered you prefer drier wines.' He looked across at her, eager for approval. Like a dog waiting for a pat on the head.

'Did you have a good day?'

'Well, seeing you has made it.' He punctuated the cheesy line with an equally cheesy smile, twisting to take his jacket off and hang it off the back support of the stool, then pulling his tie loose and unbuttoning the top of his shirt, as if he could relax now Leigha had arrived. His adam's apple bobbed as he took a drink from his stout, drawing her attention to the blonde curl of chest hair hinted at by the now open V of his shirt, the broadness of his chest and shoulders below. He was a fine looking man. She felt agreeably dark and elfin opposite him, perched high with her legs wrapped around the silver poles of the barstool. She took a deep mouthful of wine to match him, felt her worries ease off.

'Roddy, what are you doing Easter weekend?'

'Er…' Roddy consulted his phone calendar with a swift movement of his thumb. 'The whole weekend? Got drinks on the Good Friday. Why, I could cancel if you want to go away somewhere, together?' Leigha took another mouthful of wine, held it there for a moment to feel it cold against her teeth, sharp against her tongue.

'No, just the Saturday, really. Wedding. My old uni housemate.'

'Oh.' Roddy put his phone back into his trouser pocket. 'So, you're looking for a plus one then?'

'Well, yes. I'm a bridesmaid though, so I'm afraid there might be points where you'll have to, you know, fend for yourself…'

'A bridesmaid!' Roddy wiggled his eyebrows suggestively. 'Hot!'

'Hmmm, well I wouldn't count on me looking too hot. I've heard rumours of yellow dresses,' she dropped her voice conspiratorially. Roddy laughed.

'As long as you contravene tradition and please don't shag the Best Man!'

Leigha immediately flushed the colour of her wine. 'That's unlikely,' she answered, reaching down to fiddle inside her handbag in a fraught attempt to distract from the bile her tone had just exposed. She grabbed randomly at her lipgloss. 'Besides…' She paused as she pouted her lips and reapplied, 'that's meant to be the Maid of Honour.'

'You're not the Maid of Honour then?'

Leigha slipped the lipgloss wand back into the tube and closed it with a firm turn. 'Nope.'

'Ah, who is, bride's sister?'

Leigha shook her head, kept her eyes to her hands as she placed the lipgloss tube back into her handbag with exaggerated care. 'Someone else from Uni.'

'Oh, well it sounds like fun. Of course I'll go with you.'

Leigha hung her handbag back on the hook under the table. 'Great. Thanks. It's just a little way out of town, so I'll drive. It's on my old University campus, actually.'

'Oh that's even better. Get to see your old haunts and meet your old friends all in one day. Can't wait!'

Leigha smiled a tight smile. She wondered if Roddy knew her well enough to recognise that this smile was her cynical one. He probably did; she didn't care.

'Me too.'

It was late when they left the bar, and raining, so there was no chance of getting a taxi. The walk from Kensington to her flat on Gloucester Road wasn't so terrible, even in heels, so they hunkered down under Roddy's golf-sized umbrella and headed south. Leigha was feeling more companionable towards him after the better part of a bottle of wine and hooked their arms, pressing her cheek into the side of his shoulder.

A waitress stood leaning against the wall of an Italian restaurant, sheltering her dampening cigarette with her free hand. She exhaled her mouthful of smoke, purple and blue in the darkness, and watched the couple pass. Roddy talking away happily in a low baritone, the thin heels of Leigha's shoes hitting where the water was collecting in the mortar lines of the pavement, sending splashes like little sparks up behind her as she walked.

I bet you wish you had my life, Leigha found herself thinking to the anonymous girl.

Roddy excused himself to the bathroom as soon as they got in. Leigha went straight to the kitchen, taking a bottle of red at random from the rack and uncorking it with a practiced jerk of the corkscrew. She felt agreeably blurred at the edges. She didn't feel like calling it a night just yet.

She sensed Roddy in the doorway and turned around. He took up most of it, had his arms up holding on to the top of the frame, affection for her as ever in his eyes. Leigha turned and reached for two wine glasses.

'What's your magic number?' she asked, with her back to him.

'What, is that like a favourite number?' Roddy moved nearer, taking the bottle of wine from the side and pouring two generous glassfuls.

'No, it's how many women you've slept with,' Leigha clarified, taking her wine from him and dandling it in the crook of her thumb. Roddy gave her a sideways glance.

'You're not going to ask for some sort of STD test paperwork now are you?'

Leigha barked a short laugh. 'Just curious.'

'Why, what's your 'magic number'?'

'I asked first.'

Roddy took a slow sip of his wine. She could tell he was deciding whether or not to lie, and if so, whether it would be more impressive to revise up or down. 'Seven,' he answered, finally.

'Oh, so innocent!' Leigha smirked.

'Oh yeah?' Roddy frowned and took another drink. 'So what's yours?'

'Let's just say I'm in double figures,' Leigha teased. Roddy frowned harder.

'Yeah? But double figures like, ten? Or double figures like, ninety-nine?' Leigha burst out laughing, kicking off her shoes and hopping to sit on the kitchen worktop.

'Like fourteen,' she assured him. 'But that's still double you!'

'Well, it might be more than seven for me actually, I'd need to think about it properly,' Roddy blustered. Leigha grinned, pulled him closer by hooking her leg around his hips.

'Well, let's not think about it now, hey?'

Roddy, however, seemed to be stuck on the topic. 'How old were you when you lost it?'

Leigha wasn't expecting that. She reached behind her for her wine to stall her response, then decided she had nothing to be ashamed of.

'Twenty,' she answered, meeting his eyes defiantly, as if daring him to make comment. He didn't, but his face betrayed surprise. 'A little late to the party, maybe,' she joked.

'Well then,' was all he said, plucking her half-finished wine from her hand. 'We've got lots of making up for lost time to do.'

Usually Leigha slept well when Roddy stayed over, the heavy weight of his arm or leg thrown across her body a comfort. That night her mind just wouldn't settle.

Her first had been Seth. It was the only real secret she had ever kept from Harriet. Even though it was after the two of them had broken up, she knew it looked bad – a definite breach of friendship ethics.

She imagines that Seth would argue, if pressed, that it didn't count; at least, she's pretty sure that she's not included in his 'magic number'. A combination of alcohol and misery over his recent break-up had unmanned him. He'd gone in, breaking her open, but then – almost immediately – he started getting softer and fell out of her before a whole minute had passed. He had pulled completely away and sat on the edge of the bed with his head in his hands as she quickly dressed and left. To this day she associates the loss of her virginity with the smell of that room, warm with blood and rejection.

That weekend she'd pulled in the Union, brought the guy home, got it over with, sent him packing. Almost like a business transaction; they both certainly got what they wanted. Before the guy was even through the front gate, Leigha had headed straight into Harriet's bedroom, had shaken her awake.

'Just did it,' she told her, and the satisfaction in her voice was real. 'It was great.'

Harriet hadn't said anything, just sleepily made as much room in the single bed as she could and let her friend slip in beside her.

Harriet had nursed two small glasses of wine successfully until last orders.

'Down it,' Annie instructed cheerfully, reaching down for her handbag. 'Bit of a way back to the tube.'

'No, I'm fine,' Harriet said, pushing the glass away from her with her fingertip. Annie shrugged and reached across for it.

'Waste not, want not,' she said, before downing the little that remained. 'Eurgh,' she winced, closing her eyes in distaste. 'Warm…' Harriet ignored her, shrugging into her coat and wrapping her long knit scarf around her neck three, four times. By the time she'd finished with it Annie too was coated up, and moved around the table to link their arms and lead her towards the door.

'You need to chill out,' was her sage advice, as they passed from the wine bar out into the wintery drizzle. Harriet rolled her eyes. She hated that phrase and Annie knew it. 'It's just a wedding. You should be looking forward to it.'

'I just can't relax. It's there, looming.' She wiggled her fingers theatrically. 'It's a bit like exam dread. Or waiting to have surgery.' Now Annie rolled her eyes.

'For crying out loud. You're building them up to be so much scarier than they are. They probably won't even look at you. They'll probably just move rooms to avoid you whenever you're near.'

Harriet winced. 'Thanks. That sounds almost worse than a confrontation.'

'Listen to me, nothing –' Annie paused to tap her index finger to Harriet's forehead, '– will be worse than whatever you're picturing in here. That I can promise you. And then, it will be over and you can all go back to pretending each other doesn't exist.' Harriet frowned. 'Just keep your smile on,' Annie continued, 'go easy on the free bar, oh – and no relapsing and snogging that bloke on the dance floor, okay? I think that might be a bit of a flashpoint,' she laughed, unlinking their arms to fetch her Oystercard from her coat pocket as they neared the entrance to the Underground.

Harriet felt a throb of anxiety travel through her whole body and settle in the soles of her feet. The thought of even just being in Adam's eyeline again made what little wine she had had churn hot in her stomach.

'Oh sweetie, please don't look like that!' Annie hurriedly linked arms with her again. 'I'm only winding you up.'

'The last time I saw him, I slapped him,' Harriet mumbled dolefully. 'And,' she winced at her twenty one year old self's sense of drama, 'told him that I *never wanted to see him again.*'

'Well then,' Annie led her firmly down the steps into the Underground. 'He'll probably be avoiding you too, then.'

Chapter Twenty One

In the evenings her two sisters ensconced themselves in their bedrooms, but Sukie – more than a little starved of companionship some days – preferred to sit in the lounge with her father, who usually was doing two things at once, most commonly listening to the news whilst reading on his Kindle. Sukie always marvelled at this; although she had been brought up to be bilingual – indeed, her father only spoke to his daughters in Japanese – she certainly couldn't concentrate on reading kanji whilst BBC newsreaders prated on in clipped Home Counties accents in the background.

She had a Kindle too, somewhere upstairs; her father had bought a set for a whole family when they were first released. Sukie had never gotten on with it, preferring the realness of a printed book against her skin, even if she always felt the silent reproach of her father when he saw her with one in hand as opposed to the gadget.

She had never been very academic or literary; her degree had been in Drama and Theatre Studies and it had suited her to be 'doing' rather than 'reading about'. But nowadays, stuck in the house all day, most days, waiting with a perverse impatience for the washing machine to finish its cycle so she could transfer the load to the dryer, she found she had a lot of time on her hands for reading.

Her mother used to take her to the local library when she was very young, when her middle sister was just a nuisance in a push-chair. The elder Mitsuki, unlike her husband, had embraced life in Britain wholeheartedly and never stopped trying to improve her written and spoken English. To that end she checked out several books a week and back home in her sunny kitchen had read them haltingly aloud to her two little daughters.

So it wasn't very surprising that Sukie, fresh from graduation, newly motherless, jobless, found herself gravitating to that pleasant, solemn building and just sitting a while, some days, in the quiet. Eventually she registered for a membership and started to read, firstly, just classics she vaguely remembered her mother enjoying, then anything that struck her fancy. Three times a week at least she'd visit the library in the quiet of the early afternoon, sinking down into one of the scallop-edged reading chairs and losing herself for a few hours.

One day, unusually, the reading chairs in the fiction section were all in use and so Sukie had wandered through travel and into non-fiction and reference, past the bank of computer desks and to a free chair.

There had been a man, hunched over a book on the nearby desk, the heels of his palms pressed into his temples, the unmistakeable stance of a student in last minute revision peril. His black jumper had been carelessly thrown over the arm of the reading chair. Not wishing to interrupt his cramming session, Sukie had silently folded the jumper and placed it on the desk in front of him. The man had jerked in surprise and Sukie smiled apologetically, gesturing at the chair before sinking into it, opening her book and forgetting all about the student with the jumper.

Two hours later she'd stretched and craned her neck to see the nearby wall clock; she really should go to the shop, get some food in, before the girls were due home from school.

The student – still there – had pushed for her eye contact,

smiling affably. Olive skinned and dark-haired with a good broad frame, Sukie had felt a ripple of immediate interest; he was just the sort of guy she used to go for at Uni. Perhaps he sensed this, as his smile had broadened and he'd part-mouthed, part-stage-whispered: Want to go for a coffee?

Demetrious was studying Law on the Open University and was, in all ways, a ray of sunshine into her life: warm and glorious, achingly temporary. He lived just off the high street with his boyfriend Rob, who worked in the City, doing something neither Demi nor Sukie pretended to understand.

'All the cute guys are gay,' Sukie had laughed, that first day, holding her coffee mug high to her face to hide her genuine disappointment. Demi had just tilted his head and looked at her playfully, an expression she would get to know well.

'I'm not gay,' he had clarified, matter-of-factly.

'Living with a boyfriend called Rob doesn't sound very straight!' Sukie had pointed out.

'Labels!' Demi had scorned, with one of his characteristic and very Greek hand gestures. 'I fall in love with the person, not the gender.'

Sukie didn't know if he fell in love with her or not, but within a month they were going straight from a perfunctory visit to the library to exchange books, then straight back to his flat and into bed.

The closest Demi ever came to suggesting that he might leave Rob had come quite recently. Sukie had finished in the shower and with great frustration was trying to pull her tights up over her still damp legs. Demi had quietly watched her from where he sat on the edge of the bed.

'Doesn't it bother you,' he said suddenly, 'that I'm sleeping with someone else?'

'What, you mean Rob?' Sukie asked, momentarily non-plussed. Demi had rolled his eyes.

'Yes, of course Rob, how many other people do you think I'm having it away with?'

'Well, you know, I hear such things about dirty Greeks!' Sukie replied, laughing.

'No, seriously,' he'd persisted. 'I would… *hate* it, you know, if I knew you were sleeping with someone else,' he admitted. Sukie finally got her tights into place and leant momentarily against the wall, regarding her lover thoughtfully.

'As long as you didn't have another girl,' she answered, finally.

'I would never,' Demi had assured her emphatically, and there was enough respect in his eyes to make her believe that he was sincere.

They hadn't mentioned it since, but that night, stretched out on the couch, opposite her father in his customary armchair, Sukie couldn't help but wonder what it would be like to see Demi in the evenings, watch television with him, talk back to the news, eat a dinner that they'd cooked together. Literally shaking herself from this chain of thought, Sukie stood and went to put the kettle on, dropping a kiss on the head of her silent father as she passed him.

He was doing that maddening thing, where he looked at her with something a bit too close to pity in his eyes.

'There's always your sister-in-law and your cousin,' Miles tried again. Nicky expressed her displeasure by banging the pans she was washing up perhaps more than was necessary. 'Or, you know, it's quite cool and modern not to have any at all, nowadays.'

'Honey –" she cut him off, 'just leave it now, alright? Those girls were my family, before I met you. I love them.'

'Yeah, but the point is that they don't love each other.' Miles flicked the tea-towel he was using to dry up with distractedly.

'They haven't been under the same roof in like, what, five years? Last time I heard Su mention Harry, she said she wished she would die in a fire!'

'She was joking!'

'It's not funny!'

Nicky frowned as she concentrated on a particularly stubborn bit of burnt-on sauce.

'They'll bottle one another or something. They'll ruin the whole day. Please, pet, reconsider this.' Miles reached out to take Nicky's dishwater wet wrist. 'It's meant to be about us, about the future, not about ancient history.'

'Yes, but my bridesmaids are meant to be about *me*.' Nicky took back her hand and continued to scour the saucepan resolutely. Realising that they were dangerously close to argument flashpoint, Miles dropped the tea-towel to the worktop and stalked out of the kitchen.

Nicky glanced at her reflection in the microwave; she looked about as frazzled as she felt. Giving up with the pan and leaving it to soak, she dried her hands on her pyjama bottoms and began stacking what Miles had already dried back into the cupboards distractedly.

Her memory lit upon the arguments at Dell Road about the washing up. She and Sukie, the only two who usually bothered, had gone on strike to see what would happen. She remembers coming into the kitchen one day to see Leigha and Harriet doggedly attempting to share a quiche using a chopstick and cake slice for cutlery. She remembers how she laughed; it was just one of countless moments during the two years they had all lived together that she imagined this is how the closest of sisters would be.

Slipping the last plate into place in its cupboard, Nicky straightened with a sigh. She could hear the television blaring out some sort of sports commentary in the room beyond, blue flickering light thrown from it against the far wall and in through the kitchen door. Her head was still too full of a life once lived in a bright, welcoming house where all the walls were painted as yellow as the sunshine – to go and sit beside her fiancé in the dark; but theirs was a studio flat, after all – and she knew full well she had no place else to go.

The communal heat in Annie's building was always up way too high; being in the lift was stifling. Harriet tried awkwardly to unbutton her coat with one hand whilst trying to hold the paper bag of takeaway cartons steady with the other.

Annie was waiting impatiently at her open flat door, having buzzed Harriet in from the street.

'I come bearing Chinese food as requested,' Harriet announced as the lift doors opened and she caught sight of her friend. 'Now *what* is so important?'

Annie stepped aside and beckoned her friend indoors. 'Let's eat first,' she said ominously, 'I don't want to put you off your dinner.'

'Literally can't eat anymore,' Harriet groaned, putting a half-eaten spring roll back on her plate as if to illustrate her point. 'Now this had better be good.'

Annie raked her fork through her uneaten rice while she collected her thoughts. 'You know my sister?'

'Which one?' Harriet asked.

'Iona.'

'The one studying at Goldsmiths?'

'Yeah, that's the one. Anyway, I was talking to her today and it turns out that she's going to this wedding too.'

'Oh!' Harriet blinked. 'Nicky and Miles'? How does she know them? Wow! What a small world!' she laughed.

'Do you remember I told you when she got this older boyfriend?'

Annie asked, tentatively. Harriet's heart suddenly hiccupped in her chest.

'Not -?' she began. Annie immediately caught her chain of thought and shook her head vigorously.

'Oh no, not your guy. Someone called John? He's a groomsman, so, I guess you know him?'

'Johnny?' After a moment Harriet laughed.

'So is this someone else who will be avoiding you?' Annie asked, 'because that will be awkward for Iona.'

'I'm just as likely to avoid him,' Harriet rubbed her eyes tiredly. 'I blamed him for what happened for years.'

'Blamed?' Annie picked up on the past tense immediately.

'Oh, you know, in retrospect I realise that I put him in an impossible position,' Harriet answered vaguely, waving her fork in the air as she gestured. 'It was me against the girl he loved. I probably would have done the same thing.'

'Well, well! Aren't we magnanimous.' Annie stood and carried the plates across to the bin, scraping the sticky leftovers straight into it.

'Well, to be honest, I think he's the one out of all of us who's been caused the most pain,' Harriet answered softly, passing her own plate to Annie.

'I hope my little sister isn't going out with some emotionally retarded prat,' Annie frowned, scraping away at the second plate.

'Believe me,' Harriet said darkly, dropping their used cutlery into the dishwasher. 'If he's going out with your sister, he's already ten times more emotionally healthy than he was the last time I saw him.'

'I've met her a couple of times, like at Ann's birthday drinks and stuff,' Iona said, nonchalantly. Johnny put his palms flat on the desk and leant in nearer to the laptop, as if closer scrutiny would somehow change the image on the screen: Annie, a slightly plumper, blonder version of Iona, with her arm around a smiling woman with straight, dark hair.

'Harry Shaw,' he conceded finally, grumpily. 'Small world...'

'That's what I said!' crowed Iona, reaching for the mouse sensor pad and clicking through more pictures in her sister's Facebook album. 'How cool! At least I'll know someone else at this wedding.'

Johnny frowned. 'Yeah well, we haven't really kept in touch. We weren't that close.'

'The way I hear it, you practically lived together.' Iona's tone remained jovial but her eyes hardened slightly. 'You were the best of friends.'

Johnny scowled and scratched at the nape of his neck distractedly. 'My best mate was shagging her,' he said, dismissively. 'That was about the extent of our relationship. Now come on. We're going to miss the film.' Johnny twisted to snatch his coat up from where he'd thrown it over the foot of Iona's bed. Wordlessly, Iona turned back to the laptop, exiting the open browser and shutting it down.

'Speaking of relationships,' she said, in that same cheery tone, 'when were you going to tell me that your ex-girlfriend was going to be at this wedding?'

Johnny froze, one arm in and one out of his coat. Iona breezed past him, grabbing her own jacket from the hook on the back of her bedroom door.

'We'll talk on the way to the cinema,' she assured him.

Demi casually trailed paths between the moles on the back of her thigh with the tip of his finger. Sukie turned her face from where it had been buried in the pillow and smiled lazily at him. She felt so relaxed. Thank God for busy business men – both Demi's boyfriend Rob and her father were going to be back late tonight and so for once she wasn't rushing headfirst into the shower.

'I'll come,' Demi said suddenly, lifting his hand from her thigh to brush her hair back off her face. 'I'll come to this wedding with you.'

Sukie laughed. 'I haven't asked you to, weirdo.'

'I know, but I know you want me to!' Demi grinned widely, his teeth Hollywood white against his tanned face. 'And I want to see you all dolled up. I want to dance with you.'

Sukie visibly blanched. 'If you're coming, you're coming as a mate, not a date...'

'So you want me to play the gay best friend?' Demi's tone was playful, but his smile was stretched. Sukie rolled over and rested her head on her elbow.

'Surely that's not such a hardship?'

'No, I guess it's what I am,' Demi answered slowly. Sukie reached out with her free hand and caught him by the chin, already rough with late afternoon stubble.

'You're more than that and you know it,' she smiled shyly.

'Just not in public.'

'Not in public,' she agreed. And then she leant to kiss him, to distract him, before the conversation got any more uncomfortable.

It was so much harder to resist the impulse, being at home. In his office social media sites were blocked, so it hadn't been an issue. Adam had walked up to and straight past his PC three times since getting in from work. He should have called someone, gone out; he wondered if it was too late to. He scrolled through his mobile phone contacts list distractedly, opened that morning's text from Johnny again and re-read it.

He stuck a frozen ready-meal curry in the microwave and, as it slowly rotated, gave in and switched on his computer. He glowered at it impatiently as it droned to life, then for some reason chose that point in time to undertake an impossibly long series of system updates.

Finally, the microwave pinged and his desktop loaded. Adam haphazardly tipped his steaming dinner onto a plate, stuck a fork into the pile of rice and carried it over to the desk. When he logged on to his Facebook, he had four notifications, one message and two invitations to play on some sort of virtual farm, all of which he summarily ignored.

He had gleaned from comments made by Nicky and Miles in the past that Harriet too lived in London: off-hand comments, as both of them studiously avoided referring to her when in his presence; he could only assume that, vice-versa, he was persona-non-grata when they spent time with her. It was a delicate balance indeed, one this wedding was certainly poised to tip. Sometimes, when he saw a short woman with a dark pixie crop on the tube, he had to fight an immediate compulsion to dive headfirst into his copy of the Evening Standard. It hadn't ever been her though, not yet. But now he knew that she knew Johnny's girlfriend. Small world indeed, he agreed wryly with Johnny's text.

He only had to type H A R R into the Facebook search box before she came up, a result of their some fifty plus friends in common. As he suspected, her profile was set to private. *If you know Harriet,* Facebook suggested gleefully, *send her a Friend Request or Message her.* No thanks, he thought contemptuously at the website.

It was quite funny, looking at the small thumbnail of her profile picture. Jumping like a scared child at the sight of women with short hair was proved even more absurd than previously granted, as Harriet's hair apparently now hung straight to her shoulders. The picture was typical profile picture fare, taken on some beach, the top half of her face taken up with a pair of ludicrously large sunglasses.

There nearly wouldn't have been anything to recognise her by, if she hadn't been smiling – her truest one, the one that almost seemed too big on her small face. Adam remembered the first time he'd caused her to have such a wide smile, how before then he'd seen it bestowed on the other girls on occasion, but never to him until that day. He'd felt in that moment like he had some sort of superpower, smiling back at her just as broadly.

So that was the only piece of information that this locked profile was giving up: that Harriet still had people in her life capable of causing this limitless smile. Adam turned abruptly to his rapidly cooling curry, shovelling a few forkfuls into his mouth, admonishing himself for the spite rising up warm from his core, telling him that she didn't deserve it.

The whole sorry story came spilling out somewhere between the third and fourth bottle of rosé. Annie sat in thoughtful silence for some time after Harriet ran out of anything to say and simply sat back in her chair, feeling positively bloated by the combination of misery and too much wine.

'Well,' Annie said, eventually. 'You were right not to tell me the whole story before; I would *never* have been your friend if I had but known!' She waggled her eyebrows to show that she was only kidding, but Harriet's stomach contracted painfully all the same. Annie moved to top up their wine glasses with the dregs of bottle number four.

'For what it's worth,' she continued, 'I think he probably did sleep with Leigha.' Harriet glared at her friend, snatching away the wine glass and bringing it up to her lips the second Annie had stopped pouring. 'She sounds like the sort of girl that encourages men to er, think with the *lower* of their two heads,' Annie smirked, as she finished replenishing her own drink. 'But you were wrong to run out on him like that. And on his birthday too, you bitch.'

'I know,' Harriet conceded miserably. 'That's the worst. All the others, they can bugger off, because I never did anything to hurt them. But I did hurt Adam. I handled the ending of things very badly.'

'And he never tried to contact you?' Annie asked. Harriet shook her head. 'Not ever?' Harriet shook her head again. 'Hmmm,' Annie said, thoughtfully. 'He's probably cool with it now, though, it's been – what? – five years? Does he have a girlfriend?' Harriet's wine-filled stomach roiled in protest at the unpalatable thought of Adam being with another woman.

'Serial dater, according to Nicky,' she answered.' Doesn't seem to want to settle down'.

'Sounds like someone else I know,' Annie remarked knowingly. Harriet shot her an evil look. 'Don't be so crotchety,' Annie instructed, patting her friend on the back of her hand. 'Like I've been saying, this is a good thing. You've been frightened of facing those girls for years, and now you have to and you need never be frightened again. And as for the 'one that got away', well…' Annie paused to take a large gulp of wine whilst she considered her phrasing carefully. 'You should take this wedding as the opportunity to do what you should have done five years ago. Say goodbye to Adam. And forget him.'

Chapter Twenty Two

'I think we should have at least offered to give her a lift,' Iona was saying, for the fifth time. Johnny felt his grip tighten on the leather of the steering wheel. 'I mean, she might even be in one of these cars.' Iona looked out of the passenger-side window attentively, as if Harriet was going to be at the wheel of the red Corsa in the adjacent lane, waving merrily. 'Or maybe she's on the train, with all her bags. Poor thing,' Iona continued sullenly.

'She's not our mate,' Johnny reminded his girlfriend, a little impatiently. 'We don't owe her lifts anywhere. I'm sure she's making her way just fine.'

'You're going to have to see her soon enough,' argued Iona. 'And she's my sister's best friend. And I liked her fine when I met her and nothing you've told me has made me feel otherwise.' Johnny rolled his eyes. If anything, Iona was *more* impressed with Harriet since hearing the sordid details of her involvement with Adam.

'Sounds like *your ex* was being a *nasty* piece of work and Adam was a liar and Harriet just realised she didn't have to stay and put up with it anymore,' she had said. Johnny had just sighed.

'Are you only taking that view because she was *my ex*?' he'd teased, mimicking the bitchy stress that Iona had put on the words. Iona hadn't dignified him with a response.

'Well, if you're that bothered about Harriet you can sit next to her and be her friend all weekend,' Johnny said scathingly, frowning hard at the tarmac ahead of the car.

'Whilst you sit with Leigha, I suppose?' suggested Iona in an airy tone. Johnny couldn't help but take his eyes from the road and glance at her. Had he ever told her Leigha's actual name? He couldn't remember. The word sounded amazing and strange coming from Iona's lips. Iona met his gaze, mutely challenging, before he dragged his concentration back to driving.

'Of course not, don't be silly,' he said roughly.

'I can't wait to meet all these people,' Iona continued, idly twirling a brown flick of hair around her index finger. 'They feel like celebrities. I know so much about them.'

They were going to be late, so late that you couldn't even joke it was 'fashionably' so, but in her post-coital haze Sukie couldn't quite bring herself to care. She started greedily on her second cigarette, dragging the heat as deep into her lungs as she could, revelling in the fact that – for once – she didn't have to rush home. She was off the leash.

Her father had only grunted when she told him that she was going to be spending the long Easter weekend back on her University campus for her ex-housemate's wedding. Obviously she hadn't informed him about her incongruous date – or the fact that she planned to spend at least half of Friday with him inside of her. 'Good Friday', indeed.

'You,' growled Demi, playfully, 'you are insatiable. We're late.' Sukie blew a smoke ring into his face.

'We're not that late.'

'Honey, even if we had a magic teleporter thing and teleported straight to the place right this second, we'd still be considered late.' Demi slapped her playfully on the thigh. 'Get up, get dressed. I don't want to make a terrible impression on your friends.'

231

Sukie laughed, sliding her hand across his hips to his groin. 'Hi guys, sorry we're late,' she mimicked. 'It's all the fault of my gay fuck buddy here and his magnificent piece. I literally can't get enough!' Demi pulled away from her abruptly, refusing to share in the joke, sliding to sit on the side of the bed and pull items of clothing on.

'Can't you let me be your boyfriend for one weekend?' he muttered, still not facing her. 'Do we have to do the "gay fuck buddy" thing?'

Sukie bit down on the retorts that immediately rose to the tip of her tongue. But that's what you are, aren't you? You're Rob's boyfriend, not mine. Instead she mutely slipped to the opposite end of the bed and followed his lead by starting to get dressed.

An understandably harried looking Nicky opened the door after the knock. Silently Adam held his arms out to her and Nicky bestowed one of her infamous bear hugs upon him.

'It's good to see you,' she murmured into his chest. Adam straightened them out, holding Nicky at arms' length and inspecting her.

'No, it's good to see *you*,' he corrected. 'The blushing bride!' Nicky gave a roll of the eyes that suggested blushing was the last thing she was doing at the moment.

'Is that my Best Man?' came a voice from inside the room; Miles appeared over Nicky's shoulder, looking a damn sight less stressed than she did.

'Hey mate!' Adam greeted him. 'All systems go, eh?'

'All systems go,' Miles agreed, cheerfully. 'You're half an hour early. Weird being back here, isn't it?'

'Very weird,' Adam agreed. 'Gives me a craving to drink cheap alcohol.'

'Funny, I've got that craving too,' Nicky said, wryly.

'What room are you in?' Miles asked, eagerly. Adam shifted the weight of his hold-all on his shoulder to better inspect the number engraved on the key fob in his left hand.

'Eight.'

'Next to me,' Miles smiled. 'I'll go along with you.'

'Wait, this isn't your room?' Adam asked, confused.

'No!' Nicky stepped aside in the doorway to let Miles past her and out into the corridor. 'It's bad luck for the bride and groom to wake up together on their wedding day.'

'Really?' Adam asked. 'You two don't strike me as über traditional like that...' Miles shot him a look that showed his agreement.

'We're not seeing one another after the dinner until it's at the altar,' Nicky said firmly.

'Dinner?' Adam repeated. 'What dinner?' His mind lit dubiously on memories of the various campus cafés and cafeterias.

'Yes, dinner,' Nicky confirmed. 'The whole wedding party. Mauritzo's, on the high street. Seven o'clock. What, did you think we were all going to order in pizza to the rooms?'

'I can't believe that place is still running,' Miles mused. 'Especially in this economy.'

'Okay,' Adam said, shifting his bag again, restlessly. 'Seven o'clock. Is anyone else here yet?' Nicky shook her head.

'Because you're half an hour early!' Miles told him again, slapping him companionably on the shoulder.

Roddy had spent the last 45 minutes talking incessantly about his time at university, a subject matter that Leigha had little to no interest in. She wasn't bothering to make her apathy any less blatant, just stared out the car window as the featureless motorways changed into roads more familiar, until finally they were cruising at 30 mph down streets she still knew like the back of her hand.

'This turning?' Roddy paused in his anecdotage to ask her.

Leigha roused herself back to the present.

'Hmm? Er, yes. It's a one way system when you get onto campus, I think. I'll tell you where to park.'

It was the middle of the Easter holidays and campus was more or less quiet, in that sad, abandoned way that places of liberal activity felt when deserted. Despite her earlier indifference, Leigha couldn't resist the stirrings of nostalgia as they slowly made their way through her old home.

'That was where I had most of my lectures,' she blurted out, pointing at a building to the left hand side of the road; Roddy glanced over politely. 'We're going to come round on the halls of residence in a minute,' she added, leaning a little forward in her seat. 'The top couple of floors of one of the buildings is used as a Bed & Breakfast all year round. That's where we'll be staying.'

'So we're actually staying in the student digs?' Roddy raised his eyebrows.

'Oh, they're like little Travelodge rooms,' Leigha told him dismissively. 'Mini kettles and everything. Don't worry, nobody's going to ask you to use a bin bag full of rubbish as a beanbag and play Playstation with them.' Roddy chuckled.

'Boy students aren't quite *that* bad, I'm sure nobody ever suggested that,' he assured her. Leigha merely looked at him archly to remind him that she didn't exaggerate. Chastened, Roddy pulled his Audi efficiently into the parking space she'd just indicated with a mute flick of her wrist.

As the safety locks clicked off, Leigha slid as elegantly from the car as she could manage. Her professional smile moved smoothly into place as an eager looking woman emerged from the door of the halls' reception and waved enthusiastically; the campus event coordinator, judging by the clipboard. Leigha took a deep breath and mentally girded herself as Roddy walked around the car to stand by her side. Here we go.

Harriet could feel sweat beading against her hairline as she made the last push up the hill from the train station, her small wheelie bag bumping and swerving erratically behind her on the uneven paving stones. She briefly considered removing her jacket and carrying it, but she really didn't want to look even more like a bag lady than she already did.

In London it was perfectly acceptable to not own a car; the world was her Oystercard. Back out here, in the suburbs, she felt uncomfortably like a child again. Dolefully, she wished that she was sweeping up in something red and fancy that positively screamed: 'Look how well I'm doing!' instead of trudging up red-faced and perspiring.

She hated her shoulders for tensing up as she made the turn into campus. This place had been her home for three years, she had been happy here; she would never have imagined that she would be returning to it so on edge.

It was startling how everything looked exactly the same. She'd been prepared for differences, for something to jar, but nothing did. She might have only just left. Johnny and Adam might be coming over that rise from the sports' centre, studded football boots dangling from their hands. Over to the west of the older buildings was a huge tree, tall and thick and hundreds of years old. Harriet blinked away the memory of a grinning Leigha, stuffing jackets and cardigans into plastic bags and into crannies under the roots, so she wouldn't have to pay to coat check them when they got to the Union.

Harriet let her mind wander, giving her feet control to take her down the familiar route to the halls of residence. She felt 18 and 100, happy and sad, far too many incompatible things, all at once. That's what she hated them most for, the other girls; they'd ruined all the thousands of happy hours she'd had here, and with them. Almost imperceptibly her pace slowed and she forced herself to speed back up to a normal stride.

Although she'd done almost nothing else but for the last few days, Harriet decided to run through the possible scenarios again.

Scenario one. Leigha bursts into an ear-splitting squeal and flings her arms around Harriet the minute she walks into the room.

'Oh my God, I haven't seen you for ages, you look so well!' she cries.

'The gang's all here!' Sukie agrees, adding herself to the hug.

'I love you girls!' Nicky coos, making it, officially, a group hug. Adam watches from where he leans against the far wall, waiting for the excitement to abate before he moves closer. He runs the pad of his thumb along the line of Harriet's jaw.

'Hello, Trouble,' he murmurs.

Scenario two. Harriet walks tentatively into the room; a deadly hush falls over its inhabitants. Leigha storms up to her, her high heel shoes clicking angrily against the flooring as she does. In one fluid movement she removes an axe from her hand bag and – just as smoothly – decapitates her erstwhile best friend. From where he leans against the far wall, Adam applauds enthusiastically.

Harriet ruefully shook her head at herself. Frankly, both scenario one and scenario two were about as likely as each other.

Harriet felt her pace falter again as she moved into the southern part of the campus, the nearer of the residential buildings already in view. To be honest, she was hoping for scenario three – the scenario where each party maintains a feigned civility and more or less ignores the others until the end of this long, long weekend. That would do her just fine. She intended to lead by example.

She just needed to do something about her face. This place was stirring up more memories than she could keep out of her expression. In her head, she was everywhere, across the grass throwing snowballs at Sukie; then over in the bottom car park, sitting in silence in Seth's battered old Polo, watching him rest his forehead against the steering wheel and cry as she broke his heart for the last time. And over there she was walking with Adam, back before things got complicated between them, him carrying her purple book bag home from lectures for her, thrown effortlessly over his shoulder as if it weighed nothing.

She dragged her focus back front and centre. There was no need to chase memories of Leigha, Sukie and Adam, when she was going to be facing the real deals soon enough.

Leigha followed the jabbering blonde coordinator into the Reception, smiling at all the right places, whilst her attention darted about, looking for familiar faces.

As she had feared, Harriet was already there, leaning causally against the Reception desk with her back to the room. Her hair was long now – strangely long – more Leigha's own length; Leigha felt irrationally annoyed by the imitation. Harriet was talking to – Leigha felt a warm flush of pleasure tempered with guilt – Johnny, who glanced up at just that moment. Leigha saw his jaw working as he clenched his teeth.

Noticing her companion's sudden disquiet, Harriet turned her head to see what he was looking at. Except it wasn't Harriet at all, Leigha quickly realised, as soon as the angles of the girl's face moved into view. The anonymous girl blinked, her focus switching from Leigha's face, to Roddy, and back again. Roddy; Leigha had almost forgotten he was there. She reached out blindly with her hand until she connected with the solidity of his arm, and looped her own through it smoothly.

Johnny looked as if could very well grind his back molars down to stumps as Leigha approached; he didn't reach out for the girl, she couldn't help but note.

'Hey, stranger,' Leigha said softly as she arrived in front of the desk.

'Roderick McCorley,' Roddy said, putting his hand out proudly for Johnny to shake.

'John Blake,' Johnny mumbled in return, returning the handclasp gracelessly.

'I'm Leigha,' Leigha told Johnny's date; she made her voice as kind and friendly as she could.

'Iona.' The girl met her gaze politely enough but didn't move a muscle. The foursome stood in awkward silence. The events coordinator – completely forgotten up until this point – cleared her throat conspicuously. Everyone turned to stare at her and she blushed, flustered.

'You're rooms 9 and 10,' she told them, moving behind the Reception to fetch the keys. 'Mr Healy and Miss Elliott would like you all to meet down here at half past six before the wedding party dinner.'

'Dinner?' echoed Leigha. 'What sort of dinner? What's the dress code?' Johnny laughed, a deep, familiar rumble.

'You know there's really nowhere round here for you to dress up for, I wouldn't worry about it.' Leigha shot him a playful look. That did it; Iona fingers twitched and she reached to hang herself off Johnny's wrist. He didn't stop looking at Leigha – really, really looking.

It's been five years, thought Leigha, irritably, and he's still the same. His attention felt like being covered over with a thick blanket on a summer's day. It was too much; it had always been too much.

'Here are your room keys,' the coordinator said, holding out a fob to each couple. 'Don't hesitate to call down if you need anything. There are area information packs in the rooms.' Johnny chuckled again.

'I don't think we need any information about the area,' he laughed, still staring at Leigha; he hadn't looked away since the minute she'd walked into the room. Poor little Iona looked dejected.

'Why don't we get settled in and… catch up properly later?' Leigha suggested.

'At dinner,' Johnny said.

'At dinner,' Leigha agreed.

Abruptly Johnny seemed to notice that Iona was hanging off of his jacket sleeve. He curled his large hand around her small one and held her arm close to his torso.

'See you later then,' he said, gruffly, before leading Iona towards the lift. Leigha couldn't help but overhear the furious whispering that exploded from the girl's mouth the minute they were half the room away.

Suddenly feeling a little sheepish, Leigha turned to Roddy, who was standing quietly, smiling faintly, as implacable as ever.

'She looks quite like you,' he said, nodding towards Iona's retreating back, not realising he was stating the bleeding obvious.

Chapter Twenty Three

As the lady behind the desk faffed with papers and with finding the key to her room, Harriet surreptitiously blotted her damp forehead with her sleeve. The back of her neck and her shoulder blades prickled, hyper-aware of the gaping doorway behind her. Hurry up, hurry up, she mentally urged the receptionist. I don't want to be caught standing here. I need time to recoup. I need a shower.

The lady smiled, finally passing over the chrome key fob.

'Room 5,' she told her. 'Mr Healy and Miss Elliott would like you all to meet down here at half past six before the wedding party dinner.' There was a formal dinner? Harriet's felt her bottom lip twist in annoyance; the receptionist gave a tinkling laugh. 'None of you seem that keen about this dinner, I have to say!' she teased.

Emboldened by the woman's informality, Harriet pressed for more information, dropping her voice low to a conspiratorial undertone.

'Has everyone else arrived then?'

'All but one room,' the woman told her.

'Has everyone else brought… plus ones?' She couldn't bring herself to say the word 'dates'.

'Not everyone,' the woman replied with a consoling smile. Harriet flushed, realising that the woman thought she was concerned that she might be the only one without someone with her.

'Okay… thanks,' she said hurriedly, backing away from the desk and grabbing for the handle to her wheelie bag.

Her heartbeat slowed back down to a sensible pace as the lift doors closed, sealing her off from any unexpected company. Dinner. Had she brought anything to wear to a dinner? She looked down at her uninspiring ensemble of jeans, cami and cardigan and scowled.

The glower was still on her face as the lift car arrived on the top floor; Harriet moved smartly out of the lift and down the corridor. But of course – because the universe was insurmountably cruel – suddenly, there was Adam, standing at the door to room 8, stuck paused in the act of slipping his key into his pocket. He was clean shaven; back during their time together he had usually sported a lazy fuzz of stubble. His bare cheeks and jaw made him look almost younger. It was a weird feeling.

His eyes were fixed on her in a manner just as intense. His gaze slipped from her mid-length hair and down the length of her body before returning to her face. His lips pressed flat together as if he was physically stopping himself from speaking, waiting for her to go first, to decide the tone they'd maintain over the course of the weekend. Feigned civility, Harriet reminded herself.

'Hey,' she said, because there wasn't really anything else to say. She cringed inwardly at how pathetic she must look and sound. Adam straightened, finishing the slide of the key into his back pocket.

'Hey,' he echoed, and she wasn't sure if he was mocking her or not.

'Weird, huh?' she offered, unsure if she meant that that their friends were finally getting married, being back on campus, being back near one another – or all of the above.

'You're about four years and ten months late, by the way,' Adam told her, with a curious little smile, one at odds with his cold eyes. It took a second for the words to sink in; when they did, she couldn't help but wonder if he'd had them prepared, or if he'd just done a little calendar maths on the fly.

'Yeah.' She drew out the word to better shorten the awkward pause that she knew would follow. 'Sorry about that.' She tried to smile winsomely but her jaw felt like it was pinned into place and ruined the effect. So she just looked at him, trying to convey her apology in her expression. The granite in Adam's eyes didn't shift.

'I'm just going for a walk round the old place,' he said. Was that an invitation? He moved away from his room door, towards her. Blood throbbed in Harriet's temples, so hard that surely he could see her skin pulsing like a drum skin. His proximity put her body into violent fight or flight mode; the only person she'd ever consciously hurt, the only guy she'd ever loved. 'See you at dinner,' he said, moving smoothly past her and pressing the lift call button.

Trying to maintain her trembled dignity, Harriet barrelled down the corridor to the sanctuary that was room 5 before the lift had even made it up to the floor.

Adam's shoulders hunched as he walked. Although it was a warm spring day, this side of campus was heavily wooded, and it was cool in the shade of the old trees.

He'd been misremembering her, he was shocked to realise. In actuality her eyes were darker, the bridge of her nose ever so slightly wider. He'd mentally lamented the fact that the girl was branded on his memory for years, only to find out he was wrong. He'd explicitly based his type on her, dating petite brunette after petite brunette, a long line of little Harriets that he could control and dump at will. But none of them, he realised now, had ever looked anything like her; none of them compared like he'd wanted them to.

He'd been eager to take the opportunity for a walk before

dinner, a moment of quiet before the celebrations got underway. He thought that if he walked old paths and sat on benches where once she'd sat next to him, he'd know exactly what to say when faced with Harriet Shaw. But, typically, she'd surprised him, caught him on the back foot. She'd apologised; he hadn't expected that. Straight off, smiling casually, like it wasn't a big deal. So maybe it wasn't a big deal; Adam straightened up a little.

He'd been expecting to see the mouse that he remembered from towards the end, the cringing, apologetic girl who allowed herself to be made a victim. But – although she'd been as rabbit-caught-in-headlights as he – in that corridor he'd seen a disturbing flash of the old Harriet, the girl who'd glare at him for playing stupid in seminars with those dark eyes, the friend who'd helped him be a better person. That was one old acquaintance that he had not been expecting to see at this wedding.

Miles wasn't in his room so Adam backtracked to room 6. Nicky answered his knock, looking – if possible – even more whey-faced than she had earlier. She looked at him expectantly.

'Which room is Harriet's?' Adam asked, without preamble. From the depths of the room he heard Miles guffaw. Nicky shot a look at him over her shoulder.

'You'll see her in less than half an hour,' she told Adam, carefully.

'I've already seen her,' Adam said, impatiently. 'And it's because we're all about to go to dinner that I want to talk to her now. Before dinner.' Nicky looked sceptical.

'Oh, Adam,' she sighed. 'Can't you all just leave one another alone? One weekend, that's all we're asking of you. Be grownups, for one weekend.'

'We knew we'd have to have this talk with the girls, but come on,' Miles added, appearing behind his fiancée. Adam put his palms up in a gesture of surrender.

'It's not like that. I just want to clear some air.'

'That air should have been cleared years ago, if it was going to be cleared at all.' Miles' voice was uncharacteristically stern. 'Our wedding is not an opportunity for—'

'It's okay, Miles,' a voice interrupted. Harriet was standing nervously at the door to the neighbouring room, clearly having heard everything. 'Adam, come in. I hope you don't mind if I keep on getting ready.' She turned and disappeared back inside her room, leaving the door ajar as an invitation for him to follow. Adam shot the silent Nicky and Miles a look of triumph before doing so.

Harriet had seated herself at the vanity table and was using straightening irons on her hair, something he had never seen her do before; her hair had never been long enough when he'd known her. It underlined the relieving fact that this girl was more or less a stranger to him; she didn't have the power to hurt him – or he her – they'd both given that up long ago.

He must have stood in silence for too long; Harriet squinted at him in the mirror. 'You can sit down, you know. What's up?'

Adam sat heavily on the end of the bed and rubbed the heel of his hand into his eye socket. 'Look, I just wanted to say…' he started. Harriet watched him implacably in the mirror. 'You know, no hard feelings.'

'No hard feelings?' Harriet echoed, moving the straighteners smoothly down a section of dark hair.

'You know,' Adam said again. 'I'm sure you're going to have enough stress this weekend. I just wanted you to know that… I won't add to it.'

Harriet turned the straighteners off and carefully placed them down on the table top before swinging her body around in the chair to face him.

'Do you mean that?' she asked. Her voice was small and queer, her eyes shining with something indefinite.

'Yeah,' Adam answered gruffly, clasping his hands and letting them dangle between his knee, forearms resting along his thighs. He was already regretting it. Being this near to her was making his gut churn like the aftermath of a bad curry. He wanted to touch her face, stroke his fingers down her long hair and see if it was soft and warm from the straightening. She was dangerous.

Maybe this was what he had really wanted from his line of surrogate-Harriets. The bad curry feeling. The impulse to reach out and touch so strong that it made his fingertips quiver and twitch. Maybe he'd been looking for that for the last half a decade, not just another girl to hurt, like he had once been hurt. Maybe he was the romantic that he always joked he was after all.

Harriet suddenly rose from her chair; Adam jolted back as if she'd lunged at him with a knife. Casually, as if she hadn't seen his insane reaction, Harriet crossed the room and fetched a pair of high heeled shoes from her suitcase.

'Thank you,' she said, with her back to him, the shoes held tightly in her hands. 'I really am... sorry, you know.'

'You said.'

She turned around; her eyes searched his face. He wished he knew what for.

'So. Adam Chadwick. Friends again?' She shot him one of her rare gigawatt smiles; even now they could make his chest cavity feel like it was crumpling. Dangerous.

Adam stood, abruptly. The smile dropped off of Harriet's face as quickly as it had appeared there.

'For this weekend, anyway,' he qualified unkindly, moving past her and to the door. 'See you at dinner.'

They didn't have time to get changed. Nicky and Miles had been waiting in the lobby; after the obligatory hugs of greeting Nicky had chivvied them up the stairs with a sweep of her hands, like they were farmyard animals she was shooing away: hurry up, the taxis will be here in a minute!

Luckily, Demi always looked good – another plus of having a gay boyfriend. Sukie herself was a little rumpled from the car ride but was wearing black so it didn't show so badly. They barely had time to dump their overnight bags – Sukie dragging a hairbrush through her hair as she changed her shoes – before heading straight back out the door.

Before Sukie had a chance to pull it open, Demi caught her firm in his arms, spinning her to face him. He kissed her, greedily, crushing her against the wall, messing up her newly smoothed hair. It was like kissing a stranger; his kisses were normally unhurried and languid, smooth and thick as syrup but this one was wild and urgent. She didn't have time for this. Sukie pushed him away from her, smiled provocatively to soften the action, slipped through the bedroom door and hurried towards the lifts.

At some point in the last few minutes, Leigha had arrived in the lobby. Sukie hadn't seen her since before Christmas, and even then it had been a fleeting visit. She looked sleek and content, even if her collarbones did jut out a little prominently above the sweetheart neckline of her dove grey dress. The blond man beside her was a head or two taller than the average and built like a rugby player to boot, making Leigha look even more insubstantial in comparison.

Sukie made a beeline towards them and the two girls threw their arms around one another enthusiastically. Old friends are the best friends, Sukie thought, as they pulled back from one another. Leigha eyed Demi appraisingly; she didn't know who he was and that obviously intrigued her. Sukie hadn't told anyone about her dirty little secret, not even her bestest, oldest friend.

'You must be the famous Leigha,' Demi said smoothly, bending slightly to take Leigha's elbow and kiss her lightly on both cheeks.

'I've heard so much about you,' he continued, with a cheeky little half-smile, as if he knew very well that Leigha had never heard so much as a whisper about him.

Motion in her peripheral vision distracted Sukie from Leigha's response. Johnny and a slim brunette wearing a plum coloured lipstick that matched her dress exited the lift. The last time she saw Johnny – Sukie realised – he was still with Leigha. She remembered trying to be totally normal with him, although Leigha had casually confessed in a text the night before that she was just waiting for the right time to end things with him.

Johnny immediately stared at Demi, assessing this handsome stranger talking to his ex. His date hung off of his arm, looking around the lobby shyly, an embarrassingly obvious Leigha do-over, with the same glossy brown hair and cupid's bow mouth. Nicky – sweet Nicky – rushed forward immediately to put the girl at ease. Miles followed, clasping forearms companionably with Johnny in greeting.

Leigha voice started to trail off, her attention diverted. Harriet, Sukie thought, turning quickly to look again at the lift, the doors of which were just opening to expel its passenger.

It was Adam; he blinked against the bright lights of the lobby, like an actor with the spotlight turned on him suddenly. He was wearing – by chance, Sukie assumed – a slim-fit tailored shirt in almost exactly the same soft grey as Leigha's dress. He looked good, Sukie judged. He'd always been a boy too quick to smile and that had always rubbed her up the wrong way. Now his jaw seemed squarer, his face was firmer – a man's face; the past five years suited him.

Johnny made a crowing noise and moved forward to greet his best friend. Adam kissed Johnny's date on the cheek, like she was already well-known to him; they must still see one another a lot, Sukie reasoned. She was the only one rotting out in the suburbs, the only people to spend time with her ingrate teenage sisters, slipping in and out of Demi's bed, being her own person for snatched minutes at a time.

Leigha watched the boys bantering, transfixed.

Sukie sought out Demi's attention and leaned into his solid frame, surveying the group dynamics, already being reasserted. It was funny how everyone looked older, how their lives were so different, but put them all into a room, and they just played out the same old parts. It could be five years ago; they were all together, in a room, and she was watching Leigha, watching Adam.

But they weren't all in the room yet, were they. Sukie plucked at Demi's collar, drawing his ear down close to her lips so she could murmur to him.

'She's not here,' she noted. She'd run Demi through the whole thing in the car; although he'd heard the story before, it felt important to recap, make sure he understood before he met everyone. She'd watched his profile as he watched the road ahead, waiting for the big reaction that usually came when she told the story about what Harriet had done to Leigha, to Adam – to the whole comfortable friendship group – and how she had so coldly used Sukie for cover when her mother was fresh into the ground.

Demi had reached out and laid his large hand over her small one, resting against her thigh.

'My poor, poor girl,' was all he had said. 'I wish I had known you then. You must have been hurting so bad.'

Miles had moved across to the glass doors of the building and was peering through the frosting,

'I think that's the cars coming now,' he announced. He gave Nicky a loaded look, before glancing then towards the lift and the stairs, the unspoken question loud and obvious: where is Harriet? Nicky moved across and pressed the lift call button, presumably to go upstairs and wrench her missing Maid of Honour kicking and screaming from her room. Once again, it could be five years ago, with Harriet loitering around upstairs, too scared to be seen.

Even as Sukie was thinking this, Harriet appeared, slipping like a ghost from the stairwell, for some reason having chosen to teeter down seven flights of stairs in her heels than take the lift. Nicky moved across to her swiftly, locking one of her arms around her shoulders, placing her hand on the opposite arm, moving her squarely into the brightness of the lobby, murmuring to her the whole while, like she was a wild animal who needed to be coaxed and cajoled.

But Harriet didn't look wild, or terrified. She looked around, alert, taking each face in. She kept a pleasant smile pinned to her face, nodding politely at each person who made eye contact with her. Her hair was grown out, but she had it twisted up and held at the back of her head with a clip, so from face-on she really didn't look all that different from before. She was the only one of them who wasn't wearing the past half a decade like a bad outfit.

Johnny was the first to move to greet her, kissing her stiffly on one cheek. His girlfriend was much more familiar; Nicky had to move her arm to let the girl hug Harriet. Sukie watched Leigha from the corner of her eye; she had no love for Harriet Shaw, not anymore, but she had no desire to create unnecessary tension for Nicky and Miles. Leigha had always been the wronged party, so she would take her cue from her.

Leigha tilted her chin almost imperceptivity as she surveyed Harriet, considering her closely until Harriet broke away from conversation with Johnny and his girlfriend and stared straight back at her. It was like a dance; as Harriet swung to face her, Leigha pivoted towards Miles at the door, away from Harriet's eye contact, her hair bouncing over her shoulder as she did.

'So who's going in which car?' she asked, loudly.

Adam had surprised her with his quick mental maths again. 'Let's us lot grab the six-seater one,' he'd said, from where he'd moved across to the reception doors. 'Ladies?' He'd held the door open as Nicky and Iona had ushered her through and into the larger of the waiting taxis.

She sat there, staring at Adam's chino-clad legs. Last in, he and Johnny had been subject to the small fold-down seats facing the three girls on the back seat. Miles sat up front with the driver, offering directions unnecessarily. Nicky and Iona made cheerful small talk. She wished she knew if Adam was thinking about her – looking at her, even – but his knees gave up no secrets.

Johnny guffawed as the taxi pulled into a lay-by, only a few minutes from the campus gates. 'Mauritzo's?' he laughed. 'Bloody hell, Nic, we could have walked this.'

'We're grown-ups now,' Miles grinned over his shoulder from the front passenger seat. 'No short cuts through private land for us anymore.'

'Or graveyards,' Adam grinned back.

'You guys used to walk through graveyards?' Iona asked, horrified.

'It cut at least ten minutes off the walk to Tesco,' Harriet tried to reason.

'I am so glad I go to Uni in the city,' Iona said, shaking her head. 'A Tesco Metro on every second corner.'

'And a Sainsbury's Local on all the others,' Adam joked.

Through the rear window Harriet watched the other taxi glide to a stop behind them; she noticed that Johnny was watching too. She'd made a stubborn point about never asking Nicky and Miles what had happened between Johnny and Leigha. She was regretting that now.

Iona was a dear thing, whether by nature or put up to it by Annie; she caught Harriet by the arm as she got out of the car.

'Are you okay?' she asked, sotto voce. 'You can sit next to me.'

Harriet had to laugh; it was a harsh, bark of a noise. Adam turned around at the sound and raised an eyebrow quizzically. Leigha exited the second car, smoothing down non-existent wrinkles on the skirt of her dress as she did so.

'Mauritzo's,' Harriet heard her say to her date. 'Can't believe this place is still running. Mind you, it's the only good place around here.'

'Hey, you're saying Perfect Pizza doesn't serve good food?' Sukie laughed, showing her white little teeth. Their plus ones exchanged a companionable smile; they were the outsiders after all – people with absolutely no feedback to offer about the quality of food in this town – and outsiders had to stick together.

Leigha's companion had a touch of the golden-boy about him, blond and thick-necked.. Sukie's guy was metal of a different kind, all bronze skin and hair, eyes dark and watchful. He met her gaze and smiled at her. Harriet dropped her eyes, embarrassed to be caught out. He must know that he was the big question mark of the weekend.

'She's never mentioned a boyfriend,' Nicky had told those in her taxi with a light frown, 'but they seem really close, like they've been together for ages, don't they? Su isn't like that with people she doesn't know really well, is she?' Harriet had bitten her tongue, refraining from pointing out that – as far as they were all concerned – Sukie could have had a total personality transplant in recent years. She could be that sort of person, now.

The group of ten filed docilely into the restaurant. Harriet looked around at the décor as she entered, wondering if the old place had been refurbished at all, only to find that – perhaps she had since been to too many restaurants – she couldn't quite remember how it used to look.

Showing good restaurant manners, Johnny moved all the way up along the long table, seating himself in the left corner. Nicky and Miles followed suit on the other side. Harriet settled herself down next to Iona, placing her over-large handbag under the table, trying to ensure it wouldn't be a tripping hazard for any unfortunate waiters. When she looked up, it was to make eye contact with Adam, who had moved to sit next to Nicky. On the other side of him, Leigha was slipping into her seat.

Sukie paused at the end of the table for a heartbeat; Harriet felt a hot stab of embarrassment. Was she going to refuse to sit down next to her? Were they going to have to pull over an eleventh chair, sit Sukie at the head of the table and leave the spot next to her awkwardly empty? At least, Harriet thought ruefully, it would be a convenient spot for my handbag.

With a gentle hand to Sukie's back, the bronze stranger side-stepped her and pulled out the chair next to Harriet, turning a smile to her as he sat in it.

'Demetrios,' he announced, offering a hand. Harriet shook it gingerly.

'Harriet,' she murmured. Silently, Sukie slid into the remaining corner chair. Demetrios' smile grew wider.

'Oh, I know.'

Chapter Twenty Four

She was pretty much sitting the entire length of the table away from him. Aside from the right-hand corner – where her meat of a date had placed himself – you couldn't get further away. Was it by accident or by design, Johnny wondered, before getting angry with himself for even wondering. He ordered a pint of Peroni as an aperitif to the bottles of wine already ordered for the table; beer before wine, you feel fine and all that.

Iona was holding court, entertaining the upper half of the table with the tale of how she and Johnny had met. She kept looking askance at him, as if for approval, or maybe wanting him to join in with the storytelling.

Leigha – although technically sat on the lower half of the long table – had turned her head from the conversation that end and was watching Iona as she talked, her head even tilted a little as she listened. Somehow she made such a little thing – such a tiny motion – condescending; Johnny remembered that Iona was only nineteen, and at a table full of strangers, and he felt a warm rush of affection for her.

The waiter had returned with the tall, slender glass of Peroni, placing it down in front of Johnny.

'And a glass of vodka orange, please mate, thanks,' Johnny said, remembering – just in time – that Iona didn't drink wine, and realising that she might have been too embarrassed to draw attention to the fact. Her little fingers found his hand under the table and squeezed gratefully.

'So,' Demi said, inclining his head closer to hers so he could speak quietly and not interrupt Iona's anecdote. 'Do you have big plans to make trouble this weekend? Any best friend you're going to screw over – or just plain screw?'

Harriet pulled back, her heart thumping against the affront. Demi was still smiling normally; he was teasing. 'I just want to know,' he continued, 'so I can get a good seat for any fireworks.' He took a drink from his glass of dark red wine to punctuate the image.

'Look,' Harriet began, uncertainly. 'I don't know what you've heard…'

'Sukie's version, naturally,' Demi interjected. 'And I'm sure by the end of the weekend I'll have heard everyone else's version too. So why don't we just start with yours?'

Harriet reached for her own wine glass but didn't drink from it, just held it, its weight a comfort in her hand. From across the table, she could see Adam and Leigha through the curve of the glass, refracted small and disproportionate.

Finally she took a resolute sip. 'I'm sorry.' She turned to Demi, smiling pleasantly. 'It's not in my nature to talk about people behind their backs.'

Demi studied her carefully. 'Well, they certainly talk about you. You should have heard the bitchfest in that taxi…' He let his voice trail off.

Harriet took another sip of wine, swallowing cold down on top of the cold that was already inside her. She steeled her facial expression.

'All the same,' she said, shrugging.

Demi smiled at her again, and Harriet realised that all the smiles before had been somewhat less than this one.

'Harriet Shaw.' He drew out her name in a tone almost of wonder, like it was the label of some mythical figure. He subtly inclined the lip of his wine glass towards her, a toast. 'I'd really hoped that I would like you,' he said.

'So, how's everything?'

She had waited until the waiter had taken their food orders and moved off down the table. Adam turned to her, his face impassive. His eyes were the colour of his shirt, of her dress; Leigha felt an agreeable skipping down the length of her spine. He still packed a punch; he made her feel inexact and alive, not unlike the way half a bottle of vodka tended to do.

'Everything's fine,' he replied, carefully, without orientating his body nearer to her, keeping his alliance firmly to the top half of the table. 'How about you?'

'Things are really good,' Leigha gushed. 'Going really great at work. I made it to Account Executive level a couple of months ago.'

'Oh, great. Congratulations,' Adam said, sounding a little bemused.

'Roddy McCorley.' Leigha's view was temporarily blocked by Roddy's arm, shooting across her in greeting. 'Good to meet you.' Perhaps she should have already done this introduction. Adam shook hands awkwardly across Leigha's torso.

'Adam. Good to meet you.'

'It's good to meet all you fine people,' Roddy beamed across the table. 'Nice to meet some of Leigha's friends. Anyone up for some Moët?' Leigha pressed her finger tips into her temple, trying to show the group that she was distancing herself from her date's booming bonhomie. 'It's a celebration!' Roddy continued merrily.

Leigha looked up; the only person who was watching her little display was Harriet. The two made eye contact for the first time in years. Leigha tried to hold it – her first instinct was to stare Harriet down – but the hot–cold flashing of familiarity warring against distaste made her flinch away. Roddy obviously thought she was turning her body companionably into his; he beamed at her.

Miles made a joke, something inconsequential about how funny it was that they were all drinking wine. Johnny recollected that the grocery shop on campus used to sell bottles of dry white for £2.99 – it would have been cheaper to get plastered on that than the beer and spirits they'd drank instead, even when it was late in the term and they'd needed to pool together and buy supermarket value vodka at a fiver a bottle. The memory made Leigha shudder.

A bottle of chilled Moët had been speedily fetched from behind the restaurant's bar. Roddy popped it expertly, pressing a glass flute close to the neck of the bottle to catch the gush of fizz that spilled forth. He handed this first glass to Leigha. He knew that it was a quirk of hers, preferring the first glass of a bottle of champagne; it was made up bubbles and sharpness, a little bit like herself.

Leigha took a large mouthful of champagne, as if to wash out the lingering taste of the paint-stripper vodka from years ago.

The combination of champagne and nostalgia had made everyone silly and just a little over-loud. Leigha had pointed out that Nicky's drunk snigger had remained unchanged, with which the rest of the party affectionately agreed. Adam had regaled the horrified plus ones with the story of when Johnny had lost a dare and run naked up and down the length of the high street, covered in brown sauce, enthusiastically slapping his own arse cheeks. Nicky had dusted off the Miles, tequila and the Black Eyed Peas classic. By the end of the meal, the atmosphere felt a little less fake.

When the dessert plates were being ferried away and Miles had pulled out his mobile phone to call for taxis, he'd been shouted down, even by Iona; everyone wanted to walk it. The alumnae in particular were enjoying the softness of familiarity and good memories, and wanted to eke it out, just a little longer.

The party bundled into light-wear coats and jackets and moved off into the night. A cheerfully drunk Johnny immediately launched into an impression of his brown-sauce-bum-slapping dash down this very road. A groaning Leigha supported herself on Sukie's shoulder as she removed her heels, flexing her white feet against the grey of the pavement.

'Oh, I've done it a thousand times,' she said, impatiently brushing off Roddy's protests at her intent to walk barefoot.

'So,' Demi said conversationally to Adam. 'Are you going to be wearing a yellow tie to match the ladies?' The rather unusual colour of the bridesmaids' dresses had been a point of discussion at the dinner table; Nicky had only smiled. Harriet had wondered if she was the only person who remembered that their house had had yellow walls; the connection seemed obvious to her.

'Er, not to my knowledge!' Adam replied. 'Unless Miles has one hidden away in his luggage and is planning to spring it on me last minute.'

'Be afraid!' Harriet said, in a melodramatic voice. Adam laughed. They looked at one another across the plane of Demi's chest, the naturalness of that little interchange having caught them by surprise.

It shouldn't be easy, Harriet told herself, but then again, it always had been, with Adam. Every feeling had always come too easy, maybe that was what had been wrong. In the end, the distrust and loathing had come too easily, too. Besides, weren't you meant to work at friendship sometimes? At falling in love?

'I can't imagine,' Adam said, interrupting her chain of thought, 'that yellow looks great on any of you girls.'

'Well, it doesn't look good on me, I can tell you,' Harriet agreed with him ruefully. Demi turned his head; Sukie, bringing up the rear with a barefoot Leigha, was calling his name. He dropped back. 'First thing I did when I got here, try on that dreaded dress,' Harriet continued.

'First thing after our corridor chat,' Adam corrected her, with a wry smile.

'Yes, our... chat,' Harriet agreed, the tone of her voice indicating that there should perhaps be quotation marks around the word chat. A giggle rose up in her throat like the bubbles in the neck of the champagne bottle. Adam smirked.

'Bloody typical,' he said, with feeling.

'What, seeing one another in the corridor?'

'Yes, it just... couldn't have been easy, could it?' Adam said, awkwardly. Harriet thought again about just how easy things could be.

'I never thought I'd be here again,' Harriet said, quietly, the unexpected geniality of the night thus far and the alcohol making her tongue loose. Adam quirked an eyebrow at her.

'Literally, or figuratively?' he asked.

'Both,' Harriet laughed.

'You didn't think Miles and Nicky would get married?' Adam teased.

'Oh, I knew they probably would,' Harriet protested, 'and I knew we'd all be together again. All of us. But, holding it on campus... it packs quite an emotional punch.'

'Do you miss it?' Adam asked, suddenly. 'Here.'

'Not everything about it,' Harriet answered, honestly. Adam looked at her impatiently.

'I don't mean the bad stuff. Just think about the good stuff,' he told her. Harriet shook her head.

'It's all the same thing,' she told him. 'It's all tangled up in my head.'

'One bad memory, cancelling out all the good? Years of good?' Adam pressed, his tone disbelieving.

'Well, you see, I might remember my 20th birthday party,' Harriet said. 'When we took the bus into town and somehow got in to a 21s-and-over bar. We drank about a hundred cocktails on 2-for-1. They were called Jelly Baby, and Leigha and I vomited all purple on the walk home from the bus stop.' Harriet nodded at the bus stop in question, which they had come in sight of. Adam snorted at the image.

'The next day we were all completely sick as dogs, nobody could even bear to run to the corner shop, but we were craving bacon sandwiches and we didn't have any bread in the house,' Harriet continued. 'So Nicky lit on the bright idea of heating up this old packet of tortillas that we had in the cupboard. She balanced one on the toaster, and then nothing happened, and we were all looking at it, and suddenly we realised, the toaster was melting underneath it.'

Harriet broke off to smile, remembering the panicked shrieks, how only Sukie had had the consideration to stop Leigha throwing her glass of water over the active toaster and instead unplugged it and threw it out the window into the garden, where it had remained for most of the summer. Had someone thrown it away by the time of their third year start of term house party, where they'd first met Adam and Johnny? She couldn't quite recall.

'See? That's a funny story and a good memory,' Adam said, nudging her upper arm with his own.

'Yes, but now when I think about it, my brain just goes, I wonder if they hated me then.'

They lapsed into silence; Adam chewed his lip as he digested what she'd just said. 'And that's how it is with me? With all the good memories I gave you?' he asked, after a moment. Harriet gave him a pained expression.

'Don't start that, please. I thought we were going to be friends this weekend?'

'I've kissed you, here,' Adam said, gesturing at the pavement corner they were approaching. 'Any particular loathing for this corner?' Harriet laughed.

'Okay, alright. I've nothing against this corner,' she conceded. 'It's a good corner.'

'Damn straight,' Adam agreed.

'Ohhh.' Harriet tilted her head back and looked up at the bright, suburban stars. From somewhere behind her Leigha gave a drunken shriek of laughter. 'There's nothing quite like old friends.'

'Nothing quite like 'em,' Adam echoed in agreement. 'They know where all the bodies are buried.'

'Looking back, I just can't believe the sheer amount of time we *spent together*,' Harriet said. 'I mean, us as a whole, as a group,' she hurriedly clarified. 'I won't be able to spend that amount of time with anyone ever again.'

'What about when you live with a guy, get married?' Adam disputed. Harriet shook her head.

'No, because of things like, having to go to work,' she argued. 'Leigha, Sukie and I did everything together. For years. Nobody will ever know me as well as they did. It's just a sad fact. It all comes down to maths, and the dwindling volume of one's free time.' Her voice trailed off, sadly. If the people who knew you best of all ended up hating you, she thought, it was probably best to ensure that others never get to know you quite so well anyway.

She glanced up at Adam. His expression was so stung that for a moment she wondered if she'd just spoken that last thought aloud.

The campus gates were looming into view, the clock tower on the old building showing – somewhat appropriately – that the day was almost all ticked away. Here was the sense of an ending that Harriet had grasped for but not felt as her silent father had driven her away from the house on Dell Road.

'Do you know?' Harriet murmured to Adam as the archway of the front entry to campus threw a band of shadow across them, suddenly eager to get this out before it was too late. 'You were probably the best friend, the one who tried hardest to stick by me, prop me up. I really am sorry about, about your birthday, and everything. You deserved better than me doing that. I wish sometimes...' She paused to collect her thoughts. Adam's eyes bored into her, even in the darkness of midnight, unnerving her, clamming her thoughts up unspoken inside her throat.

'You wish?' he pressed, in an odd voice, after her silence had dragged on too long.

'I wish that maybe we'd just stayed as friends,' she said finally. Adam's gaze grew more intense.

'So that you would have been able to keep friends with everyone?' he asked, voice strange, and her stomach pranged in guilt that – despite all her best efforts – she was obviously hurting him again.

'So that I could have kept you,' she said, simply. 'Hindsight, huh?'

Adam didn't answer. The crunching of their shoes in the gravel of the car park they were cutting through was clumsy and over-loud. The pause grew uncomfortable, and Harriet considered making a joke, but Adam's muteness was too overbearing. They walked the rest of the way to their rooms in silence, listening to the rhythm of the conversations going on ahead and behind.

It was now – literally – only hours to go until the wedding, but still Adam couldn't sleep. Harriet's words scratched at him like the cheap linen of the hotel bed. The years had stripped away all the bluster and the immediate sharpness of pain and Harriet had, in one short conversation – probably even without meaning to – made him remember that underneath the foundations of his own pain, his own hurt, there had first been hers, and how desperately sorry he had once been for her.

He toyed with his iPhone, restlessly turning it over and over in his hand. He remembered long ago nights where he would lie awake like this, his head too full of Harriet to allow him any rest. He remembered that he used to text her at silly hours, toyed with the idea of knocking on her bedroom door, felt a little relieved that he didn't have her mobile number anymore.

She had always been so easy to talk to. He wanted to talk to her now. He wanted to ask her why she'd always been so funny about Leigha, even before Leigha had told her that they had slept together. Leigha had always been a giant self-destruct button, but he wasn't sure if it was Harriet or himself who had pushed her.

But tomorrow was not the venue for such an ugly conversation. Tomorrow, Adam would stand side-by-side with Harriet in countless photographs, smile through the Best Man and Maid of Honour dance, quite literally walk down the aisle with her; after tomorrow, he would never see her again. Over and over his phone went in his hand.

Chapter Twenty Five

'I think Nicky is racist,' Sukie said, in a tone of all seriousness, squinting at her reflection. Leigha's brows knit together in concern and she hurriedly plucked hairpins from between her teeth in order to answer.

'Why the hell do you say that?'

'Yellow? On a Japanese girl?'

'Oh, for crying out loud, behave.' Leigha stuck the pins back in her mouth and returned her attention to crafting her elegant up-do.

There was the most tentative of tentative knocks on the door. Leigha and Sukie exchanged glances in the mirror.

'It's open,' Leigha called, her words distorted around the hairpins.

As anticipated, it was Harriet. She held the neckline of her dress bunched in one hand, holding it close to her collarbones; it flapped loose at the back like a pair of stunted yellow wings.

'Hi,' she said, in an overly cheerful voice. 'I need some help, this bow thing...' Her voice trailed off, but Leigha knew what she meant.

'Yeah, you can't do it yourself,' Sukie agreed, still facing towards the mirror. Leigha removed the hairpins from her mouth again, hoping her hair was secure enough for the moment.

'Spin round,' she ordered Harriet, who dutifully obeyed. Leigha turned her fingers to the intricate corsetry bow that fastened the back of the bridesmaid dress, aware of how cold her hands were against the warmth of Harriet's back. 'There,' she said, stepping back as she finished.

'Thanks,' Harriet said, still with that fake little tone of breathless cheer. She started to back out of the room.

'Wait,' Leigha commanded. 'Nicky has told us that we need to have matching hair.'

'Matching hair?' Harriet echoed.

'Yes, matching hair.' Leigha studied her. 'Lucky thing you decided to grow your hair long really, isn't it.'

'Er, I guess,' Harriet said slowly. 'How is it I have to have my hair?'

'Half up, half down and tonged,' Leigha said edgily, gesturing at her own not-quite-finished do.

'You can use these tongs, I'm finished with them,' Sukie said, pushing the hair appliance across the vanity table without looking up.

'Thanks.' Harriet moved nearer to them and tested their heat with a light touch of her palm.

'Pin it up first, then tong the rest,' Leigha said, impatiently. Harriet's reflection eyeballed her.

'Thanks, I know.'

'Well, you may not have,' Leigha said, patting the back of her tightly pinned hair self-consciously. 'Not used to long hair and all that.'

'I've had long hair for about three or four years now,' Harriet informed her obnoxiously. Leigha just jammed another grip into her hair and didn't respond. She watched the backs of Harriet and Sukie as they shared the space in front of the mirror.

'Demi seems really nice,' Harriet offered, almost timidly, after a moment's uncomfortable silence. Sukie met her eyes, surprised.

'Yes, he is,' she agreed, with a little happy smile. Leigha stood, locked between their profiles as the old friends smiled shyly at one another.

'Yes, well,' she jeered, leaning between them to grab hairpins that she didn't need from the packet on the vanity table. 'Don't be getting any ideas now, Harriet. Although I presume you don't still sleep with other people's boyfriends?'

The malice in her own tone exasperated her; she'd have much rather come off sounding cool and unconcerned. Harriet blinked, her jaw hanging slack and stupid, obviously wondering what to say. For a second, just a brief moment, her eyes flickered to Sukie, on some old instinct that expected comfort and defence from that corner. Sukie's eye contact slid away; she focused again on applying glue along the spine of one of her fake eyelashes.

Harriet's eyes dropped and she busied her hands with hairpins; the room lapsed into silence, only broken by the hissing burst of hairspray as Leigha coated her hair with it.

Leigha had come into this weekend with every intention of being polite and civil. She'd decided to treat Harriet as if she were a stranger, some friend of Nicky's that she'd never met before, out of deference to it being Nicky's special day, and not wanting to rock any boats. But seeing Harriet – being near her – it filled her with a lava of anger and humiliation. Even now, still, she had Adam fawning all over her, walking practically arm-in-arm with her back from the restaurant, Sukie's boyfriend gossiping and laughing with her all through dinner, Johnny's girlfriend hanging on her every word.

Nicky had told her, last night, that Harriet's best friend was Iona's elder sister – completely by chance, apparently. God, that girl pervades absolutely everything, Leigha thought bitterly. In the end, everything comes back to her; especially the things that should come back to me.

The idea of Harriet even having a 'best friend' had struck Leigha as queer. She tried to picture Harriet and this faceless woman, trading chat in the steam that rose off mugs of tea; walking places with their arms hooked together, close enough to each have one earphone from the same iPod; sharing the one single bed on nights where things were hard and heartbreaking, all four legs in a tangle. The images wouldn't stick; they harder she tried to focus on them, the faster they slipped away.

Harriet had already pinned half of her hair up effortlessly and had reached for the tongs again. If she was at all distressed by the cruelty of Leigha's comment, or the oppressive silence that had followed it, her hands were steady and didn't betray her.

'How much time do we have?' Sukie asked. Leigha tapped at a button on her Blackberry to wake the screen.

'Forty-five minutes,' she answered.

'Where the hell is Nicky?' Sukie huffed. 'Seriously, Miles is not the sort of guy that would take kindly to being kept waiting at the altar if she's not ready in time. I think he'll melt into a puddle or something in panic.'

'I knocked for her, before I knocked here,' Harriet admitted. 'She's either not in her room, or she wasn't answering.'

'Maybe she's stuck in the dress,' Leigha snorted. 'By all accounts it is a bit of a meringue.' She trailed off guilty as there was another knock on the door.

'Come in!' called Sukie, padding her fingertips onto a baby wipe to remove any excess eyelash glue.

The rumours of the meringue proved to be true; Nicky entered the room sideways, like a crab. The three bridesmaids fell into a loyal and appropriately awed silence. Leigha was the first to break it.

'Nic, you look… stunning,' she told her. And she did; it wasn't particularly a dress to Leigha's taste, but on tall, well-boned Nicky it had an air of Disney Princess. A creamy off-white colour with a sweetheart neckline and little cap-sleeves, it was classic and beautiful, which was how Nicky looked in it.

Nicky's hair was still unstyled, hanging limp and loose over her shoulders and collarbones. In her hands she fiddled with the little clip-on veil that was to be fastened last at the back of her head. The pale colour of the dress was blanching her skin tone even more than usual; she'd always been a girl who needed liberal amounts of bronzer. Sukie reached across for Nicky's fingers and squeezed them.

'Come on, let's finish you up, gorgeous,' she said. 'Ley, you're on makeup. Harry, you pin, I'll tong.' Harriet obediently snatched up a handful of paler coloured hairpins and the three bridesmaids set to work on their bride.

Miles' head whipped up at the sound of a knock at the door. For one strange, terrible second he thought that it was Nicky, come to call the whole thing off; but that wouldn't, that couldn't be. He cleared his throat.

'Come in!' he called. From where he stood, across the room, fumbling with his cufflinks, Adam watched him apprehensively. Did he look that edgy? He couldn't, because – of course – he wasn't nervous in the slightest. Johnny appeared in the frame of the door, looking as casual as a tuxedo allows, holding in one hand one of the squat tumblers from the rooms' bathrooms and in the other, a bottle of Disaronno.

'Here comes the groom,' Johnny sang, tunelessly, to the familiar rhythm of the 'Wedding March'. 'Here, have some booze!' He plonked the glass down unceremoniously on the bedside table and began grappling with the awkwardly square lid to the bottle of liqueur as he hummed the remainder of the song.

'It's eleven thirty in the morning,' Adam laughed. Undeterred, Johnny poured a generous stream of the dark golden liquid into the tumbler.

'It's his wedding day,' he argued, thrusting the glass towards Miles. 'And he didn't even get a Stag Night.' Adam acquiesced with a shrug and Miles gingerly took the drink, sipping its sweetness down on top of the creeping unease he knew he really shouldn't be feeling.

Nicky hadn't said anything, or changed, not as such, but she was being brittle where before she was undemanding, looked at him more often with something like impatience in her eyes. He couldn't articulate it – and wouldn't, not to anyone – but she just wasn't as happy and glowing as a bride should be. Maybe he shouldn't have been such a stickler for the campus chapel, he thought. Maybe they should have had a longer engagement. But, then again, the fact that the wedding was being held on their old campus was the one thing that Nicky seemed genuinely pleased with.

He'd just broken up with his girlfriend when he first met Nicky. It had been the first term of his final undergraduate year. Said girlfriend was a sweet, dark-haired Biomed student, also in her third year, quick and clever. They'd had a great summer term and break together, but the October nights were drawing in earlier and earlier; the library was calling and he had grown bored and annoyed with having to fit her in.

He'd given her the spiel about them having to focus on their work now, not having the time to spend with one another, and she hadn't fought the point, not really, not like he'd egotistically thought that she would. So although the breakup had been his idea, that night Miles had found himself in the Armstrong, alone, nursing a dinner consisting of a limp Panini and sweaty-tasting pint of cheap cider.

But shrieks of laughter coming from a group of girls a few metres away had quite ruined his solitary funk. Miles had glared over at them sullenly whilst he lifted his glass to his lips.

They'd been playing pool; 'playing' being the operative word. They were whacking indiscriminately at the balls with the blunt edge of the cue stick, apparently seeing how many times they could make them bounce off the sides before they rolled to a rest. One of the girls had noticed him glaring and the humour immediately slid from her face. She'd given him a scowl that had made his glare look like a smile; Miles had hurriedly returned his attention to his pathetic dinner.

A haze of green had appeared in his peripheral vision; she'd been wearing dark jeans and a green jumper that night, he'd never forget. The blonde girl from the noisy group at the pool table had been standing there in front of him, her face flushed, holding one of the pool cues hooked in her arm like a warrior with a spear.

'Do you want to play?' she'd asked.

'What?' Miles had replied, stupidly, a little rudely. The girl had just laughed.

'Do you want to play? Or you can teach us how you're actually meant to play, if you want, if that will make you any happier.' She'd tilted her head slightly to the side and surveyed him. 'You look miserable as anything.'

And although he'd gone out that night precisely to be miserable and alone, and although it rather went against his instincts, Miles had allowed himself to be led by the blonde girl across to her waiting friends.

'There's a toll for this,' one of the brunettes had told him, eyes sparking with mischief. 'You've got to get a round in.'

'Mine's a Kopparberg,' the other brunette had informed him.

'Vodka and anything,' from the girl who had given him the death glare.

'I'll come to the bar with you and help you carry,' said the blonde girl, before Miles had had time to say anything. She'd still been holding his arm from when she'd fetched him from the table.

269

Relinquishing the pool cue over to one of her friends, she'd pulled him over to the Friday-night busy queue for the bar.

She'd pulled back her hair to air her neck, just for one second, fanning her flushed cheeks by flapping her other hand. She'd smiled at him and pulled a face at how hot and stuffy the bar was. Miles had thought she was beautiful, the most beautiful girl he'd ever seen, and if you'd told him, in that minute, that he'd be in this beautiful creature's bed that night, or that in seven years' time he'd be waiting for her at the top of the aisle, he could never have believed you.

Lost to that night seven and a half years' ago, Miles had slipped away from the conversation of his two groomsmen. Adam deftly plucked the tumbler from his limp grasp and – despite this earlier protestations – drank down a good measure himself before passing it back to Johnny who, without the need for instruction, replenished it.

'Twenty minutes,' Adam noted, adjusting his cummerbund nervously. 'We'd better get moving soon.'

'We'd better re-brush our teeth,' Johnny noted wryly, having just finished his own generous swig of the Disaronno.

'This feels naughty,' Leigha giggled, 'the four of us, like, hiding in a church.'

'I wish I'd brought a hip flask,' Sukie agreed.

Harriet exchanged a look with Nicky, that old, familiar 'what are they like?' expression. Harriet was holding up well, Nicky thought, considering that the giant elephant in the room must be slowly squashing her to death. Nicky knew she herself was not holding up quite so well. She had to intentionally will her hands quiet and steady, resting them on the slope of her dress.

The skin of her cheek felt dry and itchy where her stately and over-perfumed mother had just kissed it before slipping away to her spot on the front pew. Her father was so long-dead she didn't even know him to miss him, but the prospect of walking down the aisle alone – whilst originally her choice – was suddenly terrifying her.

Through the door she could hear the rest of her wedding guests filing into the old Victorian chapel, pictured them smiling excitedly, finding their seats, repositioning hats and fascinators and squaring off ties, leafing through the Order of Service with civil interest.

Leigha and Sukie were sharing the space in front of an age-spotted mirror, smoothing away invisible imperfections with their hair and makeup. Nicky focused on her hands again, her pale white hands on her soft white dress and the darkness of the parquet floor beyond.

'Can I ask you something?' she said, such an innocuous question. The three pairs of eyes swivelled to her expectantly. 'Do you guys… like Miles?'

There was a moment of bemused silence as her question sunk in, before the protests started, each girl talking over the two others.

'What a stupid question,' Sukie scoffed.

'Miles is great!' insisted Harriet.

'Of course we do! Why are you asking this?' said Leigha, with a shrewd look. 'You're not getting cold feet are you?' Leigha's eyes widened as Nicky hefted her shoulders in a miserable shrug. Sukie laughed mirthlessly.

'I'll go back up to the room and get Demi's car keys,' she said, rolling her eyes. 'And we'll make a dash for the borders, eh? Or maybe we can get you a horse Nic? Julia Roberts in *Runaway Bride* style.' Leigha shot her an impatient look. 'What?' Sukie said, defensively. 'Go big or go home, right? Anyway, it's only a joke…' Sukie's protestations faded away at the sight of Nicky's expression. 'You are joking, aren't you Nic?'

'I've just been thinking…' Nicky managed, her voice reedy.

'Bit bloody late for that!' Sukie frowned. A silent Harriet put all her fingers to her lips, her eyes full of concern.

'Maybe I… maybe I shouldn't have gone away, with Miles, after graduation,' Nicky continued, still staring down at her white dress. In her peripherals though, she caught all three girls exchanging worried looks. 'Maybe I should have gone to France.'

'Yeah, Nic, maybe,' Leigha said, carefully. 'But you did. You did move away with him.'

'Come on, what's this really about?' asked Sukie.

'Do you not love him?' questioned Harriet.

The starkness of the question pulled Nicky up short. Of course she did, of course she did. 'Of course I do,' she said aloud. 'It's just… I've been thinking,' she repeated. Again, those askance looks between the other girls.

'So you said,' said Harriet, warily. 'But Nic, that Wedding March is going to start in about five minutes, so you'd better think fast.'

'Do you need me to go stall? Talk to Miles?' offered Leigha.

'Do you need me to get working getting on that horse?' asked Sukie, unhelpfully.

'Where has this come from, in all seriousness?' pressed Harriet.

'It's just…' Nicky began, frustrated at how tongue-tied she was. 'I can't help but realise, especially lately, that… Miles met this girl, right? This nineteen year old, who had dreams and friends and went out and had fun and had interesting things to talk about.' Now the dam was broached, the words were falling out of her in a nonsensical rush. 'And now he's about to marry me, this twenty-six year old, who hates where she lives, hates her job. I have no friends, I never go anywhere, never get to do anything. I'm nothing like the girl he met.'

'Oh, Nicky, you have friends,' Sukie protested, shocked into uncharacteristic gentleness by Nicky's words. Nicky uttered a little scoff of disbelief.

'I haven't seen you two for years. I'm lucky if I get a Happy Birthday on Facebook, or a forwarded email joke.' She looked searchingly at Leigha and Sukie as she spoke. Her words were plain but without malice. 'And I see you, Harry, what, once a year?' Harriet opened her mouth in protest but Nicky kept talking. 'And I know, it's my fault. I moved away and I made my whole life about Miles and I never made an effort to see you guys. And now, now I have no life *but* Miles. And it's just that I've been thinking…' Nicky's voice had dropped to a murmur, 'that that's not a very good reason to be marrying someone. Because they're all you have, I mean.'

The room lapsed into silence, the noise from the chapel beyond the door swelling to fill it. Wordlessly, Leigha lifted one of Nicky's cold hands and held it between her own. 'Oh, Nic,' was all she said.

'Who wants to get married so young these days anyway?' Nicky continued, blustering now, the embarrassment at being so honest starting to ache.

'I want to,' said Sukie, simply, surprising them all. 'I'd love to have what you have, Nicky, what you've had for years. You are so lucky.'

'You two have been loved up for so long,' Leigha agreed.

'Real, grown-up love, from the very beginning,' Harriet said. 'And you may hate your job and you may hate your flat, but you can't tell me that you hate Miles.'

'No,' Nicky agreed, squeezing her eyelids tight; she refused to get weepy and send her mascara smearing; what a cliché. 'I love him.'

'It's not his fault that you've made your life so small, Nic hun,' Leigha said gently. 'Have you ever even talked to him about how you feel?'

'No,' Nicky admitted. 'I didn't… I don't want to upset him.'

'Now his PhD is over, can you guys come back to London? Can you maybe look into a teacher training course?' Sukie asked.

'I guess I always thought we'd discuss these things, you know, once his PhD was over,' Nicky said. 'But since he handed his thesis in, he's not really said a word.'

'Aside from to ask you to marry him,' Sukie pointed out, bringing a small smile to Nicky's face.

'Apart from that,' she conceded. 'He's just really happy where he is. I just… don't want it to be 2007 all over again, where I'm worried I'm going to lose him because we don't want the same things.'

'Maybe he's only happy up in Bath because he thinks you're happy,' Harriet reasoned. 'You really need to talk to him.'

'You really should have talked to him before,' Sukie pointed out. 'You see this? And this?' She gestured to Nicky's wedding dress and at the door to the chapel beyond. 'This is D-Day, Nic.'

'Nicky, you are so lucky to have Miles,' Leigha reiterated Sukie's earlier words. 'Out of all the millions of people in this country, the millions and millions of people in the world, and you find someone you can love, and he loves you too? That's like magic at work. And you've already come through so much, the two of you. I wouldn't be your friend – we, wouldn't be your friends – if we let you be silly now.'

'But, equally,' Harriet said, 'we're happy to smuggle you out the back door and deal with the aftermath for you. If that's what you really want.'

'If that's what you really want,' Sukie echoed.

The noise in the chapel reached a different pitch, the air was charged with a new expectancy; Miles and his groomsmen must have taken their place at the altar. Harriet reached for Nicky's free hand, Leigha kept hold of the other.

'Listen,' Sukie said, with urgency. 'I know I'm no loss to the world of public speaking and I know I'm not being much help. It's not that I'm particularly mad for Miles myself, I mean, I certainly wouldn't marry him. No offence.' Nicky managed a weak smile.

'Well I haven't married him. Not yet.'

'But I really don't see that you can blame him for your being unhappy,' Sukie continued. Leigha nodded in agreement.

'You're just stuck in a rut,' she said. Nicky laughed.

'In films,' she said, tone exaggeratedly critical, 'the minute the bride starts saying she's not sure, the bridesmaids all rally round, tell her they've always thought the groom is a prick, and that she's doing the right thing to call it off.'

The three bridesmaids looked at one another uncertainly.

'Well, we don't think Miles is a prick...' Leigha said. 'He's a good man. He's always been good to you. Good *for* you.'

'So we don't think calling it off is the right thing to do,' added Harriet.

'We think you're having a funny five minutes. At the worst possible time.' Sukie moved closer and put one hand where Leigha grasped Nicky's left hand and the other where Harriet was holding her right. 'Okay, you're not happy with the way your life has gone.'

'Who is, these days? Completely, anyway?' Harriet added quietly.

'But the thing is, Nic, it was all your choices that lead to this life you're living,' Sukie said, not unkindly.

'And if you're now making the choice to... you know... make different choices, better choices?' said Leigha, pulling a cross-eyed face at the inelegance of her phrasing. 'Then that's fantastic. But right now, the choice you've got to make is whether or not you want Miles in your life.'

'Because he loves you, sweetie, you're everything to him,' Harriet said. 'But you can't just leave him waiting at the altar and expect him to be okay with that. This is a big deal.'

Nicky was silent, staring down at the triangle of hands. Although she had provided the bridesmaids' dresses, the girls had been told to wear whatever shoes they wanted. Harriet wore traditional nude-coloured peep-toes, Leigha stilettos in a cartoonish, high-gloss red and Sukie in patent black wedges with a clasped bar ringing her ankle. Such disparate personalities, how had these girls ever been such close friends? It seemed so unreal, so long ago, like a story she'd once been told, rather than something she had lived, back in that house of fairy tale yellow.

Nicky's bridal shoes too seemed to speak volumes, plain white with a respectable heel, so obvious, without a shred of personality, like she wasn't really a bride at all, just done up as one for fancy dress.

'Listen,' Sukie said, impatience creeping back into her voice as time continued to slip away and Nicky still stood in a stricken silence. 'The way I see it, right, you have three options, yeah? Option number one. Just carry on. Go out there, marry Miles, and go on not telling him how you feel or not doing anything for yourself. Maintain the status quo, if you will.'

Nicky pulled a face to show exactly how unappealing option number one was.

'I thought not. Option two,' Sukie continued. 'We get you out the back door and onto any mode of transport – vehicle or equine – you desire. You don't marry Miles. You probably only ever see him again to argue about which one of you gets to keep the cat.'

'We don't have a cat,' Nicky protested feebly, but her expression was sick with horror at the finality of said second option. Sukie waved her hand dismissively.

'Whatever. You get the point. Option number three. Marry Miles and then, you know, talk to him. Job hunt. Ley will help you, she can market and sell most anything.' Leigha beamed encouragingly. 'Visit us more. We'll visit you. Make new friends, go new places, yadda, yadda, yadda. You know?' Sukie raised her hands expansively. 'Be happy and also be with Miles. They're not mutually exclusive, no matter what you're thinking at the moment.'

'You all – all three of you – independently told me that I was making a mistake moving to Bath with Miles after third year,' Nicky told them, staring at them accusingly, each in turn.

'Yes Nic, we did, but you *did* move to Bath. Not because Miles gave you an ultimatum, because – very reasonably – he was willing to go long distance…'

'That's right,' Leigha nodded.

'But because you *loved him* so goddamn much that you couldn't be apart from him,' Harriet concluded. 'So what the hell has happened there?'

The soft knock at the door sounded like rapid-fire gunshot; all four girls jumped out of their skins. The blonde events coordinator poked her inappropriately sunny face around the door.

'We all ready to go in here?' she asked, cheerily.

Nicky looked away from her, looked back down at her perfect white shoes, so stark against the darkness of the parquet tiled flooring. She pictured Miles waiting, just a short walk away, handsome and tall in his grey morning suit, Adam and Johnny standing flank with yellow carnations in their buttonholes and soft smiles on their faces.

And she realised – just in time – that although she would change almost everything about her life if she could, she wouldn't change Miles. And so there was her answer.

'Yes,' she told the woman, her voice surprisingly clear. 'One minute.' The woman nodded and slipped away, leaving the door ajar; the noise from the chapel beyond buzzed demandingly.

'Thank fuck for that,' Sukie said bluntly.

Leigha pressed her palms to her collarbones. 'You really had me worried there.'

'I'm so sorry you got like this, Nic,' Harriet said, squeezing her hand. 'You should have told me. To be fair, I should have asked,' she conceded.

'You really must talk to him sooner rather than later,' Leigha said sternly. 'Don't put it off. Or else we'll be forced to tell him, and we won't pull no punches.' Harriet and Sukie nodded in mute agreement.

'I will,' Nicky swore. Her fingers flew to her throat as the unmistakeable opening chords to the Wedding March resounded from beyond the chapel door. Harriet squeezed her hand again.

'You okay?' she asked. Nicky nodded. 'Are you sure?' Harriet pressed, and Nicky didn't know if she meant about being okay, or marrying Miles.

'Yes,' she said aloud, because it was the answer to both.

'Bugger me,' murmured Leigha, poised to be first out the door and down the aisle. She carefully gathered up her little white and yellow bouquet from its nearby vase. 'Quite nervy, this, isn't it?'

'Yeah, wish we had a hip-flask,' Sukie said, for the second time.

With a flash of a smile over her shoulder, Leigha slipped out of the door and away. With one final, searching look at Nicky, Sukie followed suit. Harriet's grasp loosened and dropped away as she completed the triad of bridesmaids moving at a stately pace down the aisle.

With one final deep breath Nicky collected her large bouquet and centred it on her torso as she stepped through the door. A hundred pairs of eyes swivelled to face her, cameras flashing, murmurs hushed. The already cacophonous music seemed to amplify, to swell, even though Nicky knew that it wasn't possible.

Leigha was just reaching the altar and was moving into position to stand opposite the front pew. Nicky focused on emulating her elegant gait; right foot, left foot, right foot, left foot, listening to the tempo of the music: *Here, comes, the bride, all, dressed, in white.*

She was about halfway when Miles suddenly turned in his place to see her, almost guiltily, as if he'd been told by someone that he wasn't allowed to look at her until she'd arrived beside him at the end of the aisle. His smile as he took her in was ten times brighter than any memory of yellow walls, any fantasy of French sunsets.

Nicky reached the altar and slipped her hand into his. The music and the talking and the camera flashes all fell away and – as she'd hoped – for that important first minute it was only them.

Chapter Twenty Six

The vows had been said; the rings exchanged; the official photographs snapped and all the hands in the wedding party line-up had been shaken. A deflated-feeling Harriet allowed herself to be taken up by the tide of people and drawn slowly into the reception hall itself. Harriet squinted to see past all the artfully placed gauze and ribbons and fairy lights; was this really the old undergrad dining hall she used to eat lukewarm baked beans in all those years ago?

At what point on the wedding day was the Maid of Honour officially 'off the clock'? Was it at the end of the formal ceremony, or at the point where the bride and groom were safely on an airplane to their honeymoon destination? She didn't know, and she felt strange and untethered as she loitered at the threshold of the dining hall, like the looseness and warmth in a muscle that had been overstretched.

The idea spooled out; would she really be missed if she ducked out now, dignity intact? – or at least, about as intact as it had been upon her arrival? She could return to her room and see out the rest of the afternoon and evening with the screw-top bottle of Jacob's Creek she had brought in her luggage as emergency Dutch courage. Or maybe she could even head home, grab the fast train into the city.

'Hey.' Adam popped up as if from nowhere, startling her as he slipped a slim flute of champagne into her limp grasp; a pointless pair of raspberries bobbed against the bubbles. 'You're with me.'

A heat spread across her ribs; Harriet's heart dipped erratically in time with the raspberries.

'I am?' she asked, in a stupid, breathy voice, not quite under-standing what he meant, but liking the sentence all the same. Adam looked at her curiously, his own glass of fizz held paused by his jaw.

'Yeah. Table one; we're sitting next to one another. Don't worry, Iona and Johnny are on your other side, so you're safe.' A pause before continuing thoughtfully: 'Guess Miles and Nic had great faith that we'd be back on chatting terms again by the time the entrees are served; they must have finalised these seating plans a couple of weeks ago.' He smiled, one of his big, disarming smiles.

Harriet felt irretrievably stupid. Of course he wouldn't be *choosing* to sit with her; for all his smiles and his overtures of friendship and his general Adamness she was always going to be the girl who didn't respect him enough to even say goodbye. On the other hand, he was always going to be the guy who slept with her best friend and lied to her about it, so hey ho.

An effervescently happy Johnny – complete with trophy Iona, sweet and traditional in a floral knee-length shift dress – appeared through the doorway and flung one arm around Adam's shoulders, the other round Harriet's.

'Good show, eh? Good show.'

'It was a beautiful ceremony,' Iona piped up.

'Beautiful ceremony,' Johnny agreed sagely. 'And now, we cele-brate. I don't know about you guys, but I plan on getting totally wankered. Wankered 2006 style. Do you think there's any Jäger? Bomb o'clock?'

'Johnny,' said Adam, mock-stern. 'This is a classy event. Nothing here will get mixed with an energy drink.'

Johnny pulled a face. 'Straight Jäger it is then,' he laughed. Iona rolled her eyes at him, but her expression was a fond one. Johnny switched his arm to her shoulders and led her away to review the table and seating plan, displayed on an A1 poster set up on an easel. With a look that somehow felt unfinished, Adam turned away from Harriet and moved further into the room.

Harriet realised that her hand was growing numb with the chill of the champagne she was holding. The berries bobbed away like nothing had happened. Don't drink, Annie had told her, sternly. Don't get drunk. Don't interact with that Adam fella more than strictly necessary. Two golden rules and you should be fine.

Well, thought Harriet, I'm already breaking the Adam rule, I might as well enjoy this glass. She took a resolute sip, in the hopes that if she filled herself up with the glitter of bubbles, she might feel less hollow, a little more tethered, a lot more comfortable in the spotlight at table one. With regret, she put all thoughts of a solitary bottle of wine or a trundling dash to Waterloo out of her mind.

When Johnny returned with their drinks, Iona was sitting patiently at the otherwise empty circular table, fiddling nervously with the little place card that displayed her calligraphied name.

'I don't know if you wanted champagne,' he said, a little awkwardly. 'I mean, I know you don't like wine, but it's not the same thing, and you had a little bit of it last night at dinner. So I brought you both.' He placed a champagne flute and a high-ball tumbler of a juice-based cocktail in front of her. 'Cocktail's called Sea Breeze, apparently. I dunno what's in it though. I can go back and ask?'

'Johnny!' Iona laughed, pulling against his elbow to make him sit down in the chair next to her. 'Calm down! Anyone would think you *have* had some energy drink.'

Johnny fussed with his cummerbund as he fidgeted on the chair. 'Sorry,' he said, with narrowed eyes. 'Bloody penguin suit.

282

And too much sitting. And now more sitting!'

'Yes, people do usually tend to sit whilst they eat a formal dinner,' Iona smiled.

'Although I'd be very much up for seeing you try to eat the pâté starter whilst trying to do keepie-uppies,' Harriet said, arriving at the table and pulling her beribboned chair out from underneath it with a dull scrape. Adam appeared, placing his glass of champagne down squarely in front of his own name card before reaching to finish pulling Harriet's chair out for her. Harriet cast her eyes down and gave a mumbled thanks.

Sukie and her boyfriend wandered over and Adam immediately pulled out her chair for her too.

'Not mine?' Demi asked, with a flash of a grin. Adam immediately went into an exaggeratedly scraping bow before holding Demi's chair out for him with a matching grin. The boys had decided they liked Demi. Roddy, well, he was a little much.

'Nobody's expecting you to like your ex's new guy anyway,' Miles had said earlier that morning, rolling his eyes. The sentence hung heavy in the room. The three men had looked away from one another, faintly embarrassed: who had Miles been talking to there, Johnny or Adam?

As if conjured up by the thought of him, Roddy appeared, his silk cravat looking a little limp and wrinkled already, a glass of champagne in each overlarge hand. Beaming around at everyone, he sat in his place to the left of Iona. Leigha followed, her fingers busy pressing hair grips more firmly into place at the back of her head, slipping into the one remaining place, between him and Demi. Johnny saw her glancing around, evaluating her placement and her proximity to everyone else.

She was directly opposite Adam and Harriet, which – at first – Johnny found a little distasteful, before he realised that – as it was a circular table – it would either have been Adam and Harriet in full view or Iona and himself. He gave Miles and Nicky a little retrospective kudos for at least attempting to navigate the mine-field that this seating plan must have been. Iona would have to physically turn to be looking at Leigha, and vice-versa; obviously, the bride and groom thought that that was the most sensitive point – interesting.

Leigha took her glass back from Roddy and took a dainty sip of champagne. Her head was tilted slightly, as if she was listening politely to Roddy's chatter, but Johnny knew his ex-girlfriend's glazed over look when he saw it. He suddenly felt a hot stab of empathy towards the guy.

Despite her pessimistic moaning that the yellow bridesmaids' dress would make her look sallow and ill, Leigha was even more peaches-and-cream than usual. She'd lost weight since the last time he'd seen her, too much, really – her arms were thin and defined like a teenage boy's – leading Johnny to suspect that her healthy glow was a combination of fake tan and artfully applied makeup. She wore two necklaces, a layered effect, a heavy-looking silver key on a long chain, and one shorter, a white gold 'L' sitting neatly in the little hollow at the base of her throat.

She'd been given that 'L' necklace by her parents on her 18th birthday, Johnny remembered. He'd taken it off for her on many occasions, whilst she held her heavy brown hair up and away from the clasp for him. Johnny dragged his attention away and picked up his champagne. The fiddly, slender stem felt like it might snap in his clumsy hold; he put it down again, hurriedly.

Iona, in conversation across his torso with Harriet, placed cool fingers over his fist. She didn't look at him, or falter, just carried on chatting away. Johnny surveyed her profile. He wished he knew the difference between wanting to love someone – someone specific – and just wanting to be able to be in love full-stop.

He turned his attention to Sukie. Out of the three bridesmaids, she was faring the worst, her genetics for poker-straight hair already reclaiming the ringlets she'd obviously spent some time creating that morning. Demi was still talking to Adam; Sukie sat in silence, with her elbow on the table and her chin cupped in her palm, watching him with a softness Johnny could never have imagined on her. Just as the thought crossed his mind, Sukie reared back, ramrod straight and glowered at Adam for something he'd just said – only half in jest – typical Sukie. Some things really don't ever change.

'Leigha is very pretty,' Iona had said, nonchalantly, as they'd unpacked their weekend things the evening before. Johnny, whose thoughts were still half down in the reception lobby with said pretty Leigha, had had to get her to repeat herself.

'I hope it's not, you know, a big thing for you, her being here,' Johnny had mumbled. 'I don't want you to feel uncomfortable, sweetheart.' Iona had just laughed as she'd stretched to hang her dress for the next day – enshrouded in a transparent dry cleaner garment bag – from the side of the wardrobe.

'Me, uncomfortable?' she'd scoffed. 'You forget, I know all about the sordid, knotty history of this group of people, and you think *I'm* the one who's going to be uncomfortable? Don't be silly.' She'd shot him a very direct, very un-Leigha like look. Still, in that instant, he remembered Leigha, Leigha of long-ago, scraping her hair back from her face with her fingers, resting her forehead on her wrists. The last time he saw her before this weekend.

'Don't be silly,' she had implored him, her voice muffled by her own arms.

He picked up his champagne flute again in an effort to distract himself and this time managed to get around to drinking from it. He changed his focus to Harriet, still talking enthusiastically with Iona. He'd mentally taken a lot of stuff out on her, he admitted to himself, thinking that if she just hadn't done what she'd done then

Leigha would have been happier, been a little less empty, maybe more willing to make a go of things with him.

He ignored the sudden and very unwelcome reflection that if Leigha hadn't been so unhappy and empty, reeling from such a big loss, she may not have gone out with him in the first place.

Things were more or less the same, he realised; Harriet was sweet; Sukie was sour; Leigha was unattainable.

'Ladies and gentlemen!' came a call from the corner, a rather animated looking chap in tails and a top hat. 'Please be upstanding for the bride and groom.'

Nicky had clung to him from the minute she arrived next to him at the altar. As they walked into their reception venue to a well-meant but rather discordant rendition of 'For They Are Jolly Good Fellows' she was pressed closer than ever, a pleased pink flush across the bridge of her face. The way she constantly sought out his eye contact was a mirror of how he was feeling inside. He couldn't quite believe she was his; he wanted nothing but to look at her.

Feeling quite majestic, Miles swept through the hall, nodding benignly at his wedding guests, piloting his bride up to the table-for-two placed on a dais at the top of the room and depositing her gently in her chair.

He didn't sit straight away; the applause and cheers grew a little protracted and strained as he stood in his place and beamed out at the motley collection of friends, family and colleagues; they all fell silent as he cleared his throat.

'Nicky and I would like to thank you all for coming.' He paused to allow the renewed applause to swell and ebb away again. 'Later, after we've had a few more drinks, you're going to hear from my Best Man, but first – before the wedding breakfast comes out and things get underway – I want to make mine.' He pulled a rather creased and folded wodge of paper from his suit pocket.

He smiled out at the sea of expectant faces and reached for a glass of champagne, one of two that had been thoughtfully awaiting them at the head table.

'I want to start with a toast to the newly-made 'Mrs Nicola Healy', Miles began, holding his drink aloft in salute. 'A name change for her, and a lifestyle change for me. You see – as I'm sure you all know – Nicky is perfect, or as close to it as a person can get!' Nicky made little mewling sounds of protest, dipping her head in embarrassment, that little pink flush of pleasure getting pinker by the second.

'Along with the usual vows I made earlier, I'm making another one: that I am going to strive to be more and more perfect myself, every single day, so maybe – after decades and decades and decades of happy marriage – I'll feel worthy of such a great wife.'

Miles had rehearsed and rehearsed this, his big moment, wanting to sound clear and confident, but already his throat was thickening up around his words, rendering him sounding stupid and over-emotional. Nicky's eyes were wet, her bottom lip caught between her teeth as she looked up at him appreciatively. He paused again to smile, this time a smile that was only for her.

'I met Nicky at university – this very one, of course – in a campus pub just through the woods there. It was grotty then and I'm sure it's grottier now, although maybe it's had a refurb, who knows?' Miles laughed. 'Sadly it's closed this weekend on account of it being Easter. If anyone gets drunk enough tonight to break into the Armstrong, please report back re: the status of the décor! Enquiring minds want to know!' Miles smirked to himself as he noticed the banter between Johnny and Adam on table one, each daring the other to actually do it, most likely.

'Anyway.' He consulted his notes. 'Nicky and her housemates were being drunk and disorderly and absolutely murdering the great game of pool. I volunteered to show them what's what – you know – what end of the cue to use to hit the balls and whatnot.' He paused to allow the theatrical protesting from the girls on table one to die down. 'And I knew, even then, that I was punching way above my weight. I mean, I had the third year appeal going for me, you know, older guy and all that, but still, I'm sure there isn't a person here who isn't thinking how I've married up!'

'Hear, hear!' joked Johnny, using his cupped hands as a megaphone.

'And since that first night,' Miles continued, 'we've had seven and a half wonderful years together. We've seen loads of couples come together and break up. She's seen me through finishing my degree, a Masters and a PhD.' Miles nodded an acknowledgement at the light smattering of applause congratulating his academic accomplishments.

'I needed to move to Bath to do my doctorate, and – rather than have us be apart – Nicky came with me. We couldn't support ourselves if we both studied, so she got a job. We haven't been able to afford nice things, or holidays, even a decent flat. Seriously. There's a reason we haven't had anyone over to stay!' he laughed. 'But all the time,' he continued, his voice sobered, 'I knew that my Nicky should be living in a palace. She could have anyone, be a glamorous footballer's WAG and be treated like the queen she is, the way I wish I'd been able to spoil her.' The room was prickly with an awkward silence; where was this ridiculous self-effacement going, the wedding guests were clearly wondering.

'Anyway, pet, I have a little surprise. I know you don't like surprises, but – trust me – this is a good one.'

'You're pregnant!' heckled an apparently already inebriated second cousin from table six.

'Yeah, that's it,' Miles deadpanned. 'Surprised, Nic?'

'A little, yeah!' Nicky giggled. 'Not to mention a little impressed.'

'The surprise is,' Miles continued, 'that I've taken a sabbatical, of sorts.'

He could see he'd startled her; she placed her champagne down on the table a little aggressively.

'What?' she asked, eyes wide. The room was the most hushed it had been all afternoon. 'Miles! You've just... you've *just* got your doctorate, *why* would you quit?' She pointlessly remembered to lower her voice by the end of the sentence, as if they were actually having a private discussion.

'I haven't quit!' he corrected her, his smile broadening. 'I said *sabbatical*. Well, I guess actually 'secondment' would be the better term for it. Or maybe there's an actual French word for it – you'll know, I'm sure.' He paused, allowing his words to sink in; Nicky just looked more confused and even wider of eye.

'What?' she repeated, after a moment.

'I've been offered secondment at the University of Montpellier.'

'The one in France?' Nicky asked, her voice rising several octaves.

'Yup, the one in France,' Miles nodded. 'I've checked. They run a term long TEFL course that would be subsidised for you if I'm on the staff. But we can stay in Bath, if you like, move into a nicer place now I'll be earning. Or I can contact the University of London board and see what they can offer me by way of a post-doc placement.' He paused; Nicky was staring up at him, lips parted, looking at him like he was a stranger. 'Who knows? Maybe there's a place for me in my old department here.'

Nicky seemed like she was in actual shock.

'The important thing is, pet, this time, you choose. Whatever, wherever you want. I am totally at your pleasure.' Finished, he beamed at her.

Nicky burst into tears.

'Why didn't you tell me?' she cried, her words muffled by the fist she was pressing tightly to her mouth.

'I... I wanted it to be a surprise,' Miles answered, blinking uncertainly. He'd been expecting a much more positive reaction than this.

'I am such a bitch!' Nicky wailed. Miles stooped to grab her in alarm; he definitely hadn't been expecting this. In the corner of his vision he could see that Harriet had risen to her feet and was crossing the short gap between their tables.

'I think the bride is just a little overwhelmed!' she announced in an overly-cheery voice, loudly, so that everyone could hear. 'Champagne on an empty stomach and all. Up you come, Nic.' She hoisted the taller girl up by the elbow. 'I'm just going to take her to splash water on her face,' she muttered to Miles. 'Great speech, Miles!' she said, louder. 'Er, to the groom!'

'To the groom!' echoed table one, with false enthusiasm. The rest of the wedding guests repeated it as more of a confused mumble. Harriet shot a look towards the rather pallid looking Leigha and Sukie, who scrambled to their feet and followed Harriet as she bodily steered the tearful bride away from her wedding reception and towards the lavatories.

Nicky had already calmed herself down by the time they entered the bathroom. It was too late to save her makeup though, she'd really done a number on her expertly applied liquid eyeliner and volumising mascara; the overhead lighting wasn't really helping either.

'I'm okay, I'm okay,' Nicky had been repeating since they left the table. 'Oh my god. Oh my god.'

'Do you have to say everything twice now you're married?' Sukie muttered under her breath. Leigha and Harriet shot her matching looks. Sukie rolled her eyes at them.

Leigha immediately ripped paper towels from the dispenser on the wall, taking them over to the sink and dampening them. Returning to Nicky, she put her fingers under her trembling chin and pushed her face up.

'Come on, Nic,' she said softly, using the corner of a wet towel to start wiping away the black smears on her cheeks. 'Let's sort you out.'

'I've ruined my own wedding day!' Nicky wailed.

'No, no you haven't,' Harriet shushed her. 'Nobody thinks that. It's natural for the bride to get a little… emotional during the groom's speech…'

'No, I ruined it by my fucking about this morning!' Nicky snapped. The three girls all winced; it was always like a little slap in the face when Nicky swore. 'I was so… horrible to him… I won't ever be able to forget…'

'Nobody else knows that…' Leigha said over her, trying to be helpful, but Nicky just kept up with her lament.

'I didn't give him even the smallest benefit of the doubt…' she continued.

'But obviously you did!' Harriet insisted, using the same bright, overly-cheery tone that Leigha had tried. 'Because – look! – you two are married. You didn't leave him at the altar. It's all okay.'

'But I thought about it!' Nicky cried.

'Fucking hell,' Sukie grumbled. 'Newsflash! Stop the presses! 'Woman gets momentary cold feet at altar'. I think not. Seriously, don't even worry about it.'

'It's sort of his fault as well,' Leigha pointed out. 'He obviously knew you were unhappy but didn't talk to you about it… wanted to wait for maximum impact on your big day.' Leigha wadded the used paper towels into a ball and placed them down by the sink. She opened her glossy red clutch bag – which Roddy had kindly been holding during the ceremony – and began to pull out various compacts and tubes.

'Yes, you're both idiots,' Sukie agreed. 'Come on now, Nic. If we don't get back out there it's going to look weird. Plus they'll

291

be serving up the soup any minute now.'

'Patê,' Nicky corrected her, with a sniff.

'Whatever.'

'Hold still,' Leigha frowned, as she carefully painted Nicky's eyeliner flicks back into place. She fumbled on the side for the mascara; Harriet was already holding it out to her. Leigha took it from her, with a flicker of a frown, just beaten down in time.

'France, Nic!' Harriet said, squeezing the girl's hand. 'Better late than never!'

'Are you going to go to France then? Not move into London?' Leigha asked, titling her head as she concentrated on applying the mascara evenly.

'I don't know…' Nicky admitted, in an astounded tone. 'How can I even choose?' She laughed. 'I've gone from no options to too many in one fell swoop.'

'I read an interesting article a few months ago. It says that women these days feel unsatisfied and unhappy because of precisely that. *Too much choice.* We can be anything we want now. We can be stay at home mothers, or we can be high-flying career women, and everything in between.' Leigha slid the mascara wand back into its tube. 'Stresses us all out.' Sukie looked at her, incredulous, just about biting back the automatic response: *what's the weather like in your world, Ley?* 'There!' Leigha said, handing Nicky another paper towel for her to blot her lips on. 'Good as new.'

Nicky turned and regarded her reflection; she bit her bottom lip. 'I need to pull myself together,' she said slowly.

'Agreed,' replied Sukie. 'Some food will help, I'm sure.' Leigha rolled her eyes and began to pack all of her makeup back into her bag.

'Can we go and have a bit of a party now?' she said, as the last lip gloss disappeared into the clutch. 'I thought this was meant to be a celebration!' she teased gently. Nicky gave a weak smile.

'You girls have been great today. I'm sorry I'm such a car crash.'

'We're your friends,' Harriet said, quietly. 'Even if we don't live with you any more, or see you all the time, that hasn't changed.' Leigha and Sukie both beamed in agreement, and Nicky's smile grew a little sturdier.

'Now, come on!' Sukie urged. 'I'm starving. I want me some soup.'

'Paté!' Nicky repeated, laughing.

'Whatever.'

Nicky had re-emerged from the bathrooms, flanked by her three little yellow soldiers, looking none the worse for wear other than having a certain tightness to the set of her mouth. Miles reached out for her immediately, face all concern, and she went to him, stance apologetic, holding his face in between her hands and kissing him as she spoke quietly.

The waiting caterers had obviously taken this as a sign that they were good to go, and a sea of monochrome-clad waiting staff began to circle, dispensing plates of paté and rustic looking breads; the three course Wedding Breakfast – interspersed with much topping up of champagne glasses – was enthusiastically welcomed and devoured.

'Do you remember, Su, I applied for this job, back in first year,' Leigha said. 'The events waitressing,' she clarified, for the benefit of the rest of the table. 'These will all be students, I bet,' she said, circling her finger to indicate the waiting staff swarming the room, clearing away plates of what had been a passion-fruit and white chocolate mousse.

'That was delicious!' boomed Roddy, leaning back in his chair and smacking his trim stomach as if it had suddenly become a full on Father Christmas belly. 'I don't usually like paté – bit faffy – but that was really nice. Great starter, not too rich.'

'I don't know, I would have preferred soup,' Leigha smirked, obviously some sort of in-joke, as it prompted titters from Sukie and even a faint smile from Harriet.

The guy with the top hat and the loud voice – the Master of Ceremonies – clapped his hands for the room's attention.

'If you wouldn't mind waiting outside, ladies and gentlemen, whilst we set the DJ up and clear the room for this evening's entertainment? The champagne bottles will be following you out, worry not!' he chortled. The wedding guests dutifully stood and filed out of the room as instructed.

Adam noticed that Harriet hung back, still at the table, fiddling with her bag, looking in it for something; considering the bag was only tiny, it seemed to be taking an inordinately long time.

Miles and Nicky had moved to join them. Nicky still seemed a bit subdued but they were holding hands and Miles seemed cheerful enough; Adam decided not to allude to the little outburst by asking Nicky if she was okay.

'Going to be hard to follow me, eh mate?' Miles smirked, smug with confidence.

'Oh ho, don't you worry!' laughed Adam, winking at Nicky, 'my speech is going to be great. I'm going to have tears, laughter, start arguments amongst your guests, horrify Nic when I reveal that a couple of years ago we all went on a boys' holiday to Vegas and you married a stripper –'

'Nah, you're thinking of *The Hangover*, mate,' Johnny said. 'Miles married the ladyboy that worked at the hotel bar.'

'Oh yeah!' Adam slapped his hand to his forehead in mock-realisation. 'How could I have forgotten that little detail?'

'I'll have you know that he was a kind and gentle lover,' Miles joked, as they all moved out into the entrance hall. 'And on that note, we'd better go mingle. You guys all okay for champagne? Hey, can we get some top-ups over here?' he called to the bottle-wielding waiters, without waiting for a response. 'See you in a bit.'

Before following her new husband, Nicky moved closer to Adam and squeezed his forearm. 'Just wanted to say thank you,' she murmured, only for his ears.

'For what?'

'I think everyone is taking their cue from you. About Harriet, I mean. You've been nice to her so nobody feels right about giving her a hard time.' Adam scratched his neck awkwardly.

'Nothing to thank me for,' he said. 'It's a non-issue.' Nicky looked at him, her expression faintly disbelieving.

'Either way,' she said, 'it's really making our lives easier. I'm sure Harriet would thank you too…'

'She already has, actually,' Adam admitted, with a little smile. Nicky nodded, and with one more squeeze floated away, the bottom of her bell-shaped dress skimming the wooden floor.

Having replenished the rest of the group's drinks, the waiter had moved towards Adam and waited patiently during the interchange with Nicky. With a grateful smile, Adam held his glass out to receive the stream of champagne. Roddy was entertaining everyone with an anecdote about his brother's wedding; Adam was only half-listening as he thanked the server and brought his drink to his lips.

'Hey,' Demi said, quietly, 'someone seems to have done a little disappearing act.' Adam looked at him, not following. 'Harriet,' Demi clarified, nodding towards the now closed double doors back into the reception hall. 'I don't think I've seen her come out. She must have slipped past us. You don't think she's going to call it an early night, now that the proper part of the evening's all done? Leigha and Su haven't been bad to her at all, really.'

Adam stared at the dark varnished wood of the doors. 'Who knows?' he said, blithely. 'Up to her, I guess.' He was picturing the wooden-panelled corridors that wormed through this old building;

you could get out to the library quad through doors at the back of the dining hall. 'Can you look after that for me, mate?' he asked, holding his drink out to Demi. 'Just going to pop to the loo.'

Demi smiled widely and accepted the glass into his free hand. 'Sure thing,' he said, in a tone that heavily suggested that he knew full well that Adam's destination was not going to be the gents.

Chapter Twenty Seven

The day still had some heat in it, as it wasn't quite five o'clock yet. Harriet sought out a patch of particularly plush looking grass and sat gracefully, smoothing her dress out carefully and folding her legs beneath her, a far cry from when she used to throw down book bags and collapse anywhere there was space to. This quad had always been thronged in the better weather, the perfect space for studying outdoors, what with its proximity to both the Old Library and the dining hall.

The quad was quiet now, all the students home for the Easter break, the campus and its amenities given over for events like conferences and weddings. Still, Harriet felt as if the ghost of her undergraduate self was going to come trotting out of the library, ring binders and text books clasped to her chest with one arm, sticking earphones in with her free hand, squinting in the brightness of the sunlit quad after the gloom of the library.

What would I say to my eighteen year old self, Harriet wondered idly, ripping up clumps of grass and sprinkling the blades. Beware false friends, the smiles of certain boys, the effect that the love poetry of Pablo Neruda will one day have on you.

She contemplated calling Annie – after all, that is what she'd come out here to do – but found she didn't quite have the energy.

She hadn't heard anyone approach, but the sun was low in the west and threw the person's shadow out in front of her; guiltily she hurriedly wiped the butchered blades of grass from her fingers. Adam sat beside her, carefully balancing the glasses of champagne he was holding, one in each hand. He took a sip from one as he settled, passing the other over to her without comment.

'So, my dissertation,' he said, conversationally, as if he were carrying on some paused, five year old chat. Harriet blinked.

'What about your dissertation?' she asked. 'Tell me you've handed it in by now!' she teased. Adam laughed.

'I'll have you know it got handed in a full fifty minutes before the deadline,' he replied, in a tone of affront. 'And I got a high 2.1 mark for it.'

'Good for you,' Harriet said, shifting uncomfortably, unsure as to where this conversation was leading.

'I changed the topic, you know,' he said, casually. Harriet trained her eyes on the little humps of grass she'd made.

'Yeah, Nicky told me at the time,' she said. 'Brave move.' The love poetry of Pablo Neruda obviously didn't have the same effect on him, she thought to herself, ruefully. She remembered Adam reading certain lines aloud to her in the dead of the night, voice hushed so as not to disturb any housemates, could picture exactly how his face had looked in the lamp light.

I love you as certain dark things are to be loved,
In secret, between the shadow and the soul.

'Anyway,' she said, hurriedly, banishing the memory of their nights together as if he would somehow be able to see the scene projected onto her face. 'What are you doing out here?'

'I was on the way to the toilets,' Adam said casually. 'Thought I'd check you weren't doing a runner.'

'On your way to the toilets with two glasses of champagne?'

Harriet asked lightly. Adam shrugged nonchalantly and took another sip from his drink.

'What are you doing out here, is the better question,' he said, turning slightly to face her more.

'Oh,' Harriet groaned, flapping her hand dismissively, 'I just wanted five minutes to sit without an inoffensive smile plastered to my face, without worrying that someone's going to think I'm suicidal with stress, or a jumped up moody bitch.'

'And running away is the better option?' Adam said. He clearly hadn't thought his words through; he was already looking away from her before the final word was out of his mouth and she knew they were both thinking about the same thing.

'I'm not running anywhere,' she said, carefully. 'Just wanted five minutes, whilst they changed the room over. Plus this champagne is going straight to my head, especially on top of last night's!' she joked. Adam didn't reply, just stared ahead to where the arch above the library door joined at its keystone; she wondered if he was talking to his eighteen year old self, too.

'So,' she said, sitting up a little straighter, trying to steer the conversation onto safer ground. 'What do you do, these days? Nicky said something to do with insurance..?' Adam turned back to her and nodded.

'Yeah, brokerage. Boring. Long hours at the moment because we're going through a merger,' he confessed. 'Pays the bills. How about you? How do you fill your time?'

'Oh, you know. Work, sleep, play. Laundry. I seem to forever be doing laundry.'

'Are you seeing anyone?' Although she had sensed they had been working towards this, the sheer suddenness of the question took Harriet aback.

'No,' Harriet said, drawing the word out. 'Not at the moment. Or I'd have him here, wouldn't I? Much needed moral support.'

'I thought I said I'd be your moral support?' Adam said, with a teasing smile.

'Only for this weekend, you said,' Harriet teased back. 'I might have meant moral support for life in general.'

'Has there been anyone serious? Any serious moral support being offered?'

'Nope. Just a rather depressing string of things that fizzle out after just a few dates.'

'A string, eh? A string sounds like rather a lot! You on that internet dating or something?'

'I think Annie – Iona's sister – I think she put me on that My Single Friend dot com once,' Harriet laughed. 'I don't think I even got any bites, despite the fact she referred to me as "a great laugh" with "a cracking bod"'!

'Hey, I don't remember giving your friend permission to quote me,' Adam laughed. Harriet laughed too, a little falsely. It was too hard to get comfortable with Adam, he kept blurring the lines; was he an old friend, with whom she had a convivial rapport, or an old ex, with whom she had unfinished business? The parameters kept shifting and she couldn't keep up.

She took a cold sip of champagne and allowed a silence to fall. She imagined finishing the glass, and another, and a whole bottle more, and telling Adam Chadwick – who was sat beside her so companionably – that sometimes, when she was in bed with a man, beneath him, she'd look up through the muddle of her eyelashes and it would be him instead.

She could imagine how well that would go down. She shouldn't even be thinking about it, let alone thinking about telling him about it. She'd better watch herself on the champagne tonight, she thought; Annie was right.

'It's probably okay to go in now,' Adam said, after a while, clearly feeling the silence had gone on too long. 'Nicky will be wondering where we are.'

And Leigha and Sukie will be salivating over the fact that we've disappeared together, Harriet thought to herself. No doubt in their minds we've broken into the library and rutted one another up against the stacks in the Reference section.

Her expression was obviously a curious one, as Adam was looking at her with interest. 'You okay?'

'Yeah, fine!' she said, a little too brightly. 'I was just… thinking. You go ahead, I – I need to make a call.' Adam looked at her, unsure. 'I'll be like, five minutes.' Still, he hesitated. 'Line me up another glass of champagne, they must be running out soon.' Reluctantly Adam nodded and hoisted himself to his feet.

He touched her shoulder as he left. It was an odd, friendly gesture, and one that left her insides feeling like the ball of wadded up paper towels that Leigha had left in the bathrooms. It was a feeling she was getting used to already, this weekend; it seemed to be coming from all corners.

She didn't call Annie, just sat and finished her champagne in solitude, staring across at the red bricks of the library archway, idly flattening out her little grass piles with her palm.

Love is so short,

Adam had read out to her, lying on his stomach in this very quad, on the first truly warm day of spring, 2007.

forgetting is so long.

Sukie had given up the ghost and was making a small hill of hairpins on the table in front of her. When she was sure she'd gotten the last of them out she massaged her aching scalp lightly with her fingertips.

301

In the centre of the room, Miles held Nicky – all elbows – in the classic waltz position as he swept her about the dance floor to the anguished vocals of Aerosmith's *I Don't Wanna Miss A Thing*.

'Bit of an odd choice, for their first dance,' Johnny murmured, frowning lightly.

'What do you mean?' Iona chided him. 'I love this song, it's a classic!'

'It's just that they aren't really, you know, *power ballad* people,' Johnny explained.

'It was playing that night.' Harriet's absence has not gone un-noted but she appeared to have slipped back amongst them whilst Sukie was occupied dismantling her hair. 'In the Armstrong. The night they met.'

'My fault,' Leigha said, stirring; she had been watching Miles and Nicky with a little smile on her face. 'Do you remember there used to be a juke box thing? In the corner by the loos? They got rid of it some time in second year. Do you remember, I went round the bar begging 10ps off strangers to make up the quid for it? And then I chose a couple of cheesy songs and *Don't Wanna Miss A Thing* was first and Miles and Nicky dirty danced to it.'

'Yeah, right in the middle of the pool tables,' Sukie added.

'How far they've come!' Adam grinned, looking fondly over at the couple. Nicky's full-skirted dress swished and swayed; it was like the end of a Disney movie.

'It's such a lovely story,' said Demi, also watching the couple. 'Shows how "The One" can appear when you least expect it. Bam! You casually go out mid-week for a couple of drinks, you're not looking for it, and there's your soulmate. Seven years later?' He gestured at the new man and wife. 'Aerosmith and a hell of a lot of tulle.'

'It's true!' Iona agreed, earnestly. The poor thing was periodically taking baby sips from a glass of chardonnay that she clearly didn't like the taste of but didn't want to say. 'My friend met her boyfriend when she was walking her dog, looking completely skanky, just two days after her high school boyfriend had dumped her. She was totally broken-hearted, couldn't even *think* about being with someone else. But then she met James and within, like, a week they were practically living together.'

Sukie managed with some restraint not to roll her eyes. Iona – or, to be fair, being nineteen – seemed utterly ridiculous to her. Had she ever been that young?

Demi smiled encouragingly at the girl. 'That's what it was like with Sukie and me,' he confided, in a gossipy tone of voice. 'I was in the library studying. I definitely wasn't looking for a girl-friend.' Sukie did not do as well at containing the derisive snort that rose up inside her at that; not looking for a girlfriend – that was putting it mildly! 'And suddenly there she was.' Demi smiled again, a smile that Sukie knew was just for her this time. It was hard to stay annoyed with him when he did that.

'Well I don't believe in there being just one person for everyone.' Leigha centred herself back towards the table and crossed her legs matter-of-factly.

'What about love at first sight?' Demi enquired. Leigha smiled, a slow, lazy smile.

'I believe in *lust* at first sight,' she corrected, flashing a – cheeky cow! – heavy-lidded look towards Adam. Adam didn't give the slightest reaction but Sukie didn't miss Harriet's knuckles whit-ening against the curve of her wine glass.

'I believe in love at first sight,' offered Johnny. Iona preened and simpered a little at this, like it was the equivalent of him saying he'd fallen for her at the first glance. Leigha turned her lidded gaze onto her ex; she – like most of the table – knew who Johnny was most likely referring to. 'Well,' he continued, nodding towards the newlyweds, 'it sure worked out okay for them.'

On the dance floor the track had changed. Nicky was being turned around and around in a very stately box-step by Miles' salt-and-pepper haired father whilst the official photographer contorted and swivelled to take pictures of them. In the opposite corner, Miles fumbled to keep pace with Nicky's mother, a grandly dressed statuesque woman, the same height as he.

'The only girl I've ever loved, well, that wasn't love at first sight.' Adam's voice was quiet, considering. 'Didn't mean it wasn't love, though.' Was he talking about Harriet, Sukie wondered? Harriet was suddenly very interested in rubbing lines in the condensation on the swell of her wine glass with her fingertip.

'I say, different strokes for different folks,' announced Roddy.

'But maybe you only believe in love in first sight when you've experienced it yourself,' Johnny argued. 'You know. Like with ghosts.' Adam grinned remorsefully.

'I really don't hold out much hope for ever falling in love at first sight.'

'How about falling in lust at first sight?' asked Leigha, more than a tad coquettishly. Roddy just laughed at her indulgently.

The wedding guests broke into polite applause as the song came to an end and Miles and Nicky were released by their respective new in-laws. The DJ came on the speakers.

Iona practically bounced in her seat. 'Ooh, I really want to dance!' she said, excitedly. 'Johnny's never taken me out clubbing, or anything, so we've never danced together.'

'Is that so?' Adam's eyebrows rose in exaggerated disbelief. 'Well, let me tell you, he was quite the mover back here in the day.'

'Really?'

'Really,' Adam repeated, cheerfully ignoring the death glares Johnny was shooting him. 'Later, we should ask the DJ to play Akon, *Smack Dat*. Johnny had a whole dance routine worked out for that, I seem to recall.'

'We *definitely* have to get hold of some Jäger if I'm going to be doing a reprisal of that,' Johnny said.

'A reprisal of what?' Sukie interrupted.

'Johnny's *Smack Dat* dance.'

'Good God,' Sukie said, with feeling. 'And maybe we can persuade Miles to do the *My Humps* routine in the background.'

'Does someone have a pen?' Leigha asked, amused. 'I feel like we should be making a list of song requests for the DJ.' As she finished speaking, so did the DJ, and the unmistakeable opening strains of Whigfield's *Saturday Night* burst from the speakers.

'Christ!' moaned Johnny. 'I said I wanted to get trashed like it was 2006, not 'party like its 1999'.'

'I think this song is even older than 1999, actually,' Leigha said. 'That's a point – do you even know this song, honey?' She smirked at Iona, who visibly wilted, her hands fumbling nervously to pick up her wine glass. Johnny felt a weird little pang of sympathy for Iona mixed with a sick pride that Leigha cared enough to actively bother his current girlfriend.

'I don't *want* a boyfriend,' Leigha had said to him, the last time he'd seen her. He'd borrowed his mother's car and driven all the way down south; they were meant to be spending the weekend flat hunting. 'I want to be able to have *lots* of boyfriends. I don't want to live with you. I want to be on my own. You can never just *leave me alone*.'

'I'm sorry, this song is just too amazing,' said Demi, pulling Johnny back to the present, as he got to his feet and held his hand out for Sukie. Laughing she let him pull her up to standing and they both joined the motley crew trying to do the *Saturday Night* dance in the middle of the room; there were about four different variations going on and Johnny wasn't sure that any one of them was the right one.

'Harry.'

The voice was a man's voice, rich and deep, but unfamiliar. Everyone in the table turned to look; it was a tall man in a good looking suit. A sweet looking red-head in a blue dress hovered uncomfortably at his elbow. Harriet was on her feet immediately.

'Oh my god!' she cried, clasping her hands together, genuine pleasure spreading across her face for the first time that weekend.

Leigha, on the other hand, had a very different expression. She looked almost as if she was dizzy, or was going to be sick. She laid her hand abruptly on Roddy's forearm, as if this stranger was wont to attack her, and she would be in need of his protection.

The man held out his arms and Harriet gave him a warm, friendly hug. 'This is Emily,' he introduced the woman at his side.

'Hi Emily, good to meet you!' Harriet beamed warmly at her.

'Leigha.' The man had caught sight of the seated Leigha as Harriet had moved closer to his companion. 'Hi! How are you?'

Johnny watched Leigha take a steadying breath through her nose; she released Roddy's forearm and stood up to her full height, imperious and beautiful.

'Seth,' she said; her voice was strange. 'What are you doing here?'

Adam quickly grasped who the interloper was; he studied Seth with interest, the person who Harriet tried so hard and failed to love the way everyone told her that she should. From the way they were talking to one another – warmly, only faintly awkwardly – there didn't appear to be many hard feelings.

'Well, Miles and I stayed in contact,' Seth explained; of course, there would have been an overlap, a time when Miles was newly with Nicky and Harriet still with Seth. 'And a couple of years ago, Em and I moved to Bristol so we've been nearby; we've met up a few times. Miles and Nicky came to *our* wedding.' He smiled inclusively at the red-head by his side.

Leigha had gotten to her feet when Seth had addressed her, but hadn't moved since. Adam looked at her curiously. He would have expected her to be right up in Seth's face, flirting and laughing and tossing her head to make her hair bounce, the way she was with everyone.

And then Adam joined up some mental dots and realised what nobody else had. He looked at the stone-faced Leigha with a renewed interest.

Even though she had known him in his early twenties, Leigha realised that when she reminisced of Seth, which she did every so often, she was more likely to picture him at sixteen, seventeen, the age at which her feelings had first grown and calcified. Seeing him here – a man grown, with a dumpy wife on his arm – was so wrong, so jarring, so galling, that surely the very building was going to come down around them.

He looked like he should be a teacher, but she knew from the grapevine that he was actually a policeman, a rugged, manly sort of occupation that seemed at odds with the new softness of his face and his torso under his thin white dress shirt. Christ, Leigha thought, irritably; it's meant to be the woman that puts on the weight after marriage.

If they had made it work between them, she thought – a little madly – he wouldn't be playing PC Plod out in the West Country, running to seed. You missed a trick there, she mentally told Seth, as he and his ginger wife reminisced with Harriet about their own wedding day; you bloody missed a trick there.

Her thoughts spooled on: Of course, if it wasn't for you falling for Harriet in Sixth Form, it probably *would* be you and me, because otherwise I wouldn't always have had this feeling that it should have been. If it wasn't for Harriet, lithe and smiley at sixteen, and the semi-indecent denim mini-skirts she used to wear, we would have eventually ended up together. Seth's life would be unrecognisable. His life would be so much better. My life would be so much better.

She felt like her eyes could bore actual holes into the back of Harriet's skull; it was a glare so heated that surely Harriet would feel it and turn around. But Harriet just continued making pleasant small talk. Leigha dragged her attention away, blinking; her eyes felt dry and gritty. Both Adam and Johnny were looking at her strangely. She felt her cheeks heat with a blush. She picked up her glass of wine, willing the movements of her hand to be smooth and steady.

Out on the dance floor, the previously jagged motions of the *Saturday Night* dance had transformed into the soft swirls of couples dancing slowly to a ballad; Leigha hadn't even registered the track change.

'I love this song,' she announced, loudly, even though she didn't. 'Roddy, let's dance.'

'What would you do,' Demi asked, as he twirled and dipped Sukie in time with the Michael Bublé track, 'if we had a fight?'

'A fight about what?' Sukie asked, confused, pushing her newly loosened hair away from her eyes with her free hand.

'This is a hypothetical question,' Demi told her, mock-stern.

'Still, I'm going to need a little bit more information than that!' Sukie rolled her eyes.

'If we had a fight,' Demi repeated. 'If we had a fight here.'

'Why would we have a fight here?' Sukie asked, confusion growing.

'Because I think,' Demi continued, ignoring her question, 'that even you wouldn't want to make a big scene at such a beautiful wedding. I reckon I'd get away with quite a bit.'

'Quite a bit of what?' Sukie puzzlement was turning rapidly

into cold concern. Demi didn't answer straight away, just dipped her again. 'Demi, what are you talking about?' Sukie pressed, as soon as she was back right-side-up.

'I told Rob that there was someone else.'

Sukie's mouth opened and closed like a goldfish. 'Well, bearing in mind that you're still living in his flat, he appears to have taken it quite well.'

'He wants me gone by the time he gets back from his trip,' Demi said, so damn nonchalantly. He went to dip her again but Sukie braced against it.

'Where are you going to live?' she asked him, appalled.

'I have plenty of friends to let me sofa surf, but thank you for your concern!' he laughed.

'Why did you tell him?' Sukie asked. 'You know that we're not *serious*.'

'But I feel seriously about you,' Demi insisted.

'You're gay!'

'I told you the first time we met. And I keep telling you.' Demi attempted to dip her again, and this time he was successful. 'I'm not gay. I'm *bisexual*.'

'I don't believe there's any such thing.' It was an old, old argument, and one that was very strange to be having on the dance floor at the wedding of an old friend.

'That doesn't make it any less true,' Demi said, softly. 'I've been with men, and I've been with women, but now I just want to be with one woman.'

The track changed again, into the second power ballad of the night. Sukie allowed Demi to gather her up and press her tightly against him as they swayed to the music. Neither of them spoke. She digested his words.

Even if her father never found out about Demi's colourful past, she couldn't imagine him approving of a relationship between them. He wasn't by nature a cruel man, but he was a stern one, and the weight of his potential disappointment just simply wasn't survivable.

If her mother was still alive, it wouldn't be such a problem; she had always been magical at softening her severe, traditional husband. But the hard cold fact was that her mother was dead, and her father was all she had left. She couldn't risk alienating him for a fuck buddy – albeit a fuck buddy she could genuinely, seriously, truly see herself falling in love with, if she ever allowed herself to; but the pressure of her father's phantom condemnation was as much of a wall between them as ever.

'Your father,' Demi said suddenly, almost as if he had eavesdropped on her thoughts. 'You always give the impression that he doesn't speak English.'

'What?' Sukie was still caught up in her thoughts, and the razor-sharpness that was missing her mother; she didn't follow.

'Your father,' Demi repeated. 'His English is fine.'

Chapter Twenty Eight

After a polite length of time, Seth and Emily took their leave from the conversation. Harriet turned her attention to her handbag as soon as they were gone, retrieving her phone from it and typing out a text message. She was wearing a large silver cuff-style bracelet, which had been catching Adam's eye on and off all day as it fell down towards her elbow joint whenever she lifted that arm. As she finished her text she impatiently pushed the bracelet back to her wrist and slipped her mobile back into her little bag.

'I'm going to get another drink,' she announced to the table – only Johnny, Iona and Adam himself remained – 'and a bottle of water. It's getting hot in here, with all the dancing. Does anybody want anything from the bar?' Johnny and Iona shook their heads, indicating their still quite full wine glasses. Adam stood.

'I don't know what I want,' he lied. 'I'll come with you.' Harriet didn't seem to hesitate, or think it was odd, just smiled and got up and led the way across to the area where the drinks were being served.

'Hey, can I tell you something?' Adam murmured, as soon as they were away from Johnny and Iona's earshot. That made her look hesitant; she fiddled with her bracelet as she nodded, slow and wary. 'Has it ever occurred to you that there might have been something between Leigha and your ex?' Adam's face coloured as he reconsidered his words too late. 'Seth I mean, not… not me,' he clarified awkwardly.

Adam watched as realisation warred with denial on Harriet's face. In an obvious attempt to stall for time, she gave the barman her order instead of answering. When the exchange was over and she had a new glass of white wine and a plastic bottle of water in hand she turned back to Adam, her expression still unsure.

'Why do you ask?'

'I was just picking up on some weirdness there, especially from her side.' Adam scratched underneath his jaw as he tried to articulate what he'd noticed. 'And I remember from back then, how you said she was randomly really batshit crazy, bringing up Seth, saying how you had treated him so badly and all that.' He paused, needing her to connect those dots by herself. 'You know?' he finished, weakly.

'No,' Harriet said, slowly. 'No,' she said again, but she sounded like she was talking to herself, not him. 'It was never like that,' she insisted. 'They were, you know, just mates.'

'Me and you were just mates,' Adam pointed out, quietly. Harriet chewed her bottom lip. It was an entirely un-Harriet like thing to do and it made Adam feel odd watching it.

'I think I would have known,' Harriet said, finally. 'I mean I know… I knew both of them so well.' They were nearing their table again now. Leigha and Roddy had returned from their impromptu turn on the dance floor. Leigha was staring into the dark depths of her glass of red wine, not interacting with anyone.

'It was just a thought,' Adam said, as they approached earshot. 'Leigha's probably just drunk.' Harriet shot him a censoring look. 'What? She was verging on being an alcoholic at twenty, and from the looks of what she put back last night at dinner, and what she's had tonight, she's only gotten worse with age!'

Harriet playfully smacked the unopened plastic bottle of water against his arm. On reflex Adam caught it in his hand, giving it a tug and dragging Harriet – already a little unsteady in her heels thanks to the two glasses of champers and one of wine – closer to him. Leigha chose that moment to look up, her eyes narrowing as she caught the flirty exchange.

Iona had gently needled him for ten or twelve tracks before Johnny begrudgingly got to his feet and led her out onto the dance floor. Although it wasn't a ballad that was playing, Iona wrapped her arms around his torso and pressed the side of her face into his chest, holding him tightly and swaying left and right, eyes closed, as if this was the best thing in the world.

Despite the gorgeous young thing in his arms, Johnny felt his attention literally dragged back to Leigha, like the two of them worked like magnets. She was on her own; ostensibly, Adam and Harriet were still sat at the table, but there was never going to be any friendly chit-chat from that quarter; Demi and Sukie had disappeared; Roddy was finally getting bored with being ignored by his date and had struck up a conversation with the table behind them, in particular an equally thick-necked rugger bugger' type, the boyfriend of one of Nicky's colleagues.

He only really registered that Iona had said something because he felt the vibration of her speech against his ribcage. He angled his head closer to better hear her.

'Hmmm?'

'I said I wish you wouldn't keep looking at her.' It was no wonder he hadn't heard her the first time; Iona's voice was pitifully quiet, embarrassingly sad. For a brief moment he considered feigning ignorance, before deciding that she would probably find that even more insulting. He sighed.

'I'm sorry, sweetheart. I don't mean to. I just haven't seen her for so long, you know?'

'She's not a nice person, you know.'

'Sweetheart,' Johnny repeated, plastering on what he hoped was a reassuring smile. 'Nobody expects you to like your current partner's ex!' He remembered Miles putting forward that very same sentiment that morning, in his room. Was it really only that morning?

'It's not about that. It's not that she's your ex. God, I wish you had *more* exes, to be honest and not just her being the be all and end all.' Iona shook her head slightly, as if curtailing herself before she went too far. Johnny pulled their torsos apart so he could look her in the face.

'Look, I know you feel loyal to Harriet because of your sister,' he said. 'And, you know, having spent time with her again this weekend – yeah, okay, she's a nice person – but you can't hate Leigha for what happened years ago, because Harriet was the one that caused everything. Everything was just really complicated—'

'No,' Iona interrupted him. She sounded strong but still Johnny had to strain to hear her over the music, which they were still automatically dancing to. 'She *made* everything complicated. She *makes* everything complicated. She ruined Adam and Harriet's chance of being happy together. And now they're both such sad people. Seeing them interact tonight, they're sweet. They look good together. I think they could have really been something.'

Johnny remembered Adam, sitting in their lounge as the clock ticked past midnight and his 21st birthday was officially over. He'd held a bottle of beer in one hand, the other was wrapped in First Aid Box gauze. His face had been matt and tacky; Johnny had suspected that there had been some tears before he'd arrived home.

'I think we could have really *been something*,' Adam had mumbled, pressing the mouth of the beer bottle to his lips before he'd even finished talking. 'I really thought that we had *something*.'

'She ruined your life, too,' Iona continued, stubbornly. Johnny sighed.

'No she didn't.'

'Yes she did. Because of her you gave up that internship. Harriet told me. So you changed your whole life to fit around her and she just dumped you anyway?'

'Iona, stop it. So because of her my life was changed. That's not necessarily a bad thing. That's what people do to one another, come into their lives and shake things up. It would be a pretty boring world if that wasn't the case. And besides.' He pressed Iona close again. 'Is it such a bad thing that my plans changed, and I came to live in London? Have the job I have now? If I hadn't I would never have met you. And I like knowing you, you know; I really do.'

He was sincere, he realised, after the fact. He must have sounded so, too, because Iona quieted and settled against him again. They swayed wordlessly to the music for the remainder of the track.

After the cake had been cut and distributed and Adam had delivered a flawless – and only mildly risqué – Best Man speech, Miles took his chance, taking his new wife gently by the hand and leading her outside.

It was the first moment of their marriage they had been truly alone. Miles reached and took Nicky's face in his hands, running the pads of his thumbs softly underneath her eyes, which – at close inspection – were still a little puffy from her earlier crying.

'Miles…' Nicky began, as if she was dying to tell him something. Whatever it was, Miles thought it could wait.

'Pet.' He shushed her by moving one of his thumbs to her lips. 'Don't worry about it. We'll talk about it another time.'

'Are you cross?' Nicky's voice was so timid that Miles had to swallow a laugh.

'How could I be cross? You've married me, you've goddamn married me. I feel like I could never be cross again! But, of course,

I'm sure I will be.' Nicky immediately looked concerned. Miles smiled at her, angling her head down so he could kiss her on the forehead. 'We'll argue. About money and the kids and unfinished DIY and who's turn it is to do the washing up.' Nicky had slowly begun to smile too as he spoke.

'We could always get a dishwasher,' she said, thoughtfully. 'That would negate that one, at least.'

'Can't negate everything though!' Miles said. 'I'm just going to have to be sometimes cross with you, Nicky Healy.' Her new name was thrilling, like a secret. 'I get to be "sometimes cross" with you for the rest of our lives.'

'How romantic!' Nicky laughed, putting her own hands up to lay them atop of Miles' hands, still framing her face.

'To be fair, the threshold for romance is a little high today.' Miles pressed close, pressing their noses together, inhaling the familiar scent of her usual cosmetics. This woman was home to him. 'Now, we probably have another five seconds before someone comes looking for us, or someone wants to take a photo. Kiss me like I'm going to take you to live on the French coast.' Nicky laughed and did.

It was officially night time and the air was almost too cool on Sukie's bare shoulders and arms as she stepped out into the openness of the north quad, trailing Demi behind her with a firm grip on his wrist like he was her errant child.

Over beneath the balustrade there was a couple mostly in the shadows, so much so they would have been anonymous were it not for the white glare of Nicky's wedding dress. Sukie made an impatient noise in her throat, pulling Demi on, feeling lucky that she – unlike most of the guests – knew this place like the back of her hand and could mentally catalogue all the places where people could be alone. She walked with purpose through the darker shadow of the stone arches over the library door and into the library quad itself. As she had hoped, it was deserted.

Sukie fumbled with her bag for a moment, desperately needing to soften the moment with a cigarette, before remembering that she'd left her packet back in her room, due to the limited space inside her tiny, formal bag. Irritation levels rising, she dropped the bag in disgust, and it swung manically from its strap, banging against her side.

Demi had hung back from the moment she'd dropped his arm to open her bag. He leant back against the dark red brick of the wall, watching her.

'Okay,' Sukie said. She took a steadying breath through her nose. 'Okay,' she repeated. 'What are you talking about?'

'I think I was talking about how much I care about you,' Demi answered, his voice uncharacteristically quiet. 'How much I want to be with you.'

'No, not that. About my dad.'

'And how he speaks perfect English?'

'Yes, that.' The bite of annoyance in her tone was getting sharper and sharper with each exchange. Demi shrugged, a long, languorous movement.

'I went to see him.'

'You're lying.' Sukie's jaw clenched so hard that her back molars ground together.

'When you were having your hair cut last weekend. I knew you'd be out then so I went over.'

'How did you know where I live?' Demi shot her an impatient look.

'That town is only so big. And it's not exactly crawling with Japanese people. I just asked around.'

'Oh God.' Sukie took a moment to digest this information. 'Are you actually serious?' she asked, clinging to the faint hope this might be one of his weird jokes. Demi nodded his head. 'Fucking hell.' She exhaled. 'He didn't say anything to me.'

'I know. I asked him not to,' Demi explained; he finally had the grace to look a little awkward and apologetic.

'And what exactly was the topic of this conversation you and my dad had, in such great English?'

'You, obviously.' Demi was starting to react to Sukie's angry tone, his answers getting more and more sarcastic.

'And what about me in particular?'

'About if he cared that you've been graduated five years and you haven't been given the opportunity to look for a job, so your CV looks like shit. How you have had to take on the mantle of a middle-aged mother of teenagers instead of moving out, living your own life. How lonely you are. How unfulfilled. I asked him if he knew that you write and upload stories and little scripts and stuff online...' Sukie felt blood rush to her face.

'How did *you* know?' Demi smiled at her; she caught the pale flash of his teeth within the shadow as he did.

'Googling you, love. You use that one email address for every account, so...'

'Fuck.'

'He didn't know, though,' Demi continued. 'So I told him. And I told him they were damn good. You could be a writer, a proper writer. You should be *doing something* with all that spare time you have. Some sort of course, or internship.'

'I know,' Sukie tried, 'but the girls need me at home—'

'The girls?' Demi repeated her, interrupting. 'Those "girls" are, like, sixteen years old!'

'Seventeen and fifteen,' Sukie corrected, mumbling. Demi rolled his eyes.

'Whatever.'

'I'm *happy* to help out,' Sukie argued. Demi just looked at her, patiently.

'No you're not.' His voice was gentle, matter of fact, not accusatory or exasperated. 'Not *happy* to.'

'And how exactly did you introduce yourself to my dad?' Sukie drew herself up to full fighting height, eyes flashing. 'A concerned bystander? Or, "hi, I'm the guy that's been fucking your daughter"?' Demi winced at the phrasing; Sukie barrelled on, strengthened by it. 'Because if you say that he took *that* well, I'll *know* that you're lying.'

The quad fell into silence as Demi stared her down, obviously choosing his words with care. Finally he shifted, pushing away from the wall and approaching her.

'Although I pointed out that it was totally secondary to everything else that I'd come to say, I did say that I had feelings for you, yes, and I asked if he would be adverse to us ever being together.'

Sukie covered her face with her hands. 'Did you tell him that you were gay?' she asked, miserably, voice muffled. Demi made an impatient sound and moved even closer.

'I told you, I'm not gay!' His voice was the closest to angry that she'd ever heard it; Sukie stopped herself from shrinking away. 'And even so, what business is it of his? Who I've slept with is only my business, *mine*. And yours, if you wanted to be with me. That's it.'

Sukie had no immediate answer. She kept her face hidden in her hands. 'And what did he say to all this?' she asked finally. When Demi hesitated before answering, she repeated herself, volume rising to an almost-shout. 'What did he say?'

'He said he didn't realise. And that he wants to talk to you. At first he just told me off for telling him off but he calmed down pretty quickly.' His voice grew gentle again. 'He said he thought you wanted to be at home still. He thought you were doing it to stay close to your mother.'

Sukie stiffened. Her immediate reaction was to argue against this ridiculous, insulting over-simplification.

'I reckon it's a bit of both,' Demi said, softly, before she could formulate a response. 'He wants you near, and there's a part of you that wants to be there. It's only natural.' Demi tilted his head, considering her.

'I always thought your dad was some sort of monster, like a step-mother from a fairy tale, keeping you locked away at home, cooking and cleaning. But he's actually a good man. He just wants you to be happy. It's been you as much as him, all along; you've been trapping yourself at home and projecting all your shit onto him, haven't you?'

Sukie finally dropped her hands, feeling the evening air blow cold onto her flushed face.

'It's not like that really,' she insisted, although a small part of her was realising that it could well be. 'I thought he'd be disappointed if I left home, moved into a bedsit, got some dead-end job to support me whilst I wrote. He's a businessman. He's ridiculously practical. And I thought, I really, really thought that he'd totally disapprove of you.' She looked at him, glumly. Demi finally breached the remaining space between them and put his arms around her.

'Honey,' he said, 'why ever would you think that? I would be a fantastic boyfriend. You can get a reference from Rob.' Sukie groaned at the bad taste of his joke. 'And kind of like what Miles said earlier, about Nicky: I would be an even better man, every day, for you, but – to be honest – I don't even think I'd have to try that hard to make you really happy, and calm, like I think you haven't truly been for a long while. What's not to approve of there?'

There was silence for a while as Demi kissed her, and she kissed him back, with a little more *something* than she'd ever let herself put into it before. They were startled apart by clanging, the building's old clocktower striking the hour. It was seven o'clock, so much of this strange day already slipped away and gone forever.

'Besides,' Demi said, against her ear; his voice was husky and hushed, like they were back in the library on the day that they first met. *Want to go for a coffee?* he'd murmured, just like that. 'By the end of the year I'm going to be a fully qualified lawyer, remember? And your dad sure liked that.'

Leigha sat down without preamble. She was half-cut and looking bad on it. Her make-up was caking in some places and she was sweaty and shiny in others. It was the first time they'd been alone since she'd broken up with him.

'I see your *girlfriend* –' She gestured erratically towards Iona with the hand that held her drink; the wine slopped dangerously against the sides of the glass. '- has found someone more her own age to talk to?' She laughed; it turned into a bit of a snort, but at least she was still sober enough to look embarrassed by it.

Iona was over on another table, deep in conversation with Miles' sixteen year old sister, giving her UCAS and university application advice, of all things. Johnny felt a stirring in his chest, but it wasn't the one he normally felt when Leigha was involved. It was annoyance; almost distaste.

'Where's Roddy?' he asked. Leigha shrugged. Her wine swilled around inside its glass again.

'Have I told you that you're looking good, Johnny?' she said suddenly, her focus sharpening. Johnny waited for the elation he expected to feel at the compliment to hit; he felt nothing. He looked almost accusingly at his bottle of beer. *Wine before beer and you'll feel queer*; was that what was going on? Leigha took a big drink. Her lips were the same dark red as the wine; Johnny wasn't sure whether it was a lipstick or stain from the drink itself.

'You haven't gotten fat or anything,' Leigha continued, much to Johnny's bemusement.

'Yeah, well…' Johnny scratched his nose in confusion. 'That

wouldn't be a real good look for a sports presenter, would it?'

'I don't think I've ever seen you in a suit, either,' Leigha said.

'What about Graduation?' Johnny asked. Leigha was in all his graduation photos, smiling out at him from the walls of his parents' house whenever he went home to visit them.

'I guess,' she said, nonchalantly. They lapsed into an uneasy silence.

On the dance floor, Harriet and Nicky held one another, like they were hugging instead of dancing. Adam and Miles stood to the side, talking and half-watching the girls. Adam snapped a photo using his mobile phone; the girls protested faintly that they hadn't been ready for a picture. Demi and Sukie had reappeared after a notable absence but looked none the worse for wear as they too just held each other and swayed to the music. The song was *Total Eclipse of the Heart*, which Johnny found a little depressing for a wedding reception, but what did he know.

Across the room, Iona and Miles' sister rose to join the others, Nicky and Harriet pulling apart to include them. The four girls danced in a loose circle, giggling, all sweeping, enthusiastic movements, shouting out the lyrics along with the track as the song headed towards its crescendo. Iona was especially beautiful in that moment, her face flushed, her dark hair spilling out behind her as she moved. Of course, the image of her dancing this way with Nicky and Harriet couldn't help but evoke memories of Leigha, who for years had danced in this same, silly, natural way with those same two girls.

Johnny glanced at Leigha; she too was staring out across the dance floor, a sad little slope to her mouth; Johnny guessed she was remembering too.

'Ley,' he said, softly. 'Can I ask you something?' She nodded, eyes still locked on the other girls. 'Did you ever love me?'

She turned immediately and stared, her posture stiffening, obvious alarm penetrating through any buzz caused by the wine, her old walls rising straight up.

'Johnny,' she said, and at least her tone was apologetic. 'I never said I did, did I?'

No, no she hadn't. He'd forgotten that. How could he have forgotten that?

'Could you have? Ever loved me, I mean?' Despite his earlier numbness towards Leigha, this was hurting him for sure; he wasn't sure though if it was the equivalent of picking a scab or of cauterising a wound, or why he was even asking, not really.

'Johnny…' She sighed out his name, as if this was hard for her. 'I don't know. You are…' She caught herself just in time to correct her tense. 'You were just too much, you know? I told you all this at the time…'

'So tell me again,' Johnny insisted. Leigha sighed again. For a heartbeat or two, nobody spoke.

'All this raking over ancient history is boring,' Leigha said finally, before pausing to see off the remnants of her wine. 'I'm going to go find Roddy and another drink. See you later?' She was standing before she'd even finished her sentence, and gone before Johnny had a chance to reply.

Johnny sat in silence – alone at the large table – seeing off his own drink, feeling objective for the first time in forever. He couldn't quite believe it. He'd given up his dreams, changed all his plans for a flighty, boozy girl who had never even told him that she loved him? God. He wanted to shake his twenty-one year old self. What were you thinking? You are one lucky fuck, he told himself, sternly. So you'd better not pull any shit like that again; your lifetime luck quota has probably been exceeded.

There was still part of him – not even that deep inside – that wanted to follow her, take the drink from her hand, sober her up, look after her, and somehow make her love him; but that part of him was quieter now, and felt a little ashamed of itself.

The track changed and drew his attention back to the group on the dance floor. Iona was laughing, holding her hair bunched up in her hands as she flapped her hand in her face in an effort to cool down after her exertions dancing. The lights from the DJ booth shot colours across her: pink, yellow, blue.

Maybe his luck wasn't out, not quite yet. It would be interesting to see though, if he could ever love Iona; if there was something true there, or if he'd only been drawn to her thanks to the looks and little idiosyncrasies that she unknowingly shared with Leigha. He knew one thing for sure, though: either way, he wouldn't mess her around.

Iona seemed to sense his attention on her and caught his eyes across the span of the room. She smiled – really smiled – waving enthusiastically. Johnny felt a flutter in his chest again; a nice one, this time.

The new track was Journey's *Don't Stop Believing*. Much more appropriate, Johnny felt, rising to his feet to join his friends and his girlfriend on the dance floor.

The feel of the evening was getting loose and informal enough that she didn't think anyone would mind, so Harriet kicked off her heels when she returned to her seat, rubbing her bare toes against the prickly carpet as she stretched out the ache in her feet.

As if her leaving the dance floor had been the invitation they'd been waiting for, Leigha and Sukie moved in on Nicky. Harriet watched them, trying to feel detached, and failing. The night was wearing on, and the more tired she got and the more she had to drink, the sadder about everything she felt. Once again she considered retiring to her room. She wasn't wearing a watch, but surely it was getting on to nine o'clock? Guests with young kids or those who had a long drive home were already saying their goodbyes, so she wouldn't be the first to leave.

Her thoughts were interrupted by the arrival of Adam. He thumped a glass bottle of clear liquid down in front of her, and liberated two shot glasses from the pocket of his suit trousers before sitting down. Harriet reached out and turned the bottle around so that she could read the labelling on the front: Grey Goose vodka.

She arched an eyebrow at Adam. 'What's this?'

Adam reached for the bottle again. 'Best Man and Maid of Honour perk.' He poured two healthy shots of vodka. Harriet shook her head.

'No thanks.'

'Oh come on,' Adam laughed. 'I know it isn't pilfered Malibu but…' With a quick motion he did his shot.

'Adam,' Harriet laughed. 'No. Two things I was explicitly told not to do tonight was hang around too much with you or get drunk; therefore doing shots of neat vodka with you is really not on the agenda!'

'Who told you not to hang around with me?' Adam asked, his interest immediately piqued.

'Ah, nobody. My friend.'

'Annie?'

'Yeah, Annie.' Harriet reached out and toyed with her empty shot glass, listlessly. Not for the first time that night she reflected on how much easier she would be finding things if Annie were there too.

'Well, Annie sounds like a sensible lady,' Adam smiled. 'So let's drink to her.' Harriet gave him a 'nice try' look. 'To Annie?' he tried again, holding the vodka bottle up and giving her what he hoped was a gold medal level smile. Harriet rolled her eyes.

'To Annie,' she agreed, pushing her shot glass towards him to be filled. 'Not too much.'

Adam watched her profile as she threw her head back and did the shot, the corners of her eyes crinkling at the vodka's bite.

'Never ever, have I ever…' he chanted, as he filled up his own shot glass with about a half measure.

'Uh-uh, no way.' Harriet shook her head, but there was a smile on her face all the same.

'Harry. You will probably remember from your time as a student here that it is much more socially acceptable to mask the unhealthy and rapid consumption of shots by saying that it's a drinking game.' She laughed.

'Fine,' she said, reaching for the bottle and pouring herself her own half measure. 'But I start. Never ever have I ever been a boy called Adam.' Adam rolled his eyes.

'That's so not the point of this game,' he said, taking his shot all the same. Harriet was poised to refill his glass the moment it returned to the table top.

'I thought that this was just a pretence to conceal the fact that we are rapidly consuming an unhealthy number of shots?' Harriet asked, voice mock-innocent. Adam felt a laugh twitching on his lips.

'Fair enough,' he conceded. 'If that's how you want to play it. Never ever, have I ever, been a girl called Harriet…'

A contrite-looking Roddy had returned to her side. His equivalent of dancing was to stand in one spot and awkwardly shuffle.

'Dance with me,' Leigha ordered, pressing herself against him, catching him at each wrist and placing his hands on her hips. The song playing was something currently in the charts, with a heavy bass line and the occasional interspersing of rap – not really a track conducive to a couple dancing - but Roddy manfully attempted it nevertheless.

Roddy was too tall for her to be able to look over his shoulder;

Leigha lay her cheek flat against his chest, feeling one of his shirt buttons pressing on the delicate skin underneath her eye.

Seth and his wife were sitting in one of the corner tables, almost blocked from her view completely by a rather rowdy table of Miles' Bath University colleagues. The wife was showing something on her phone around the table; probably a picture of her own wedding. Seen them, Leigha thought: nothing to brag about, sweetie. She closed her eyes, shutting them out, concentrating on the thump-thump-thump-thump of Roddy's heart, louder at this close range than the bass line of the song.

For her fifteenth birthday she had had a sleepover; just her, Harriet and Sukie and a couple of other girls from school. One of them had just read a book where the hero and the heroine were from different dimensions – or something – real cheesy stuff. But it had sparked up a conversation about alternate realities, multiple universes, where as simple a decision as what to have for lunch sent manifold versions of you spinning out through time and space, one for each possible possibility.

That had delighted the fifteen year old Leigha, the idea that somewhere in the universe there would be a Leigha living the perfect life. It made everything seem suddenly much more achievable, like she could conceivably engineer it so that she *was* that Leigha.

She tried to picture the Seth of the reality where the two of them had been able to be together, no Harriet Shaw to come between them. She tried to picture that Leigha; she found that she simply couldn't.

She opened her eyes; their dancing had slightly shifted where they were in the room. She was facing inwards, to where Miles and Nicky and Sukie and Demi were dancing, the latter couple laughing as they skipped and swerved to avoid treading on the skirt of Nicky's dress.

Leigha considered going over and asking Seth to dance; he must have noticed that she'd blown him off earlier, and knowing him he was probably feeling awkward and bad about it. Or embarrassed; the last time she saw him he was naked and crying – that is pretty pitiful, after all.

She imagined how dancing with Seth would feel. All those years ago, when he'd first put his arms around her – breathing hot and beery over her face, into her mouth – and still she'd melted, wanted them to press closer together than physics allowed, wanted them to occupy the same time and space, for always.

The track blended into the next: a love song. The couples drew one another closer. Demi cupped the back of Sukie's head, his fingertips disappearing into the blackness of her hair. Miles and Nicky murmured quietly into one another's ears as they began to dance cheek to cheek. Leigha found herself feeling something that was just short of wishing that she had the same.

A project, she thought to herself, the thumping-thumping heartbeat under her ear all but drowning out the romantic lyrics of the song. A project to find a man who could overcome her natural distaste for anyone who seemed to like her too much. A man like an alternate reality Seth. What a man that will be.

Roddy wasn't such a man, of course, and never would be. She knew she shouldn't have brought him to this wedding – he would be thinking that he meant more to her than he ever could – but she hadn't been able to face it on her own. She never had liked being on her own.

Leigha was lulled by the rhythmic movement of muscles beneath the cotton of Roddy's shirt as he gently circled her around and around in time with the music. She closed her eyes again. When they got back to London tomorrow she should finish things with him, or maybe some time next week, when he called to make their usual mid-week dinner-and-drinks date. Either way, it should be soon, to clear the path for Alternate Seth.

Now she had a focus, killing time with Roddy felt a little bit too much like stringing him along, and Leigha didn't like the prickles of guilt that that thought brought on. It made her think of Johnny. They'd not seen one another for about a month, by the time he'd driven up to take her flat-hunting and she'd realised, belatedly, that she'd let everything get a little too far. She hadn't wanted to hurt him, but had known that letting things go on would just end up hurting him more, so she'd bitten the bullet she'd been avoiding biting since the summer.

'You're a cruel cow, Ley,' Johnny had informed her – voice oddly toneless after an hour of pleading and wheedling – as he'd shrugged back into his jacket. 'I don't understand you, or what your problem is.'

Of all the many things that she'd been called over the years, that one had stayed with her, felt particularly unjustified.

So then – tomorrow afternoon, when they arrived back at her flat, it would be cruel to put it off. She could do it in the car when he pulled into the car park, even; he didn't have any belongings at her flat, wouldn't need to come up. One short, sharp, uncomfortable conversation, which was all it ever took.

The DJ apparently had a line of sight on them and a sense of humour – or it was a rather wonderful coincidence. The track changed to Pat Benetar's *Hit Me With Your Best Shot* and Adam and Harriet subsided into giggles.

'Ahhh, I'm quite drunk,' Harriet lamented. 'You total pain in the arse.'

'Bet you're feeling a little less stressed though,' Adam beamed at her. 'And it kept you from leaving early.' Harriet's face tightened.

'How did you know I was thinking of leaving?' she asked. Adam shrugged, suddenly evasive, looking away.

'Guessed. I bet I would have felt the same. There isn't much here for you to hang around for. Except for me and the premium vodka.'

'The two things I was told to avoid,' Harriet reminded him.

'Yup,' Adam agreed. 'Those same two things.' Harriet rubbed her fingers over her temple; they were tacky with the splashback from pouring so many shots of vodka.

'What's your game?' she asked Adam, but not in a tone that suggested she expected an answer. 'I can't work it out.'

'No game,' Adam answered. 'Aside from Never Ever, ha. Just trying to make things a little easier for you, like I said that I would yesterday.' Harriet shifted, a dry smile on her face; she had her right arm crossed over her torso, her fingers resting lightly against her left shoulder. With her left hand she fiddled with her bracelet.

'Make things easier for me?' she echoed. 'Oh, Adam, mate… I doubt you've ever made anything easy for anyone, especially not me.' She smiled to soften the force of her words but she could see that they had stung him all the same. He poured himself another half-shot of vodka, not meeting her face.

'Yeah, well.' He quickly downed the shot. 'I'm just being a friend. Like you wanted.' Confusion creased Harriet's forehead. 'You wished that we'd been friends,' he clarified.

'We were friends…' Harriet said slowly, still muddled.

'No, like how you said yesterday,' Adam muttered. 'About how you wish that we'd *just* been friends.'

'Oh.' Realisation dawned. 'Oh, I didn't mean it like that. It was a compliment. It meant that I – you know – would have preferred to have stayed friends than nothing. Like, I would rather have us never been together and still been good mates today, than what actually happened. You know?' she repeated, weakly. Adam glanced up.

'No,' he said. 'I don't feel that way at all.'

'I just mean that ignorance is bliss, or something!' Harriet flustered, trying to undo the damage. Adam's stare hardened.

'I guess,' he said, slowly, finally dropping his eyes again. Harriet exhaled uneasily. 'It's just that you were a better lover than you were a mate,' Adam finished, shrugging. Harriet's mouth fell open.

'What?'

'What?' Adam asked, innocently. 'It's a *compliment*,' he said, in a sing-songy tone, repeating her earlier excuse.

'Excuse me?' Harriet was rankled. 'I think I was – I *am* – a really good friend!' Adam shrugged again, nonchalant.

'One who left me standing in your emptied-out bedroom on my 21st birthday,' was all he said, still in that irritating, sing-song voice. Harriet scowled.

'Well, it wouldn't have *gotten* to the point where that was my only option if, you know, you'd been more supportive!'

'Supportive!' Adam looked incredulous. 'How the fuck was I not supportive? Holed up with you in that little room every night, bringing you takeaways because you were too timid to go downstairs and use the kitchen! Telling you I loved you, trying to counter all the poison that those bitches dripped in your ear. Don't you dare tell me that I wasn't supportive.'

Harriet briefly closed her eyes. 'It just... it wasn't... you just weren't supportive enough,' she managed, finally.

'And what was it you were expecting?' Adam asked, sarcastically. 'What could I have done to fix it? All you ever said was that I shouldn't get involved.'

'I—' Harriet began to protest.

'Oh, don't make a scene, Adam!' Adam put on a high-pitched voice to imitate her. 'Don't go and talk to them about it! Don't make it worse!'

Harriet had no response; they fell silent. Harriet felt a warmth stinging in her chest, and behind her eyes, the wine and the vodka churning in her stomach. Now, she thought, now is the time to say my goodnights.

'I'm sorry,' Adam said, gruffly, unexpectedly. 'I promised I wouldn't get in to all this with you. It doesn't matter.'

'No, I'm sorry,' Harriet said. 'But that seems to be all I'm saying to you this weekend. I think I'm going to call it a night.' As she spoke she rose to leave.

As she rose she lifted her hand to her face; her bracelet raced along the length of her arm; something caught his eye.

'Hey,' Adam said, standing too. 'Show me.' He reached out and took her right arm; three little black Vs were inked onto the inside of her wrist and forearm.

'Oh, yeah,' Harriet said, uncomfortably. 'Hence the bracelet. Wasn't sure Nicky would approve of a tattooed bridesmaid.'

'What, are they birds?' Adam asked, running his thumb over the first one; Harriet nodded. 'Wow. You're still full of surprises, Shaw. Didn't have you pegged for a tattoo. You always said they were tacky.'

'It's hardly a big skull or a thorny rose or a scroll that says 'Mother' across it,' Harriet rolled her eyes. 'And I only said that tattoos should be meaningful, not just for their own sake.'

'Okay,' Adam nodded. 'And what does this mean?' Harriet hesitated, tilting her head as she considered her answer. Suddenly Adam remembered the bird earrings he'd once bought her, and how they had dangled and spun whenever she had tilted her head like that.

'They remind me,' she said, finally. 'Of what's important. Of before.'

'Christ!' Adam said, looking down at the three little birds again. 'I hope it's not: this one's you, this one's Sukie and this one's Leigha?' He traced the birds outwards from her wrist as she spoke. Harriet shook her head and brought her own fingers down next to his.

'Not at all,' she told him. 'They are all me. Where I've been, where I am, and where I'm going.' Adam looked at her, their faces close; he still held her arm.

'That's very... zen, or something,' he said finally, not really knowing what to say. 'Harry, come on. Stay. No more forced shots, I promise. I'll even get you some water.' She hesitated; the expression on her face looked like a no. The pulse in her wrist jumped under his fingertips. 'Harriet.' He said her name again like the repetition of it could make her stay. 'Don't go. It's been really good to be with you.'

And it had. There was still so much he wanted to talk about: whereabouts did she live now, what her job involved day to day, had she voted and how, what did she think about London having the Olympics? He wanted to know more about this grown-up Harriet. He hadn't intended to bring up the past – not at all – but it was everywhere, inescapable, sitting on the chair next to them, within the lyrics of the music, in the taste of the vodka, in the look in her eyes.

But still, the no on her face wavered and became a half-smile.

'I'm quite tired,' she said, apologetically. 'It has been nice to catch up, though.' She stepped to the side, sliding the chair back into place under the table. Adam felt something like panic rising up, a heat inside his body.

'Come on,' he tried, one last time, speaking before he had time to consider his words. 'You owe me.'

He regretted the words the second that it was too late. Harriet's brows snapped together and she pulled her arm away from in between their bodies.

'Good night, Adam,' she said, her voice clipped.

'Look, do you want to take my number?' Adam tried. 'Maybe we should try a proper catch up in a less stressful environment?' Harriet shook her head.

'I don't think it's a great idea. Anyway, "just for the weekend", wasn't that what you said?'

'Oh, come on,' Adam snapped, his patience thinning. 'You're just being difficult, as per usual.'

'As per usual?' Harriet echoed in disbelief. 'What does that even mean?'

'Whatever. Nothing.' Adam underlined his indifference to the conversation by sitting back down, clamping down on the anger roiling inside his belly. She was so many extremes to him, it was unsettling; the person who being with was the easiest thing in the world, and the person who seemed to live to make things hard. With one last dark look Harriet swept her little beaded clutch bag from the table top and began to move away. 'See you at the Silver Wedding Anniversary party,' he called after her, desperate for the last word. 'Maybe by then you'll have grown up.'

Harriet turned on her point and marched the few steps back, throwing her bag back on the table and placing her hands on her hips; Adam rose to his feet to meet her wrath.

'Just leave me the hell alone,' she hissed.

'Oh, poor Harriet, Harriet the victim,' Adam mocked. 'Running off again. Do you know? I was really pleasantly surprised by you this weekend. I thought you were "old Harriet", back from the dead. Clearly, I was wrong.'

'What the hell do you mean, "old" Harriet?' Harriet balled her hands into little fists. 'When are people going to understand that there's just *Harriet,* not as many versions as there are opinions; just one, just me!'

'Well, according to your own arm there are at least three Harriets,' Adam jeered. She stared at him; he imagined that she was also wondering how they'd deteriorated so damn quickly.

'I'm sorry that right now I'm not acting like what you *expect* of me, or fitting nicely into whatever *box* you think I should, but, don't you dare presume to tell me that I'm "not myself". You don't fucking know me.'

'And whose fault is that?' he shot back.

'At the end of the day,' Harriet said, dropping her volume. Adam realised that their angry voices had drawn the attention of some strangers on neighbouring tables, but he couldn't quite bring himself to care. He *was* angry, damn it. His very veins were pulsing hot, like they had no blood in them, only a mixture of resentment and vodka.

She's dangerous: isn't that what he had told himself upon first seeing her again? She's dangerous because you want her – still – and she'll lure you in and fuck you up again, and after a second time all the petite brunettes in the world won't make you feel right again.

'I didn't "run away",' she continued, 'so much as I was chased away. And I didn't deserve it. I don't deserve to be the *persona non grata* at this wedding. I didn't do anything wrong.' Her tone was infuriating; she did, but didn't *quite* say: *but you did.*

'That's what you think?' He could hear the sneer and the poison in his voice and wondered detachedly at how absurdly easy it is to flip between love and loathing. Or maybe it was just with her. He started counting on his fingers. 'You kept us a secret. That was wrong. You never – not once in your life – stood up to Leigha. You let her get used to getting her own way, no matter what it was she wanted. That was wrong. You hid away in your room instead of confronting matters. That was wrong.' Harriet's fists were white and bloodless, she was holding herself so tightly.

'And then you pushed me away and just left me when I had bloody *ripped* myself open and laid everything out there, trying to make it work, trying to make you happy. And that was wrong. Because I told you and I told you and I am fucking telling you again now – that despite the fact I think, deep down, you actually want it to be true – *I never slept with Leigha!*'

It might have been muscle memory, a flashback from that night in the computer lab. Adam registered the tell, the tensing in her shoulders, and caught Harriet by the wrist, neatly blocking the intended slap. Her cuff bracelet landed at her elbow joint. Harriet glared at him hotly across their crossed arms.

'Not this time,' he told her, quietly.

She didn't say a word, or even look at him again. She scooped up the bag and walked out of the hall at a dignified, even stately pace, like she was reprising her earlier walk down the aisle.

Adam watched her until she was lost through the far doors. And that, he promised himself, is the very last time that Harriet Shaw ever walks out on me.

Chapter Twenty Nine

When it became painfully clear that Adam wasn't following her, Harriet sped up, moving swiftly from one quad into another and out, out past the office buildings and their car park and through the front gates. Her feet carried her down the most familiar route whilst her thoughts pitched and rolled.

When she happened upon the first bus stop of the high street she stopped abruptly, sitting down hard on the shiny red plastic bench and wrapping her arms around herself. She didn't have a wrap or a coat and the night had turned cold. Now that the heat and adrenalin of the argument with Adam was seeping away she felt the skin on her forearms goosepimpling and became aware of the ache in the balls of her feet. She slipped her heels off and picked them up, leaving her feet bare on the gritty pavement.

Two girls came down the road, laughing, arms interlinked, pausing at the sight of a lone woman in a sleeveless yellow dress sitting in a bus shelter.

'Sorry?' the shorter of the two girls said. She was wearing a navy hoodie with the initials of the university emblazoned across the front. 'The buses stop at six.'

'Oh,' Harriet said. 'Thanks. I know. I was just, having a sit.'

'Oh. Okay.' Exchanging an uncertain look the two younger girls moved on, off to the 24 hour garage a couple of streets away, perhaps. Suitably embarrassed, Harriet got back to her feet and continued her aimless wander.

Although, of course, it wasn't aimless. Minutes later Harriet found herself walking down Hatcher Road and came to a stop at the exact same spot she and Adam had shared their first kiss, their faces damp with snow, breaths visible and mingling together in the dark. *I never slept with Leigha*, he had shouted. Probably the most adamant and believable he had ever been with his denials; not that it mattered, not now.

The stunted tree that used to block the light into Nicky's bedroom had been felled, the patch of crab grass upon which it had stood paved over and made into a parking space. The knee-high wall that circled the right hand side of the house and curved Dell Road into Hatcher had been fully restored – perhaps plain rebuilt – and was painted a twee white. The front door had been red and peeling a little the last time she closed it behind her, and now it was a glossy black. The new driveway was empty, the curtains all drawn open, even though it was night. The house looked empty and dead and full of ghosts; the house looked completely different.

How many lives must each student house see, Harriet wondered; how many friendships and fights, make-ups and break-ups? Do the bricks and mortar absorb all the energy, the happiness and the sadness? Maybe so – as standing there had much the same effect that walking through campus had had, drawing out more images, more and more. Harriet couldn't believe how much was inside of her, had been just lying in wait for her to come back to it.

Sukie's dark head framed in the right-hand window as she worked away at her desk, catching sight of Harriet returning after a week back at her parents' and standing up and waving eagerly through the glass. Leigha draping bunting across the old tree on birthdays, and tinsel each Christmas, laughing, laughing. All four girls, latched arm-to-arm in the darkness, drunk, giggling, helping one another over the crumbled section of the wall rather than walk the extra ten foot to the gate.

Harriet startled. Leigha was standing on the corner, wearing a beige pashmina wrapped across her torso, her arms folded across her chest, Sukie standing behind her with a cropped leather jacket thrown on over her dress. Harriet turned fully to face them; Leigha eyed her, impatiently.

'Nice scene back there,' she said, without preamble. 'Nice of you to ruin Nic's wedding day.'

Harriet frowned, finally, finally out of patience. 'I just want to be left alone,' she snapped.

'Well, you can't just have a shouting match and storm out of the room,' Sukie said. 'Nicky wanted to come after you but she couldn't really, could she? So she sent us. Funny that we all knew you'd come here;' her tone was only slightly mocking.

'The old place looks good though,' Leigha said, looking appraisingly at the renovations. 'Our dick landlord would never have put this sort of money into it, he must have sold it. Hey!' Harriet had begun walking off down Dell Road. 'Where are you going?'

'Away!' Harriet shouted. 'To be alone! Christ.'

'Oh, don't be so dramatic,' Leigha said, rolling her eyes. 'Always gotta make a scene, play the victim.' Her words were painfully close to what Adam had said, hit on the bull's-eye; Harriet hesitated.

This could be the last time she saw these two girls, now that there wasn't a hypothetical mutual friend's wedding hanging somewhere in the future. She remembered how she'd watched them walk down the garden path and away out of the sight, that last night, the night of Adam's birthday. They were standing in almost the exact same spot now; it had a neatness to it.

'What should I have done differently?' she asked.

Sukie raised an eyebrow. 'Differently? Ha! Well not getting totally pissed on contraband vodka and shouting—'

'No, not tonight,' Harriet interrupted her. 'Before.'

'Uh!' Leigha made an incredulous noise. 'You could have tried *not* sleeping with Adam.' Harriet looked at her, hard.

'Did you?' she asked, quietly. 'Did you *actually* sleep with him, Ley?' Leigha frowned, biting down on her lower lip, nervous and unsure; Harriet could still read her like a book.

'Yes, of course I did,' she said, finally. Harriet's heart constricted painfully; deep down, she still wanted it to not be true. *Let's just say that I visited Australia. Many times.*

'You know I didn't know that though, right? When I, when we… got together.' Harriet had meant to sound matter-of-fact, and cringed when it came out sounding vaguely apologetic. Leigha looked unimpressed.

'Whatever. We spent hours – *hours* – talking about him, me and you. Don't you dare for one minute think you can tell me that you had no idea that I liked him, that I'd claimed him.'

Harriet flinched. 'He's not a… piece of land.'

'Whatever.' Leigha's eyes flashed. 'He certainly didn't complain at the time.'

'Guys,' Sukie interrupted, still hanging back. 'Do we really have to go through this? Does it even matter anymore?' She shook her head. 'We should get back; Nicky will worry. Just hold it together a little longer and then you'll never have to come near one another again so long as you live.'

All the more reason to get these things said, Harriet thought.

'Leigha, what's the deal with you and Seth?' she asked, and was gratified to see the smugness immediately drain away from the other girl's face. 'Because there is something, right? Adam said he noticed something.'

'Adam?' Leigha repeated, in a choked-sounding voice.

'Things got weird between us back when I broke up with him,' Harriet said, slowly, thinking back. 'You always did seem more on his side than mine.'

'Your side?' Leigha twisted the fringing of her pashmina in her first. '*You* broke up with *him*, what do you even mean, 'your side'? Christ! You broke his heart!' Leigha's face was as heated as her words, her fingers bone white where they gripped the material of her shawl hard enough to chase away the blood.

Harriet just looked at her, even now feeling the impulse to comfort this beautiful, angry woman, the corpse of their friendship turning over in her heart; and she wondered how she'd ever missed the obvious.

'You and Seth,' she tried.

'I don't want to talk about Seth.' Leigha turned away abruptly. 'Come back, don't come back, I don't care.' She began to walk away and after a flicker of hesitation, Sukie started to follow. Harriet's time was up.

'I would have forgiven it of you,' she called after Leigha's retreating back. Leigha paused, glancing back over her shoulder.

'Well, I would never have done it in the first place,' she said, in an odd little voice.

The two girls looked at one another in silence, separated by the length of the house where they'd once lived together.

How to articulate in this one, final instant the pain that had been caused? How to explain that in her darker moments Harriet had found herself wishing that Leigha and Sukie had just been dead, because then at least the grieving and the missing of them wouldn't come hand-in-hand with the knowledge that she had been so definitively, so personally rejected. How that if there was a time machine, Harriet would go back and try her hardest to cut out the cancer that would one day kill their friendship. Even if she had to relive all that pain again she would always do so, just to be able to spend just one day with her best friends – when that's what they still were.

There was no way of getting any of that across, no way and no time. Harriet dropped her eyes.

'It wasn't just something seedy. I did love him, you know,' she offered, almost by way of explanation. Leigha's lip curled. I loved you too, Harriet thought. And – just like what you do with everyone else's love – you took it for granted. You wasted it. And when it came down to it, you threw it away like it was nothing. But I let you.

'Good for you,' was all Leigha said.

'We should get back…' Sukie said again, impotently, half to herself.

'And I wish that we had been able to stay friends,' Harriet continued. 'I guess what I'm trying to say is…' She met Leigha's eyes again, for the last time. 'I'm not sorry for what I did. But I'm sorry for it.'

Leigha turned away.

'That's nice, Harriet. The thing is though, you can be the best friends in the world, but some things are unforgiveable.' Without looking back she started walking away again, back in the direction of the campus. Sukie looked between the two of them, uncertain. Harriet smiled ruefully.

'You know what, Ley? I completely, completely agree.'

Leigha gave no sign that she had heard her. She was almost at the far end of the road.

'Are you coming back to the do?' Sukie asked, gruffly.

Harriet shook her head. 'No, I don't think so. I think I'm done.'

Sukie nodded, awkwardly, giving Harriet and the old house one last look before hurrying after Leigha. Harriet was left alone, standing in the spot where – one evening in February – her friend had kissed her, and set all of this in motion.

Annie would probably call this closure. Harriet didn't know about

342

that. She felt empty and hollow, the way you did after a good cry. She felt a strange sort of peace, too, standing there, like on this corner she could reach through the membrane of time and space, clap her twenty year old self on the shoulder and tell her that she's going to be fine. That there will be other best friends: gorgeous, funny, supportive Annie. In time there may be other Adams, who knew?

She dallied, saying goodbye to the corner and to the house, giving Leigha and Sukie enough time to make it to the intersection with the main road before starting her own walk back to campus. That bottle of Jacob's Creek and the oblivion of sleep was calling to her. She focused on her feet – still bare – as she walked, watching out for anything she didn't want to step in, tired of thinking about anything harder. So she was almost upon Leigha, waiting at the intersection, before she noticed her.

Leigha had an expression that even Harriet didn't know how to read. She didn't – she couldn't - look Harriet in the face. She opened her mouth to speak, but nothing came out for a moment or two.

'I just wanted to say,' she managed, eventually, looking into the middle distance. 'I didn't.'

'Didn't..?' Harriet echoed, hardly daring to breathe in case Leigha didn't finish her sentence.

'Didn't,' Leigha repeated. 'Sleep with him, I mean. I was lying. He wasn't.' She gave a shrug. 'I wanted to hurt you.' She toyed with the longer of the two necklaces she was wearing. 'Because you hurt me.'

There was an excruciating pause where neither of them spoke. Leigha hesitated, as if she were waiting for a thank you. Harriet couldn't speak; pain had risen up inside her like bile. Leigha stared down at her own fingers, fiddling with her chain.

Without another word, Leigha turned and marched across the intersection, walking away and out of sight. She walked under a streetlight at the last possible minute, coming alive suddenly in a riot of dark hair and yellow dress, before being consigned to the shadows of the campus wall, leaving Harriet alone with a regret that felt physical enough to choke her.

Nicky laughed delightedly as the DJ and the congregation of women behind her egged her on.

'Okay!' she called. 'Okay! One!' She swung the now slightly worse for wear bouquet up and then brought it back down to her chest. 'Two!'

She pitched the flowers gently over her shoulder as she shouted 'three', causing the women behind her to jump and scatter.

'Christ!' Leigha mumbled, smartly stepping sideways and out of the trajectory. Miles' teenage sister squealed and shot forward, arms outstretched for the prize. The bouquet grazed her, bouncing off her shoulder and smacking the nearby Sukie in the face, forcing her to catch it in her arms. She looked across the tangle of whites and yellows and greens, giving Demi – sitting nearby – a look of mock horror.

Demi, Johnny, Iona and Adam were seeing off the rest of the bottle of vodka; waste not, want not. As the excitement of the bouquet toss faded and the crowd of onlookers dispersed back to their own tables, the DJ announced that he would be playing his final song of the evening: safe journeys one and all.

'There's a game I played in my halls last year,' Iona said, excitedly.

'I don't think there's a single drinking game in the world that you can tell us about that we haven't played,' Johnny interrupted her, smugly. Iona glared at him.

'It's the one where you have to give a statement about yourself, something you haven't done—'

'Never Ever,' Johnny interrupted again, smirking. 'Standard!'

Adam shifted. 'I don't like that game' he said. The room filled

344

with the strains of Aerosmith's *Don't Wanna Miss A Thing*; apparently once in one evening just wasn't enough.

'I love that game,' Johnny laughed. 'If you play it properly you find out some wicked stuff. Like, do you remember? That weird Jed guy from down the hall in first year, he admitted that he had herpes and I don't think he ever got laid again, the whole three years.'

Adam laughed. 'I don't even think he understood the rules, poor git.'

'And you get to find out loads of quality stuff about your mates, too,' Johnny continued. 'Like Sukie had kissed a girl.' Demi's eyebrows shot up in amusement. 'Or about your weird genital mole,' he nodded towards Adam, who practically spat out his drink in alarm.

'Excuse me!' he said, laughing through the coughs, 'I have no such thing!'

'You said you did!' Johnny insisted, laughing too. 'You said it was in the shape of Australia, or something.'

Adam stopped laughing, very abruptly. 'It's a birthmark,' he said, finally. 'How did you know?'

'You told me during a game of Never Ever,' Johnny said, looking a bit worried. 'Way back. First year. Might have even been our Freshers' Week?'

'I did?'

'Yes,' Johnny asserted. 'How else would I know? Wasn't exactly into peeking at you in the shower, mate, God!'

Adam poured himself a full shot of vodka, glanced at the doors once, then settled back in his chair, letting it go.

The intricate lacing that had been impossible to tie on her own came apart with one tug of the ribbon bow; the dress fell and pooled around Harriet's feet. She dutifully hung it up.

She considered having a hot shower to chase the chill from her skin but didn't quite have the energy, slipping straight into her pyjamas instead. She grabbed the glass tumbler from the en-suite and the room temperature bottle of wine from her bag, taking both over to the window and settling herself down on the wide sill. She opened the window as far as the restrictors would allow, swung her legs out of the gap and let them dangle as she poured herself an unsatisfying glass of wine.

She stared out across the rooftops of her old campus, placing and recognising each building, even in the dark. Diagonally to her left was the building where she'd lived in her first year; she tried counting up from the ground and across from the right to work out which had been her window.

She'd just got it worked out when there was a knock at the door; soft, tentative. All the same, Harriet almost spilt her wine.

She'd made the decision not to seek Adam out, even after what Leigha had revealed. There was no point; there was too much water under too many bridges.

But maybe – just maybe – he didn't agree.

'One second!' she called, her voice croaky and odd-sounding. It seemed much more difficult to get her legs back into the room that it had been to swing them out. They didn't quite seem to support her when she got them back underneath her, and made her way to the door.

Nicky was stood on the other side of it, still splendid in her white wedding dress, although she'd loosened her hair and lost the clip-on veil by now. She looked at Harriet, face all concern.

'Are you okay?' she asked.

'Ah, Nic,' Harriet said, stepping aside to let her in the room. 'It's your wedding night. I'm not the person you should be with.'

'I wanted to check on you,' Nicky insisted, as Harriet closed the door behind her.

'I'm fine,' Harriet assured her. 'I'm sorry if I made a scene.' Nicky waved her hand, dismissively.

'Well if you did, then I did first, anyway,' she said. 'Did Adam upset you?'

'No.' Harriet hesitated. 'No, it was just me being high-strung. I owe him an apology, really, but I'm too chickenshit to give it to him. He never did sleep with Leigha, apparently.'

'I never really thought he did,' Nicky admitted, quietly. Harriet twisted her mouth.

'Well. I guess it's good to know.'

'You guys were getting on well,' Nicky began, gently. 'Miles and I were excited; we always hoped you would take this opportunity to put all the old crap behind you. You guys were good together.' Harriet laughed mirthlessly.

'Apparently not!' she said. 'Right person, wrong time is the best we can chalk everything up as, I think. Either way, it doesn't matter now.'

'Harry.' Nicky took her shorter friend by her upper-arms, holding her out in front of her. 'What have we learned this evening? That it can be – it should be – *all* about the person. You can make it the right time, if you really want to. If it's the *right* person, there's nothing that's insurmountable. Love is all about the two people that share it. Everything else… it's just context. It's just background noise.'

Harriet gave her a weak smile. 'You're a great friend, Nic.' It was the highest compliment she could think of. 'Love you.'

'Ah, Harry.' Nicky enveloped her in a bear hug. 'I love you too. But promise me you'll think about what I just said.' The two girls disentangled themselves.

'I will,' Harriet promised. 'Now, please get back to your marital bed.' Nicky laughed.

'Okay. I'll see you soon though, yeah?'

'You bet,' Harriet said, firmly. 'Call me when you're back from the honeymoon. I want to hear everything. Not least of all, where you guys are going to be living!' Nicky laughed again.

'Will do. Night.'

'Night,' Harriet echoed softly, as her friend slipped out into the corridor and shut the door behind her with a quiet click.

June 2005

That was the term that Sukie had taken up smoking with a vengeance. The impending weeks at home back under the sharp eye of her mother was soon to curtail her short of full addiction, but for now Sukie was lighting up at every opportunity, non-smoking halls be damned.

That night she was perched on the radiator boxing so she could exhale straight out the window – in deference to the fire alarm – her badly-mixed G&T in a mug and balanced on the sill beside her. The world outside was muffled. The first years' exams were over and all over campus freshers were sitting together like this, at loose ends – drinking, smoking, talking – whilst the second years and finalists remained secluded in the hush of revision.

Leigha had opted for a couple of bottles of pre-mixed Sex on the Beach, Sainsbury's own brand, which she drank from the only glass that had survived the year.

'We really need to remember to buy some glasses,' she laughed, as she refilled it. 'Some house-warming party it will be, our guests drinking out of bowls.' Sukie laughed her sharp laugh and took another long drag of her cigarette, momentarily throwing an orange glow across her face, reminding Harriet of how in primary school – tiny and skinny in long, white socks – they used to cup buttercups under one another's chins, confirming that – yes – they all liked butter.

Leigha lazily rubbed her fingertips on the wall she was leaning against, collecting small little curls of Blu-tac. Harriet had done her best to get it all off, but still you could see patches where the photos had been all year.

'This year's gone so fast,' Harriet said suddenly. Leigha looked across the bed at her, eyebrows raised as she brought her glass to her lips to communicate agreement; Sukie reached her arm outside the window to grind her cigarette out on the brick of the building.

'Way fast,' she agreed, jumping back down into the room and manoeuvring herself onto the single bed as well, facing the other two, crossing her legs so that a knee rested on the shin of each friend. She placed her mug of gin atop a nearby cardboard box packed up with text books, a handy table.

They would be moving into their new home over the next week, in dribs and drabs, walking suitcases down the student village streets in convoy, coordinating a taxi for their heavier stuff. Tomorrow they would get together with Leigha's friend Nicky, their new housemate, and celebrate endings and beginnings, but tonight they had wanted it to be just the three of them, in this room, one last time.

Harriet tried to take a mental snapshot; the tobacco-spice of Sukie's breath as she spoke, the fruit and sugar on Leigha's as she replied, the warmth of the early summer evening outside and the body heat and alcohol fug pressing close in the small room. As if she could sense the run of her thoughts, Leigha chose that moment to drop her head to Harriet's shoulder, closing her eyes and turning her face down, making a contented, drunken noise. Sukie immediately slapped out at Leigha's foot.

'Come on, stay with us Ley; you haven't had that much to drink.'

Harriet rolled her head back against the wall - letting Leigha's head fit in all the better underneath her chin.

Sukie and Leigha launched into an old routine – the usual teases, nothing sharp enough to hurt – but the sort of things that only the best of friends could get away with saying to each other.

Even though the end of an academic year wasn't quite the same as the end of a calendar one, Harriet found herself making resolutions. She'd work even harder in her second year, do all the seminar reading, ensure her First; she'd somehow manage to jettison Seth, hopefully without breaking his heart; she'd be happy – and make sure that everybody that she loved was too.

Harriet sealed the wishing with a hearty sip from her mug of gin

350

and grinned, at her best friends and in the face of the interposing future.

Epilogue

August 2012

Summer had been lying heavy on the city for months; travel by tube was a punishment. Adam decided to head off early, jump off public transport at Waterloo, and walk the rest of the way to the bar along the Thames, a ribbon to his left, the dirty silver of coins.

He thought he'd left good time, but Johnny was already there waiting when he arrived, seated at a low, square booth in a nook to the right of the bar, waving enthusiastically to catch Adam's attention.

'Alright, mate,' Adam greeted him, slipping into the seat opposite. 'You haven't got the beers in!' he chastised. Just as he finished speaking a waitress appeared with two honey coloured beers in sweating pint glasses on a tray. Johnny smirked as she set them down.

'I always get the beers in, mate, you know that.' He thanked the girl and she left.

'So how's tricks?' Adam asked, helping himself to one of the beers. 'How's Iona?' A small smile spread across Johnny's face.

'She's fine. She got a 2.1 grade for her second year.'

'Ah, good for her!' The two men sat and drank in companionable silence for a moment.

'Anyway, before you get settled,' Johnny said, placing his glass back on the table top. 'I have to admit an ulterior motive in getting you to come out for a drink today.'

Adam arched his eyebrow. 'Well, you're barking up the wrong tree if you want to borrow some money,' he teased.

'I saw Harriet, last month,' Johnny said, without further preamble. 'She came to Iona's birthday drinks.' Adam felt a frown creasing his forehead and straightened his expression.

'Oh yeah?' he said, drawing a line in the condensation on the outside of his pint glass with his fingertip. 'She good, yeah?'

'She's good,' Johnny agreed. 'She told me that you never slept with Leigha.'

Adam shot his best friend a look. 'You what?'

'She said she knows for sure that it never happened. Leigha was lying.'

'No, I mean…' Adam struggled to grasp the words. 'For years, you've thought… you thought that I had?'

Johnny shrugged. 'Leigha Webster is quite a persuasive person.'

'Apparently,' Adam groaned. 'Fuck's sake, man.' They took another moment to drink from their pints in silence. 'So Harriet knows that I didn't, now,' he said, after a moment. 'Good. I hope she feels bad.'

'I do, actually,' Harriet admitted. Adam jolted and turned; she was sitting with Iona in the booth behind them, smiling awkwardly. Adam sighed, and shot Johnny a glare.

'I warned you mate. Ulterior motive,' Johnny smirked, lazily stretching as he got to his feet. 'Anyway. This place has got a great beer garden, apparently. Me and Iona are going to go check it out.' Iona slid elegantly across the leather booth seat to stand and Johnny collected his beer. 'Catch you kids later.' Iona reached back to squeeze Harriet's hand before she followed Johnny out through the far doors and into the sunshine beyond.

Harriet meekly dropped down on the side of the booth that Johnny had just vacated. 'I'm sorry,' she began.

'I'm going to stop you there,' Adam said, leaning back against the back of his seat. 'Because I don't know where this is going, but I have a pretty good guess. Now that the old impediment of me having shagged Leigha is out of the way you wanna pick things back up, yeah? Well, I'm sorry – I'm really sorry – but that's not going to happen.'

'It's not about that all,' Harriet said. 'I just wanted you to know that I know, and I wanted to talk to you.'

'Okay then.' Adam gestured expansively. 'Talk.'

'Well. I wanted to say I was sorry—'

'You've said it,' Adam interrupted, mercilessly.

'Okay.' Harriet tilted her head, nervously fiddling with her hair, pushing it back behind her right ear; a tiny silver bird spun in the space between her earlobe and her shoulder. 'I'd like the chance to be friends again,' she said, plainly.

'Friends?' Adam echoed.

'Yes, friends. And – okay, yes, who knows? – maybe in time, more than friends, like before.'

'Ah, Harriet,' Adam said, feeling uncertain, uncomfortable. 'You know that's not possible. There's too much shit there, too much… anger.'

'I'm not angry anymore,' Harriet said, gently. 'And as for all the old rubbish, well, that's why I want us to be friends – just friends – so we have the chance to create new rubbish.' She gave the ghost of a smile. Like before, like at the wedding, being in proximity to her made him irrational, made him fill up with the thought of her; wherever they were together, the universe always shrunk itself down to just that point, just that room, just her.

'You once pressed me, laid yourself open, when I told you no,' she continued quietly. 'And so I'm doing it now. I'd really like…

another chance… to maybe one day,' she smiled, 'get a second chance.'

Harriet scribbling notes to him in the margins of his notepaper during lectures; Harriet teaching him the girls' signature dance moves in the Union; Harriet smiling softly at him across the study tables of the library, her chin cupped in her hands as she listened to him read poetry to her in a whisper; Harriet with the taste of snow on her lips.

'After all,' Harriet concluded, 'when it comes to each other, what have we got left to lose?'

And Adam recognised the warm feeling in his chest; it was hope that she could be right, and it was brighter and stronger than he ever thought it would be.

'So, we start again?' he asked. 'Blank slate? Is that even possible?'

'We're in charge of what is or isn't possible,' Harriet laughed. 'So, yes, we can try for a blank slate, if you want.'

'Okay,' Adam said, smiling at her for the first time that afternoon. 'I guess we could always try. So. Hi there.' His smile became a grin. 'I'm Adam.'

'I'm Harriet.' Harriet stretched out across the table and cupped his hands in hers. 'It's really good to meet you.'

Erin Lawless

I live a happy life full of wonderful friends, in love with a man who buys me books instead of flowers. To mix things up a little, I write books where friends and lovers hit obstacles and (usually) overcome them. When I'm not doing that I read absolutely everything I can get my hands on, spend an inordinate amount of time in pyjamas and run a fun-but-informative blog on British history.

You can follow me @rinylou or visit my blog http://erinlawless.co.uk/.

About HarperImpulse

HarperImpulse is an exciting new range of romance fiction brought to you from the women's fiction team at HarperCollins. Our aim is to break new talent from debut authors and import the hottest trends from the US, bringing you the very best in romance. Whether that is through short reads for your mobile phone or epic sagas that span the generations we want to proudly publish romance fiction that gets everybody talking.

Romance readers, come and meet the team at our website www. harperimpulseromance.com, our Facebook page www. facebook. com/HarperImpulse or follow us @HarperImpulse!

Writers, we are simply looking for good stories! So, what are you waiting for? To submit, e-mail us at romance@harpercollins.co.uk.

LOVE ROMANCE?
WE'VE GOT THE LOVE.

If you'd like to find out about the latest HarperImpulse romance titles, as well as exclusive competitions, author interviews, offers and lots more, join us on our Facebook page! Why not leave a note on our wall to tell us what you thought of this book or what you'd like to see us publish more of?

/HarperImpulse

You can also tweet us
@harperimpulse